For Mat & Maisie,

with much love

from

Piri

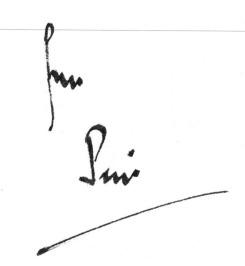

THE COLOMBIA SYNDICATE

THE COLOMBIA SYNDICATE

Peter Rawlinson

CHAPMANS

Chapmans Publishers Ltd
141–143 Drury Lane
London WC2B 5TB

BRITISH LIBRARY CATALOGUING IN PUBLICATION DATA

Rawlinson, Peter
The Colombia syndicate.
I. Title
823.914[F]

ISBN 1-85592-043-3

First published by Chapmans 1991

Photoset by Rowland Phototypesetting Ltd
Bury St Edmunds, Suffolk

Printed and bound in Great Britain by
Clays Ltd, St Ives plc

For Elaine

ONE

When she died he was lying in her bed.

He had felt her slip from beside him and he had seen her naked figure silhouetted in the door when she had turned on the bathroom light. He had cradled his arm over his head and shut his eyes. He opened them when he heard the half cry. Then he heard the crash.

He found her lying beside the bath, a glass in splinters on the tiles around her feet. He lifted her and turned her. Her eyes were open. He carried her into the bedroom and laid her on the bed and stood above her, he as naked as she. Then he gathered her up and shook her roughly. Her head fell back; her eyes remained open. He put her down and lowered his head to her chest; then he grabbed her wrist feeling for her pulse. She was quite dead. He did not even know her name.

For a moment he stood, looking down at the dead girl. He must not become involved in the enquiries that would follow her death; he would have to get away – and quickly. He turned and went across the room to where he had left his clothes but in the half-light his foot caught in the lead of a lamp and he stumbled into a small table, which crashed to the floor taking with it the lamp and the telephone. By his feet he could hear the buzz of the telephone receiver, which had separated from the handset, and he knelt, cursing, fumbling for the light. But when he found it the bulb had broken in the fall. Beside him lay the small table, its drawer half open, books and papers scattered on the carpet. He got to his feet and went to the bedside table to turn on a light. Then he knelt again to pick up the telephone. Suddenly, on one of the papers beside him, he saw his own name. It was not only his last name, but his full name – not the false one that he had given the girl – neatly

1

typed and underlined, the heading of a report. Beneath was his correct date of birth and his address, not the office address where he had first encountered her, but that of his home, which he had not told her and which, during their evening together, she had never enquired. Yet all the time, back in her room, she had a report with his true name and his true address.

He had first seen her the day before in the narrow lift that took him to his second-floor office. She had appeared suddenly just as the doors were closing and he had kept them open for her as she slipped in beside him. She had not looked at him but he had at her. He had asked which floor she wanted. The fifth, she had replied, and he had pressed the button, number five, three floors above his. There was little room for more than the two of them and he had looked down at her head as she stared ahead of her. She had dark hair and colouring with a short, rather plump figure. He liked the scent she had been wearing, heavy and strong.

When the doors opened she had left without a word.

That evening he had seen her again. She came walking down the stairs, turning the corner just as he had come out of his office. She must, he now realised, have been waiting for him.

'Good evening,' he had said.

She had smiled and went on down the staircase. He noticed her large brown eyes and broad, slow smile.

The next morning, this morning, it had been almost exactly the same. She had suddenly appeared and followed him into the lift. This time they had spoken.

She said she was going again to the fifth floor. He had asked her if she worked there but she had said no, she was just visiting.

At midday he had gone to the bank at the corner of Bond Street to cash a cheque as he always did each Thursday, money for himself and for Sally, his secretary. As he had waited in the queue he had caught the scent of her perfume. She had been standing immediately behind him.

'You must think that I am following you,' she had said.

'I wish you were,' he had replied.

After a pause, he had asked, 'Have you come from that office above mine?'

2

She had nodded.

'Are you in a hurry? Would you like to go in front of me? I have plenty of time.'

She had accepted gravely and he had stood aside and behind her, studying her long, very dark hair. There were several customers in front of them. The girl turned slightly as they waited and smiled.

'If you are not in too much of a hurry,' he had said, 'would you like to have a cup of coffee, or a drink – when we have got our money?'

'Yes,' she had replied, and turned away.

At the counter, he noticed that she had received a bundle of fifty-pound notes. Perhaps, he calculated, a thousand pounds. She had waited for him and they had crossed Piccadilly to the Ritz and drunk champagne. While he talked, she had looked carefully at him, smiling as though to herself. After an hour she had said that she must go back to the office which she had to visit again. She did not say why. He had asked her how long she would be there. All afternoon, she said.

'Would you care to repeat our drink this evening?'

Yes, she had replied.

'I will meet you here – at six-thirty.'

Later he had taken her to a small Italian restaurant at World's End in Chelsea. Again she had spoken very little and had not asked him his name or what he did. He had said, and it was a lie, that his name was Max and that he lived in Hampstead. She had not seemed interested and when he had asked her for her name she had said that it didn't matter – yet. She kept looking at him, intently, her large brown eyes rarely off his face. Her silence had disquieted him and he had talked and began to drink more than he had planned.

They had gone back to her flat off Sloane Square to make love and when she had opened the front door she had gone straight through the hall into a bed sitting-room and switched on a light beside the bed. The apartment was quite small and remembering the money that she had drawn from the bank, he was surprised that it was so modest.

At once she began to undress as silent as she had been all evening. In bed she was, surprisingly after what had passed,

3

passive and unresponsive, as if she were not particularly interested. He had wondered why she had ever agreed, and he became rough and irritated and in his turn perfunctory. They had not spoken. Then she had slipped out of the bed – and died in her bathroom.

Now she was lying naked where he had laid her, while he was naked and kneeling on the floor beside her bed with the report she had on him in his hand. He began to read.

MARTIN FRANCIS MAITLAND

Born: June 4th 1961. Address: 16 Maddern Road, Fulham SW10.

1. Enquiries into the subject have been difficult but with the help of your photograph we have identified him as a Martin Francis Maitland born on June 4th 1961 in London, the son of Brian and Joan Maitland, maiden name Messenger.

2. On the birth certificate the father, Brian, was described as 'Accountant' employed by the American Gulf Petroleum Corporation in Dubai. Enquiries at the London office of the Corporation have revealed that Brian Maitland retired from this company in 1973 shortly after his wife had died of cancer. We suspect that there was some financial trouble, for Brian Maitland was retired early without pension and in December of that same year we were informed that he killed himself by taking an overdose of sleeping tablets.

3. The son, Martin, was at the time at a boarding school in Seaford in Sussex. The Corporation believe that thereafter the subject was brought up by the mother's spinster sister, Anne Messenger, but know nothing more.

4. The Probate Register at Somerset House shows that Brian Maitland left estate, estimated at £60,000 net in trust for his son until the boy reached the age of 21 in 1982 when he was to receive the capital. The trustees were Anne Messenger and Terence Wells of Wheatcroft's, solicitors of 18 Lincoln's Inn Fields.

4

5. The Electoral Register revealed that Martin Francis Maitland resides at a small house No. 16 Maddern Road in Fulham. For much of the time the house is left locked and unattended when the owner is believed by neighbours to be overseas.

6. From Maddern Road the subject was followed to a small office with a single secretary in a block called Clandon House in Old Bond Street from which the International Oriental Trading Company purport to engage in trading in precious stones. The Company is not a limited company but is registered in the Business Names Register. It is presumably this business which takes the subject so frequently overseas. Recently he has been attending the office daily. He banks at the Midland, New Bond Street, to which he went on Thursday at midday to cash a cheque.

This is as much as we have been able to discover but there is another matter which we must bring to your attention.

During the week when we had him under observation we became aware that the subject was also being observed by others. Last evening in Fulham a man approached our operator and threatened him in such terms that we are not prepared to continue this assignment. The work of this firm is limited to personal and matrimonial enquiries and we do not wish to become involved in matters which are clearly outside our normal practice.

We enclose our invoice in respect of the balance of our account.

There followed a signature that he was unable to decipher.

Nothing was attached to the two sheets of the report so he bent forward to search for the invoice, which would reveal the name of the detective agency. But it was not among the other papers, which consisted of notes of expenses, taxi fares and meals, and receipts from large stores, Harrods and Fortnum and Mason – for food and expensive clothes all paid by cash. Among these he found a note in handwriting on blue writing paper.

'Darling,' it began, 'I don't think that we should go on. You must be very, very careful. I am getting worried.'

He lifted the paper and smelt the heavy scent. It was the same as that worn by the dead girl. Beneath the note was a photograph, a picture of two girls with their arms around each other, sitting on the grass in a garden in front of a white house. One was the girl lying on the bed behind him. He turned the photograph and on the back was written a single word.

Still naked he got to his feet and began to search the flat. There was no food in the kitchen, only a few bottles of liquor and some white wine in the icebox. In the drawers in the dressing-table were some make-up and one change of under-clothes. A single dress hung in the wardrobe. Of the clothes to which the bills related there was no sign.

He went to the desk, opening and searching the drawers. They were empty. One was locked but he saw on the dressing-table the handbag that the young woman had with her earlier in the evening. In the bag there was a small key but none of the money that she had drawn that morning from the bank, only a few coins. He put the key into the locked drawer of the desk and the lock turned. Inside was a small revolver. It was loaded.

He carried it in his hand as he walked past the body of the girl to search the bedside table. As he did so he turned and looked down at her as she lay, her eyes still open, her face very white and very restful, the few lines that he had earlier noticed beside her mouth now smoothed away. He closed the eyelids with his forefinger and then turned away and began to dress.

He put the report, the note, the photograph of the two girls and the revolver into his pocket. He picked up the table, replacing the lamp. He rearranged the objects on the desk, put the bills in the drawer from which he had taken the revolver, relocked it and returned the key to the handbag. Each object that he had touched he wiped carefully with his silk handkerchief. Then he turned out the light and left.

It was now one o'clock in the morning. In Sloane Avenue he picked up a cab, and as they drove he watched through the back window to see if the cab was being followed but he could identify nothing. In Maddern Road before he entered the house he looked around. The small street was empty.

From the wall safe in his bedroom he took three passports, one a stiff British passport, the second thin and coloured maroon, the third green. These, with two thick bundles of dollar notes, he packed into a briefcase. As he left the house he set the alarm, then went out into the Fulham Road and began walking east, watching as before. After a time he found a taxi.

'Clandon House,' he said. 'Old Bond Street.'

In his office he drew the curtains before he turned on a single desk-lamp. He took some files from filing-cabinets and fed them into the shredding machine. The telephone began to ring in the office. He stopped shredding and he stood, waiting. Then it stopped. After a time he went back to his work. Before he was finished the fax machine stuttered out a couple of pages. He read them and put them with the other documents through the shredder. He went into the secretary's office and sat at a typewriter.

'Sally,' he typed, 'I have to leave early in the morning for Jo'burg in South Africa. I'll get in touch with you as soon as I can. I am sorry that we shall not be able to go this weekend to the country. Look after yourself and the office. Martin.'

He left the note on the desk. Then he called Air France and in the name of Jacques Simonet he booked a seat on the 7.30 flight to Paris from Heathrow. He switched out the single light and drew back the curtains and sat in the darkness.

At five o'clock, as dawn was breaking, he left the office and walked down Piccadilly to the Underground station at the Circus. He bought a ticket to Heathrow and sat on the empty platform waiting. At 5.46 he caught what was the first train to the airport and arrived at Heathrow at 6.30.

A quarter of an hour later he checked in for the flight, produced his maroon passport and in the name of Jacques Simonet passed through Immigration. At seven o'clock he boarded the Paris plane.

At Charles de Gaulle, in excellent French he told the taxi driver to take him to the Crillon Hotel. There he drank coffee and read *Le Figaro*, looking up now and then from behind his newspaper. Then he left the hotel and walked up the rue du

Rivoli beside the Louvre gardens. He hailed another taxi and told the driver to take him to 17 rue Casimir Perier. He let himself into the building and then into the apartment with his own keys. Inside he went straight to the telephone and dialled. There was a long delay before it was answered.

'*Midi*,' he said and replaced the receiver.

He shaved, took a shower, and with a towel around his waist and the briefcase beside him he lay down on the bed and slept.

TWO

Precisely at noon the front door of the apartment was opened by a smart and fashionably dressed woman in her late forties, her dark hair shot with silver, her oval face carefully made up, her perfume discreet – very different from that worn by the girl who had died twelve hours earlier. The woman used her own key. Inside she stood for a moment in the hall, listening. Then she went silently into the bedroom where the man was sleeping.

The curtains were drawn but the light filtered into the room. She crossed to the bed and stood staring down at him, her arms folded, one foot slightly cocked on its high heel. He lay on his back, the black hair curling on his forehead, his face very pale, more lined than it should be, she thought, for a man so much younger than herself. Her eyes wandered over the strong, hairless torso and flat belly, and then moved back to his face and traced again the worry lines at the corner of his eyes and beside the thin mouth, shut tight, like a trap.

As she watched he stirred faintly and sighed, moving his head to one side. The fingers of his right hand were curled around the handle of the briefcase on the bed beside him. She knew that if she touched them or it, he would awake – and awake violently. She placed a chair beside the bed close to the sleeping man.

She sat in the darkened room, facing the door, motionless for three hours, her hands in her lap, her eyes either on the door or on the man – until he woke.

He opened his eyes very suddenly, and immediately his fingers gripped even more tightly around the handle of the briefcase as though to make certain that it was still beside him. Then he sensed her presence for he knew her scent. He turned his head towards where she sat and smiled.

'*Chérie*,' he said, and held out his arm – the other arm, not the one with the hand on the briefcase.

She took the hand and rose.

'It is three o'clock. I have been here since noon, which is when you asked me to come. As you know, I am very obedient.'

'I know,' he said drawing her onto the bed beside him.

She sat, and he put his head in her lap still holding her hand in one hand and his case in the other. Then she bent forward and kissed him and he pulled her towards him. She jerked away and he stretched forward and unbuttoned her blouse.

When she was naked she lay on top of him, looking down on him, loving the extraordinary light blue eyes, which never left hers, loving the lines on the tired face, enjoying his enjoyment, moving with him. They turned, and now she looked up at the handsome face above her.

She thought: Who is he? Who really is he? Then she was lost in the climax, calling out the name she knew him by, clawing at his shoulders.

Afterwards, as she lay beside him, she turned to him and, loosening her hand from his, she smoothed back the hair from his forehead.

'You were very tense. Are you in trouble?' she asked.

He should not have answered but he did.

'Yes,' he said.

'Is it serious?'

'Very – I think.'

She went on caressing his forehead.

'You had better tell me.'

He looked up at her and improbably for him, was moved by her beauty and the look of understanding, compassion even, on her face. He was very tired and he could not stop himself telling her. As soon as he had he knew that he should have remained silent.

'I am being watched. There are people following me.'

'Following you? For heaven's sake, why? Because of us?'

'No. These are enemies.'

10

'Enemies? What do you mean? Why should you have enemies?'

'Because of what I do.'

'What you do? You have never really told me.'

'There is no need.'

He sat up in the bed but she pushed him gently down.

'I have just come from London. There was a girl whom I had seen once or twice hanging about my office.'

'A girl? I suppose she was a pretty girl?'

'Yes, she was. But not beautiful like you.'

The woman's hand kept smoothing back his hair, running her fingers through it, gently and slowly.

He went on: 'I kept seeing her in the lift or on the staircase, she was even beside me at the bank. Then she spoke to me.'

The woman remained silent, her hand still caressing his hair and his forehead.

'She suggested we have a drink.'

'And you agreed.'

'Yes.' He sat up again, leant across to the table and took a cigarette and a lighter. The woman got up and wrapped his towel around her and returned to the chair in which she had kept her vigil. He lit the cigarette. He should never have said anything. Now he had to go on.

'The girl said that she had an office above mine and had often seen me in the building. She said she was giving a party in the evening, that is last night.' He passed a hand over his face. 'And she asked me if I'd like to come. I understood that she had meant a party in the office upstairs so I thought I would drop in before I went home. In the evening, on my way up to her office, she met me at the lift and said that the party was at her flat, and she suggested that we share a taxi.'

'What was her name?'

'She did not tell me and I did not tell her mine. That was one of the surprises. Anyhow we went to her flat. It was quite small, in a block in Sloane Avenue. Then, when we got there, I found there was no one else expected.'

The woman was looking at his face in profile as he sat on the bed, his elbows upon his knees, smoking. She got up and drew back the curtains and turned and faced him.

11

'Was that such a surprise?'

'Yes, it was. I said to her that I thought this was going to be a party, and she said that it was and didn't I want a drink. Then, as she crossed to a table to fix a drink, she suddenly stumbled and stopped and began to fall. I ran across the room and managed to catch her.'

'What had happened?'

He stubbed out his cigarette. 'I don't know. But she died – literally in my arms.'

The woman said nothing. She was standing by the window, her arms folded across the towel over her breasts.

'Is that the truth?'

'Yes,' he said, not looking at her. 'As I ran over and caught her and when I was trying to lay her down, I knocked over the telephone and a table. On the floor I saw a paper with my name typed on it – my full name, which I had never given her, and my address. It must have come from a drawer in the table, with a lot of other papers. It was a report – on me and where I lived.' As he spoke he kept thinking, as he had ever since the scene in the flat in Chelsea, why had that girl had him followed and who were the other watchers who had scared off the detective?

'A report on you? In your name, Jacques Simonet?'

'Yes. It was a professional report, ordered by the girl. It described my father and how my mother had died. But it also said that there were others who were interested in me and who were following me. When the girl fell I was going to telephone for a doctor or an ambulance but when I had read the report, I didn't. I just left her there. And came here.'

They were silent for some time.

'Perhaps it was just the girl. She had seen you and wanted to know about you and had enquiries made?'

'I think that it is more serious than that.'

He got up and walked towards the shower. He should never have spoken. He had never before told her anything about himself or about the people with whom and for whom he worked. It had been the anxiety and his exhaustion that had made him speak.

'What are you going to do?'

12

'Move on,' he said.

'You had better come to Gauville – this evening.'

'No. I must go further away than that. They may know about us.'

'They? Who are they?'

'I don't know. The people who were having me watched. I shall go to Rio tomorrow.'

'Why to Rio?'

'I have business there.' He leant towards her and took her hand. 'There are people who are not very fond of me. And they aren't very scrupulous. I cannot tell you any more, Marie-Claire. I will when I return.'

'When will that be?'

'Soon. In about a month. When I have made enquiries. Someone obviously wants to find out more about me. That is why the girl picked me up. And then these other people. It is they who concern me.'

'Will you come to me when you get back?'

'You know that I will.'

She had never enquired what he really did. Trading in precious stones, he had told her, importing them from Brazil. And ivory from East Africa, which he had said he took to Hong Kong to be carved and that there were those who wished to end the trade in ivory. She had not wanted to ask more. If she were to keep him, she had to be content with what he cared to tell her and with what he gave her. He had never before told her so much. That there were other women she had always suspected. From when they had first become lovers she had known that she was now involved with someone and something strange and mysterious. It had been part of what attracted her.

They had met a year ago. The woman friend with whom she had been lunching at the Brasserie Lippe had to leave and she was at the table waiting to pay the bill. It was only then that she had casually glanced to her right and seen the man sitting alone at the next table and for the first time she had looked into those pale blue eyes. He had begun to talk and she had replied off-handedly and called again for her bill. But the bill had never come to her. He had paid it. So their talk went on and she had stayed. That was followed, month after month, by secret meetings, rendezvous always in the apartment in the rue Casimir Perier after sudden summonses, which she always obeyed. Only once, when her husband was away, had they driven into the country to an inn. He had told her so little about himself, nothing about his background or his family.

Now he had spoken as if he were in danger, something to do with his work and with the secret life of which she knew nothing and from which he had so firmly shut her out. But was he telling the truth? Was the story all invention, to provide an excuse for leaving her?

'Are you telling me the truth?' she asked.

He looked at her with those startling blue eyes and she heard him say: 'I swear that I am. Marie-Claire, look at me. I left London with this briefcase and nothing more. What I told you is true. There are people who do not like what I know or what I do and they are looking for me.'

What do you really do? she thought to herself. What do you *really* do? But she said nothing and took his hand in hers.

'Where will you go?'

'As I said, move on. For at least a month. And find out who they are and what they want. But first I need information. I must get it tonight, here in Paris. Tomorrow South America.'

She sat on the chair while he was in the shower. She felt sad – and old.

'I need to buy a clean shirt,' he said as he dressed. 'Will you come with me? I don't want to be alone. Then we can dine. But first I had better make the arrangements.'

As she herself showered she heard him speak to VARIG, the Brazilian airline, and book his flight to Rio for the following day. Then they left together.

At half-past eleven that night he said goodbye. It was raining hard as she got into the car. He kissed her on the lips and then closed the door. She lowered the window and looked up at him.

'Goodbye, Marie-Claire,' he said. 'I shall be back, I promise.'

14

'Take care,' she replied. 'Take great care.'

Then she drove away to Normandy.

When he got to the club he asked for a table by the wall. The show was still on, he was told as he was led to a seat, but it would be over very shortly. This was the finale. As he and the waiter threaded their way to the table, they were caught for a moment in the spotlight. He was still carrying his briefcase. At the table he ordered *fine à l'eau* and two glasses.

'A bottle of Remy Martin. Unopened.'

The figures on the raised stage pirouetted and flounced, more extravagantly, more vivaciously than ordinary showgirls, exaggerating their twirls and the conventional chorus-line routines while a tall singer, tall as a conventional man and with blonde hair reaching shoulder-length over the sequined evening gown, patrolled among the tables with a hand-mike. For a second, almost imperceptibly, the singer paused in front of Maitland's table. Then, the tour completed, the patrol ended in the centre of the stage surrounded by the dancers as they twittered and caricatured the final movements that signalled the end of the show.

After the final crash of cymbal and drum, the chorus swept off their wigs and held them behind their backs and then flourished them above their heads, smiling and pouting, looking naked with their short hair above their painted faces. The singer alone stood still, the long blonde hair in place as the acolytes waved their wigs at the audience, who, save for a few who clapped and one man who cheered, remained silent. He bowed, then swept a deep ironical curtsey and the performers tripped off stage.

The lights came up and then were lowered again as the dance music began and couples took to the floor, some obviously pairs of women, others more dubious as they begun in a desultory fashion to circle in the gloom of the dance floor. After a time the singer appeared at Maitland's table by the wall, still in costume.

'Why are you here?' he asked, towering above Maitland as

15

he sat at the table. His voice was two tones deeper than during the performance. 'What do you want?'

'I want help. Sit down.'

A couple at a nearby table turned and looked across at them, and then grinned at each other. The singer held up two fingers in an obscene gesture. Maitland grabbed the hand, twisting it roughly and holding it against the table.

'None of that.' He poured a drink. 'I must find Josef,' he said. 'And I need to stay the night.'

The singer flung back his blonde hair, which had fallen almost to the glass. In close-up and in the light of the single candle with the red shade on the table his face under the paint with the exaggerated crimson of his lips looked gaunt.

The singer drank and asked, 'Why?'

'Trouble. I came from London this morning.'

'But why Josef?'

'I must speak with him. It is important. How can I find him?'

The singer said nothing, peering at the man through his blonde hair.

'I will pay,' Maitland said. 'Five hundred dollars.'

There was a silence while the singer drank some more of the brandy.

'The last I heard of him he was in Berlin. But he may not be there now. So much has changed. As you know, he moves around a lot. I have not seen him for many months. But I have an address at my place. You might find him through that.'

'Good. And tonight,' he said, 'I need to stay.'

It was a command.

'Come with me.'

They both rose and Maitland, still holding his briefcase, followed the singer through the tables to the entrance and then through a curtain into the back of the club.

In the dressing-room the singer took a key from a bag, and said, 'I will call Tomas and tell him that you are coming. In case he is out, here is the key. Let yourself in. 28 rue Parnasse. I shall not get back until late, when I am finished here. I will give you Josef's address then. The dollars?'

Maitland took the notes from his wallet and handed them over, taking the key.

'This is half,' he said. 'The rest when I get the address.'

Then he turned and left.

He used the key to get into the apartment in the rue Parnasse. As he opened the door a tall black man was standing in the small hallway, facing him, leaning against the wall.

'I am Jacques Simonet,' Maitland said, shutting the door behind him.

'I know. I was told that you were coming. I am Tomas.'

The black man turned and led him into the sitting-room.

'You will have to sleep here, on the couch. There is only our room. Do you want a drink?'

'Coffee. I shall wait.'

Tomas shrugged and went into the kitchen, leaving the door open. Maitland looked at the couch. It had two dolls in flounced dresses propped at either end. The walls of the room were decorated with posters, advertising the club and the shows with drawings and caricatures of the singer, the name in large lettering. On every table and shelf stood photographs, some in silver frames, photographs of the singer looking young and glamorous. Many were of film stars with their arms affectionately around him. The prime of the singer, he thought! One was of him in Tangier after the operation, looking strained and altered, as indeed he had just been.

He tossed the dolls onto a chair and sat on the couch.

Tomas returned bringing a mug of black coffee and a rug.

'I am going to bed. You will have a long wait. The club won't close until after four o'clock.'

'I know,' said Maitland, taking the mug.

At the same time as the singer returned from the club in the early hours of the morning, on the other side of the city two figures in raincoats were standing in the shadows at the corner of the rue Casimir Perier. They were trying to find some shelter from the rain but from where they had stationed themselves they had a clear view of the entrance to number 17. At dawn they went away.

Later that morning, when Maitland left on the early morning flight to Berlin, the two were seated in the airport lounge, casually reading their newspapers and watching the check-in desk for the VARIG airline and its flight to Rio. They only left when the flight had closed and the plane was airborne.

At noon in Normandy Marie-Claire de Tourneville, braving the torrents of rain and the high wind and accompanied by a retriever and a small Jack Russell terrier, walked out of the front door of the Château de Gauville. She went through the rose garden beside the house and through the gate into the beech woods. She did not notice a grey Renault being driven slowly past the entrance to the drive.

When, an hour later, she emerged from the woods and returned to the garden, the car was parked out of sight at the corner of the drive behind the tall hedge. It was empty.

In the hall Marie-Claire pulled off her rain hat, shaking it so that the rainwater fell onto the stone floor. As she hung her raincoat in the closet and took down a towel to dry the dogs, she saw through the small window a figure standing in the wet in the rose garden.

She tapped on the glass, gesticulating to her husband to come in out of the rain. But the figure did not move.

She opened the window and with the rain slanting across the garden she called out, 'Bernard, come inside. Come out of the rain.'

There was no reply. The figure had disappeared.

She closed the window and stood for a moment, remembering. She wondered how far the aeroplane might have gone on the long flight across the southern Atlantic – and whether he was safely on board. She walked through the hall and into the library where she found her husband sitting and reading in front of the fire. She did not tell him about the figure she had seen in the rose garden.

THREE

It was half-past six on the Monday morning and there was a ground mist as the car turned out of the drive and into the lane. It was going to be hot in the city.

Godfrey Burne was being driven to London from his home in Wiltshire. When he had got into the car he had noticed that they had once again changed the registration number. It was rather silly, he thought, as the car itself was always a black Rover. He ought to have a word about that. But as he settled into the back seat he knew that Webster, his driver, would object to any change; Webster enjoyed the Rover. So Godfrey would leave it alone. Webster was more important.

On Sunday he had sat in the sun in the garden working on his papers and as a result his face was burnt a brick red beneath his full head of iron-grey hair. With his square figure and broad shoulders clad in his light grey suit he looked the very picture of the countryman. It would not have been easy to place him as the Chief of the Overseas Intelligence Service, MI6; or C as the Chief was always known. He took out his key and opened the box, which they had brought with them in the car from London, and prepared to work on the fresh papers that had come in overnight. In the front with Webster was a duty Special Branch officer from the Protection Squad. On the previous Friday afternoon he had been in the car in Winchester. As they had left the city an approaching truck had slowly pulled out to overtake a stationary vehicle, completely blocking their passage. Webster had been obliged to stop abruptly and wait while the truck completed its manoeuvre. The braking had led Godfrey to look up from his papers and he had seen the Special Branch man take his gun from his shoulder holster and hold it ready in his lap. England, he had thought, in this day and age!

19

Today it was a new man, or rather a different man from the Special Branch officer who had been with him on Friday. Godfrey was used to studying the napes of their necks. Webster's he knew well. This was a nape he did not think he had seen before. It looked reassuringly competent, fitting snugly into the white shirt collar.

'Good drive down?' he enquired.

'Very easy indeed, sir,' replied Webster. 'Only an hour and a half.'

'It must have meant an early start for you both. I can't think why you won't stay Sunday night.'

'We prefer it.' Webster turned his head to the man on his left. 'If we did, you wouldn't get your overnight box. And it means a few more hours with the wife.'

The Special Branch officer nodded.

'How is she?' said Godfrey. 'Have you arranged your annual visit?'

'Yes, we have. Lady Burne has asked us all for the first week in August. The whole family. So I expect you will go away.'

Webster had been with him for four years. They were friends. Godfrey often thought that he spent more hours in the week in Webster's company than in that of anyone else – including Angela.

'Nonsense,' he said. 'And don't forget to meet Lady Burne this afternoon, the four-thirty at Paddington.'

'I won't, sir.'

Godfrey turned back to his papers and from then on they drove in silence.

The first was the sheet with his daily programme typed out by the Duty Officer in the small hours of the morning. It was headed: 'C's Programme.'

Underneath he noted the confirmation that he and the Director-General of the Security Service were to talk. '1000 hours. DG MI5 at your office.'

Then below, 'Accompany DG MI5 to the Home Office. He is due to see the Home Secretary at 1100 hours?'

He noted the question mark. The Home Secretary was not directly his minister; his was the Foreign Secretary. The item for discussion at the Home Office was the responsibility of MI5.

It would be unusual for both of the Heads of the two intelligence services to attend such a meeting but if the Director-General wanted his support, he would go.

Godfrey went quickly through the messages about the find of the dead girl in the flat in Sloane Avenue so that he would be prepared for the visit of the Director-General and then worked steadily at the other papers in his box until the car drew up at the office. Before he got out of the car to go inside with his guard patrolling beside him, like, he sometimes thought, a fussy tug shepherding a ship to the dockside, he said to Webster, 'Stand by at ten-thirty. We may have to go to the Home Office.' Then, as an afterthought: 'Oh, and meet Lady Burne off the four-thirty at Paddington this afternoon.'

That's the second time he has said that, thought Webster. He must be worried about something.

Alone now in the car Webster drove off to the garage and to the canteen.

The Home Secretary, a stout man with horn-rimmed glasses, affected in his political life an air of good humour and bonhomie that those who knew him well knew was false. On the public stage he played the role of friendly uncle and in the constituencies he was much admired by the Party stalwarts who enjoyed his incoherent speeches and identified with the bluff figure with the quarterdeck manner and Royal Navy tie. In Parliament the House of Commons relished his use in debate of phrases that somehow conveyed more than the words he had actually used so that subsequent study of Hansard gave the Administration, and especially the Home Secretary, plenty of room for evasion. He assiduously cultivated the backbenchers in the Party, drinking and indiscreetly gossiping with them in the smoking-room in the House. He was also an especial favourite of the Parliamentary Lobby, those privileged journalists who had access to Ministers and to whom the Home Secretary's 'off-the-record' comments about his colleagues, inevitably unfavourable, were an agreeable source of copy, much used in political stories by the Lobby but attributed to 'sources close to the Administration', a device that deceived no one – no one, that is, in the know. All in all the Home Secretary was the most powerful minister in the present Administration.

Godfrey could not stand him.

When the Director-General and Godfrey were shown into the large room with its high ceiling leading off the long corridor of the vast Edwardian building, the minister was seated behind his desk. A young Private Secretary sat to one side. Godfrey noticed with some irritation that the Attorney General was sitting in front of the Home Secretary. There was no need at this stage for the Law Officer to be involved.

The two ministers rose when the visitors were announced.

'Come on in, Director-General. Come on in, C. Both great mandarins together! Well, well! What a signal honour. Most unusual but, of course, most agreeable. I was told only a few minutes ago that you were both coming. Quite a surprise.'

'The Foreign Secretary,' said Godfrey, 'is in Tokyo and we spoke last evening on the telephone. As the matter also involves my people I told him that the Director-General might bring me along this morning in case I can be of help and he approved.'

'Good, good. I am sure you can help, C. You always do help. And if you can't, well, it will have been very nice to have seen you.'

The Home Secretary laughed pleasantly but for all his heartiness his manner, if not his words, did not conceal his irritation at being interrupted.

'As you can see I have the Attorney with me. We're working together on the difficult debate in the House this afternoon about the riots. Rather an anxious occasion for us politicians, as you fellows will appreciate. But I have been told that you will not keep me long so I am sure you won't mind if the Attorney stays. Privy Councillor's oath, eh? He and I are rather pressed for time.'

The Home Secretary, with a show of much friendliness, bustled around his desk and led the way to the conference table surrounded by straight-backed chairs, which stood in a corner of the room.

'Come over here. We can all sit more comfortably at the table and you can tell me all about it.'

The Attorney, a thin, lugubrious man, his tall forehead bald, with what hair he still retained over-long at the back so that it protruded untidily above his collar, took the chair next to Godfrey. He had about him an air of detachment as if he found talking to people extremely tiresome. The Attorney, Godfrey considered, remembering his early days at the Bar before he had joined MI6, would make a singularly awkward judge when the time came. Moreover it was rumoured that the time when the Attorney left the political arena for the Bench might not be long delayed for it was said that the Home Secretary wanted him replaced as Senior Law Officer of the Crown by someone more amenable, one of his own cronies, the Solicitor General.

When they were all seated at the table, the Home Secretary said sharply, 'Where is Sir George?'

As he spoke the Permanent Secretary slipped into the room and settled down a little apart from the others next to the young Private Secretary who, his pad at the ready, prepared to take the note.

'We can now begin,' said the Home Secretary testily.

The Director-General took a file from his briefcase.

'It concerns the death of a girl whose body was discovered last Friday morning.'

'The death of a girl?' interrupted the Home Secretary, as though someone had suddenly insulted him. 'I was told nothing about any death. Have you come to see me about a murder?'

'No, Home Secretary, it is not about murder, not of this girl. The autopsy report says that she died', the Director-General read from his file, 'as a result of a massive haemorrhage due to a congenital aneurysm in the brain.'

'An unusual condition,' murmured the Attorney softly.

'It is,' said the Director-General flatly. 'But that is how she died. Her death occurred in a flat in Cavendish Mansions, Sloane Avenue, Chelsea on Thursday night. Her body was discovered by a woman friend who had arranged to meet the girl at this flat the next morning. When the woman could get no reply she became extremely agitated. She seemed certain that something must have happened to her friend.'

'As indeed there had,' said the Attorney. The Director-General ignored him.

'The woman forced the porter to let her into the flat with his passkey. When they opened the door they found the dead body of the girl, who was known as Mary Traynor, lying on the bed, naked.'

The Home Secretary looked only half surreptitiously at his watch.

'This is very interesting, Director-General, but as you have said there was no question of murder, you will forgive me for hurrying you along and you must excuse me for being, as I usually am, so obtuse –' Here the Home Secretary smiled and looked over to the Attorney who to the Home Secretary's annoyance merely looked down at his fingers and failed to register the answering smile that had been expected – 'It wasn't murder. So why are we all here?' He looked genially around the room. 'As I explained, the Attorney and I are rather busy.'

The Director-General was used to his minister. He went on doggedly: 'When they found the body the woman friend became even more hysterical, telling the porter that she had warned her friend that something terrible would happen to her. It was what she said next that aroused our interest. For she spoke excitedly about a man called Maitland. Apparently from the moment when she could get no reply to her knocking she at once assumed that a man called Maitland had in some way harmed her friend.'

'Maitland?' said the Home Secretary.

'Yes. That is what interests C and myself.'

Godfrey inclined his head suitably gravely and looked straight at the Permanent Secretary. He wondered if Sir George remembered that Maynard Keynes had once said it took him a week to recover from a ministerial conference and that afterwards he always felt like a woman outraged and had to retire to solitude or reflection ro recover from what Keynes called the rape of his reason. But Godfrey supposed that the Permanent Secretary was used to it. Sir George without a change in his expression conveyed that he knew exactly what Godfrey was feeling.

The Director-General went on: 'What increased the interest

24

of both the security service and C's people was that the hysterical woman was a South American, a Brazilian.'

'Why? What has that to do with it?'

'Because a few days earlier I had been given the name Maitland from a source in Colombia,' said Godfrey. 'It was suggested we look into his activities. We were told nothing more.'

The Home Secretary looked at Godfrey and then back to the Director-General who was studying his notes.

'The name of the woman is Pilar Olivella and she was on a visit to London where she rented a furnished flat for a few weeks. She comes from an important Brazilian family. Her father is a government minister.'

'Who alerted MI5?'

'One of my people had spoken on the previous Tuesday with the Chief Superintendent at Chelsea advising him of our interest in anyone with the name Maitland.'

Godfrey came to his aid. 'It is the South American factor which interests my branch. We are getting intelligence that the drug barons in Medellin in Colombia are bringing their civil war to Europe and infiltrating assassination squads to deal with rivals.'

'Assassination squads!' The eyes behind the owlish spectacles began to narrow. The Attorney continued to look profoundly disinterested, as though the whole conversation demonstrated the absurdity of the world in general and of the two security services in particular. The Home Secretary turned his eyes on the Attorney. He saw that it would not do to appear too ingenuous.

'The drug dealers have been coming to Europe looking for arms,' said Godfrey. 'They have been to Tripoli and recently one faction met two IRA leaders, one a former priest, in Amsterdam.'

The Director-General went on, 'At first the police thought the death of the girl might have been murder.'

'But it was not,' murmured the Attorney wearily, looking at the pelicans, which he could just see on the grass by the lake in St James's Park.

'No. We had an immediate autopsy. There was evidence

consistent with her having had sexual intercourse shortly before she died.'

The Attorney looked down at his folded hands, his posture conveying the impression that in that case death had served the lady right.

'Well, who was this girl?' asked the Home Secretary. 'Was she also South American?'

'We don't know. The name she used as a tenant of the flat was Mary Traynor. We believe that the man she was with at the time of her death might have been Maitland.'

'Why should you think that?'

'We had traced a Martin Maitland of Maddern Road, Fulham with an office in Old Bond Street. The morning after the body of the girl was found there was no trace of Martin Maitland either at his home or at his office.'

'Why was not this Martin Maitland immediately put under observation?'

'We had been given only the name Maitland and we had only just targeted this Martin Maitland as one we should investigate.'

Either, Godfrey thought, the Home Secretary was being, to use his own word, obtuse; or more probably he was preparing the ground so that if any political embarrassment ever arose out of this he would be able to blame it on yet another example of incompetence by MI5.

'So the man with whom she had', the Attorney put his fingers together under his chin, 'sexual intercourse just before she died might have been Martin Maitland. On the other hand, it might not.'

'Yes.'

The Home Secretary began to feel that the Attorney was intervening too much. He said sharply, 'Well, what has happened to this Martin Maitland?'

'He may have left for South Africa, although no one answering his description was on any flight on the Friday or over the weekend. He has, for the moment, wholly disappeared.'

'There is a little more, Home Secretary,' Godfrey said. 'From the general description of Martin Maitland obtained from neighbours at his home and office, his build at least corresponds

26

with the description of that of the man who assassinated Brigadier Sullavan in Frankfurt last month, for which the IRA claimed responsibility. It could mean that we are searching for a professional killer.'

'Mary Traynor', said the Attorney softly, 'was not killed by anyone; she died of natural causes and no one knows if anyone was with her when she died.'

The Home Secretary shifted irritably in his chair. It was time to assert his authority. 'Rather a lot of speculation, don't you think? Rather a lot of "ifs" and "buts", eh?'

'If he were the man with the girl when she died,' said Godfrey, 'he may have learnt something when he was with her which may have led him to disappear. Many could be interested in this particular man.'

The Home Secretary looked at Godfrey and then at the Attorney. He rose to his feet. 'Well, it is very interesting, but inconclusive, wouldn't you say?'

'Of course,' said the Director-General.

'I presume that it is on what you have told me that you base your application for telephone orders?'

Godfrey glanced again at the Permanent Secretary who stared back, the look in his eye telegraphing, Never mind.

The Director-General said briskly, 'I would like an order for a telephone tap on both Martin Maitland's home and office.'

'Very well, if you think it worthwhile.'

By his tone of voice the Home Secretary certainly did not. He hoped that the Attorney had noticed it.

'And a tap upon his secretary at her home in Clapham and on Pilar Olivella who is staying at 85 Gilstone Road, Notting Hill until she leaves for Rio in two days' time.'

'Very well,' repeated the Home Secretary, signalling to the Permanent Secretary. The young official made a note on his pad. The Home Secretary had started to move from the table to his desk.

'But at the moment, gentlemen, and you will forgive me if I speak frankly, it all seems to me a little far-fetched. A girl dies of natural causes and you are linking her to South American assassination squads because a South American woman friend is distressed to find her dead and a man whose general

27

description might possibly correspond with that of an IRA killer in Germany might have been her lover.' He laughed genially. He was behind his desk now. 'Still,' he went on rapidly sensing that Godfrey might intervene and worse still might start the story all over again, 'you can have your orders, Director-General. They will be confirmed. And now if you will forgive us, fascinated as I was to hear about your speculations, the Attorney and I have serious work to do and I think that even you, gentlemen,' and here the Home Secretary gave one of his hearty laughs although without any twinkle in the eyes behind those concealing spectacles, 'even you will understand that is not unimportant. The life, I am told, of the Administration may depend upon how the Attorney and I perform in the House this very afternoon.'

They were dismissed.

Bastard, thought Godfrey as Webster drove him away from Whitehall and the car joined the queue of traffic slowly moving south across Westminster Bridge. Godfrey offered up a silent prayer for the relief of his friend the Director-General by an autumn reshuffle of the government and the removal of the egregious Home Secretary. But he knew that the man was too powerful ever to be shifted unless it suited himself. All the Home Secretary's other colleagues might go, go quite easily, significantly helped on their way by a discreet shove from the man they believed was their friend. But not him, never him. As he got out of the car he said to Webster, 'Don't forget to meet Lady Burne at Paddington.'

Something has certainly got into the Old Man, thought Webster.

Back in his office, as he ate the sandwiches slightly rough at their edges and drank the infamous department coffee that had been brought to him from the canteen, he studied again the transcripts of the decoded messages from Carlos at the beleaguered Colombia station.

Godfrey's Deputy, James Kent, believed that Carlos had become unreliable. He was drinking, Kent had said, and was ill, demoralised by the collapse of the local station. But Godfrey

28

knew more about Carlos than did Kent. Many years ago when Godfrey had been serving in Caracas he had personally recruited the then young Carlos. Now Godfrey had Carlos' latest messages. They had been sent 'For C's eyes only' and the full text with Carlos' proposal had not been distributed, not even to Kent. Only the name Maitland; Carlos' plan Godfrey had kept to himself.

About Maitland Godfrey had a pretty shrewd idea what he was. Maitland was dangerous but, for Godfrey's purpose, his importance lay in that sooner or later he would inevitably surface at the home of his masters in Colombia and he might therefore provide a trail to that place for which Carlos was searching.

Godfrey pushed aside his cup and spoke on the telephone to James Kent, asking him to come to his room. His relationship with Kent was uneasy. It had always been, ever since Godfrey had joined the service some years after Kent. Then Godfrey had overtaken him and when it was decided to look for C from within the ranks of the service, and not introduce a Chief from outside as so often had been the practice, Godfrey had been preferred. James Kent had been resentful for he rated his own talents superior to those of Godfrey whose insights into intelligence developments he contemptuously called 'C's hunches'. In Kent's opinion, the gathering and servicing of raw intelligence required primarily the talents which he, James Kent, enjoyed. The style of leadership presently exercised by Godfrey could, Kent believed and sometimes secretly hoped would, lead to fresh disasters and the service had enough disasters in the not very distant past.

When the Deputy was seated opposite his Chief, Godfrey tossed a file across the table to him.

'I am going to ask him to go to Latin America.'

'For what reason?'

'To talk to the woman Pilar Olivella and to try and find the link between her, the girl and Maitland.'

Kent took the file. He was a short, pale-faced man with shiny black hair as yet not even flecked with grey and a habit of pursing his pale lips whenever he spoke. His appearance was spruce, his manner spry and his movements quick, bird-like.

Together they made an oddly disparate couple: C so square and robust with his ruddy complexion, heightened by the summer sunshine; the Deputy so slight with the sickly complexion of the man who lived permanently in the city. Godfrey watched as Kent studied the file on a man whom Kent knew and heartily disliked, one of those whom Kent privately called 'gentlemen amateurs' in the mould of C himself, the kind whom Kent considered had done so much damage to the reputation of the service in the past.

With the file still in his hand, Kent said, 'Do you think that he is the right man?'

'For this task, yes.'

'Has he the judgement or the experience?'

'The experience? No. The judgement? I hope that he has. It is not a difficult task. While he is there I shall also ask him to check out Carlos. He speaks the local languages and I believe that he is in any event contemplating a trip to the Argentine. He is presently engaged in some Latin American study.'

'Is there any need? I can get someone to talk with the woman and do a check on Carlos, if that is all that there is to it.'

He suspects, thought Godfrey, that what I have in mind to invite the man selected to do is more than that.

But for the present Kent had no need to know.

'I have decided to send in someone new,' Godfrey said shortly.

'These situations are rarely straightforward. They usually escalate; he could easily become deeply involved.' Kent tapped the file he was holding in his hand. 'When he was with us I was always unsure of him. I thought that he was unsure of himself. And he is hot-tempered. Perhaps it is the foreign blood.'

'His Spanish mother? What has that to do with it?'

'It has to do with temperament. When he was with us I never sent him overseas because I feared that in the field he might be led into doing something foolish.'

'I am prepared to take the risk. As he will primarily be in Latin America for his academic work, his presence will not arouse comment.'

Kent placed the file with distaste onto the table between them.

'I only hope that he will not do anything foolish – for all our sakes.'

Godfrey got to his feet.

'I shall require you to brief him. I shall be in Cambridge this evening. I think that I shall be able to persuade him to help.'

And so it was decided. But when the time came to review and enquire into the operation, James Kent intended to ensure that it was on record that the Deputy had been kept in ignorance of what was the real purpose behind C's irregular selection.

FOUR

Maitland had left the city far behind him and had driven all day along the autobahn, which in the old days had been fenced to form a corridor for travellers to and from the West.

Two nights earlier, on the evening when he had arrived, he had left the Hotel Bristol at ten o'clock and taken a taxi to the address in the city that the singer had given to him. The last time he had been in Berlin the wall had loomed stark and impregnable, keeping him out as well as his friends officially in – save for their expeditions when passage to and fro had been accomplished without much difficulty. He had good friends in the East under the old regime; now with their past connections with the secret police, the Stasi, they had mostly gone underground.

He had been surprised at the meanness of the neighbourhood to which he had been directed and when the taxi had dropped him in a street of tall and grimy apartment blocks it reminded him more of the drab streets he remembered of the East. He had not expected that the man whom he wished to see would have cared to live in such a squalid area. But perhaps it was just an accommodation address. Or had the singer tricked him?

Inside the building the light was so dim that he had used his cigarette lighter to illuminate the stairs and on each landing to check the numbers of the doors. He had climbed three flights before he reached the number written on the paper that the singer had handed to him.

A thin-faced, elderly woman had answered his ring, keeping the door on the chain.

'I am looking for Josef. I am a friend and I have come from Paris.' He spoke in German.

'Who are you?' she said.

32

'Simonet, Jacques Simonet.' He held up a passport and showed the photograph to the woman. 'I was told that I might find him here. I have money for him.'

'He is not here.'

'Will he be back?'

'I do not know.'

'Can you pass a message?'

'If they telephone I shall tell them you called.'

'Will they be telephoning tonight? It is urgent. I want him to have the money which I have brought him.'

'I do not know. They may or they may not. What was the name?'

'Jacques Simonet. I am staying at the Hotel Bristol.'

The woman with her chin almost on the chain peered down at his clothes. The name of the hotel had impressed her.

'Tell them to telephone me at the Bristol. As soon as possible. Tonight or tomorrow, at the latest. I cannot wait long. It is a large sum of money.'

'Very well,' she said and closed the door.

He went down the stairs. The singer had not cheated him.

Back in the hotel he waited in his room. No message came and at midnight he went to bed.

The next day he had returned to the mean building and again rang at the door. This time there was no answer. He wrote his name on a piece of paper and pushed it under the door. That night he received the telephone call and next morning early he hired a car and was on the road.

As he drove Maitland remembered the last time he and Josef had driven west; they had been held up at the checkpoint on entering the autobahn because there was a telephone in the car and they had been obliged to complete endless formalities. Today he just drove.

At Padeburg he checked into a hotel, the Weisses Rossel, nondescript and almost hidden on a corner. After he had garaged the car, he found the post office and cabled an address in Repulse Bay in Hong Kong that he expected to arrive in three days. Then he returned to the hotel and waited for the man from Baghdad, Heinrich Bucholz.

Heinrich Bucholz was a tired-looking man of about fifty,

33

with little hair and gold-rimmed glasses in front of narrow, sharp eyes, looking the wearier because he had only returned to Germany that morning after the flight from Damascus. But he turned up at the hotel promptly at seven o'clock and the two men went up to the bedroom. As they went to the staircase, they passed a man sitting reading a newspaper, a briefcase on his knees. When they had disappeared the man left the hotel for he had accomplished what he had been sent to do. He had his photograph of Bucholz in whom he was interested, taken by a camera in the briefcase. He knew nothing of Maitland, save that he was English. As a matter of routine they would send London a print of the photograph.

Later that evening Maitland and Bucholz dined together.

At eleven o'clock, after Heinrich Bucholz had left, there came the telephone call for which Maitland was waiting with the directions for the next day. He took the call in his bedroom. The voice was that of a man but it was not Josef's.

The following morning he left for Eyendorf at 6.45. Twice he lost his way. At last, at the outskirts of the town, he found the country road for which he had been searching and at the end of which lay the place to which he had been bidden. From the road he could see that it was a large white house, isolated and screened by trees and surrounded by a garden with high hedges. He drove past slowly, observing the house and grounds. Then he turned the car at a farm gate and came back up the lane so that the car was facing the way from which he had come. He parked on the grass verge close to the tall hedge out of sight of the entrance. He locked the car and, taking his briefcase, he went through the gate into the garden and stood under some laurel bushes that over-hung the drive.

The house from close at hand looked decayed and dilapidated, the white paint peeling from the walls, one gutter broken and leaning away from the roof. The grounds were ragged and unkempt, the gravel green with weeds. To the front, beside and above the main front door, all the windows were closed and shuttered. To one side, where an outside stair led up steeply to an entrance, he could see evidence of occupation, curtains in the upper windows. Before going as he had been directed to the stair, he skirted the house, keeping under the shadow of the eaves of the deserted front with its shuttered windows. By the closed main door he stood for a time looking over the lawn, which led to the high hedge on the boundary and beyond that to the flat fields.

He took something from his pocket and seemed to be comparing it with the view in front of him. Then he made his way back around the side of the main house and climbed the stairs.

A woman answered his ring, the cleaning woman. She had on her hat and coat and was on her way out. She told him that he was expected and she directed him to what was the sitting half of a low-ceilinged room obviously converted from what had once been an attic. The room was divided into two, with steps in the centre leading up to another level where there was a bar with shelves lined with bottles and with stools before it. He heard the woman clatter down the stairs and from a window he saw her disappear at the end of the drive. He went over to another low window, which looked out over the front garden. He could see the lawn bordered by the high hedge and he moved closer to the glass, studying the view intently.

'Yes?'

He had heard no one enter the room and at the sound of the high-pitched voice, he drew back and swung round, expecting to see a woman. But standing close behind him was a large stout man, with a head as round as a football and a fat red face and eyes that almost disappeared into the blubber of his cheeks. He wore a check shirt and his belly bulged grossly from grubby canvas trousers. On his feet were a pair of felt carpet slippers.

'I was expecting Josef,' Maitland said.

'Who are you?' asked the fat man, in the shrill voice so surprising in one of such bulk.

'I am Jacques Simonet. I believe you expected me.'

Maitland went through the same routine for the fat man as he had with the woman at the apartment in Berlin, holding up a passport. Then he slipped it back into the inside pocket of his jacket.

'It was not you with whom I spoke on the telephone.'

'No,' said the man moving up the steps to the bar. 'I was told someone would be coming. You fit the description. They did not recognise the name you are using.'

35

By now he was behind the bar and he took a bottle from the shelf and two glasses. He put them on the bar.

'Schnapps?'

'No.'

The fat man shrugged, poured a glass and drank.

Then he said, 'Josef is in Geneva, or at least he was. He is leaving for the East, either tonight or tomorrow, whenever he gets a message. If you are quick and he hasn't left, you might catch him at the Hotel du Rhône. He does not want you to telephone.'

'Why was I brought here?'

'To see what you looked like.'

'That could have been done in Berlin. But, as it happens, I had good reason to come to Eyendorf.'

Maitland walked up the steps and sat on one of the bar stools, opposite to where the fat man stood with his glass in his hand. From his inside pocket Maitland brought out what he had been studying below in the garden. It was the photograph which he had removed from the girl's flat in Sloane Avenue.

'Will you look at this.' He handed the photograph across the bar to the man who slowly and carefully pulled a pair of spectacles from his shirt pocket. 'Look at the back first.'

By now the man had his glasses on and he turned the photograph over.

'You see what it says.'

The man read and then looked up.

'Yes,' he said.

'What does it say?'

'What it says. Eyendorf.'

'Yes. Eyendorf. Just the one word, Eyendorf. Now turn it over and look at the picture.'

The fat man did so, deliberately and sullenly.

'Do you know the two women?'

The man was studying the picture.

'I repeat, do you know the women in that photograph? Look at the background, the garden behind the women? Do you recognise it? Do you recognise that garden?'

Before the fat man could reply Maitland suddenly half rose and with extraordinary speed stretched across the bar, gripping

36

the fat man by the shirt with both hands, dragging the round head close against his, knocking the spectacles onto the bar. The bottle and the glass crashed onto the floor and the tumbler broke on the tiles. Then Maitland raised his right hand and in rapid succession slapped the fat cheeks, first with the palm and then, more brutally, with the back of his hand, repeating the pattern of the blows three times across the face. The man began to scream in his womanish voice and fell against the shelves, rolling bottles to the floor. Maitland, with one hand still gripping the checked shirt which had torn as the man fell, slid around behind the bar and pushed him violently, chopping with the side of his hand at the fat face, breaking the nose, until the fat man fell to the floor and Maitland stood astride and over the prostrate figure, his shoes crushing the broken glass. Then he leant down and pulled the man to his feet, almost throwing him into a chair.

The photograph had fallen onto the bar. Maitland picked it up and wiped the schnapps from it with his silk handkerchief. He went back to the figure slumped and blubbering in the chair and he held the photograph close in front of the fat man's eyes.

'Who are they? Who are the two women in the photograph?'

The man was moaning in his high shrill voice, wiping the blood from his nose with the back of his hand.

'Friends of Josef. I don't know their names. He brought them here.'

'Where had they come from?'

'I don't know. Don't hit me.' The fat man cringed, expecting another blow.

'Where did Josef say they were from?'

'He said they came from Berlin, they had all come from Berlin.'

'Who else was with them?'

'No one. Only the three of them.'

'When was this?'

'A month ago. They were only here one day.'

'What were their names?'

'I don't know. I tell you, I don't know.' The high-pitched voice was now a whine, broken by sobs. The fat man cowered back in the chair, the blood flowing from his face.

'They were just women. He brought them, I tell you. He had picked them up in a nightclub. They were lovers, Josef said. They made him laugh. He wanted to photograph them. You know what he is like.'

'Where had he met them?'

'I told you. In Berlin, in a club. He just brought them. For fun, he said, for the day, to photograph them together. He made them pose. Then they had a picnic in the garden. Then he drove them away. They were going on somewhere. I don't know where. I have not seen them since. He said they made him laugh. You know him.'

Maitland looked down at the fat man who was mopping the blood from his face with his sleeve. Maitland put the photograph back into his pocket.

'When did you last see Josef?'

'A week ago. He came and took some clothes for his trip.'

For a minute neither said anything. Maitland looked around the room. 'Where is the telephone?'

The fat man, one hand still to his face, the blood from his nose now staining the front and sleeve of his shirt, pointed to the lower part of the room and stayed sprawled in the chair into which he had been flung. Maitland backed down the steps and picked up the telephone. He asked the operator to give him Lufthansa in Hamburg.

Maitland missed Josef in Geneva. When he enquired at the Hotel du Rhône after the night flight from Hamburg, he was told that Josef had checked out the day before. He spent the night at the hotel, much of the time on the telephone. The following day he flew to Zurich and took the Swissair flight to Hong Kong. At the airport he took a taxi, which drove him through the tunnel under the harbour to Hong Kongside and then up the hill to an apartment block on the mid-levels. No one saw him. He let himself into an apartment in the west tower block; it smelt unused, musty. He switched on the dehumidifier and the air conditioning and then lay on the bed, stripped, smoking and drinking liquor, which he had bought on the plane, remembering what he had told Marie-Claire in

38

the rue Casimir Perier. He knew that he should not have spoken as he had. He slept. When he awoke it was dark. A storm was beginning and the thunder rolled round the Peak. Then he dressed and left. Outside it was raining heavily but after a time he found a cab in Kennedy Road.

When he returned two hours later the room was fresher and cooler. His clothes were very wet. He took some tablets from his briefcase and drank some water. He had a shower and lay on the bed, hoping that the pain in his head would lessen. The thunder had ceased and eventually he slept. When it was scarcely light, he rose and left the apartment, switching off the machines. He picked up a taxi opposite Bamboo Grove and told the driver to take him to the rear of the Hong Kong and Shanghai Bank building. He walked through the open deserted atrium into Stanley Street and turned east. He drank tea in a bar, killing time until the bustle of the city began in the street outside. Then he retraced his steps west towards the bank. Before he reached it, he entered the Swire Building and on one of the glass-enclosed bridges on a walkway above the street he stopped and stood for a time apparently studying some papers from his briefcase, which he had placed at his feet. In fact he was watching the people passing, both below and beside him. Then he doubled back through another building into the rear entrance to the Mandarin Hotel where he had more tea in the coffee shop. After about an hour he returned to the bank where he mounted the moving staircase to the second level. He waited in the queue behind the rope and when his turn came he paid in US dollars and drew out local cash. Then he walked west to the Bond building, took the elevator to the thirtieth floor and walked into the offices of the International Oriental Trading Company.

The Hong Kong Chinese receptionist looked up from the desk.

'Good morning, Mr Brandt,' she said. 'We were not certain when you would arrive but they are expecting you.'

He smiled at her and passed into the inner office. There were two men in the room, one a very old Chinese, the face lined as if it were a map and above it incongruously dyed black hair tied in a pigtail. The other was younger, a European, and he rose when Maitland entered. The old Chinaman remained seated, looking out of the window at the panorama of the harbour far below.

'When did you get in?' the European enquired.

'Last night,' Maitland replied.

There was a silence. Then the old Chinese man turned and looked at Maitland.

'Josef is dead. He was found this morning in his apartment in Wan Chai. His neck had been broken, by a blow of an open hand. So we knew that you were here.'

FIVE

The Master of St Peter's was enjoying himself.

It was the first Midsummer Feast for the Fellows and their guests over which Sir Alexander Murray had presided since his retirement from the Diplomatic Service and his election to the Mastership of this small but delightfully rich Cambridge College. In full fig, emblazoned with star and decorations, he sat at the centre of the High Table furnished with the fifteenth-century silver chalices and seventeenth-century bowls. With a smile of satisfaction on his distinguished face, he looked down the hall where, at four long sprigs lit by candlelight, the gowned figures of the Fellows were dining in splendour. On his left was his wife; on his right was the wife of his principal guest. Once upon a time she had been his mistress.

It was now nine months since the diplomatic career of Sir Alexander Murray had ended in high style in the Embassy in Paris. But to his disappointment he had not been selected as the Head of the Diplomatic Service, an appointment for which he believed that he was well qualified and would have adorned. He knew who had been responsible for his early retirement, the Foreign Secretary, whose handling of foreign affairs Alexander Murray was wont to describe as 'bizarre' and which he had endured with ever mounting acerbity.

Sir Alexander Murray's disapproval of what was to some the invigorating if erratic conduct of foreign affairs which this minister favoured had been ill concealed even from the minister himself. But to the exasperation of Sir Alexander and some of his cronies, the minister had from time to time enjoyed some success with the international community although his impetuosities and flouting of convention had often got him into trouble, to extricate himself from which he had needed all

41

his natural talent for debate in the House of Commons. It was said by the enemies of both the senior ministers at the Home and Foreign Offices that the man had only been appointed Foreign Secretary at the instigation of the Home Secretary who was confident that a spell at the Foreign Office would inevitably end in personal disaster and thus remove another potential rival to the succession to the Premiership. But so far the Foreign Secretary had gone his merry way, driving roughly his subordinates in the Foreign Service but on occasion demonstrating agility in negotiation at international council chambers so that he had continued to survive, if precariously, at the Foreign Office. The Home Secretary was having to hide his chagrin but, it was said, was only biding his time, confident that in the end the unorthodox behaviour of the Foreign Secretary would at last pull him down.

While to Sir Alexander the Foreign Secretary was a buffoon, to Godfrey Burne in his work at MI6 he was supportive and robust. None could deny the man's charm; nor his insatiable appetite for vintage champagne.

Sir Alexander Murray, whose looks suggested central casting had chosen some knight of the London stage to play the part of an immensely grand and wise ambassador, was no one's fool and in his youth had been as dashing as he was handsome. But with success had come what was, for his contemporaries and subordinates alike, an almost intolerable pomposity. Serving under so unorthodox a chief as the present Foreign Secretary, he had made no secret of his preference for a more conventional conduct of overseas affairs and from the start the relationship between minister and ambassador had been, to say the least, cool.

Then last summer the Foreign Secretary had unexpectedly appeared in Paris on a day when Sir Alexander and Lady Murray were in the evening giving a ball at the Embassy, the Hotel de Charost in the rue du Faubourg St-Honoré – the great house with the garden running down to the Champs-Elysées that Sir Alexander's predecessor the Duke of Wellington had purchased from Napoleon's sister, the amorous Princess Pauline Borghese. What was to have been a glittering occasion for the Murrays, to bid farewell before returning home to assume the expected position as Head of the Service or Office and an evening eagerly anticipated by the social and diplomatic community in Paris, was transformed, for the hosts at least, into a singularly tiresome and, as it turned out for the hopes of Sir Alexander, fatal occasion.

It had been only at the last minute that the Foreign Secretary had arrived in Paris and had imposed himself upon the Ambassador. The reason for his sudden descent was because he had insisted that the Ambassador seek for him a meeting with the French Foreign Minister at the Quai d'Orsay in order that the British minister could further press upon the French Government the need to support the stand of the British Government over economic disagreements with Bonn, a dispute only recently exhaustively discussed in Brussels. Sir Alexander, his mind much upon the swan song entertainment that he was to give that night but in any event sincerely doubting the wisdom of any immediate Franco-British meeting, had advised against this proposal. But when London insisted he had with difficulty made the arrangements to which the Quai d'Orsay had reluctantly consented, with the proviso that the meeting must unfortunately be brief as the French minister had on that evening another pressing commitment – which Sir Alexander well knew was the minister's weekly rendezvous at Choisy with a certain lady to whom the minister was much devoted.

The meeting had not been a success. The Foreign Secretary had been impulsive and clumsy. His man-to-man approach of downright common sense had been met with coolness. As a result he had grown heated and more vehement than was wise. The more he had blustered, the chillier had become the Frenchman, who had never wanted this meeting and was, understandably, anxious to get away. As an exercise in the particular style of diplomacy affected by the British Foreign Secretary, it had been a disaster.

Back at the Embassy the Foreign Secretary and the Ambassador had discussed the meeting in the library. The minister called for whisky and soda and helped himself liberally. The Ambassador, riled at having been instructed to ask for the meeting with the French which he had advised was inopportune, was at his most lofty and had hinted at the inappropriate nature of the approach that the Foreign Secretary had chosen to adopt in the discussion with his prickly and extremely formal opposite number. The Ambassador counselled that, with the French in particular, a more subtle approach was always more likely to attract acceptance of what the Foreign Secretary had in mind. The Foreign Secretary, sensing correctly that he was being patronised, had reacted violently, refusing as he said to have to follow the 'stuffed-shirt style' so fancied by officials and Sir Alexander in particular, and clutching his replenished whisky glass he had stumped off to change for dinner. His bad temper was exacerbated by the knowledge that he had handled the interview with the French minister foolishly and that the pompous Ambassador had been right throughout. This did not make it any the easier to accept the lecture which had been read to him in the library and which he therefore the more resented.

Although Sir Alexander did not know it, after that conversation in the library his fate to be passed over for the appointment as the Head of the Foreign Service was settled. The subsequent events of the evening, which were much enjoyed by the irreverent, only applied the seal.

At the dinner the minister talked loudly and drank steadily, watched frigidly by his host. At the ball, in a remarkable demonstration of affability quite uncharacteristic, as the Belgian Ambassador remarked, of the Anglo-Saxons, he happily mingled with the guests, playfully addressing all the pretty women with considerable freedom, indiscriminately pinching the anatomies of ambassadresses and several of the most icy of the ladies of the Faubourg St-Germain. Some of the more exuberant South American ladies much enjoyed it, slapping the minister playfully with their fans. The ladies from the Faubourg St-Germain did not. As the night wore on, well fortified by the champagne and reflecting after each glass more emphatically on his complaints about 'stuffed shirts', and in order, as he told the company, to liven up the party, he insisted upon executing enthusiastic Irish reels, which he had required the orchestra to play for an inordinate length of time.

His performance had culminated when he had lurched up

to the Papal Nuncio and invited His Eminence to dance. This surprising invitation had been, understandably, declined and the Ambassador had finally felt obliged to lead the Foreign Secretary away from the ballroom. On the stairs leading to the bedrooms, the minister had become abusive and the Ambassador had lost his temper employing words so rough that for all his apparent inebriation the Foreign Secretary next morning had well remembered them.

As the Italian Chargé d'Affaires later commented, it is always dangerous to assume how tight any man ever was and, in any event, the invitation to the Nuncio to dance may not have been due to any confusion brought about by a blurred vision of crimson ecclesiastical skirts but rather was a subtle Protestant joke. Anyhow that October the Foreign Secretary had survived the annual reshuffle, but Sir Alexander had been retired to wander restless and disconsolate around his study at his home in Derbyshire until, to his consolation and delight although not to that of his wife, Margaret, he had been invited to become the Master of St Peter's.

Margaret had had her fill of official pomp, which with Alexander as a consort was rarely negligible. When her husband was passed over, she secretly rejoiced. She looked forward to staying quietly at home and looking after her dogs, having earned, she felt, some relief from the stream of guests, official and family, which for forty years had flowed through her various drawing-rooms and which during the last four in the great house in the rue du Faubourg St-Honoré had swollen into a torrent. Now to her regret she was, although housed during the week in the more manageable although elegant eighteenth-century Master's Lodge, nevertheless obliged regularly to entertain dons and their wives, some of whom were decidedly dusty; and batches of undergraduates many of whom were decidedly raw. Tonight she was once again having to attend another of those grand official banquets that last autumn she had fondly believed were for her occasions never to be repeated.

As was the custom she sat beside her husband at the celebration of the 550th anniversary of the founding of the College, reserved and rather silent, although consoled by having as her neighbour at the dinner table her husband's principal guest, a particular friend who had been at the Quai d'Orsay when they had been *en poste* in Paris and who had flown from Charles de Gaulle that evening especially to be with them for Alexander's first Midsummer Feast and the celebration of the anniversary. He was the agreeable Bernard de Tourneville, and he was talking to her about the garden at Gauville.

On the other side of the Master sat Marie-Claire de Tourneville; beside her, Godfrey Burne, an Honorary Fellow of the College who had his own particular reason for attending the feast at St Peter's.

Marie-Claire and Godfrey had known each other for many years although not so intimately as she and Alexander who had now turned his handsome silver head away from Marie-Claire and towards Margaret on his other side.

'I am so glad that you both managed to come over. It is giving Alexander such pleasure to have you and Bernard here,' said Godfrey.

Marie-Claire put out her hand and let her long fingers rest for a moment on the lip of the silver cup in front of her, a gift to the College, Alexander had told her, from Cardinal Wolsey.

Godfrey went on: 'And we are delighted that you are coming down to spend next weekend with us at Finches. I don't believe that you ever came in the old days.'

'No, I never came. But Bernard has been, has he not? I am looking forward to seeing the place and to being with you in Wiltshire, especially if it stays as warm as it is tonight. Normandy last weekend was full of rain.'

Marie-Claire's English was formal, rather stilted.

'Alexander is enjoying his evening. He is certainly looking very grand.'

'Yes. I am so happy for him that he has this position. I was sad to hear that he had been passed over.'

Godfrey thought back to when Bernard had been serving at the French Embassy in London and when the handsome and in those days dashing Alexander had been at the European desk in the Foreign Office. How long ago was it? Twenty years? Marie-Claire was still very good-looking, he thought. 'Very well turned out', was how Margaret would describe her, in the black

46

dress that showed off the whiteness of her shoulders.

He noticed her fingers moving restlessly over the damask tablecloth. She seemed very tense, overwrought. Was it because she was sitting next to Alexander? How old would she be now? Forty-five? He remembered how she had looked when she was the centre of all attention in the London diplomatic world in the seventies and how he had been the one who had been obliged to warn his friend Alexander of the gossip about Alexander's affair with Marie-Claire. Godfrey himself had seen them together, quite by chance, at the Hind's Head Hotel at Bray one summer evening. They had not seen him, so absorbed had they been in each other. It was after that sighting that Godfrey had decided that he ought to ask Alexander to lunch with him at Boulestin. He had not liked what he felt he must say and at first Alexander had stayed silent and resentful. Then Alexander had said that he did not think that Margaret knew about the affair but that he was thinking of giving up the Foreign Service and going away with Marie-Claire. Godfrey had told him bluntly not to be a fool.

Shortly after that lunch he had heard that Marie-Claire had suddenly gone home and over the subsequent years Alexander had proceeded remorselessly from post to post and to ever grander embassies. Godfrey had seen little of Marie-Claire since those days in London, although over the years he had often to meet with Bernard on the business of their respective governments. Quite recently they had been involved together in the European effort to identify the route and the organisers of the drug traffic that now flowed across Europe from the East and South America. It was because of what he needed to discuss with Bernard about the developments and to seek his help that, when he had learnt that the de Tournevilles were to be at Cambridge, he had asked his wife, Angela, to invite them for the weekend.

'Alexander looks so well,' Marie-Claire said. 'Unlike the rest of us, advancing age suits him. But I am not so sure that Margaret is so happy as he. I believe that she would have liked to have stayed with her dogs in the country.'

'You are much too modest,' Godfrey replied. 'You look as enchanting and as beautiful as ever.'

She smiled, flattered, as he went on, 'But you are right about

Margaret. That is all she ever wanted, time for her dogs and her garden. She never enjoyed all the formal entertaining of the diplomatic life which was such meat and drink to Alexander. But she has played a great part in his success. She was such an asset and support to him, perhaps more than Alexander ever appreciated.'

Marie-Claire was silent and he wondered if he should have said what he had. She had spoken of Alexander's advancing years suiting him and Godfrey had meant what he had said about her. She remained very beautiful, but not the calm beauty she used to be. He was conscious of the tenseness and strain beneath the poise. Were the wounds of that old love affair with Alexander still open, even after all these years? He wondered how Alexander had ended it. With grace, he hoped. If he had not, she surely would not have been here. Or was her attendance just a duty, because of the diplomatic friendship and the professional connection between her former lover and her husband?

Godfrey had often asked himself if he had been right to speak out as he had. To interfere in two people's lives, to act the conscience, was no light responsibility. Had Bernard and Marie-Claire thereafter been happy? For that matter, had Alexander and Margaret?

As he pushed around on his plate the rich food of which he ate very little, he reflected on the pain which these affairs brought with them. He remembered Angela and how passionately she had once loved the man she had met on that holiday in Italy.

Godfrey and Angela had been married ten years when Angela's affair had begun. Godfrey had been obliged to go on an official trip to Langley, the CIA Headquarters in Washington and Angela had taken the chance to go with a group on a painting holiday in Tuscany. It was there that she had met the man who became her lover. Later in London the two had for a time shared a studio in which during each day they painted together. It would halve the cost was Angela's excuse. At first Godfrey had not understood how it could have come about. He had thought that she was content with their life together and he had suffered more than he had believed possible, but he had brought himself to understand. Nothing had ever been said between Angela and him but as he had known of the affair soon after it had begun, so he knew when it was over. Only later had he realised how lonely she had been and that her loneliness had been his fault. He had been too absorbed in his work to think enough of her and of how conscious she must have been of the passage of the years and of life slipping by. In the end it had not ruined their life together. They had survived. More, they had been very happy.

He could see Angela now, on the other side of the table large and comfortable and friendly. She was laughing with her neighbour, a biochemist from whom it was actually a feat to extract even a wintery smile. But she had him laughing! How lucky they had been. But, as his gaze moved back and along the table, he was not so sure about Margaret.

He turned to his neighbour on his other side. She was another scientist, a physicist, and garrulous. She only knew that Godfrey was something to do with government, a civil servant, and she became very earnest about embryo research and indignant about its opponents – the myopic medievalists, she called them. She spoke so much and so fast that Godfrey was able to nod and smile occasionally and think about the real purpose why he was here, the talk he had planned when the dinner was over. For it was then that he would attempt to persuade the man whom he had chosen to return temporarily to the service and to carry out Carlos' plan.

At the same time, on Godfrey's other side Marie-Claire had turned back to Alexander. Only now and then did she look up to his face and into his eyes. But she was not, like he was, remembering. Save for a moment of wonder at how handsome he had remained and how pompous he had grown, she was not thinking of him at all.

Although neither knew it, both she and Godfrey, as they smiled and nodded at their neighbours, were thinking about the same man. To Marie-Claire the man was called Jacques Simonet, the lover who so disturbed her peace; to Godfrey he was the man Martin Maitland, the quarry who needed to be hunted down.

49

SIX

At about the time when the Master had led his guests into the hall to dine, the Home Secretary with his Personal Assistant in attendance had crossed from the House to the small television studio where the BBC conducted Parliamentary interviews when the House was sitting.

The Home Secretary had ended his speech, which had opened the debate on the prison riots, at about five o'clock and he had then sat on the government front bench to hear the speeches that followed his. As soon as he had sat down, he had felt irritated and petulant. On this occasion there was none of the exhilaration that followed a Parliamentary or platform triumph. He knew that his speech had not gone well. His bluff and deliberately waffling style had on this occasion not amused his own troops. The backbenchers in his own party had been restless and, unusually, several had interrupted him. His sallies against the opposition had not been received as he had intended. When he sat down the Prime Minister had not said anything, just patted his knee as though to comfort him. The gesture had enraged him. He had been followed in the debate by the Shadow Home Secretary who for once had been rather effective. That had increased the irritation. The debate would go on until 9.30 in the evening, when the Attorney General would make the last speech for the government before the vote at ten o'clock, the 'winding up' speech, as it was called. After the Home Secretary's failure much would depend upon a successful performance by the Attorney General. So the Prime Minister was looking pensive when the Home Secretary slipped out of the Chamber to be interviewed on television.

He took out his annoyance on the civil servant.

'Why on earth have you fixed up this interview?' he said

50

testily. 'I ought to be on the bench listening to the debate.'

'But this is an important programme, Home Secretary, and I thought that you should like the opportunity to explain the government's position to the public.'

'Which you feel that I have singularly failed to do in the House,' he said savagely.

But when they reached the studio the show of heartiness returned. On the programme he did better than he had in the debate and he began to feel better. After they were off the air, the interviewer lingered to gossip with him.

'I spoke with the new Chancellor this afternoon. He seems to have settled in well,' said the interviewer as he gathered together his notes.

'Ah, Ambrose. You spoke with Ambrose, did you? A good friend of mine, Ambrose. Known him all my life. You are right. He has settled down very well at the Treasury. Excellent appointment, excellent. Just the right man for the job. All those damn dots, wasn't that what Disraeli said? Or was it Randolph Churchill?'

The Home Secretary laughed heartily. Then he stopped abruptly and shook his head, the genial expression succeeded by one of concern.

'Off the record, I'm just a little worried that Ambrose may not have sufficient, what they used to call in the eighteenth century, sufficient "bottom" for these extremely difficult days. You know what I mean, the gut determination for the job. After all, he's got to take some pretty tough decisions. I hope I'm wrong, of course. Just a slight worry.'

He shook his head again sadly. This 'slight worry' about the ability of his colleagues, especially the more prominent, constantly plagued the Home Secretary, a worry that he often felt constrained to share with the media although not with his colleagues.

The interviewer who knew his man well had deliberately cast a fly and had been rewarded. So he cast another: 'I understand that the Attorney is winding up your prison debate tonight. I wonder how long he will stay before going on the Bench. But he's a useful performer in the House. A safe pair of hands, isn't that what they call it?'

51

By now they were strolling together towards the exit to the studio.

'Yes,' said the Home Secretary. 'Yes. The Attorney is winding up. A safe pair of hands, yes, that's what they call it.' He sounded unenthusiastic. Then he stopped and said gloomily: 'But with him it is not "bottom" I worry about but whether he's got what I like to call the "brio", which is needed for making a successful winding up speech. Is there enough fire in his belly, for that's what the fellows like at the end of a debate, you know? Something to send them off happy. Some of the fellows don't think that the Attorney can manage that.' He shook his head gravely. It was clear that he agreed with the fellows. 'Not his fault, of course. It's just not in his nature. He'd make a good judge though.'

Then he brightened up. 'Well, thank you, old fellow. Nice to see you again. Splendid interview, as usual. Fierce but fair, eh? I can understand why they pay you so much.' Laughing heartily and shaking the interviewer warmly by the hand he bustled back to the House.

'Bloody prima donna,' he said to the civil servant as they crossed the road.

Later in the evening, after the ten o'clock division, the Home Secretary sat at one of the round tables in the smoking-room drinking whisky and soda surrounded by his cronies. Among them was the Solicitor General, who was pleasantly conscious of the Home Secretary's favour and who was accordingly solicitous in attending upon him in these sessions with his supporters. The Solicitor wanted the Attorney General's job, and the Home Secretary was the man to get it for him. So he smiled indulgently but not too obviously at the Home Secretary's jokes.

Brian Pepper, the Prime Minister's Parliamentary Private Secretary crossed the room and came over to the group.

'Well, I'm glad that's over. The debate ended far better than I feared it might. The PM was particularly pleased with the Attorney. He thought the Attorney pulled it round superbly. Very sound. It was just what was needed.'

'You are right,' said the Home Secretary. 'A sound wind up by the Attorney. Quite sound. But . . . ' he paused, 'perhaps

52

not quite enough "brio" towards the end, if you know what I mean. The fellows like to go away with a bit of "brio" or a bit of a laugh. And not much of that from Mr Attorney, eh?'

He laughed, beaming around at the cronies. The Solicitor General confined himself to a judicious smirk.

By this time on that same evening the party at Cambridge was dispersed between the Fellows' Common Room and the Master's garden. Godfrey had sought out the man he had come to persuade and had steered him deftly from the Master's Lodge to the end of the garden where they could be alone. It was a warm June night, such a night, Godfrey reflected, as only England can produce – and then all too rarely. They sat, smoking cigars, on a bench before a small lily pond. The moon was full and by its light and that from the open windows of the Lodge, they could see in the distance the figures of the diners sauntering around the garden, some in couples, others gathering in groups, the women more easily visible in their long coloured dresses. From time to time the two men could hear the laughter and see the girls suddenly clutching at the arms of the men in their dark coats, occasionally darting at each other like tropical birds.

Godfrey's companion was Edmund Hamilton, a slim man in his mid-thirties with a strong, angular face which, when he smiled, had a quizzical, slightly mocking appearance. He had the dark handsome looks and colouring of his Spanish mother. A bachelor, he had only recently been elected to a Fellowship and was an historian; his period was the sixteenth- and seventeenth-century Spanish and Portuguese Empires in Latin America on which he was presently engaged in producing a substantial work. He spoke both languages and a decade earlier, as a young man straight down from the university, he had been spotted by Godfrey and recruited into 'the friends', as MI6 was generally known, although so far as the outside world was concerned Edmund, on leaving Cambridge, had joined the civil service in the Ministry of Defence. He had served for a few years in the office, never overseas, and then suddenly he had resigned and had left for St Peter's.

'How are you enjoying yourself, Edmund?'

'Very much. It is a different world from that of your office, although I find that some of the work is strangely similar to that which I did with you.'

'Not the same element of intrigue?'

'There wasn't any intrigue when I was with you, unless you are talking about the in-house Whitehall variety. That was vicious enough.'

Godfrey smiled. 'There's always plenty of that.'

'Not that academics are innocents. My colleagues are a splendidly feline lot, but strangely unworldly, especially those who have never strayed outside. It is sometimes hard to take their opinions as opposed to their scholarship seriously. No, I found that working for you under James Kent meant little more than being engaged in the humdrum compilation of facts and analysis. That is why what I do now is so familiar.'

'But more intellectually stimulating?'

'Perhaps. But your work could be demanding enough. I suppose that much must have changed since '88 and '89?'

'Strange, wasn't it? Two hundred years after the fall of the Bastille came the fall of Marxism. The end of two *anciens régimes*.'

'Did you anticipate it?'

'Neither its extent nor its timing. No more than did Louis XVI. Do you remember his entry in his diary for July the fourteenth 1789 when the Bastille was stormed?'

'No.'

'"*Rien*".' Then Godfrey said quietly, 'I hear that you have a study in hand on the early Spanish conquerors in South America.'

'Yes. And it is proving far more of a labour than I anticipated. The scope is, perhaps, too ambitious and I shall in the end have to limit it. At present I am engaged in the research.'

'I was told that you were thinking of going to the Argentine shortly to do some work in BA. Will you be spending the whole Long Vacation there?'

'Probably. I need to locate some sources which I can only do in BA. Also there is a personal quest. I have an ancestor, a soldier who died somewhere in Colombia in the sixteenth century but whose grave the family never located. I would like to try and find out more about him.'

'That would take you to Colombia?'

'Possibly. It's just an idea.'

'Would your research take up all your time?'

'Most of it.'

'When do you plan to go?'

'In a few days.'

There was a pause and Edmund watched the smoke of his cigar spiral up between his eyes and the figures standing in front of the windows of the Lodge. When the stroll down to the seat by the lily pond had been suggested by Godfrey Edmund had thought no more than that his old Chief had wanted an opportunity to gossip. Now he reflected upon how expertly he had been manoeuvred into this agreeable but isolated spot. Godfrey, he suddenly realised, was up to something.

Then it came, casual, unforced.

'When you are in South America, could you do something for me in Colombia? It might fit in with your programme.'

There was a silence. Then Edmund said wryly, 'I suppose you have in mind a visit to Medellin, the centre for all the drug barons in South America.'

Godfrey did not rise. 'No, I wasn't thinking of a trip to Medellin. Near there, but not actually to Medellin itself. What I want is some information.'

'Why do you need me? You have many more experienced people than me.' Edmund stretched his arms lazily above his head. 'After all, C, as far as "the friends" are concerned, I am retired.' But he smiled as he spoke.

'No one ever retires from our business,' said Godfrey. 'It is a life sentence as you well know.' Then he went on: 'You ask why you and why not my people who are on the Colombian station? Well, there have been casualties, too many casualties, and they have not been accidents. Now they have identified the one man whom I still trust and God knows how long he will survive. I need someone new, someone to go where he cannot. I thought of you because you know Latin America and you could have good reason to be there.'

Godfrey paused. Edmund watched as a girl at the far end of

55

the garden darted at a man, who turned and ran from her laughing until he allowed himself to be caught. Edmund saw the man lead the girl away from their companions. They stopped by a tree and the girl leant with her back to it and the man bent forward and kissed her.

'If you want nothing from Medellin –' Edmund began, but Godfrey interrupted him.

'I did not say that. I shall, in the end. All roads in this business eventually lead to Medellin. But that is later. The people I am interested in originally came from Medellin but they have established themselves somewhere nearer to Cali. It is over the mountains into that area where I would want you to go. For somewhere in that region there has been set up a new centre for a highly organised and disciplined group which over the past two years has grown increasingly significant in the traffic with Europe.'

The man and the girl were now strolling back to the Lodge, her head against his shoulder.

'What is this centre?'

'If I am right it is the base which controls what I call a "railway".'

'A railway?'

'Yes, an odd kind of railway, one which crosses continents and oceans. The part of the line in which I am interested starts from this special depot or station in Colombia. It is the head-quarters which controls a "railway" which runs from the growing fields across the Atlantic to Europe. It has branch lines to Libya, Iraq – and to Belfast.'

'Drugs?'

'Drugs by themselves, no. Rather drugs, money and arms, for as I said there are branch lines. Drugs to buy the arms to protect the drugs which provide the money. This place is the nerve centre. I need to find it. And identify not just the couriers or foot soldiers but the commanders.'

'Have you identified any of them?'

'None of the leaders, although we may have identified one man who might lead us to the people who control it.'

'Who is he?'

'He is an Englishman. He was in London last Thursday. Now

56

he has disappeared. Something frightened him off. It could have been the death of a girl.'

'A girl?'

'Yes. She died very suddenly but naturally from some condition of the brain and I think that this man, Martin Maitland, may have been with her when she died. Now he has disappeared. Either her sudden death alarmed him because of the enquiries which would follow or it was something else. He may have found out something from the girl which caused him to run. We had only just heard of him. Now he has disappeared. When the body of the girl was found by a Brazilian woman friend called Pilar Olivella she at once assumed that a man called Maitland must have been involved. We need confirmation but I believe that we will find that he is known in Colombia.'

'If you are right, what would be his role?'

'That of their professional killer, used by them and by others. If I am right he will surface sooner or later in Colombia and if we can get onto his tracks he might lead us to the place for which I am searching. But that is just a means to an end. To find the place, that is the real task.'

'So it is important,' said Edmund.

'Yes,' Godfrey replied. 'It is very important, far more important than many of those east–west operations in the past. Today the drug traffic is the real threat and it has come to Europe with a vengeance.'

For a time they smoked in silence. There was still one last group of those who had been at the feast in the hall, standing and talking at the far end of the garden by the Lodge.

Then Godfrey said, 'So there are two tasks. The first and less important is to speak with Pilar Olivella to discover what was the connection between the dead girl and Maitland. The second, the real task, is to find that centre.'

He got up and stubbed his cigar into a tub of wooden slats, a waste basket near to the seat. Then, looking down at Edmund, he went on: 'James Kent would be officially in charge of your briefing but he does not know what my real objective is.'

'James Kent! You know what he thinks of me.'

'Kent would make the arrangements solely in BA and in

finding Pilar Olivella. In Colombia you would get your instructions from Carlos in Bogota and Carlos is my man. Kent knows nothing about slipping you over the hills beyond Cali.'

Godfrey turned to face up the garden, now empty in the moonlight for the last group had disappeared into the Lodge. The noise of laughter from the house as well as from the garden had ended. The people, his colleagues, Edmund thought, were now on their way home, back to their quiet and safe Cambridge houses while he in this peaceful garden was talking to a man who was asking him to go on a trip to a country thousands of miles away and find for him a place that was the head-quarters of a drug ring and the home of a killer.

Godfrey turned back to Edmund who was still sprawled on the seat, the cigar dead in his fingers.

'I don't want any confrontation or any heroics. All that I want is the report of an intelligent observer. I want information. That is all.'

'When I was with you I never served overseas. I wanted to but Kent would not have it.'

'It is not Kent who is asking you now. It is I. Kent does not know what Carlos in Bogota and I have in mind. But I repeat, I want no heroics. That will come later and from other people, once we know where this place is. But I must not disguise from you that what I ask you to do could be dangerous.'

Edmund rose from the bench and plucked at a spray from the bed of shrubs beside it. He began to strip it, petal by petal. He did not look at Godfrey.

'When I was a child I had a grand-uncle who used to tell us tales about the "Great Game" played by our grandfathers on the North-West Frontier, Kipling country, the borders of Afghanistan and the Raj. You remember? Subalterns disguised as Pathans wandering about the tribes gathering information. The stories were probably invented but as tales went they were none the worse for that. It was one of the reasons why I joined you. But I found that all that you set me to was analysis and research.'

'At which you were very good.'

'I was sorry to leave because I thought that I had lost my only chance for adventure. I would like to have seen if I could live up to the heroes in my grand-uncle's stories.'

Godfrey said sharply, 'There will be none of that nonsense. I told you, I want no heroics. Just information.'

When Edmund next spoke it was so softly that Godfrey only half caught what he was saying but later it was the part of all that had been said that evening that Godfrey was best to remember.

'I would enjoy the adventure of proving myself to myself.'

'What do you mean? What I want from you is to observe and listen and report. Nothing more.'

With a cricketer's arm, Edmund threw the stub of his dead cigar deep into the bushes. Then he turned back to Godfrey.

'I was talking to myself, to the secret me, to the child who listened to those tales so many years ago. I will go, C. Of course I will go.'

'How soon?'

'As soon as you like.'

'Then I want you on the flight to BA tomorrow night. Tomorrow early, come to the office for a briefing. I will have your papers ready.' He put his arm on Edmund's. 'You must forget your romantic old grand-uncle.'

'He was only a storyteller, telling tales to children.'

They began to walk to the Lodge, Godfrey with his hand still on the younger man's arm.

'It should not take long. A few days easing you up to Bogota from the south. Then only a couple of days when we have got you in. But I don't want any misunderstanding. It could be dangerous.'

'I know,' said Edmund. 'That is why I shall go.'

They went into the Lodge.

In the dimly lit hall, before Godfrey went to collect Angela and find Webster to drive them home, Edmund said, 'A strange end to a Midsummer Feast.'

'When next year we celebrate together the Midsummer Feast of St Peter's,' answered Godfrey, 'all this will be over and done with and half-forgotten.'

SEVEN

On the evening of the Saturday before the helicopter landed in the garden at Finches, the seventeenth-century stone manor house that had been the home of the Burne family for generations, Godfrey had removed the hoops from the croquet lawn so that the machine could land where the previous afternoon the house party had so inexpertly been trying to propel the coloured balls beneath the rectangular hoops now stored away in the garden shed. As the helicopter descended the wind from its rotors bent the rose bushes almost double and swept the grass that had not been taken up at the cutting on the Friday scurrying in small whirlpools across the lawn.

The noise of the machine's approach and then the clatter as it arrived had broken into the quiet of the Sunday morning of the Wiltshire village of Chapel Iford and especially into the reflections and studies of the vicar, the Reverend Henry Makepiece now back from his church and with his books in the library in the vicarage. They were not, in truth, his books; they had been the gift of an eighteenth-century predecessor who had bequeathed a remarkable collection of volumes and manuscripts to the use and benefit of the incumbent vicar of the parish of Chapel Iford while he held the living, on condition that they remained housed in the vicarage and access to them was allowed to visiting scholars. Succeeding incumbents had imitated the generosity of the founder of the library so that after two hundred years the number of volumes had swollen until they stretched from wall to wall in handsome mahogany bookcases with the collection of documents laid out in the drawers beneath.

Matins and Holy Communion were safely over so the noisy arrival had not disturbed the few who had attended the vicar's service but it did disturb him as he rose from his desk and peered crossly out of the window of the library as the helicopter appeared over the top of the clump of tall chestnuts in full bloom, which stood at the corner of the lane and his neighbour's drive. There it hovered like an ungainly bird of prey over its quarry until it began to descend and disappeared from sight although not from sound.

That the village should have to put up with this intrusion and that all the inhabitants should be obliged to hear if not to witness the ostentatious arrival or departure of the people who lived literally over his garden wall aroused in the vicar far from Christian sentiments. He resented not only the arrival of the noisy machine but also the power and importance that it represented, more even than he resented the absence from his church that morning, like most Sunday mornings, of any of the house party presently at Finches.

Henry Makepiece had only recently arrived in the parish; his neighbours, the Burnes, had been in the village far longer than he, indeed their family for centuries. The vicar and his wife, Anne, had married late in life and they had come to the vicarage only twelve months previously. When they came they both had known that she was suffering from leukaemia. He had hoped that the beauty of the surroundings and the charm of the vicarage and its garden might somehow encourage the disease to leave her alone, or at least to delay its progress. He had prayed that they might have several more years together for he knew of some who had lived long after the diagnosis. But then, only three months in their new and graceful eighteenth-century home, her condition had suddenly deteriorated. Within weeks she was dead.

He buried his Anne in the churchyard and his loneliness began in earnest, his house lifeless and empty. Often as he sat in the library cataloguing and listing the volumes and documents or preparing the sermons that so few came to the church to hear, he stayed late into the night in order to postpone the time when he had to mount the stairs to what had been for so short a time his and Anne's bedroom. Sometimes he would look up from the pool of light on his desk into the shadows at the far end of the room and think that he could see her in her chair working at her embroidery. But it was only a wraith and then he would surrender to his despair and to an ever increasing bitterness, which had made him turn against his God who had rejected his prayers.

At first he had prayed for the strength to drive from him this rejection of his God but these, like his prayers for Anne, were not answered and his bitterness increased. The practice of his office now became no more than the routine performance of professional duties. He told himself that he ought to go away and leave this place that had witnessed the last weeks of his beloved Anne, but their marriage had been childless, he was growing old and he had nowhere to go. Also, as he had to admit, he was too fond of the celebrated library and his role as its custodian ever to leave voluntarily. He knew further that he had begun to enjoy the solicitude of his parishioners who treated him as the victim of tragedy and gave to him a special place in this parish. Whereas if he were to leave he would be just another elderly clergyman widower. So he determined to stay.

When Anne had died, his neighbour Angela Burne had been kind, doing all that she could to help and mitigate his loneliness. He was regularly invited to come through the gate in the wall that divided the garden of Finches from the vicarage to dine or lunch at Finches where he was treated more as an old friend of the family than as a neighbour of only a few months' standing. But in his loss and loneliness there had perversely arisen a bitterness directed not only at the God who had permitted Anne to be taken from him but at the neighbours who were doing their best to provide him with support. The Burnes became the human focus of his pain and of his resentment at the blow life had dealt him. Their hospitality, which he regularly accepted, he regarded secretly with contempt as he compared the happiness of their home with his sour life and empty house. Back in the vicarage after an evening as their guest, he would sneer to himself about his hosts and at their important friends and at the comfort in which they lived.

He told himself that this resentment of the Burnes was demeaning but he grew to nurse his obsession until it gave to him almost a purpose without which his life would have been the emptier. His secret hatred was not lessened, indeed he tried to make it somewhat excused, by his knowledge that, in religion, Lady Burne was a Roman.

The noise of the engine of the helicopter, which had lessened while it had idled on the ground decanting or receiving its passengers, increased as the machine rose again and Henry Makepiece watched as it gathered height above the trees and swung away out of sight.

Then the telephone rang. He walked across the room and picked it up. At once he recognised the voice.

'Mr Makepiece, it is exceedingly late in the morning and you will probably have made your arrangements for luncheon, but if you were free and would like it, we would be so delighted if you would care to come over and join us. I know it is unforgivable to ask you so very late,' the voice went on, 'but Godfrey has been called away. You must have heard the awful racket from that machine.'

'Indeed, Lady Burne, I did. Indeed I did,' he purred into the receiver.

'Wasn't it hideous? Such a noise! And on a Sunday morning! Very inconsiderate for all of us, and especially for Godfrey who has been whisked off to some government conference. Anyhow, I was talking to one of our guests who is staying with us from Paris and I said that the helicopter must have greatly disturbed you when you were probably in your library and I mentioned the collection which you have in the vicarage and he was so interested. So I wondered if you would care to take Godfrey's place with us and perhaps afterwards, if you were agreeable, I could bring our friends over and take a look at some of your treasures?'

'How kind, how very kind of you, Lady Burne, to think of me,' he said. 'But I have already, alas, prepared my modest Sunday repast and I ought not to let that go to waste, as I am sure that you will understand. But, pray,' he went on, 'do bring your friends from Paris to the library in the afternoon. Indeed this morning I have been studying something which might well interest them, some sixteenth-century books published in Paris and a 1530 Basle edition of St John Chrysostom.'

'I knew that it was much too late to ask you and I do hope you did not mind –'

'Of course not, of course not,' he interrupted. 'I appreciate your kindness in thinking of me, which, dear Lady Burne, you do so regularly.'

'Nonsense, Mr Makepiece. So long as you were not offended. It was just a last-minute thought. Well, could we come at about half-past three? Would that be convenient?'

'Excellent,' he said. 'I shall, as ever, look forward to seeing you. Three-thirty, then.'

He replaced the receiver and went to his kitchen and savagely cut himself a slice of cheese.

At Chequers the cast for the conference was assembling. As the helicopter that had brought him from Wiltshire prepared to land, Godfrey saw on the ground another, which he presumed had brought the Foreign Secretary from his official house at Chevening in Kent and with whom Godfrey had spoken earlier in the morning. When they had landed Godfrey crouched beneath the still turning propeller and made his way from the field to the garden gate. Inside the house, he was greeted in the hall by the Director-General and the Permanent Secretary at the Home Office.

'You are late, C,' said the Permanent Secretary.

'Fashionably late, George. Where are all the Great Men?'

'In the white sitting-room, with the American Ambassador. The Home Secretary brought the Solicitor General in his car. Apparently the Attorney is at The Hague.'

Very convenient, thought Godfrey.

'When did they pick up the Libyan?' he asked.

The DG replied, 'Last evening, at Heathrow. Quite by chance on a fairly routine check, routine that is for Libyans. They found on him a small quantity of cocaine and then, after a search, the writing on a small piece of paper.'

'Pretty careless, wasn't it?'

'It was. He was en route to Bogota, changing in London and would not ordinarily have had to pass an inspection. I suppose he couldn't do without his cocaine. But we take special steps with such people.'

'Where was the paper found?'

'Rolled up inside the top half of a hollowed-out lead pencil. The top unscrewed and the paper was inside the tube. Ingenious and well made.'

'But old-fashioned.'

'Yes, we had seen that before. On the paper were a series of numbers, some we believe may be telephone numbers and others could be times and dates for a meeting. There were also four capital letters, grouped in two pairs, BV and LP. It was alert of them to have found the coke.'

'It was,' said Godfrey. He knew what the letters stood for but all he said was: 'Now they will know that we know.'

'Not necessarily. The man was not present when we inspected the pencil, which we handed back to him with his other belongings. He would not know for certain that we had found the paper. He will be charged with possession of the drug and remanded in custody. It might give you time before the trial. You have sent someone, I am told.'

'Yes,' said Godfrey and wandered over to the French window. He was not going to discuss it further.

It was warm in the house and the men were formally dressed in suits and ties. Godfrey thought of his garden at Finches. This meeting would probably be a waste of time. What could the politicians contribute? But he supposed that they had to be involved. The Americans were putting on the pressure. Still, it would have been better to have left it to the professionals. He had said this earlier to the Foreign Secretary on the telephone and that surprising man had agreed.

The Private Secretary came out of the white sitting-room.

'We are going to have lunch before the meeting as the American Ambassador has to get away,' he said.

'That is a relief,' said Godfrey as they walked onto the terrace for a drink. Then he reflected that having lunch before the meeting would probably prolong it. Especially if the Home Secretary and the Foreign Secretary got at each other.

But at the meeting in the Long Gallery the Home Secretary was, for him, unusually silent. So too was the Foreign

Secretary, perhaps because he was in further trouble with his Cabinet colleagues due to another clumsy confrontation, this time with the Germans, which had infuriated the PM. But at the luncheon he had eaten the salmon and drunk the surprisingly good English white wine enough for two. He had sat next to Godfrey.

'You and Angela must come again to Chevening, C,' he had said. 'What about next weekend?'

Godfrey groaned inwardly. It would take him from Finches and, agreeable a host as the Foreign Secretary was on such occasions, marching his guests up the tall hill to a gap in the beech woods that gave a spectacular view of the Palladian house below and then walking them back around the lake, a visit would take up time when time over the next weeks might be short.

'We would love to, but it may depend upon what develops from what we are going to talk about after lunch. I might be busy.'

At the meeting Godfrey, when invited by the Prime Minister, corroborated what the Americans had said in the message from the President brought by the Ambassador, and reminded the ministers of the double civil war being fought in Colombia: first the Colombian government against the drug barons; then the drug barons between themselves, Escobar versus the sophisticated Cali cartel who had become the principal suppliers of drugs to Europe. Now the dealers were looking for arms to protect themselves and their sources of raw coca in the Popyan-Cacua region and assassination squads had been brought in to deal with rivals. Recently, he said, they had identified one operator in London.

'Identified?' the Home Secretary interrupted. 'Stumbled upon, wouldn't you say?' He laughed pleasantly.

It was one of his few interruptions. Godfrey concluded by advising that both the CIA and the MI6 organisation in Colombia had been penetrated.

'I have sent in a new man to take a look and report.'

Soon thereafter the officials were dismissed leaving the ministers to continue their discussions among themselves.

'How do I get home?' asked Godfrey.

'I'll get you a car, C,' said the Private Secretary.

'First class to work, by helicopter,' grumbled Godfrey. 'Second class home.'

At Finches Bernard de Tourneville was still in the vicarage with Henry Makepiece. After a time, Angela and Marie-Claire had left the two men together and had gone for a stroll through the garden and into the beech woods. As they walked they had chatted desultorily. Angela was distressed by the tension from which Marie-Claire appeared to be suffering and which Angela and Godfrey had both noticed at the feast at Cambridge. She had hoped that the country and their weekend together might have relaxed her friend. But it had not. If anything, Angela thought, the look of strain on the beautiful face of Marie-Claire had increased.

It was too hot to walk for long and the two soon returned to the garden and to the shade of the summerhouse. They sat in silence, neither looking at the other but ahead of them towards the tall scarlet poppies and the clumps of peonies that stood out so prominently in the herbaceous borders, which stretched back to the house.

After a time Angela said, 'What is wrong, Marie-Claire?'

Marie-Claire jerked her head and turned towards Angela. 'Wrong?' she said. 'What do you mean? Why do you ask that?'

'You seem so tense and troubled, so unhappy. I have felt this since we were all together in Cambridge. Forgive my interfering, but we have been friends for so long. I cannot help feeling that something is wrong.'

There was a pause. Marie-Claire looked down at her hands in her lap.

'Yes,' she said, almost in a whisper. 'There is. I am very unhappy.'

For a time neither spoke. Then Angela asked, 'Is it Bernard?'

Angela was startled at the strength of the other's reply: 'No! No, it is nothing to do with Bernard. Nothing at all.'

Angela remained silent. When Marie-Claire spoke again Angela saw that there were tears in her eyes.

'It is to do with me. It is nothing to do with Bernard. I love

Bernard. It is what I am doing, what I have been doing with someone else. What I cannot stop.'

When Marie-Claire said this, Angela thought back to a time in her own life many years ago, to a scene that she would never forget in a tall studio off the King's Road in Chelsea, with a man standing with his back towards her looking out of the window at the rain. Angela could still hear her own voice telling the motionless figure by the window of her unhappiness, that the pain was too great and that what was between them had to stop. She remembered stumbling down the wooden, uncarpeted stairs out into the grey London rain, certain at that time that all happiness for her had fled for ever and that nothing save emptiness remained.

Angela looked at the unhappy figure of her friend in the chair beside her and then beyond to the garden and the rose-coloured brick of her house in which for so long she had been and still remained so happy, her life so fulfilled, the unhappiness of that affair now only a distant memory.

'Are you so much in love?' she said.

'Yes.' It was a whisper. 'Only it is not love. I wish it were.'

'Do you want to talk about it?'

Marie-Claire did not reply and Angela saw the fingers twining and twisting, the fingers she had noticed at the College feast which were so rarely still.

Then Marie-Claire said, 'It has been going on for a year. He is younger than I am. It is very shaming.'

'What is so shaming?' asked Angela. 'That you are having an affair or because he is so much younger than you?'

'Because I cannot stop seeing him and because of the kind of man that he is.'

Again, neither spoke.

Then Angela asked, 'Is he very unkind?'

Marie-Claire put her hand to her eyes and gave a laugh, but there was no humour in it, more like a cry.

'I do not think he knows what it is to be kind. He is not like Godfrey or Bernard, or even Alexander who has become so pompous. You know,' she added, 'that Alexander and I, long ago when we were in London, were lovers?'

'Yes,' replied Angela. 'I knew.'

'This man is not like any of them. He is certainly not like Bernard, whom I love. No, he is another kind altogether. He is from another kind of world.'

'What kind of world?' Angela asked. Then she went on quickly, 'But I should not ask questions.'

'No, I need to talk. I want to talk. I am glad that you began this. I must talk to somebody.'

Angela stretched out her hand and placed it for a moment on the other's arm.

Marie-Claire went on, almost to herself: 'He never speaks about the world he lives in but the other day, for the first time, he told me something. I know now that he is involved in something strange and that he is in danger. But I don't care. When I am with him, I can think of nothing and of nobody else. When I am away from him, when Bernard and I are living our life in Paris attending official functions at the Elysée or at home at Gauville, I think of this man all the time – wondering where he is and what he is doing, to whom he is talking and with what other women he is sleeping. Because he is, I know. And then, one day he will telephone and he will tell me to come to him and I will obey. Me! Me! At my age, with the life I have, and he so much younger than me and involved in things of which I know nothing and dare to ask nothing.'

Again they both kept silent; Angela with her eyes straight ahead of her on the garden, Marie-Claire's on her hands, still turning and twisting in her lap. Angela broke the silence.

'Does Bernard know?'

'I hope not. He does not know the contempt I feel for myself. But they say that people usually do know when the person they are living with is having an affair. And you, a friend, knew, didn't you?'

'I saw that something was wrong, that you were unhappy. And when a woman is so unhappy I suppose one always thinks that it may be a man, especially with someone who is as beautiful as you.'

Marie-Claire put her hand on Angela's but she did not look at her.

'Me! At my age! Behaving like this! Bernard knows that I shall always love him but he probably suspects. I have not been exactly good company lately. But he cannot know of the shame.'

'You keep speaking of shame, as though this was something more than having a love affair –'

'It is not a "love affair" in the way you are thinking. It is not a *love* affair. That is part of the wretchedness. There is no love, only this humiliating passion. There is no love,' she repeated. 'He is not capable of love. That is why I feel so ashamed. He tells me lies which I know are lies and now I know that he is involved in something terrible. But I also know that when he summons me, I will go back.'

'When did you last see him?'

'The week before last, just before the weekend. On the Friday, but I feel that he is still here, with me, beside me, inside me. He has gone away but he said he will be back soon. But I don't know, I don't know.' Again Marie-Claire stretched out her arm and grasped Angela's hand, gripping it tightly. This time she turned and looked at Angela. 'And Bernard, with his official position with the government. What can I do, what can I do?'

Shadows were now moving over the lawn and Angela could see Godfrey and Bernard come out of the house and stand talking on the lawn.

'Would you like to stay here for a little with me? I am not going to London next week. I shall be here on my own. Why don't you stay with me, in the sunshine, away from it all, just for a few days and take time to rest and to think?'

The two men were now starting to walk slowly down the long lawn flanked by the herbaceous borders towards the summerhouse.

'Do you mean that?'

'Of course I do. It might help. It will be just the two of us and it will be very peaceful.'

'Then I would like to, just for a week or so. I don't want to be in Paris.'

'We shall be quite alone together,' said Angela.

The men were approaching. Angela got up and kissed Godfrey on the cheek.

'Welcome home. How did you enjoy your trip in that noisy

70

machine? But we never heard you return!'

'No,' said Godfrey. 'They are always generous in getting you to their meetings but when the meetings are over they let you find your own way home. So I had to scrounge a car from the government car pool. I hear that Bernard has spent the afternoon with the vicar looking at his books.'

'And very interesting books he has,' said Bernard. 'Some very rare sixteenth-century volumes which were printed in Paris. But, my friends, if you will forgive me, I did not altogether fall in love with your abbé.'

'Oh, he is all right,' said Angela. 'He is just sad and lonely.' Then she took Bernard by the arm. 'And during Godfrey's diplomatic excitements with helicopters and yours with your ancient books, I have had my own triumph. I have persuaded Marie-Claire to stay on and keep me company for a few days so that we can lie in the sun and gossip about the two of you. Then I will deliver her back to London and she can fly off and join you in Paris. I hope you won't mind, Bernard?'

Bernard looked down at Marie-Claire who was still sitting.

'I mind nothing which will make her happy.'

Marie-Claire looked up at him and he smiled at her, very gently.

'I shall of course miss her painfully and I shall have to pass my evenings in the Jockey Club and lose a fortune at the bridge table while I think enviously of her in this delicious garden with you.'

Then Angela understood that of course he knew about Marie-Claire and knew that it was serious and that Marie-Claire was suffering. She could not prevent herself from throwing her arms around him and kissing him.

'Leave my adorable husband alone,' said Marie-Claire, and they all walked back into the house.

EIGHT

Edmund Hamilton had forgotten how cold it could be in June in Buenos Aires. It was raining hard as the taxi brought him from the airport to the hotel. In the city he had the driver take him to a store and he bought himself a raincoat. It would be too hot and heavy to wear further north but here he would need it. He would abandon it when he began his travels and charge it to Godfrey.

The hotel was not ostentatious – gloomy in the dark Spanish style but comfortable, very appropriate, London had suggested, for a visiting academic.

Originally Edmund had planned to do nothing about Godfrey's business until he had completed his own but when he had been briefed he had learnt that his travels north would have to begin not when he had finished his own work in BA but soon after he had started it. At the office, James Kent, as Edmund had expected, had greeted him coolly and when Edmund spoke of the amount of personal historical research he wished to do while he was in BA, Kent had said that their matter was now more urgent than they had at one time thought.

'For some reason C wants you up north as soon as possible. I presume it has to do with your meeting with Pilar Olivella. But I am, of course, being kept in the dark.'

To Michael Robertson, the Chief Clerk and Head of Administration in the department, Kent had said, 'This assignment did not require any special agent but C has selected Hamilton and plucked him out of Cambridge, an inexperienced man who has never served overseas. When he was with us, I personally considered the fellow wholly unreliable.'

'But he has the qualification of having good reason to be in

72

the region,' Robertson objected. 'His academic work is good cover.'

'But quite unnecessary. He has only to talk with the woman and take a look at Carlos, both tasks which a local might have done. All that is needed for this assignment is an observer who will form clear judgements and who will send in a sensible report for us to analyse. C is up to something and he has certainly not consulted me.'

At Edmund's briefing Kent told him that in BA he would be approached by his local control who would direct him until he was on his way to Bogota. Edmund had protested that he must pass some days in BA working on his own research and Kent had been obliged to agree. He said that in order to help with the genuine academic work and thus get Edmund the sooner to Rio where he was expected to meet Pilar Olivella he would provide a local researcher. Later, just before he left his club for Heathrow that same evening, Kent had telephoned.

'I have identified a research assistant for you. An historian called Macdonald, who has also worked with me in this office. You will be contacted in BA. That', he concluded, 'is all that we can do for you here in London. Now it is up to you,' and he rang off.

On his first day in Buenos Aires Edmund, nursing his jet lag, presented his credentials from Cambridge to the National Library, a vast nineteenth-century building, and was led up a great marble staircase to the office of the Deputy Director, a round bald-headed and affable man with whom Edmund had corresponded from Cambridge. After an amiable interlude over immensely strong coffee while Edmund explained in detail what he needed, he had been handed over to a department Head who, after an hour or so of discussion and some telephoning to other librarians, had directed him to the university across the city.

Edmund resisted the temptation to stay in the hotel and rest. He was reluctant to start work but he remembered the pressure of time of which Godfrey had spoken in London so he made his way across the city and spent the afternoon at a table in the icy library surrounded by the documents that he had come to examine and which had been located for him and courteously and promptly brought to him. Soon, as one document led him to another and volume followed volume, the hunt warmed his blood and, the weariness temporarily forgotten, he stayed at his table until seven o'clock covering pages with notes and references before he went back to the hotel. He arranged to return to the library on the following day.

As he passed through the dark foyer and was walking to the desk to collect his key and disappear thankfully into his room and to his bed, he was confronted by the figure of a girl dressed in navy-blue leggings and a cardigan over a T-shirt with a halter. Her dark hair was cut short; over her arm, a shoulder-bag.

'Dr Hamilton?' the girl said in English with a pronounced Spanish accent. Edmund stopped.

'Yes, I am Edmund Hamilton.'

'My name is Macdonald,' replied the girl. 'Teresa Macdonald. My former tutor in London told me that you were staying in this hotel and that you wanted someone to help with the historical research which you have come to Buenos Aires to do. I believe that he gave you my name.'

'You?' he said. 'You are Macdonald?'

'Yes. I would be very interested to help. I am an historian and I would like the employment.'

'You said your tutor –'

'Yes,' she interrupted. 'Mr James Kent. I believe that you know him. I worked with him in London two years ago. He tells me that you are here for research on a study of the seventeenth-century Spanish and Portuguese settlers and that you need an assistant. I am sure that I could prove useful. Mr Kent suggested that I contacted you after you had arrived. I hope you found today what you needed in the National Library and the university?'

'You know that I have already been there?'

'Oh, yes. I thought it wiser to greet you this evening when you might know more about the extent of the work which you need to do. I expect that you may be tired after the flight and the work which you did today but I believe that it is urgent

74

that we settle the programme of your research project as soon as possible and of course arrange the terms of my employment. I too have other arrangements which I also must make. If you are willing, perhaps we could discuss how you think I may be able to help. I think that I can reassure you about my credentials. As a researcher,' she added.

Edmund hesitated.

The girl went on: 'I am sorry to be troublesome, but I would like to settle the matter this evening.'

She looked, he thought, unusual and attractive, but her voice had an unexpected note of authority. He glanced at his watch.

'Very well. If you could give me half an hour to have a bath, perhaps then we might dine together and discuss it over dinner.'

'I would be happy to do so,' she replied gravely. 'I will take you, if you will permit, to an agreeable and quiet restaurant which I know. I shall wait for you here in the foyer. I expect that you may now wish to make some enquiries.'

She turned and left him. As he stood in the elevator waiting for the door to close, he could see that she had curled up like a kitten on one of the sofas, her legs tucked beneath her. Oblivious to the other people around her who were regarding her with some surprise, she was studying a book which she had taken from her shoulder-bag.

From his room he telephoned to London. Kent was still at the office. Edmund was abrupt but James Kent was not perturbed. He sounded as if he were enjoying Edmund's surprise. He confirmed the girl's authority. Although irritated by Kent, Edmund nevertheless went downstairs to accompany the girl to dinner feeling surprisingly elated.

The restaurant to which Teresa Macdonald led him was certainly quiet and discreet, the tables widely separated. The staff seemed to know her well. When they began to eat and the waiters had retired, she wasted no time.

'You have checked?' she enquired.

He replied that he had spoken to London. He admitted that he had been taken aback when she had approached him.

'Mr Kent had not told you?'

'No,' he said. 'He had not.'

75

The girl expressed no surprise but went on to tell him that he could be allowed only two more days at the university before he had to fly north to Rio. It was not a suggestion, he noted, but a command.

'"Allowed"?' he queried.

'Yes,' she replied shortly. She was more than his assistant researcher; she was his Control.

'Why only two days?' he enquired.

Teresa replied that she was instructed that Edmund had come to discover the connection between the man Maitland, the dead girl and her companion, Pilar Olivella. She emphasised the word 'companion' to make clear to him that she knew of the relationship between the two women and she told him that an opportunity had presented itself to meet and speak with Pilar at a reception in Brasilia, the capital of Brazil, in four days' time. The reception was an engagement party to be given by Pilar's father, who was a minister in the Brazilian Government, in honour of Pilar's younger sister.

'I will be attending this reception. Inez was at school with me and I have been invited. I do not know so well her older sister whom I have not seen since I was a child. If you were to attend this party I could introduce you to Pilar. It would be quite natural to do this if you were to accompany me to the reception – as my companion.'

Again the girl emphasised the word 'companion'. She looked at him steadily.

'Your companion?'

'Yes. We meet this evening following an introduction from Cambridge where I also studied, and we make the arrangement between us for me to assist you in your research. As you see, we dine together. London suggests that I attend the university with you on each of the next two days as your assistant. This will serve a double purpose. To help you in your work and for us to be seen together. It would be thought reasonable, London believes, that as we have become academic colleagues we also become friendly.'

'By London, you mean James Kent?'

'Yes. We shall repeat this dinner tomorrow and the following evening. The day after we shall fly to Rio in order to conduct

76

further research in Brazil. The tickets must be booked by you from your hotel, in both our names.'

She looked down at her hands now folded demurely on the table in front of her.

'On the evening before leaving Buenos Aires together, you may care, for the better verisimilitude, to spend the night at my apartment.'

She paused. Edmund could not conceal his smile. She was so serious, so matter of fact. He liked the 'verisimilitude', especially in her accent. But the girl raised her dark brown eyes and stared severely at him.

'I have in my apartment two bedrooms,' she said. 'As we have become friends I accompany you on your further research which takes you north to Rio. I will secure for you an invitation and you will accompany me to the reception given for Pilar's sister – as my new friend.'

Once again the emphasis, this time on the word 'friend'. It conveyed the interpretation that others were meant to put upon the friendship that was to have developed between them.

'That way,' she said, 'it is very natural.'

She had not taken her eyes from his. He replied looking at her equally steadily, but with his quizzical, slightly mocking smile.

'That, as you say, would be very natural. I do not find your plan at all disagreeable.'

For the first time he saw on her serious little face the hint of a smile.

'And after that?' he asked.

'That is not a matter for me. I have to bring you to Pilar and I shall ensure that you meet at the reception. Then it will be up to you to persuade her to meet you on further occasions to talk.' She added, with a hint of mischief, 'I would have thought that for this task they should have sent a woman, but we shall have to make do with you.' She lowered her head. He smiled again.

'You are probably correct but as you say, you and London shall have to put up with me. So those are my instructions and

77

you and I are to work as a team. I confess I was surprised when I saw you.'

She dropped her eyes as he went on, 'There is one matter which I must make clear. Since I have only two more days here for my personal work, my new assistant must be prepared to work very hard indeed – academically. For I have much I want to do.'

'I am ready for that. London anticipated that. They warned me.'

'London, or rather Mr Kent, I am beginning to realise, thinks of everything.'

When he said this she stretched out her hand towards his involuntarily, and then withdrew it sharply.

'Do not be so certain of that. London is far away and it can look very different when you are safely in an office on the other side of the Atlantic ocean. I must warn you that if you go to Bogota it could be very different.'

For a moment neither spoke. Then Edmund said, 'Perhaps. But when I am there all I have been asked to do is to take a look around and meet a man, a friend of the Chief's.'

'C,' she said.

'Yes.' He picked up his glass. 'To Mr Kent, young Miss Macdonald's tutor! Does he appreciate what he is letting his pupil into?'

'We both do,' she replied quietly. 'I have been working here for several years.'

He had meant something different, something more personal. He looked across the table at her. She looked very young and vulnerable.

'Then you must have become involved when you were a child.'

'Almost. I began when I was at the university, at the time of the Malvinas war. My father was a British naval officer but he died when I was very young. Then I went to Cambridge and later I worked for a time with Mr Kent.'

'And are you also a good actress? For that is what you will have to be if we are to stage my attendance at the reception to meet Pilar Olivella.'

'All of us in this business need to be able to act.'

He was smiling but she remained serious.

'That is what we all have to do.'

'Very well. Then by the time that we reach Rio we must appear to be what the press call very good friends.' He copied her intonation when he spoke the word 'friends'. 'We have not much time. It may be harder for you than I am sure that it will for me. Do you think you can manage the charade?'

'I think so,' she said softly.

'So now we had better start our adventure and practise becoming friends. You must look as if you were enjoying it. That, after all,' he mimicked her, 'would be only natural.'

Then she smiled, properly.

The following day she accompanied him to the university where he introduced her as his research assistant and they worked steadily together. She had been right: she was competent and had been well trained. She sat opposite him at the table and he found himself watching the small head, with its short dark hair, bent low at an angle over the documents, writing quickly on her pad beside her with, he noticed, the pen gripped deep between the thumb and forefinger; writing, he thought, like a child. He noticed her very small, finely shaped ears.

At midday they went to a bistro and drank coffee and ate a little, and then worked on until seven o'clock. That evening they went to another more popular and grander restaurant. She still wore leggings but with a very short dress above them. When he dropped her at her apartment he kissed her cheek before walking back to his hotel. The night was warmer and already he had discarded his raincoat.

He asked the concierge to book two tickets on the VARIG flight to Rio for two days ahead, giving his name and Teresa's.

The following day it was warmer. He collected the air tickets and checked out of the hotel. They worked at the university as before. In the evening she said that she was taking him to an *asada*, a cook out in a garden in a suburb of the city. When they arrived the party was assembling on the lawn, the family

79

of the hosts busy over the brazier on which the meat was turning on a spit.

As they walked into the garden she said, 'Francesca Thompson will be here tonight and she will be at the engagement party in Brasilia. She also flies to Rio tomorrow.' She slipped her hand into his. 'So you must forgive this,' she said, and they entered hand in hand.

All those to whom Edmund was introduced had names which sounded English or Scots but they all spoke in Spanish, and only in English with an accent. During the evening he stayed close to Teresa. There was dancing, rather old-fashioned, with the couples holding each other closely. He danced with the hostess and many times with Teresa. Then, all that he could see was the top of her head but he felt her body pressed close to his. He enjoyed dancing with her and he forgot the work that they had to do together in his delight in being with her. On the way home to Teresa's apartment he kissed her properly.

She showed Edmund to her second bedroom and said good night gravely. He lay on the bed. He wanted to go to her room but instead he lay sleepless, thinking of her.

The next day they flew to Rio, Godfrey's raincoat, as Edmund had christened it, abandoned on the bed in the second bedroom of Teresa's flat. He had only used it once. When the aircraft circled the mountain prior to landing at Rio Airport he took her small hand in his. He found it difficult to think of anything save of her.

They booked two connecting rooms in an hotel that rose like a great white ship from the strand of golden Copacabana beach. When they said good night he tried to kiss her on the lips as he had the night before but she turned her cheek to him. The next morning he went out onto the balcony and stood letting the sun warm his back and looking over the great stretch of sand, watching the early sun-worshippers playing their volley-ball and running into the ocean. Teresa joined him.

'I am not finding it difficult,' he said, 'to play-act.'

She remained silent. Damn you, James Kent, he thought. C would not approve of what was happening.

He put his arm around her but she broke away from him and said that she would meet him later when they must go together to the university where he was expected. When she had left him he stayed on the balcony watching the people and the couples on the beach below him.

He began to fantasise, pretending to himself that he and Teresa were real lovers together for a short time before he left for war. But they were only pretended lovers, acting a part. Soon he would have to leave her to go north to where the real danger would begin – in Colombia.

NINE

The reception was held in a white, low villa matching those of the embassies and of the government ministries that housed the diplomats and government servants of Brasilia, the artificial capital city of Brazil. The city had been born in the fifties, laid out on the virgin plain many miles from Rio. It was populated with officials – ministers, civil servants, diplomats and their families. Nations had vied with each other to build modern residences and chancelleries for their embassies and many were of striking architectural distinction. When it had been completed the reluctant diplomats and politicians and civil servants had been obliged to remove themselves from Rio and emigrate many miles into the interior to inhabit their new quarters in the brand new but boring city in which the roads radiated out from one another in orderly spokes bordered by the official buildings and the embassies.

The engagement party for Pilar's sister was in one of these official residences, for her father was the Minister for Development. Another reception, after the wedding, would be held later in Rio.

Teresa and Edmund, after a two-hour flight in the early morning, had arrived in Brasilia and then separated. In Rio his invitation had been secured and Teresa had gone to stay with the host's family; Edmund to the British Embassy where he spent an hour with the Ambassador and then another with the MI6 attaché. He was given a message from C, instructing him that he was wanted in Colombia as soon as possible. In the Colombian capital, Bogota, Carlos was waiting for him. That was more important, the message emphasised, than the extraction from Pilar Olivella of information about Maitland, whose whereabouts were still unknown.

In the evening the British party from the Embassy, the men in white dinner jackets and the women in full evening dress, set out in the Ambassador's Jaguar and together they joined the receiving line, which led to the hosts and the engaged couple. After he had been presented Edmund went to find Teresa. When at last he found her she was among a group of friends on the terrace outside the ballroom and the sight of her took away his breath. He stood transfixed, watching the flickering light from the naked flame of the tall sconces on the balustrade shining on her bare shoulders and sparkling on the diamond studs in her ears. She was wearing a blue and white polka-dot organza dress, strapless and tight over her breasts and waist until it fell away into a series of ruffles down to her ankles. When she turned the dress moved as if it had a life of its own; and then she saw him standing in the shadows looking at her. She smiled and came over to him, slipped her arm through his, and they walked together down the broad stone steps into the greater privacy of the garden.

'We can talk here,' said Teresa. They stood watching the water from the fountain falling over the ribs of a cascade each of which was lit with a different coloured light. From there it ran between banks of oleander and frangipani trees, through a necklace of pools to a lake at the far end of the grounds. The whole garden seemed to be alive with water, its sight and its sound. In the distance they could hear faintly the music of the orchestra.

'You look very beautiful,' he said and bent as though to kiss her but she smiled and turned her head and put her finger over his lips.

'We came here to talk. Pilar is not staying with the family but with friends. I met her again this afternoon. I must warn you, she is very formidable. I have told her about you and that we are working together.'

As she spoke his eyes never left her face but he scarcely heard the words she was speaking, so moved was he by the way she looked in the moonlight in that magic garden. He had been enchanted enough by the Teresa of their working days in BA, clad in her T-shirts under wrapped cardigan and the dark blue leggings, with the shoulder-bag and the files of notes so

83

carefully compiled in the libraries, the serious Teresa who was his researcher, the capable Teresa who had organised their adventure. Now here she was in this place where she had been instructed to bring him, radiant and beautiful and he knew for certain that he loved her.

'Pay attention, Edmund. You must not forget why I have brought you and what you have been sent here to do.' But she was smiling and she laid her hand on his arm. 'When you get the chance to speak with Pilar, tell her the story we have planned about your seeing her outside the flat of Mary Traynor in London. All she knows is that I am working with you on your book. She may not stay long at the party. I do not think that Pilar likes to dance. We must find her before she leaves.'

'Not until you and I have danced.' He took her hand and kissed the fingers and then turned the hand and kissed her palm. He led her back through the garden to the terrace and into the ballroom.

They danced without speaking and he held her very close to him. He was conscious of the attention they were attracting but he could think of nothing but her. All he wanted was to make love to her.

After a time she broke away from him and said quietly, 'Come, we must find Pilar. As I said, she will not be here for long.' He followed her off the dance floor out again to the terrace and into the garden.

'You do not want to let her see us dancing,' he said.

'Be sensible, Edmund. You must know what she is like and now you must do what you have been sent to do.'

She took his hand and they wandered slowly around the garden, Teresa inspecting the groups and couples whom they passed, searching for Pilar Olivella. From the garden they made their way back into the house and then in a corner of one of the reception rooms away from the music Edmund saw two women talking together, one young and one older. Teresa pressed his arm and directed him towards them. He saw that it was the older whom he had been sent to find.

The younger was a girl hardly out of her teens; the elder a woman in her mid-thirties, tall and thin, with a handsome face framed by jet-black hair, which she wore full and long. Her complexion was sallow and in repose her expression severe. He noticed how smartly she was dressed, in a crimson sleeveless silk shantung dress, and a heavy gold necklace at her neck and triangles of gold at her ears. As they approached she looked up from the girl with whom she was talking. At once she broke into a smile. It was a brilliant smile, transforming the austere face. The smile was for Teresa, and her eyes moved over Teresa's hair and face and body, lingering over her, drinking in the vision of the girl who was coming towards her, looking at Teresa as a man would at a woman with whom he was entranced.

'Teresa,' the woman said, 'little Teresa, you look absolutely divine.' She pushed her face towards Teresa and Edmund saw that she did not kiss Teresa's cheek but the corner of her mouth. If Teresa had not slightly moved her head, she would have been kissed full on the lips.

'Thank you, Pilar,' said Teresa in Spanish and Edmund saw that she had coloured. 'You look wonderful yourself. I have brought Edmund Hamilton to introduce to you. He is –'

Pilar interrupted her. 'Your dress is quite enchanting. It sets off your skin to perfection. Teresa, you are quite exquisite, like a creature from a Fragonard.'

'You are embarrassing me, Pilar, and in front of Mr Hamilton whom I was presenting to you.'

The woman turned towards Edmund and the smile faded from her face; it was as if a lamp had been suddenly extinguished.

'How do you do,' she said in English. 'Teresa told me of you.' She looked him up and down, insolently, Edmund thought.

'Mr Hamilton is from Cambridge University in England and as I told you I am helping him with the research on a book he is preparing on the seventeenth-century settlers. A part of his family came from the Argentine.'

The woman turned again to Edmund and said, 'I saw you dancing together.'

'My research assistant dances divinely.' He smiled at Teresa.

'You are fortunate to have hired', the woman stressed the word, 'so talented and becoming an assistant.'

She was weighing him up, he thought, like a potential rival.

'The work you have in hand sounds a most ambitious project.'

Before he could reply Pilar turned back to Teresa. 'I did so enjoy meeting you again, my dearest Teresa. The last time we met before this afternoon, you were a little round frump in a pinafore – and now look at you. Quite the beauty! I shall come over early tomorrow to see you. Let us have luncheon together. I want to hear all about you.'

'That will depend upon when I must return to Rio and about that you will have to ask Mr Hamilton. I am uncertain how much work he may have for me.'

Pilar took Teresa's arm. 'Well then, let us take the chance to talk now.' She turned to Edmund. 'There seems to be an intolerable absence of servants. Would you be so kind, Mr Hamilton, to find for me a glass of lemonade, and perhaps one for Teresa? I think that you may find the refreshments in the next room beside the ballroom. We will look for a table so that we can sit and talk. I am finding this heat quite suffocating.'

With one hand she steered Teresa towards the door while with the other she worked her fan. The young girl seized the opportunity and fled. Edmund was left standing alone. He turned on his heel and went in search of the bar. He needed to cool his rising temper.

When he returned there was no sign of Pilar and Teresa. With a glass in either hand he wandered from room to room and eventually he found them seated at a table in the shadow in a corner of the terrace, away from the crowd and the light and heat of the flaming sconces. On the table in front of them were two glasses. Pilar, he saw, had her hand over Teresa's.

'Ah, the gallant Mr Hamilton, bearing drinks. He has managed to track us down. It is very kind of you but in the meantime we found one of the elusive waiters and the saucy Teresa ordered champagne.'

Edmund put the glasses on the table.

'I do not like to mix my drinks.' Pilar pushed aside the glass Edmund had brought and smiled at Teresa as at a fellow conspirator. Edmund, unbidden, pulled up a chair and sat. He stared at Teresa who dropped her eyes and he spoke to the woman in Spanish.

'It was very kind of your family to invite me this evening. I know that I owe my good fortune to Teresa.'

'You do indeed. It must be agreeable to be indebted to the delightful Teresa.'

'In time I hope to be even more indebted for she is proving of great help to me in my work. As I have already discovered, Teresa is quite the scholar.'

'You are talking about me as if I were not here,' said Teresa.

'No,' said Pilar. 'We talk about you because we are both so interested in you. It is certainly a massive task which Mr Hamilton has put you to.'

'Yes,' said Edmund, 'as you indicated earlier it is an ambitious project. I shall probably have to reduce its scope. At present I am engaged in the research.'

'With the help of Teresa.'

'With the essential help of Teresa,' he repeated. 'Indeed, at the moment it seems as though it might be the work of a lifetime.' He was looking directly at Pilar. 'Of course I do not know yet if Teresa would agree to such a formidable commitment.'

Pilar leant across the table and picked up her handbag. She rose abruptly.

'Come, Teresa, shall we move back into the house?'

She began to walk along the terrace. Edmund remained seated and as Teresa followed Pilar she put her hand lightly on his shoulder. Then he too got to his feet and walked after them along the terrace and through the French windows, which led into the ballroom.

It was the supper interval and the music had stopped. The dancers were standing around in groups on the dance-floor.

Teresa said, 'There are my cousins, Luis and Aminta Ibanez. I have not seen them for months. Forgive me, I must speak with them.'

She went over to a young couple in the centre of the floor and embraced them. Pilar followed her with her eyes, momentarily turning them to Edmund as though surprised that he should be still beside her; soon they were back fixed upon Teresa. The crowd began to move off the dance floor and Pilar followed the throng, which was now making for the corridor that led to the supper-room. Edmund, determined, accompanied her.

'She is very beautiful,' he said.

Pilar turned, looking at him up and down, now making clear her objections at his continued presence.

'She is, as you say, very beautiful. She is a good friend of my young sister. They were at school together. I have known Teresa since she was a child, longer I presume than you, Mr Hamilton.'

By now Teresa was well ahead of them, talking and laughing with her cousins, the man with his arm around her.

'Your sister must be very happy to have been given so magnificent a reception,' he said. 'Teresa and I walked together in the garden. It is a very romantic setting.' He could not resist the provocation.

They had to wait as the crush ahead of them moved through the door.

'My sister and her fiancé are to be married in Rio later this month. As a friend of Teresa's, you are, of course, most welcome to be here.'

She did not mean it, he thought. Not that it mattered. He watched her as she searched vainly for Teresa, who by now had disappeared into the crowd entering the supper-room and he observed the sullen expression on her face as she accepted that Teresa had gone and that she was left with this unwelcome intruder. He determined that he would now do what he had come to do and after what had passed he did not care if he caused her distress.

'Do you know England, señorita?'

'A little. I have travelled in Europe.'

'Do you know London?'

'A little.' They were now in the corridor still behind the last of the people approaching the supper-room.

'I thought that you did. Were you not there recently?' She stopped and looked up at him. 'I ask because I feel certain that I have seen you in London.'

'Seen me in London?'

'Yes. As soon as Teresa pointed you out to me and brought me over to introduce me, I recognised you.'

'I am quite certain that we have not met.'

'No, you are right, we have not. But I have seen you quite recently, and in London.'

She looked away from him and then back, surprised.

He began the story that he and Teresa had planned.

'My sister has a flat in an apartment block in Cavendish Mansions in Sloane Avenue, in Chelsea. Do you know Cavendish Mansions?'

A flush heightened the colour in the woman's sallow face but she said nothing.

'About ten days ago I was staying with my sister when there was an incident. A girl who lived in the flat next door was found to have died during the night.'

Pilar was standing very still, but she had turned away her head.

'It was in the morning and there was considerable commotion. My sister and I came out of her door and we stood watching what was going on. The porter had to open up the flat and then the police arrived.' He paused. 'The name of the girl who died was Mary Traynor.'

Pilar put her hand to the heavy gold necklace at her throat. 'Why are you saying all this?'

'Because I saw you there. You are the friend of Mary Traynor. It was you who discovered her body.' Then he spoke in English. 'Miss Olivella, I need your help.'

'My help?'

'Yes. There was a name which you spoke to the porter and to the police when you found the body of your friend. It was the name of a man.'

'I do not know what you are talking about.'

'Oh, you do,' Edmund said roughly. 'You know very well.'

She started to push past him but he put his hand on her arm. 'Leave me alone,' she said. 'Leave me alone,' and she brushed off his hand.

'You called the man Maitland. I want to know what you know about him.'

'Who are you?' she asked.

'That does not matter. I must know why you spoke that man's name when you found the dead body of your friend.'

89

Again she started to walk from him and again he put out his hand, this time gripping her arm tightly.

'It is important. It is not possible to talk here tonight but I must come and see you – and as soon as possible.'

Her sallow face was now blotched and her eyes stared at his full of either anger or fear. His hand still gripped her arm.

'Does Teresa know about this?'

'Of course.'

'So that is why you are here?'

'It is. Teresa knows how important it is for me to talk to you. She knows everything.'

As he said this Pilar drew herself up and looked at him full in the face. Suddenly she was fully in command of herself.

'I order you to leave me.'

She had raised her voice and a couple just ahead of them turned and looked at them. He dropped his hand. Then she swept past him and out of the room.

He watched her disappear and then walked back through the ballroom and out of the French windows. He stood on the terrace, his hands on the balustrade. From a passing waiter he took a long frosted glass in which swam berries and other fruit and he drank thirstily. He stood watching the people below him in the garden and the play of the fountains. In the end, he told himself, she would talk; fear would make her talk and later, tomorrow when she had time to think she would tell him what he wanted to know. But as he stood alone on the terrace with the sound of the people at supper in the villa behind him he was uncomfortably conscious that his dislike of the woman's behaviour with Teresa had made him act more roughly than he had intended.

He went back into the house and walked through the supper-room. He saw Teresa's cousins, the Ibanezes, at a table but Teresa was not with them. He searched the other rooms but there was no sign of either Teresa or Pilar. He walked back to the terrace and down the stone steps into the garden to where earlier he had stood with Teresa by the cascade and the pools that led down to the lake. He could find her nowhere so he made his way into the hall. He would go home, back to the Embassy. In the morning he would speak to Teresa and ask her to arrange another meeting with Pilar. The woman would be frightened into talking.

He asked a servant to call him a taxi. At the Embassy he was the first of the party to have returned. He poured himself a whisky and soda and as he sat in the library thinking about the evening he began to grow increasingly uneasy. What if he had frightened off Pilar altogether? He tried to comfort himself with the thought that Teresa herself would be able to approach the woman; Teresa would be able to discover what they needed to know about Maitland. In any event, as C had emphasised, his real task was not here with Pilar Olivella but in the north, in Colombia where with Carlos he had to find the hidden place that lay over the mountains beyond Cali.

Nevertheless his unease grew because he knew that he had failed in the first task that he had been set. He should not have allowed the woman to anger him. He finished his drink and went unhappily to his room. After lying awake thinking of Teresa and the manner in which Pilar had behaved with her, he slept.

In the morning early there was a message from Teresa instructing him to return to Rio and that she would call him at the hotel in the evening. There was no indication whether she herself would come and join him.

He told the Embassy MI6 man that he had made contact with Pilar Olivella but he said and was asked no more. He took the morning flight back to Rio alone, and waited.

No word came. The following morning he went back to work at the university on the outskirts of the city where the archivist expected him. He found it difficult to concentrate on what he was doing. In the late afternoon he telephoned the hotel but there was no message for him. The young librarian offered to drive him back to the hotel and he accepted gratefully. While he waited, he sat in the garden watching a pack of small monkeys climbing down the trunk of a tree to collect fruit that had been left for them. When they had grabbed it, they scampered back up the bole into the branches, chattering with pleasure.

In the car the librarian asked, 'Is this your first visit to Rio?'

Edmund replied that it was; he had arrived from BA three days ago and then had gone to Brasilia to a reception from which he had just returned.

'Then you must see the *favelas*,' the young man said grimly.

He drove Edmund to the other city, only a few yards from the city in which Edmund was living in his luxurious hotel. This was a place of hovels, a shantytown on the side of the mountain, which rose behind the city of expensive shops and hotels where open-topped, torpedo-shaped motor-cars nosed along the streets, hooting at the tourists for passage. As they drove into the alternative city high above them a small airplane towed a banner advertising some expensive scent.

'This is the Pavaozinho slum,' said the librarian.

The paths between the hovels ran with mud and filth, and grimy children ran after the car, demanding money when it stopped by a large concrete building several storeys high, some kind of community centre where rough-made artefacts were for sale and simple home-made mechanical exhibits were on display. The walls were covered by posters announcing community events. As they wandered about a priest attached himself to them. He served, he said, in the *favelas* and this was a club that he was trying to create, a place where at least the children could play out of the filth of the paths. After a time he led them to the roof and pointed silently first to the hovels immediately below and then to the city beyond with its high-rise office buildings and the great white hotels with the golden Copacabana beach and the ocean in the distance. Edmund could think of nothing else but to empty his pockets and wallet of all his cash and hand it to the priest who took it gravely and thanked him. Then the young librarian drove him away.

As he sat on the balcony of his room, which faced the ocean and not the squalor of the mountainside behind, Edmund knew that the magic of the place that he had felt when he had first come with the girl with whom he had fallen in love had fled, and he wanted to get away. Above all he wanted to see Teresa.

*　　*　　*

But he did not see Teresa until the following day. He had a message that she was in the hall. She did not come to his room and he went down to her. She was dressed once more in her T-shirt and leggings, very different from the girl at the ball with whom he had danced. She looked tired and strained. He wanted to take her in his arms but when he greeted her she merely nodded to him and then walked ahead of him to the terrace overlooking the pool. They sat at a table and Edmund ordered coffee. He stretched out his hand and covered hers. She withdrew her hand and did not look at him.

'I am going home,' she said. 'Today.'

'Why? he asked.

'Because Pilar is leaving and there is nothing more for me to do here. I brought you to her but what you said to her that night, or how you said it, has alarmed her. To have mishandled her so badly was unforgivable.'

'I am sorry. I know that I was clumsy.' He paused. Then he said quietly, 'She angered me.'

'Angered you?' She raised her eyes to his and looked at him full in the face. 'She angered you?' she repeated.

'Yes.'

'May I ask what you think that you came here to do?' He tried to interrupt, but she went on, ignoring him: 'Do you think this is all a game, some childish game between boys and girls which stops when someone angers someone else? You were given a task to do and you agreed to do it. You knew how important it was to get information from that woman. But she annoyed you and you got angry! Well, let me tell you that you have frightened her and angered me.'

'I am very sorry to have angered you,' he said quietly. 'I know that I did not handle her sensibly. I said all that we had planned, that I had been there in the block of flats when the police came. I suppose that it was the way in which I spoke.'

He wanted to say that he had been so aggressive because of her, Teresa; because of the way that the woman had been behaving towards her. But he did not.

'You have frightened her. Now you may have destroyed any chance of finding out the connection with Maitland, which is what you were sent to discover. She will not talk to you again.'

Then he said it. 'I did not like her behaviour with you.'

'You did not like her behaviour with me? What has that to do with what you were sent here to do? Her behaviour with me!'

He put out his hand. 'Teresa,' he said. 'Please. You must understand.'

'You knew what kind of woman she was and you knew that I had set up the meeting so that you could gain her confidence and encourage her to meet with you again. All that you have succeeded in doing is to make certain that she will not see you again. And all because you did not like her behaviour to me!'

'Yes,' he said, staring at her. 'Yes. Just because of that.'

'Then you are irresponsible.'

'Perhaps I am. Because of you.'

'Listen, we had a job to do, you and I, a task, an official task involving this woman Pilar. Now you have frightened her and all that she did for half the night was ask me questions about you and rebuke me for bringing you to her father's house. She wants to know with whom you are involved and why. I have told her that as far as I know you are a scholar who has hired me to help in your research. Then I had to tell her that you had told me the story of Mary Traynor in London.'

There was silence. Then he said, 'I can only say that my temper got the better of me, my Latin temper. I got angry because I was jealous at the way Pilar Olivella had been behaving to you. I did not like her and I did not like the way she was looking at you.'

She put her hand to her forehead. 'We were given a task, a professional task, and you allowed your feelings for me to get in the way.'

'I am not a professional.'

She looked up and said quietly, 'If you could not behave professionally then you should never have come.'

As he heard her words he did not care about his failure, all he cared about was her disappointment in him.

'I know that I failed you.'

'You have not failed me. I shall be given other tasks. You have failed those who trusted you and sent you. Pilar now is going to leave Rio and will not even wait for her sister's wedding. She plans to go to the States. I shall go home. As for you, they want you in Bogota the day after tomorrow. I do not know why nor why it has become so urgent. Do not fail them in this, as you have failed with Pilar. Have you completed your own work here at the university?'

'Another morning. Just a few more hours.'

'Then you must go north as soon as you have completed it.'

'When will I see you?'

'I do not know.'

She must know what I feel for her, he thought. She cannot fail to know.

'What is the point? When you have finished what London wants of you in Colombia, perhaps you will be allowed to come south again.'

But he remembered that C had warned him that after he had gone to Bogota he might have to be brought out and home, quickly. He put his hand on hers but again she pulled away.

'Let me come with you. Then I will go north. I am not ready to say goodbye.'

'But you have to. We all have to in our business. This is all nonsense. It has caused enough trouble already.' But she spoke more gently. Then, businesslike again: 'If I get any information which may help you I shall get a message to you in Bogota.'

'I shall come back to see you,' he said. 'Whatever happens, I shall come back.'

'We shall see.' She stood up. He remained seated. 'I have a car to take me to the airport. It is waiting. I am very late and I must hurry. No,' she said as he began to get to his feet. 'I do not want you to come with me, even to the airport. You must finish your work here and go north as you promised. That is why you have come. And that is the reason why we met and why you and I have worked together.'

She seemed as if she was going to turn and leave, but then as he sat before her she stretched out her hand and laid it gently on his cheek. Then she was gone.

Edmund turned and looked down over the rail of the terrace to where the half-naked figures lay like salamanders sunning themselves by the pool. One man had his arm around a girl. She was topless with only a silver triangle around her waist.

He watched the pair and cursed himself.

At Rio Airport Teresa had to run to the check-in and she was the last to board the VARIG flight to BA.

The passenger in the seat beside her said, 'You cut that very fine,' and put a hand lightly on Teresa's knee and kept it there.

'I know,' Teresa replied. 'But I had someone to see.'

Pilar turned her head away and stared out of the cabin window as the plane took off and rose to circle the Christ figure on the Corcovado mountain.

TEN

In Hong Kong the man who had been greeted as Mr Brandt by the Chinese receptionist on his arrival at the offices of the International Oriental Trading Company remained inside the offices of that company for the whole of the day on which he had arrived. In the evening, after it was dark, he was driven in a bottle-green Rolls to a villa overlooking the South China Sea above the site of the old Repulse Bay Hotel, which had long since been redeveloped. During the drive he received a telephone call. As he got out of the car and was giving the chauffeur instructions, a small figure hurtled out of the door of the villa and grabbed him from behind round the waist. He held on to the small hands clasped in front of him as he finished what he had to say to the chauffeur. Then he turned and lifted the slight figure high up into the air, holding her above his head at arms' length.

The eyes of the child, slanting but blue like his own, beamed at him from beneath the fringe of a pudding-basin haircut.

'Tommy,' the child said ecstatically, 'Tommy.'

He pulled her to him and kissed her and then lowered her to the ground.

'Where is Fan Sen?' he asked.

'I am here.'

They were joined by the child's mother. She handed him a letter. He looked at the English stamps and postmark and put it unopened into his pocket. Then he put his arm around the woman, and the three went into the house.

The following morning a junk anchored in Repulse Bay and a launch collected Maitland from the slipway where he was waiting. He was carrying only his briefcase.

'I shall see you tonight,' he said to the woman, who had

come to see him off. He kissed the child who waved to him as he was taken out to the junk, which, after he had come on board and disappeared below, weighed, and made for the sea beyond the mouth of the bay.

He was led to the stateroom. At the table sat the old Chinese man with the lined face and dyed black hair who had been present when Maitland had arrived at the office in the Bond building on the previous morning. On either side of him sat two younger Chinese. They were in conference. None rose to greet him; the old man waved him to a chair.

The old man, the principal among the three, was speaking to his companions in Mandarin. The newcomer was ignored. Maitland understood enough of the language to know that the old man was talking of an agent in Macao and a venture in northern Thailand that had failed and the need to warn Vincente Consuero in Colombia. While the old man was speaking Maitland lounged back in his chair; he would match their manners with insolence of his own. He rose and crossed the room to stare out of the porthole.

'Please remain seated,' the old man said in English.

Maitland strolled slowly back to his chair and lit a cigarette. None of the others, he knew, liked the scent of tobacco and he deliberately puffed the smoke into the air above them. The scene, he suspected, was being carefully staged. He puffed his cigarette even more contentedly and sprawled deeper in his chair, waiting for the real purpose for his summons to the junk to be revealed.

The old man then began to speak in English, although he still did not look directly at Maitland but continued to address his companions. He spoke of the need for discipline in their organisation and of the rules that bound them all together. It was when he began to speak of Josef that he turned for the first time to look directly at Maitland.

Josef, the old man said, had become drunken and unreliable. Sooner or later he would have had to have been dealt with; but his 'elimination', as the old man described it, had not been authorised by the Central Council. Personal feuds and private retribution were impermissible. He paused. Maitland had kept his gaze directly on the old man whose eyes as he spoke never met those of Maitland but swivelled around the stateroom from the papers before him to the ceiling above Maitland's head. Maitland waited, listening to the words of the old man above the throb of the engine of the junk as it sailed on into the South China Sea.

Then the old man flicked his fingers and one of his companions handed to him a slim file and laid it carefully on the table in front of him.

The noise of the engine ceased and was succeeded by the rattle of the anchor chain. Maitland rose and walked slowly to a porthole and looked out. They were anchored in a small bay.

'Sit down, if you please.'

Maitland strolled slowly back to his chair. He lit another cigarette. The old man began. He wished to receive an explanation about Maitland's relationship with a young South American girl in Germany, which had received some notoriety and had brought undesirable attention upon him.

Maitland smiled. 'A pack of lies,' he replied coolly. 'The child blamed me for her pregnancy but it was not true. The girl was on drugs; her family had to take her home.' He stubbed out the cigarette that he had just lit. 'But is that the reason why you have invited me here? If it is,' he said contemptuously, 'I am intrigued that such important people should concern themselves with such triviality.'

The old man made no reply but lowered his head to study the papers in the file in front of him.

'In any event,' Maitland said, 'I do not see that whatever may have happened in Germany is any business of yours.'

'You have a woman in France?' said the old man.

'If I have, what business is that of yours?'

The Chinese on the old man's right now spoke. 'We have kept you and this woman under observation. We are fully informed over places and dates when you meet her.'

The old man picked from the file some photographs and held them close to his eyes.

The other went on: 'We know that you were with her Friday a week ago in Paris. When you left her, your mistress was followed to her home in Gauville.'

Maitland tilted back his chair. 'What I do with my women is

my business. It is not yours. Your business is when you hire me. I have given you no reason to be dissatisfied.'

'We shall see,' said the old man softly, 'we shall see.'

Maitland bent forward across the table, thrusting his face close to that of the old man who stared back at him impassively.

'Take care, take very great care. You would not easily find another to do for you what I do. Or do it so well. I work for you and you pay me. What I do with women is my business.'

He sat with both hands on the table, leaning towards the old man who stared back at him, still passive and inscrutable. Maitland turned his head to look at the other two men, one after the other.

'You bring me all the way out here to lecture me about women!' He stood again and leant against the bulkhead. He lit yet another cigarette. 'I protect both your skins and your profits and you had better not forget it. And what I do for you, I do at the risk of my life.'

'For a price,' murmured the old man. 'For a handsome price.'

'Of course.' Maitland blew rings of smoke into the air above his head. 'And if you are so distressed about my sexual morality, you might care to remember how many wives each of you allows himself. How many is it? Two, three, four? As well as your child concubines and your boys.'

One of the men half rose but the old man put out a hand and he sat.

Maitland went on: 'So you have had the impudence to have me watched with a mistress whom I rarely see in a city I rarely visit. And I presume that it is you who I found out were having me followed in London. Well, let me repeat. What I do for you and Consuero in Colombia is your business. My private life is my own.' He came back and stood by the stateroom table. 'Now unless you have anything serious to say, order the Master to take the junk back to Repulse Bay and allow me to leave.'

There was silence and the noise of the sea could be heard slapping against the hull. Maitland stubbed out the cigarette in the ashtray, pushing it from him and nearer to the man who had attempted to interrupt him. As he did so the old man very slowly and deliberately took a sheet of paper from the file in front of him and began to read.

100

'Marie-Claire de Tourneville, aged 48, the daughter of Henri de Remusat, Councillor of State, and wife of Bernard de Tourneville, nominally of the Quai d'Orsay in the French diplomatic service but actually Chief of the DGSE, the French Secret Intelligence Service.'

The old man raised his eyes and for the first time looked direct into the blue eyes of Maitland.

No one spoke. The old man tossed the paper across the table towards Maitland who let it lie where it had fallen. Then, slowly, Maitland sat, picked up the sheet of paper and read.

'Not,' said the old man, almost to himself, 'not the wisest choice of mistress for someone in your profession and for someone associated with us.'

The third man, who had not yet spoken, said, 'Do you now understand why we had you watched? Such a relationship raises at best the question of your judgement and . . . ' the man paused and then added quietly, 'at worst the question of your loyalty.'

Maitland put down the paper. His face had grown paler and the blue eyes were narrow and cold. The insolence had gone.

'I did not know,' he said simply.

The questioning then began, a cross-examination that lasted for more than two hours. One took notes and when Maitland answered the old man studied the papers before him, comparing what Maitland said with what had been written on the reports. First they wanted to know how he had met her; then where he used to take her; then what he spoke about when he was with her; then what he had said to her about himself and what she knew about him.

It was this last on which they pressed him hardest. Most of all they wanted to know what she knew of his life. He said that he had never spoken of his life, she did not even know his true name and she believed that he was what he held himself out to be, an international trader in precious gems whose business took him across the world. His relationship with this woman was, he said, no more than a casual sexual connection with an attractive woman whom he had met in a restaurant in Paris and of whose husband he knew nothing. He met her to have sex and for sex alone; she was no more than a convenient

101

sexual partner. She had kept their relationship secret because she had a husband of some social position who, she had told him, was an elderly official of no great importance.

'You did not enquire?' the old man asked.

No, Maitland replied. He had not thought there was any need. He met the woman in an apartment; they were rarely together outside the bedroom of that apartment.

'Do they know in Colombia of this woman and what post her husband holds? Does Vincente Consuero know?'

'I do not know,' Maitland said. 'I have not spoken about it.'

The questioning went on. Maitland was no longer smoking. They had not eaten all day and as it grew dark the engines of the junk were started and the ship sailed from the bay where they had lain at anchor. As the lamps in the stateroom were lit, Maitland said that now that he knew who the husband was he would terminate the association.

'I shall not see the woman again.'

The three men across the table sat in silence for several minutes. The old man suddenly closed the file and handed it to one of his companions.

He said, 'That would not be enough. You will understand what you have to do.'

Then he rose and without another word or a glance at Maitland he left the stateroom. The two others remained watching Maitland.

The man who had spoken first said, 'You will disembark at the Star Ferry. There are flights to Europe tonight. You have your passport?'

He knew what he had to do, if he himself were to live.

'Yes,' he said. 'I have my passport. I shall return tonight to Europe.'

No more was said. The unspoken alternative lay heavy on the humid air in the stateroom.

It was early in the evening when the junk threaded its way through the traffic in Hong Kong harbour and came alongside the jetty near to the Star Ferry terminus opposite the Mandarin Hotel. Maitland disembarked; none of the three appeared on

102

deck to see him leave. The green Rolls that had taken him to Repulse Bay drove him to the airport. He told the driver to inform Fan Sen. The reservation had been made from the junk and he boarded a Swissair flight to Paris.

On the aeroplane he ordered champagne but did not eat.

While the Boeing 747 thundered west and north back to Europe he passed the night thinking of what had been said in the stateroom of the junk and of what now he had to do. He sat chain-smoking, occasionally drinking champagne.

He had not told the men on the junk that when he had last seen Marie-Claire he had said to her more than he had ever said before and more than he ever should. She knew now that his life involved secrecy and risk and danger. Now if he were himself to live he had no alternative.

On arrival at Charles de Gaulle he took a taxi and ordered the driver to take him to a small hotel in Montmartre. In his room he slept for several hours and when it was dark he took a taxi, which dropped him by the church at the end of the rue Casimir Perier. He walked down the street passing the entrance to number 17. He found another taxi and returned to the hotel.

Next morning he checked out and once again was dropped at the corner of the rue Casimir Perier. Carrying his suitcase he again walked past number 17 but this time he stopped at the end of the street and entered a *tabac* where he bought some cigars and newspapers and spent a few minutes leafing through magazines, observing the street outside. Then he retraced his steps and, sure now that no one was watching, he entered number 17 and let himself into his apartment. In the sitting-room he picked up the telephone and dialled the same number that he had called when he had arrived from London after the death of the girl. He stood listening to the ring at the other end. There was no reply and he replaced the receiver.

Over the next hour he repeated the telephone call. On each occasion he got no reply.

He rang the exchange, asked for enquiries and sought a country number. The request was refused. The number was not to be disclosed. He went to a shelf and took down a copy of the *Auberges de France* and studied the entries for Normandy.

103

Then he made one more telephone call and booked a reservation for the night at the hotel he had chosen. Taking with him a pair of field glasses and a small grip, he picked up a taxi and was taken to an apartment block in the Boulevard Suchet. He told the driver to wait and after studying the list of names on the bell-board outside the front door, he rang a bell. There was no reply. He returned to the cab and ordered the driver to take him to a telephone. From the call box he rang the Travellers' Club in the Champs-Elysées. He spoke to the hall porter.

'Is Monsieur de Tourneville in the club?' he enquired. 'If he is, may I speak with him? I am calling from his office.'

He was informed that M de Tourneville was not in the club. He next telephoned the Jockey Club and repeated his enquiry. This time the Hall porter said he would fetch M de Tourneville and told him to hold on. After a moment and without speaking further Maitland replaced the receiver, returned to the taxi and instructed the driver to take him to the Hertz office at 27 rue St-Ferdinand. There he produced a driver's licence with a photograph in the name of Bertrand and hired a large Citroën which he drove out of Paris through the Porte d'Ateuil en route to Normandy.

He arrived late at the inn where he had earlier made the reservation. The hotel was 20 kilometres from Gauville and next morning he left the hotel soon after first light and drove to a lane near to the château at Gauville. He parked the car in a turning a little way from the house and, crossing a field on foot, he entered the woods that bordered the garden.

From the edge of the wood he observed with his field glasses the back of the château. The windows were shut but no curtains were drawn across them, save for one at the very top of the house. After about an hour he saw a woman pull back the curtains in the top room window. Through his glasses he could see that she was in her nightdress. Then he circled the château keeping under cover until he took up a position where he could observe the front of the house. Here again he saw that none of the curtains in the windows were closed. Then the woman, whom he had seen framed in the top window but who was now dressed, opened the front door to let out the dogs. She stood by the door while the dogs raced around the rose garden. Then she called to them, shouting loudly and noisily and whistling. There was obviously no one in the house to disturb. Eventually the dogs came to her and she took them inside.

Maitland lay on the ground inside a large clump of rhododendrons, his field glasses trained on the house, and waited for a further hour until he was satisfied that there was no sight of anyone else. He made his way back to where he had parked the car and drove it slowly into the wide sweep of the drive, which led between the rhododendrons and some tall poplars to a circle of lawn in front of a balustrade and the broad stone steps, which led up to the front of the house. He drew up the car, got out and climbed the steps to the front door. When he had pulled the old-fashioned bell handle he could hear the dogs barking. After a wait the woman whom he had seen earlier came to the door.

'Good morning, madame,' he said, smiling at her. 'I am sorry to disturb you and I hope that it is not too early but I am a friend of Madame de Tourneville. When I last saw her at Fontainebleau I told her that I might be in the neighbourhood today and she invited me to call. I am on my way from Bordeaux to Paris and I wondered if it would be convenient for me to pay my respects. If it is too early I could come back later in the morning. My name is Henri Lepage.'

He was still smiling and she noticed the remarkable blue of his eyes.

'I am sorry, m'sieur. Madame is not here.'

She tried to prevent the dogs from coming out of the door but they escaped her and a retriever came to him, welcoming. He bent and patted the dog, taking its head in both his hands and fondling its ears.

'She is not here? That is most unfortunate! I am so sorry but I was certain that she told me that she would be here today. I must have made some mistake. Then I must hope to see her at the Boulevard Suchet when I arrive in Paris.'

He was still playing with the dog.

'No, m'sieur. She is not in Paris either. She and M'sieur de

Tourneville went to England for a visit and Madame is staying on. We do not expect them down here for at least another ten days.'

'I see. Well, that is most disappointing. I must have mistaken the dates. I don't think that I can follow them all the way to England.' He smiled at her again as he patted the dog. 'And you are left looking after the dogs, and very nice dogs too! Well, it is a good time of the year for M'sieur and Madame to have a holiday in England.' He made no move to leave.

She returned his smile.

'I don't think that Madame thought that it would be much of a holiday. She was not very anxious to go. It was, she said, a kind of official visit.'

'Poor Madame! She does not enjoy those kind of visits, the official visits. That will not amuse her and I do not blame her.' He straightened up. 'Well, I might as well get on the road. My detour has been wasted. Thank you, madame. You have been very kind. I am truly sorry to have disturbed you so early in the morning. Will you tell Madame de Tourneville that I called and that I shall get in touch with her when she is in Paris?'

He shook her hand and began to descend the broad stone steps that led down to the drive.

When he was halfway down, and before the woman had gone back into the house, he turned and, looking up to her, he said, 'By the way, madame. There is no need to tell Monsieur de Tourneville that I called. You understand? A little secret, just between you and me – and Madame de Tourneville. Look after your children,' he said pointing at the dogs now at either side of her feet.

Then he ran down the rest of the steps and got into the car. She stood on the steps watching as the Citroën sped up the drive and turned out of her sight into the lane.

When Maitland arrived in Paris over two hours later he went to the offices of the British Council in the rue de Constantine. He asked if he might see copies of *The Times* published during the past two weeks. He took the bundle of newspapers on their wooden library handles to a table and calculated the date when he had last been with Marie-Claire and had watched her as she had driven away through the rain to Normandy. Commencing with the edition dated two days thereafter he examined the Court page of each edition of the days following. He studied the reports of every function, noting every single name that was listed as having attended each occasion. Then he found what he was seeking.

The item was headed 'St Peter's College, Cambridge'. Beneath was the text:

The Master (Sir Alexander Murray, GCMG), Fellows and Honorary Fellows of St Peter's College, Cambridge, last evening celebrated the 550th anniversary of the foundation of the college on the occasion of the college's annual Midsummer Feast. The guests included the Vice Chancellor Professor Sir Harold Vincent and Lady Vincent; the Master of Trinity College, Lord Harrington of Ashstead and Lady Harrington of Ashstead; the Master of Christ's College, Professor Sir Hans Kornberg, FRS and Lady Kornberg; M and Mme Bernard de Tourneville; General Sir Francis and Lady Black; Sir Peter and Lady Reynolds; and Professor James Winthrop and Mrs Winthrop.

He noted down the names, returned the newspapers to the desk and asked for a copy of *Who's Who*. He checked the ages, careers and addresses of each of the guests listed in the announcement in *The Times*.

Then he recalled an occasion when Marie-Claire had been with him and he had seen in her eyes that she was measuring the difference in their ages. She had said, a little sadly, that she wished that he could have seen her in her prime. When she had been in London, she had boasted gently, the world had been at her feet. He had told her that he loved her as she was.

So de Tourneville must at one time have served at the London Embassy. Sir Alexander Murray, he knew, had lately been the British Ambassador in Paris. That would be the link that had taken the de Tournevilles to Cambridge, the occasion to which Marie-Claire had not looked forward and from which the husband had since returned to Paris and she had stayed on. But why had she stayed if the *bonne* had been right and she had been reluctant ever to go? Was that reluctance because of his promise that he would soon be returning to her? That, he thought grimly as he carried the book back to the counter, was exactly what he was about to do.

The entry for Sir Alexander in *Who's Who* had given the Murrays' address as the Master's Lodge, St Peter's College, Cambridge and Wetherby Place, near Buxton, Derbyshire. It would be at one or the other of these addresses that Marie-Claire would be staying. It would not be difficult to discover which.

That evening Maitland returned to the nightclub where he had gone earlier in his search for Josef, but this time he did not enter through the main entrance but bribed the man at the stage door and was shown into the singer's dressing-room. While he waited he examined the posters, which, as in the apartment in the rue Parnasse, decorated the walls, and he picked up and studied the photographs on the dressing-table. He examined them idly, wondering if for sentimental reasons the singer might have one of him. If there was, he thought, it would have been taken before the singer had gone to Tangier to have the operation. But he found none. He was not, he was glad to note, important enough; or, what mattered more, well known enough. He sat and smoked until the singer returned at the end of the first show.

The singer, entering the dressing-room in full costume, was startled at the sight of him sprawled in the chair by the dressing-table, and stood, a hand on the door, staring at him.

'How did you get in here?'

'The usual way when one wants to visit the star of a show. Money.'

The singer closed the door.

'What has brought you back? What do you want?' The singer took a dressing-gown from the rack and put it over the low-cut frock, knotting the cord in front.

'Just paying a visit. Once more I need some help.'

'Did you find Josef?'

'No, I missed him. But the address in Berlin which you gave, or rather the address which I bought from you, was correct.'

'You thought that I had cheated?'

'It had occurred to me, but you did not.'

The singer looked at him, brushing the long hair back from his painted face.

'In the end it did not matter. Eventually I found what I wanted.'

The door of the dressing-room burst open and one of the chorus still in make-up and dressed in bodice and black net stockings ran into the room. He looked as if he were about to cry.

'Not now, *chéri*, not now.' The singer shepherded the youth out of the room and locked the door.

'What do you want this time?'

'First, I need to stay. Is Tomas at home?'

'He is.'

'I want to see him for I need help to arrange a trip. And I have not much time. If he can help, then I won't bother you for long. So I am confident that he will. I shall of course pay.'

He took out his wallet and put some dollar notes on the table by the pots and bottles of make-up.

'Come with me,' the singer said.

They left the dressing-room and went down the corridor to the telephone by the doorkeeper's lobby. Maitland waited while the singer telephoned.

'He will expect you,' the singer said, replacing the receiver. 'You will not need the key. I do not want you to stay long.'

'I do not wish to stay long.'

As he left through the stage door he saw the singer walk back along the mean corridor to the dressing-room, joined by the boy from the chorus. The singer put an arm around the boy, comforting him.

Four days later he took the morning train to St Malo. He was dressed in a seaman's dark sweater, a check shirt, faded light blue jeans and grubby white rubber-soled shoes and he carried a canvas grip. In the evening he went to a restaurant, L'Escale, on the quay. It was full. He picked his way across the room to a table where two men and a girl were eating. They looked up as he approached. They were expecting him. He greeted them affectionately as though they were old friends. They asked no questions. The older of the men, with a weather-beaten face and grizzled hair, was obviously the skipper. They spoke in English, the younger man and the girl with an Irish brogue.

Most of the diners had come ashore from the yachts in the basin. At about nine o'clock many of them rose to leave and Maitland's party went with them. There was a tide to catch. Before they left the table Maitland handed an envelope to the younger of the two men. Outside, this man said goodnight and slipped away into the dark. The skipper, the girl and Maitland joined the other diners who had left the restaurant and who were walking back in groups to their dinghies moored at the quayside. Maitland insisted upon taking the oars and he rowed expertly amid the small flotilla making for the yachts.

'I was well trained,' he said grinning at the girl and the skipper. 'In the service of the Queen.'

The three of them boarded a 20-foot ketch and, when the dinghy was stowed and preparations completed, they motored out of the harbour accompanied by several other craft. When clear of the harbour they hoisted sail for the night voyage to Salcombe in Devonshire. The sea was high and the wind fresh so they made good progress and the following afternoon, after waiting a little for the tide in company with three other yachts of the same class, they crossed the bar at the entrance to Salcombe harbour. They lowered the sails and motored up the river to a mooring. When the Customs launch came alongside they declared a case of wine and three bottles of cognac; the skipper handed over their three passports together. They were cleared with little fuss and about five o'clock the skipper rowed Maitland and the girl ashore.

The two shared a taxi to Exeter. He bought two second-class tickets and they caught the night train to Paddington. The girl spent most of the night dozing, cradled in his arms. They separated at the station and Maitland booked into a small hotel in Praed Street.

Later he telephoned the Master's Lodge at St Peter's. Margaret Murray answered the telephone and, speaking in French, Maitland asked to be put through to Madame de Tourneville. He said that he was speaking from the Château de Gauville, Madame de Tourneville's home in Normandy, and that he had some bad news about one of her dogs which he felt that she should know. Margaret expressed regret and told him that Marie-Claire was no longer with them. She understood that she might be staying with friends in the country. She did not say with whom. He said that he did not want to trouble Madame unduly but he felt that he ought to inform her as Madame was very fond of the animal and they had been obliged to summon the vet. He asked for her address in case he needed to contact her and she gave him a telephone number that he might try. She did not know the code but gave him the name of the village. It sounded familiar to him. He dialled the number, someone answered, 'Finches', and he again asked in French to speak to Madame de Tourneville. When he was not understood, he repeated the name. He was told to hold on. He waited and before anyone else spoke, he replaced the receiver.

Then he remembered why the name of the village was familiar. It was Chapel Iford, in Wiltshire, the name of the village where the aunt who had looked after him as a boy, and whom he loved and to whom he sent money, had gone to live with the clergyman whom she had married late in life. In Hong Kong he had opened a letter that had been waiting for him for several weeks. From it he had heard that his aunt had died and had been buried in the village. He had never met her husband, but at Chapel Iford he would keep clear of the vicarage.

So he began his final preparations for the last stage in his mission to set at rest the anxieties of the men in Hong Kong.

ELEVEN

'There is something you should know, C,' Harvey Thompson had said. 'We need to talk. This evening.'

His voice was unhurried but the tone conveyed to Godfrey that what Harvey wanted him to tell him was important.

'I have to be at the House for the ten o'clock division this evening. Can we meet earlier and then dine together at Peyton's? That is if you like breakfast food for your dinner.'

'You forget, I too am a member,' Godfrey had said.

'Of course you are. Well, see you at my rooms in Albany at seven o'clock. We can talk privately there.'

Sir Harvey Thompson was the Parliamentary Undersecretary at the Foreign Office and, as it so happened, Godfrey's Member of Parliament, for Finches was in Harvey's constituency in Wiltshire. They were of the same age, the middle fifties. They had been at the university together and then for a time in the same chambers at the Bar, until Godfrey had left to join MI6, and Harvey for the City and then the House of Commons. They had remained close friends and Godfrey relied on Harvey as his informant on the political and Parliamentary scene.

Although not a senior minister, Harvey was a man of influence both in politics and in the City. He had never aspired to high office in government, content to represent in Parliament the county in which his family had long been established. He had to be persuaded to serve in government and he had consented only on condition that it would not be for long. Not for him the scramble up 'the greasy pole' to high office and it was because he stood aside from the game and was thus no rival that he was the confidant of most of the principal chieftains in the Party including the Prime Minister himself – a man not given readily to accept the judgement of others.

112

As Webster turned the car into Albany courtyard off Piccadilly, Godfrey reflected that Harvey Thompson was perhaps the
last in the House of that now almost extinct breed the knights
of the Shires. There had been a time when they and their
opposites in the other party, the solid trades unionists, had
provided the ballast in the House of Commons. For all their
political differences, the two groups had been very alike. The
knights and the old-timer trades unionists used to regard the
political 'high-flyers' with a demonstrable scepticism, and as
the two groups drank together, as they usually did in the downstairs bar in the House of Commons, they would discuss in
similar terms horses, greyhounds and the career politicians.

But now, thought Godfrey as, accompanied by his watchdog
detective, he was led by the porter to Harvey's staircase, the
old stalwarts of Parliament had gone; the House was full of
merchant bankers on the one side and university lecturers on
the other. Both he considered equally suspect. Some indeed,
he had noted, had even attracted the attention of his friend the
Director-General of MI5.

Harvey greeted him at the door. He was a thin, spare man,
who held himself very erect. His white moustache beneath a
prominent nose made him look older than his years. He led
Godfrey into his chambers and into the drawing-room, with its
high ceiling, which overlooked the glass-covered walk and the
small front gardens, which ran the whole length of Albany
from Piccadilly to Burlington Gardens and the mouth of Savile
Row.

'Byron once inhabited these rooms,' Harvey said. 'I don't
think he would approve of me, snob though he was. He'd
consider me too much of a Castlereagh kind of man. Whisky
and soda?'

When they were seated, Harvey asked after Angela and
about the establishment near to Finches of a Buddhist settle-
ment whose monks with their saffron robes and cropped heads
were causing considerable local consternation; not to Godfrey
and Angela who enjoyed the introduction of this touch of the
exotic, but primarily to a group led by the vicar, Henry
Makepiece. Then Harvey came to the point.

'Tell me about Kent. He's your Deputy, isn't he?'

113

'Yes. What about him?'

'Is he a good fellow?'

'He is extremely efficient.'

'That is not quite what I asked. But never mind. I have been hearing his name lately. When you were appointed as C, you jumped over him, didn't you?'

'Well, he had joined before I did, but when I got the job we both had comparative responsibilities. What have you been hearing about him?'

'His name has been cropping up lately in certain quarters. There seems to be developing a faction which rates James Kent very highly.'

Godfrey was nettled and, uncharacteristically, showed it.

'And why not? He is very good at his job.'

'I am sure that he is. It is his supporters or, as I would call them, his promoters who are worrying me.'

'Promoters? What are you getting at, Harvey?'

Harvey rose to his feet, glass in his hand, and stood looking out of the window at the flowers in the small gardens in the covered walk. He could see Godfrey's 'minder' at the entrance to his staircase chatting to the porter in the swallow-tailed coat and tall hat.

'Just some gossip which I happened to pick up. It comes from the Home Office and that is what has distracted me.'

'The Home Secretary and I', said Godfrey, putting his glass down on the table beside him, 'are not friends.'

'No, he is not a friend of yours and I thought I should warn you. He calls you "the Secret Mandarin" and he has been talking about you with his cronies. I gather he has been dropping a hint here and there that he is concerned about the management of your service.'

'The Home Secretary?'

'Yes. Apparently he is questioning your judgement, suggesting that you have become over-obsessed with theories about murder squads and suchlike coming from South America.'

Godfrey laughed. 'I have said something like that to him. Perhaps I alarmed him. He is not a man I would choose to go tiger-hunting with.'

114

Harvey swung round and faced his guest. His expression was serious.

'Don't underestimate him. I like him as little as you but I have a high regard for his power within this Administration. The PM relies on him and he is impregnable politically. So he is a formidable enemy. He has few rivals when it comes to Westminster or Whitehall street-fighting and as you know he collects people, his people, whom he gathers around him, and he works them into the posts where he wants and they will support him. You have heard about the Attorney?'

'No.'

'Well he's out. He is going to the Bench, to the Court of Appeal. The Solicitor has succeeded him. The Home Secretary's crony.'

'The Attorney will make an awkward judge,' said Godfrey reflectively. 'I shall miss him in Whitehall. I enjoyed his acid comments to his less intelligent colleagues. But his successor will certainly suit the Home Office better. He is more malleable and an indifferent lawyer. The other at least was clever and had standards. I suppose that he championed the independence of the Law Officers too stubbornly to suit the Home Secretary.'

Harvey brushed aside Godfrey's comments impatiently.

'I told you about the Attorney because it is another demonstration of the man's power. Tell me, Godfrey. Have you recently sent someone to South America, someone special?'

Godfrey looked at him. There was a moment of silence.

'You and I are old friends but if I have or have not sent anyone to anywhere in the world on the business of my service, it is none of your damned business.'

Harvey was not to be put off.

'I know that it is not my business. But I am telling you as an old friend what I think that you ought to know. It is being suggested, very discreetly of course, that lately the leadership of "the friends" has become rather erratic. As I said earlier, it is being hinted that you are overreacting to stories of the drug runners and their murder squads and now it is being said that you have upset the service by dispatching on a mission some untried academic who is a friend of yours.'

'That is nonsense. He is a friend but he is also the best man

115

I could find for a very particular job.'

'Of course I accept that, but that you selected a man they call an inexperienced young don is what the Home Secretary and his cronies are putting about and they are using it as an illustration of your lack of judgement. Very discreetly of course, just a whisper here and there in Whitehall, but when I picked it up I recognised it as the start of one of that man's whispering campaigns which he initiates when he wants someone out.'

'I have no doubt that you are right about that,' said Godfrey drily. 'But I have allies, the PM and the Foreign Secretary, quite apart from the Cabinet Secretary.'

'The Foreign Secretary is going through a particularly bad patch both with his Cabinet colleagues and with the back-benchers. More clumsiness, this time with Bonn. He may not survive the autumn reshuffle if he even lasts as long as that. The PM relies on the Home Secretary because of his influence with the Party in the country and this Cabinet Secretary will do as he's told. He's not like some of the earlier breed. No, Godfrey, what is happening looks to me like a campaign against you orchestrated by that unpleasant man at the Home Office. At present it is just the hint that it may be time for a change of C. They are building up a case against you, Godfrey.'

Godfrey remained silent. It was helpful to have been alerted. He had certainly taken a risk by sending Edmund, but for Carlos' plan to succeed, Edmund was the only one they might be able to slip in – and later slip out. Only Edmund's qualifications fitted; there had been no one else.

But Godfrey was disturbed by the accuracy of the leak. Not many outside 'the friends' themselves would know of the detail about who had been sent. He himself had told the ministers' conference at Chequers that he had sent someone in, but the identification of the 'inexperienced young don' indicated that the leak must have come from within the department.

'Thank you for telling me,' he said. 'But I would like to go back to the beginning of what you said. You spoke of James Kent. What is this talk about James Kent? That is what interests me.'

'Nothing direct. Just that Kent is a very competent Deputy.

116

I suspect that they may be preparing the ground if ever you should go.'

He means *when* I shall go, thought Godfrey.

'Kent is said to have a rather different style to yours and a style of which the Home Secretary appears to approve.'

Godfrey smiled. 'That is true. He might very well appeal to the Home Secretary.'

He thought again about who would know the mission of Edmund Hamilton. None knew the real purpose of the mission, and that included Kent. Kent had been against sending anyone, let alone Edmund; he had made that plain. But that Kent should be responsible for a deliberate leak surprised him. If, of course, it had come from Kent. Others, cronies of Kent, may have shared Kent's reservations. If so, the Whitehall grapevine could have picked some gossip from within Kent's office. The links between the two services, MI6 and MI5, were close and Kent's disagreement could have filtered through to the Home Office. What mattered now was that Edmund should pull it off without running into trouble. But in the field, as Godfrey well knew, trouble had rules of its own.

Harvey had been watching his friend. He now poured him another drink and as he handed the glass to Godfrey he said quietly, 'It will be all right. You have friends and much support. But I wanted you to know what might be brewing. I don't trust that *faux bonhomme* at the Home Office.'

Godfrey laughed. 'Neither do I. Thank you for alerting me. I have taken a risk in sending the man I chose but I know that he was the right man for this job. Indeed no one else could have done it.'

They walked across Piccadilly into St James's Street, followed discreetly by Godfrey's minder. In Peyton's they ordered scrambled eggs and bacon and pints of beer in pewter tankards. They sat at a round table in the low candle-lit dining-room and Godfrey found himself next to William Blaze, the Government Chief Whip, a man whose appointment had surprised many of Blaze's contemporaries in the Commons. The Chief Whip was complaining to his neighbour about television, which he considered was regularly biased against the Government. Still concerned by what Harvey had told him of the leak over Edmund's mission and of the whispering campaign in Whitehall, Godfrey found Blaze and his complaints tiresome. When Blaze turned to involve him in the conversation and appealed to him for an opinion, Godfrey answered too shortly and turned away to talk to his other neighbour. Blaze coloured and soon got up from the table and went into the inner room.

As he watched Blaze walk from the room, Godfrey regretted his hastiness. The snub had been obvious and he knew that he had been foolish. He determined to seek out Blaze after dinner and put it right but when he and Harvey had finished their scrambled eggs and followed into the inner room, Blaze, after muttering to Brian Pepper over his coffee about the airs which 'the civil service mandarins' allowed themselves, had left for the House.

On his way home in the car, Godfrey cursed himself for being so impolitic with a man who wielded much political power. Blaze was the type who would be particularly sensitive to what he would consider to be a slight from an official.

I must be more careful, Godfrey thought, especially if the knives are being sharpened for a bout of Whitehall street-fighting. I have already one sufficiently powerful enemy in the Home Secretary. It was not clever to have made another.

As Webster drove him home to the flat in Chelsea, which he used during the week in London, he determined that here was a fence that he must take care swiftly to mend. The Chief Whip was important and he might well regret that encounter.

As Webster pulled up the Rover at the traffic lights at the fork in the Brompton Road by the London Oratory, a dark green Ford Escort drew up alongside them on their off-side. Webster glanced to his right at the single occupant in the car. The driver's face was momentarily illuminated as he lit a cigarette. When the traffic lights changed, Webster drove the Rover left into the Fulham Road on the way to Godfrey's flat. The Ford Escort with Maitland at the wheel drove straight ahead along the road that would take him west, to Godfrey's home in Wiltshire.

TWELVE

Martin Maitland drove the Ford Escort down the motorway making sure that he kept within the 70 m.p.h. limit. He was taking no risks. He did not wish to be stopped by any police patrol, although he had with him a valid driving licence in the name of Mathews. He was wearing a striped shirt and a tie and black kid gloves. On his head was a flat check cap, which he had bought that morning at Lock's in St James's Street. In his service days, just back from the Falklands, he had been in the truck when his Platoon Commander had stopped in St James's and had emerged from Lock's with what the platoon sergeant had described as a 'flat 'at' which the Platoon Commander had worn jokingly with his service assault jacket. Maitland had admired the cap and now he had one himself. Beside him on the passenger seat lay a Barbour jacket purchased at Simpson's in Piccadilly.

The car itself, which had 50,000 miles recorded on its mile-ometer, had been purchased for cash the previous day in the second-hand car market at Warren Street by an Irishman who had driven it to a lock-up garage in Victoria Road, Hackney in north-east London where the Irishman had sprayed the red vehicle a dark green and tuned its engine, replacing as neces-sary the worn parts. Apart from the change in colour, the body, which was relatively unmarked, was left alone. Then the mech-anic had filed away the chassis and engine numbers as well as he was able, making them indecipherable at least to the naked eye or inspection under a magnifying glass. Finally he had fitted replacement number plates and filled the tank from cans in the garage.

At half-past six on the following evening, Maitland had arrived. Inside the lock-up garage he had lifted the hood and watched while the Irishman revved the engine. Satisfied, Maitland had handed over a bundle of fifty-pound notes and, throwing a holdall onto the rear seat, he had driven away. At the traffic lights between Thurloe Place and Brompton Road he had lit a cigarette. He had not noticed the black Rover with the driver and the single passenger seated in the back.

On the motorway he drove in the centre lane regularly keeping his eyes on his rear and side mirrors to watch the headlights of the following cars, slowing to allow them to overtake. After three-quarters of an hour of steady driving he left the motorway and then followed the dual carriageway of the A303. Soon he came to the edge of Salisbury Plain and he could see the great stones at Stonehenge lit by the moon and by the modern floodlighting surrounded by the fence which now protected them from vandals. As he drove past he touched his cap and smiled. When he was a boy his Aunt Anne had told him that it was wise to propitiate any god or devil who might be lurking amid those mysterious stones. She herself used to make the sign of the cross.

The only person Martin Maitland had ever loved had been that aunt, Anne, the sister of his mother. She had cared for him after the death of his parents and he had never forgotten her kindness to him when he was a small boy, how she had taken him from the preparatory school to which his parents had sent him to board and had let him go to a day school so that he came back to her each evening. The memory of his cold and formal parents had soon faded and the aunt, the surrogate mother, was the one who stayed close to his heart.

Then, at the age of sixteen he had run away, and for a long time no one could find him. His reason for breaking with the comfortable home that Anne Messenger had provided, and escaping from that kind but stifling life, had been simply a desire for adventure. He had hated school; he had no friends. He had looked at the world surrounding the small, neat semidetached house in its neat garden in the then neat borough of Ealing and he had decided that it was not the life for him. So he had taken a fifty-pound note from his aunt's purse and slipped away and lived rough among a pack of fellow runaways.

120

Sometimes he would think of being back with her, of being pressed against her comforting, comfortable figure and of her scent of lavender. But despite such occasional yearnings in times of despair when he was cold and hungry, he never seriously considered exchanging the independence of his life on the streets for the respectability and comfort of the house in Ealing. There was also pride, and he had always had plenty of pride. To have slunk home would have meant humiliation and defeat. He had never spoken with Anne Messenger after that last evening before he had stolen her money and left. For two years he had lived in the sleazy world of the West End of London, living in squats, thieving, dodging the police and the officials whom he knew were searching for him. At one time he hung around the amusement saloons at Piccadilly Circus where packs of youths congregated around the pinball tables ogled by grey-faced men in shabby raincoats. Very soon he had become streetwise. But he had stayed resolutely clear of the personal use of drugs. Like many, he traded in them but that was for money. After two years, in a moment of sudden revulsion at the life he was leading, he had enlisted in the Royal Marines.

When he began recruit training he bitterly regretted what he had done and fought like a street rat against the discipline, the authority and the regimentation of his new life. After a time he had settled down and he began to enjoy the harshness and the physical demands on his undernourished body, which grew strong and wiry. He acquired a pride in what it could be made to endure. Within a few months there had been grafted onto the street urchin the toughness and resourcefulness of the trained soldier. He found that he had an aptitude for the skills of the man taught to use gun and knife, the man trained to fight and to kill.

On enlistment he had been obliged to give the name of his aunt as his next of kin and when she learnt of his whereabouts she had rejoiced, hoping that the discipline of the service would wipe away what she had regarded as the stain of the months when he had lived among the pack of rent boys who haunted the Circus. She used to write to him care of the Royal Marines long and chatty letters but he never replied and refused to meet

121

her. When she discovered that he was stationed at the depot at Deal she came and visited but he would never see her, despite the urging of his Commanding Officer. The last time he ever saw her, he had stood watching her from a corner of a barrack-hut as she turned sadly from the guardroom and walked disconsolately down the street. For a moment he had longed to run out and call to her but he had stood until she was out of sight and that was the last he had ever seen of her. Soon thereafter he had been posted to various ships and stations overseas. He never saw her again but she continued to write.

During the next three years he lived the life of a hard and competent Royal Marine, taciturn and unfriendly; he was, according to his companions, more a fighting machine than a fighting man. He shared their whoring but rarely their drinking. He was admired but not liked; he refused all offers of promotion to non-commissioned rank. He volunteered for the Special Boat Section and was engaged early in the Falklands campaign. He saw much action, doing all that was demanded of him with a cool and ruthless efficiency. By the end of the fighting he had become expert in the techniques of killing.

Then, when he was twenty-one, three years after he had joined, he learnt of his inheritance under the estate of the parents whose existence he had long before wiped from his memory. He bought himself out of the service and made for Hong Kong where he had previously served, and disappeared into the maze of dwellings in Wan Chai. He emerged as a man who would kill for money.

Before he had left England after discharge from the Royal Marines he had instructed the solicitor executor to send a third of what he had inherited to his aunt. Thereafter he had heard of her through the solicitors to whom he gave a poste restante address in Hong Kong. He instructed them to keep him informed about her and from time to time he had sent her money. She would write thanking him and the solicitors forwarded her letters to a bank in Manila. In this way he had heard of her marriage late in life to the clergyman Henry Makepiece and of the move with her husband to the vicarage in Chapel Iford in Wiltshire and he was glad that she had found companionship and security. Then he had been informed by the letter Fan Sen had given him when he had returned to Repulse Bay of her death and burial in the graveyard at her home.

It was odd that it should be to that place where her life had ended that he was now headed.

By half-past midnight he was deep into Wiltshire.

He went over in his mind the plan that he had made. He had allowed himself two nights in which to accomplish his purpose and on this, the first of those nights, he had decided to reconnoitre. During the day he had studied a large road map of the area and the Ordnance Survey map, the scale a half-inch to the mile, which showed the country around Chapel Iford and on which was clearly marked the house Finches and the vicarage. He would keep clear of the house of the widower of his aunt, the clergyman he had never met.

During his study of the Ordnance Survey he had noted a track that led from a narrow twisting lane into what appeared to be dense woodland about half a mile from Finches. It was two o'clock in the morning when he found the lane and he drove slowly with only his side lights lit until he turned off the lane up the track that twisted through the woods. At a clearing, well out of sight of the lane, he turned the car and reversed it carefully into the undergrowth. He took a pistol from his pocket, screwed on the silencer and laid it on his lap. It was a warm night and with the side windows open he sat for half an hour motionless and listening. Then he removed the cap, tie and jacket that he had worn during his drive into the country and slipped on a pair of dark blue overalls and a woollen dark blue balaclava helmet, which he took from the holdall. He put a pistol, a compass and the night-glasses into the pockets and using a torch and a long knife he cut branches from the bushes and covered the front windshield of the car. He searched for and found some long twigs of dead wood. After he had trod on one and tested it to ensure that it snapped under his foot, he laid the others carefully on the hard ground around the car.

Then he set out. He had now less than three hours of darkness for his reconnaissance.

He anticipated that the house would be protected by a burglar alarm system and perhaps household dogs, and he had come prepared for both. He planned to enter the house to look around and establish the whereabouts of the bedrooms. But even if the opportunity presented itself, he would be reluctant to accomplish what he had come to do on this night for it was late and to get away he would have a long drive ahead. On the following night he would return at an earlier hour and then he would have plenty of time to catch the boat, travelling while it was still dark.

He made his way easily enough through the woods and then over a wall, which he presumed was the border of the property, until he stopped and lay in the undergrowth inspecting through his night-glasses the dark mass of the house beyond. He began to pick out features, concentrating on the downstairs windows. They were of a kind that he would be well able to force, although he expected that they would be linked into an electronic burglar alarm system. He began to sweep with his glasses the side of the house searching for signs of the alarm control box or of the electronic links.

He was about to shift his position in order to examine the other sides of the building when he saw the patrol. There were two of them and they came around the corner of the house from what appeared to be the stable block. They moved silently onto the lawn where they stopped and stood talking quietly. A third man who came from the opposite corner of the house, leading on a leash a German shepherd police dog, joined them. Maitland was able clearly to pick out with the glasses their flak jackets, their radios, side arms on their belts and the automatic weapons that they were carrying.

His shirt beneath the overalls became stained with sweat. Not for a moment had he reckoned on this. He kept his glasses trained on the patrol ready to slide back deeper into the woods, but he knew that once the dog caught wind of him he would be finished.

What kind of house was this with armed guards patrolling the gardens? What was Marie-Claire doing at a place such as

124

this? He had assumed that she was a guest of friends in some country house although not, as he had discovered in London, of the ex-Ambassador to Paris. Who the owners were of the house called Finches he had been unable to discover but that had not troubled him. He had been confident that he would be able to make an entry. It had not occurred to him that Marie-Claire would be staying within what amounted to a fortress.

Could the reason for the armed guards be her husband's connection with the French Security Service, which he had learnt at the conference in the junk? It seemed unlikely; her husband was back in Paris and in France, at Gauville certainly, she was not so protected. The reason for the patrol must be to protect not the guest, Marie-Claire, but the owners. Whoever they were, he now had to accept that he would not be able to force an entry into Finches.

As he lay concealed in the bracken at the edge of the wood watching the group on the lawn, one of the patrol began walking towards him. It was the man leading the dog. That was the danger, the trained dog. He watched the man approaching in the moonlight; he had only a few seconds to decide whether to withdraw silently hoping to remain undiscovered – or to stay and fight. But even if he moved the animal would get on to his track; if he shot and destroyed the dog, the men would be upon him and any battle could not last long. If he succeeded in dropping the man who was approaching and who was now within range, the others would see and hear what had happened and as well as radios to raise the alarm they carried automatic weapons.

A few yards more and despite the slight breeze that was blowing away from him, the dog would get the scent. He took the pistol from his pocket. He would use it on the dog and the man nearest to him, then on the others, then on himself. He would not allow himself to be taken. One of the two on the lawn by the house whistled faintly. The dog handler stopped and turned. The two near to the house beckoned to him. The man looked again to the edge of the wood where Maitland lay hidden as though the man sensed that something was there; the dog was pulling on the leash, anxious to get free. But the others whistled again and the man turned and retraced his steps to join his colleagues, hauling the reluctant dog with him. After talking together the three moved on and disappeared around the side of the house. He heard a latch click in one of the outhouses by the garages and he saw light flooding out of an open door. Then the door was pulled to and the shaft of light went. That was their guardhouse, he thought.

He withdrew the way he had come, moving skilfully and carefully as he made his way back to where the car lay hidden. When he was near he circled the car keeping to the woods and away from the track. After he was satisfied that all was clear he came out of the wood and onto the track, walking slowly towards the camouflaged car, keeping the beam of the torch low on the ground in front of him as he examined the carpet of twigs which he had laid before he had set out. He saw that they were undisturbed and he repeated his inspection around each side of the car before opening the door. He climbed inside and sat considering what he should do.

He could abandon or postpone what the men in Hong Kong required and take his chance with them. But if he abandoned, he knew what would happen. From the moment when the old man had said in the stateroom on the junk that for Maitland to cease the association with Marie-Claire was not enough, he had known that it was his life or hers. To postpone and wait until Marie-Claire was back in France meant delay and neither the men in Hong Kong nor Vincente Consuero in Las Paza who had summoned him to Colombia would tolerate delay.

From what he had seen of the patrol guarding that house he had to accept that he could not get to her; somehow he would have to get her to come to him. And time was short. As he sat in the car pondering how he could accomplish what he had come to do suddenly he thought of the clergyman at the vicarage at Chapel Iford, Henry Makepiece, the widower of his aunt. Makepiece would know the people at Finches where Marie-Claire was a guest; Makepiece then might be the tool to bring her to him. He thought of what he knew of the clergyman and of what his aunt had written to him about her life and her husband's custody of the library in his vicarage in the letters to which Maitland had never replied, and a plan began to form in his resourceful mind. But if he were to answer Consuero's urgent summons to join him in Colombia, one matter was certain: he would have to make use of Makepiece on the night of the day which was now beginning to break.

The first light of dawn was showing through the trees when Maitland clambered out of the car, removed the camouflage from the windscreen and drove the car slowly out of its hiding-place and onto the track. He got out again and walked back to where he had parked. Using the light of the torch he restored as well as he was able the bent and crushed brambles and with his foot eased leaves and debris back over the tracks left by the car. He rubbed earth into the stems from where he had cut the branches. He stripped off his overalls and balaclava, stowing the kit that he had used during the night in the holdall, save for the torch and the pistol from which he unscrewed the silencer. These he put into the wide pockets of his country jacket, tuck-ing the pistol itself into the waist of his trousers. He took out a battery-driven electric razor and shaved himself and put on the tie and the cap. As dawn was breaking he eased the vehicle slowly out into the lane.

There was a ground mist, which helped concealment but made the driving difficult. After nosing the Ford slowly up the lane he came to a wider road down which he drove until he came to a farm gate. He knew that to avoid any chance of being noticed it was unwise to stop but he had lost his bearing and he needed to consult the map. It was still very early and the chances of other traffic on the road at such an hour could not be great. He stopped the car, checking the road both in front and behind him; the mist, although thinning, still limited visi-bility. In the car he examined the map and saw how to get to the vicarage. But it was too early for that. He would make for the motorway and lose himself in the traffic.

As he put the map aside and started up the Ford, a farm lorry came up suddenly and passed him. He jerked his head away and the lorry disappeared down the road ahead of him.

Soon the sun dispersed the mist and he followed the road towards Warminster. He drove north for over an hour until he

127

reached the M4 motorway and headed west for Bristol. He was surprised that at that hour the motorway was so busy until he remembered that it was the holiday season and that many made an early start from their homes so that they could reach the West Country before the build-up of the traffic. Tucked in among the stream of cars and campers he decided that it was now safe to draw into a service station where he mixed with the families stopping for an early breakfast. He ate eggs and bacon, drank the coffee with the distaste of one used to better, and pretended to read the first editions of several morning newspapers as he sat formulating his new plan.

THIRTEEN

On the morning on which Martin Maitland had breakfasted soon after dawn at the service station on the M4 motorway, Henry Makepiece went to his church ostensibly to conduct daily matins. It was well before seven o'clock. There was no congregation and he had expected none. He said no prayers but busied himself for a time in the sacristy before he left the church to return to pass another agreeable day in his library with his books. He locked the church door behind him and it was only when he had turned and began to walk through the churchyard towards the vicarage that he saw a figure standing by one of the graves. He was surprised to see anyone in the churchyard so early in the day.

The figure was that of a man, dressed in a country jacket and light coloured corduroy trousers, holding in his hand a check cap. He was staring at the stone at the head of a grave on which had been placed a bunch of fresh flowers. What made the clergyman halt so abruptly was that the grave was that of his wife. Resentful that a stranger should be standing over the grave of his beloved Anne, he gathered his black cloak about him and marched over the grass to where the man was standing.

When he came within a few feet, he said, 'Can I help you?'

The man did not speak nor did he turn but stood with his head bowed as he had from the moment when Henry Makepiece had first seen him.

'Can I help you?' he repeated.

'I have placed some flowers on the grave,' said the man and he turned and stared at Henry Makepiece with eyes of a strange pale blue brilliance. 'They are not very much. I got them from where I stopped on the motorway. I did not know that she was

129

dead until yesterday. I came straightaway. It is the grave of my aunt.'

Then, to Makepiece's consternation, the man leant forward and gathered the clergyman into his arms, bowing his head until it lay upon the shoulder of the black cloak. Then the man pulled himself back but kept both arms still outstretched, his hands still gripping tightly the upper arms as he stared into Makepiece's eyes.

'The grave of your aunt! What do you mean?'

Makepiece tried to break clear but the hands gripped him securely and he could not.

'What do you mean, your aunt? I don't understand. That is the grave of my wife, Anne.'

'I know. She was also my aunt. I am Martin Maitland. I had not seen her for fifteen years.'

The hands still held Makepiece's arms and the pale blue eyes now appeared to be filled with tears.

'Martin Maitland!' said Makepiece. 'The boy who ran away! You?'

'Yes. The boy who ran away.' The hands dropped and the two stood facing each other. 'I would like to talk. Can we go to your house?'

Maitland indicated with his head the vicarage which lay beyond the lich gate at the end of the churchyard, and before the other could reply he took the clergyman by the arm and authoritatively turned him and started walking him across the graveyard to the path.

'I am sorry if I startled you. I should have telephoned, but all I could think of was to get to the place where she lies. I have come a long way and I am very tired.'

The hand gripped Makepiece's arm and the clergyman could do nothing but allow himself to be propelled towards the gate.

'Martin Maitland,' he repeated and looked up at the tall figure walking beside him, driving him towards the gate. 'She told me about you but she did not know where you were. She had not seen you for years. Why have you come back?'

'To see her grave and to pay my respects to her and to you.' They were now through the lich gate and approaching the vicarage. 'May I come in?'

Henry Makepiece was uncomfortably conscious of the man's gaze and prayed that he would be spared more embarrassing embraces. They stood before the front door of the vicarage.

'In?' he said haltingly. 'You want to come in?'

'Of course. As I said, I have come a very long way and I am very tired.'

Maitland's eyes never left those of Makepiece who fumbled for his key in his pocket under his cloak.

'Oh, yes, of course,' he said. 'Of course you must come in.'

When the door was open Maitland followed the clergyman quickly inside. He was glad to be out of the open and within the privacy of the house. He did not think that anyone had seen him. No one had been about when he had parked the car among some others in the courtyard of the pub, which appeared to be used as the village car-park, for the inn was not open but there were several cars in the yard. From there he had walked to the churchyard reckoning that the clergyman might go to the church early in the morning. If he had not, Maitland had decided to go to him in the vicarage. But from behind the tall yew hedge of the churchyard he had seen Makepiece come from his house and walk to the church. When the clergyman had disappeared, Maitland had searched for the grave. He knew that the gravestone would be new and it had not been difficult to find. He placed his flowers and while he waited for Makepiece to reappear, he had looked over the hedge and between the tall chestnut trees at the gables and roof of the mysterious house where Marie-Claire was staying and which he had viewed in the darkness only a few hours ago.

'You will have some tea?'

Maitland followed Henry Makepiece into the kitchen.

As he busied himself with the kettle and spooned out the tea into a pot, Makepiece said, 'She used to speak of you and she wrote to thank you when you sent her money.'

'I know. There was no need to thank me. I was glad to send it. I owed her much. She was very kind to me when I was a boy. I wanted her to have it.'

'Your money was very useful when she became ill. Why did you never reply to her letters? Did you not get them?'

'I did but I was very far away. I was glad when I heard that she had married.'

When he said this Maitland saw that Makepiece stopped what he was doing and stood with both hands on the table, his back to his guest, his head lowered. Maitland, measuring and assessing, noted the back of the neck above the collar and the slight figure in the black cassock.

'We had so short a time together. She was a very kind and gentle woman and we were very happy. I cannot get over her leaving me.'

The words were spoken almost in a whisper. Then the clergyman straightened and went back to the tea-making, collecting cups and saucers.

'Would you like something to eat?'

Maitland shook his head.

'Then come into the library.' Carrying the tray Makepiece led Maitland out of the kitchen and across the hall.

'Push those books aside,' he said. They sat at the table and Makepiece poured the tea. He found it difficult to look at his visitor, trying to avoid the stare from those strange eyes.

'Why did you run away from her?'

'I did not run away from her. It was from the life into which I would have been forced had I stayed. I wanted a different kind of life.'

'You became a soldier she told me.'

'A Royal Marine. Yes, for a short time. Then I went into business in the East.'

'You refused to see her. Why was that?'

'I am not really sure why, but I loved her and I thought that I had shamed her, shamed her standards.'

'By running away?'

'Yes. And by the life I then led.'

But it was not only then that he had shamed the gentle, kindly Anne. It was afterwards. It was now.

'She would have liked to have heard from you but you never answered her letters.'

'I could not bring myself to write. I knew she thought that I had been ungrateful and that I had failed to repay her for all the kindnesses she had done me. That was why when I had succeeded in business I sent her money.'

'She told me that you had made over to her part of your inheritance.'

That was good money, clean money.

'I did. The executors forwarded to me her letters and gave me news of her. That is how I knew that you and she had married. She wrote of your happiness together. She deserved that.'

Makepiece made no reply. He was thinking of Anne at her embroidery sitting there in her chair in the corner of the library while he wrote his sermons.

Maitland went on, 'I had come from Paris to London to do some business and as I was in England I thought that I would try to see a friend of mine who is visiting in Wiltshire. She left a message for me at my club, telling me the name of the house but she did not say the name of her hosts. When I got her note I recognised the village – your village, Chapel Iford.'

'You knew that we had come here?'

'Yes, I knew.'

Maitland got to his feet and walked around the room, looking at the shelves of books. 'You have a remarkable collection. In one of her letters Aunt Anne said that scholars from many lands came to visit and study them and that gave you much satisfaction.'

'The books are not mine. They go with the living and the vicarage. The incumbent is their custodian. It is a condition that he should allow visitors to consult them. By advance arrangement, of course. They are a great consolation – the books that is, not the visitors.' He smiled weakly.

Maitland was now at the window, looking across the garden towards the house beyond.

'When I saw the address which my friend had left for me was in the same village as your vicarage, I decided that at last, after all those years, I would come and see her.'

'She would have liked that.'

'I spoke with the solicitors to get your telephone number. It was then that I learnt that I was too late and that she had died.' He was still staring at the house over the garden, his back to Makepiece. 'So I came to her grave.'

133

Then he said casually, 'What is the name of the house which I can see across the garden?'

'Finches.'

'As I thought. That is where my friend is staying. Who owns the house?'

'A family called Burne. The house has been in their family for generations. They are very grand indeed.'

Maitland did not miss the inflection in the tone of Makepiece's voice. 'You sound as though they were not friends of yours.'

'Oh, they are friendly enough to me, and since Anne's death they have tried to be thoughtful. But I find them a trifle condescending, condescending to an impoverished widower who is the local parson. But then', he added by way of explanation, 'the wife is a Roman.'

'Why should they condescend to you? You are a scholar. What are they?'

Makepiece passed a hand over his face. He should not have spoken as he had.

'It is perhaps my imagination. They are rich or appear to be. The husband is a government official, a civil servant. So I don't know where the money comes from.'

So that was the reason for the armed patrol. But what kind of civil servant, Maitland wondered.

'There is always much coming and going, with government cars and grand people visiting. And when they are short of an extra man, they will ask me over. To make up the numbers, I imagine. They only come to church on special occasions. I suppose that she thinks that to come to my church is a sin.'

'Is he a very senior official?'

'He must be. The other Sunday they sent a helicopter for him. It made a vile clatter and disturbed us all. It took him off to some conference. A helicopter on Sunday morning and in a country village!'

'I suppose at weekends they have parties. Are many staying there now?'

'I do not believe so. There was a Frenchman there that weekend. I believe he left on the Monday with Sir Godfrey.'

'That would be Monsieur de Tourneville,' Maitland said. He had rejoined the clergyman at his table.

'So it was. That was his name, Tourneville. How ever did you know?'

'Because my friend is Madame de Tourneville. She is at Finches and it is she whom I have come to see.'

'He came to visit my library. I did not find him agreeable. I went to great trouble to get out some volumes which I thought might interest him but he was, like the others, supercilious. He was probably hoping to be shown something salacious. You know what the French are like.'

'And his wife? Have you seen her?'

'Only in the village, walking with Lady Burne. She looks out of place. Over-dressed for the English countryside.'

The tea was finished. Makepiece rose and picked up the tray. How long, he thought, was the fellow going to stay? Did he expect to be given a bed? Makepiece thought of the pleasurable tasks he had set himself during that day in the library and now this visitor would upset his programme. But the man was a blood relative of Anne, the only one in the world and he must be hospitable and polite.

As though he had read the other's thoughts Maitland said, 'I shall not trouble you for long. I have a journey to make. Here, let me help you,' and he took the tray from Makepiece's hands. 'I must not put you to any inconvenience. Have you anyone who helps you in the house?'

They went together into the kitchen and Makepiece emptied the teapot.

'Yes,' he said. 'But she only comes once a week. She will not be here today. She will be here tomorrow, Thursday.'

That is fortunate, thought Maitland. Then he put his arm around Makepiece's shoulder in another of those extravagant gestures that so embarrassed the clergyman.

'I have two favours to ask you. The first is simple. May I rest here for a few hours?'

'Of course,' Makepiece replied, breaking free. 'That goes without saying.'

'My second request is a little more delicate.'

Once again Maitland took the other by the arm, the grip as forceful as it had been when they had been in the churchyard.

135

Makepiece was propelled firmly back into the library and sat at his desk.

'I have to see Madame de Tourneville and I do not want anyone to know that I am here. It is a matter of great importance and if you can help then I shall be able to leave you and not disturb you further. If I can see her this evening I can leave tonight for overseas.'

When Maitland said that he would be leaving that night, Makepiece could not restrain a fleeting look of relief. Maitland noticed and smiled.

'But it will call for a little innocent deception on your part.' He held up his hand to stop Makepiece interrupting. 'It is not much of a deception. It is only over a name.'

'A name?'

'As I said, it is a matter of some delicacy, concerning Madame de Tourneville and myself. I have to go away for a lengthy visit and I must see her before I leave. I have to tell her something which may be painful for her. It is also important, for the sake of the lady's good name, that it should not be known by her friends that I am meeting her, especially not by the owners of Finches. If you can arrange for me to see her, I shall not trouble you after tonight.'

'I do not understand. Her husband was here the other week-end,' Makepiece protested.

'I assure you that it is not what you think. There has been nothing between the lady and myself which you as a priest might consider wrong. We are friends, good friends, and it is true that we have developed an interest in each other. But it is, I promise, quite innocent. However, I realise that this must stop. Now I have to go away to the East and for a long time, which will be for the best. But I must see her and explain to her that we cannot meet again. It is the honourable thing to do.' He added quietly, 'I give you my word of honour that if you can arrange for her to come to talk with me here this evening I shall never see her again.'

His eyes were once again fixed upon Makepiece who shifted uncomfortably in his chair.

'It would be most irregular, most irregular. I really do not wish to play any part in this matter between you and this married lady.'

'Not even to help me do what is honourable?'

'Of course I would like to help you do that, but how can I possibly arrange for you this – this assignation with this French lady?'

'By telephoning to her and passing a message, asking her to come and talk with me. There would be nothing wrong, I promise you, and you would be here in the house while I talked with her. Then I would go.'

'But what is the deception that you want me to practise?'

'The deception, the harmless deception, is the name which she and I agreed that I should use if ever I had to get in touch with her. The name we agreed upon is Jacques Simonet. All that I would ask you to do is to telephone, speak only with her and ask if she could come here this evening as Jacques Simonet from Paris will be here and wishes to see her.'

'Jacques Simonet? But when I give her that name she will ask how I should know a Jacques Simonet and why I am giving her such a message.'

'I have thought of that. You must say that you understand that Monsieur Simonet is a scholar from Paris and he has asked if he might pass an hour in your library and that he requested you to pass on this message because he had learnt that his friend Madame de Tourneville was staying in the neighbourhood.'

'A scholar from Paris! But you say that the name is a false one.'

'I assure you that she will understand once you give her the name. She will know that it is a story which I have given to you so that I can arrange a meeting with her. She will understand and she will not question you. As I need to rest before I travel on, tell her that Monsieur Simonet will only be arriving at the library at six o'clock this evening.'

'But why do you not telephone yourself? Why should I have to telephone? It is all so very mysterious and complicated.'

'It is not mysterious, I promise, but I must have regard for the lady's reputation. I cannot telephone myself because I would have to give the name Simonet and it would involve

137

her in much explanation with the Burnes and she would not like that. Whereas you could ask to speak to her and it would be quite natural to invite her to come and see some book of interest as you did her husband. It would avoid any suspicion. As I said, her good name is at stake. I must see her but, as you will appreciate, I must not jeopardise her reputation. Surely you as a gentleman and a Christian priest understand that?'

He rose and began to prowl around the library. He picked out a volume from a shelf, watched nervously by Makepiece who did not like the books to be handled by anyone other than himself. Maitland turned to face Makepiece who was still sitting at the table.

'I beg you to do this for me, perhaps just a little recompense for the help I tried to give my aunt. And once I have met her,' he added, 'I shall be away. I only wish to talk in this room with you not far away and only for a short time. For her sake, the Burnes must not know that I am here and that I want to see her.'

Makepiece played with a pen and some pamphlets lying on his table. Those Burnes, he thought. They and their grand friends.

Maitland came across the room and placing both hands on the table leant over Makepiece. It was yet another act of intimacy and Makepiece again felt the disquiet that the man aroused in him.

'Do this for me, and for Anne. I did what I could for you both when she was alive and if you help me now I shall continue to do what I can for you.'

There was just the hint of a bargain, and it was followed by silence while Maitland still leant across the table his face close to that of Makepiece.

If I do what I am asked, thought Makepiece, the man could be gone by nightfall. Moreover the financial help, which had been so useful during Anne's illness, might overcome the difficulty of remaining in this large house with the library to which he was so devoted.

'You promise me on your word of honour, on Anne's grave, that your relationship is wholly innocent and that all you wish to do is talk with her for a short while here in this library?'

'On my honour and on Anne's grave.'

There was a pause while Makepiece played with the papers on his desk.

'Very well,' he said at last, 'I shall do as you wish.'

The strong hand once again gripped his across the table and then pulled him to his feet and once again he was led, this time to the telephone.

Maitland stood beside and above him while Makepiece was connected to Finches. He spoke with Marie-Claire and said what Maitland had told him to say.

When he had replaced the receiver, Makepiece said, 'She sounded very surprised when I gave the name. But she said that she would be here.'

Maitland put his arm on Makepiece's shoulder. 'Thank you, for now I can do what in honour I ought to do although it will be painful both for her and for me.' Then he said briskly, 'But I am keeping you from your work. Have you services or appointments during the rest of the day?'

'Fortunately, no,' replied Makepiece. 'I am devoting the whole of the day to cataloguing. I shall be working here on my books all day. I shall not be going out.'

'Then may I retire and leave you to your labours? You were kind enough to say that I might rest and I am very tired. I have to get back to London tonight before I leave for the East. Thanks to your help I shall have accomplished all that I set out to do and I have paid my respects at the grave of Aunt Anne. I am greatly in your debt.'

Makepiece led him upstairs and into the bedroom opposite to his and Anne's, a tall room with print curtains and a four-poster bed.

'Will this suit you for your rest? There is a bathroom through that door. Can I get you anything else?'

'Nothing. You have been very kind. I am very glad to have met you and I promise that in memory of Anne I shall continue to be of what help I can. I now understand why my aunt wrote to me so happily describing her devotion to you.'

When Maitland said this Makepiece turned abruptly away but Maitland called after him, 'It would be kind if when you are having some tea in the afternoon you would come up and make sure that I am awake? I am so weary that I fear that I might oversleep.'

'Of course. I shall bring you some tea to your room at about four o'clock.'

As Henry Makepiece spent the day alone with his books and the catalogue that he was compiling, and since no one called at the vicarage to disturb him before he took the tray of tea up to the room where his guest was resting, those were the last words that Henry Makepiece was ever to speak.

FOURTEEN

After Godfrey had left for London and Bernard for Paris on the Monday morning following the conference at Chequers and Marie-Claire's confession to Angela of her troubles, the two women had spent the following days agreeably and lazily in the golden weather. Godfrey came down for the following weekend and then left for London. Then they were alone in the house save for the housekeeper and her husband, the gardener, who lived in a flat above the stables where the police who patrolled the ground had established their guardroom. A cleaner came in from the village for a few hours each morning. During the week the housekeeper prepared the evening meal in the afternoon and then retired to her flat and to her television. At the weekend there was more to do and more help was recruited.

So Angela and Marie-Claire were left undisturbed, eating their lunch on the terrace and after their evening meal sitting under one of the great chestnut trees in the moonlight. During the day they worked together on the herbaceous borders, which stretched from the lawn down to the summerhouse, and sometimes Marie-Claire took herself off alone for long walks in the woods, the black retriever puppy bouncing at her heels.

Angela enjoyed having Marie-Claire with her, never ceasing to be struck by how beautiful Marie-Claire had remained, her skin still so clear and her figure still so slim. Quite unlike her own, she thought ruefully but without the slightest resentment or jealousy. Over the years Angela had grown ample enough despite, as she complained, her regular hard labour bending and twisting and turning over her garden, which, with the house, was her passion. She rarely painted now as she had at one time. That part of her life had ceased with the end of that love affair so many years ago. She had learnt by the pain that those few months had caused Godfrey, her lover and herself and she had hated herself for being its cause. When it was over, the years of real happiness and contentment had begun. She knew how fortunate she was in having such a husband and friend in Godfrey and so beautiful a home to tend and love.

She had grown comfortable with herself and her life in the country, playing the part expected of her in the village charities and with her own Church's charity for the poor, the Society of St Vincent de Paul in Westbury where she drove each Sunday to Mass. She attended regularly the meetings of the Women's Institute and this year was President of the area Red Cross. She did all that was expected of the chatelaine of the manor house in the village, supporting generously the Anglican parish church that lay just over the wall. She knew, however, that some in the parish still regarded her with suspicion as a Roman Catholic, more she suspected since Henry Makepiece's arrival as vicar. His predecessor had been more friendly to her Church and much easier than Makepiece, although he had been less of a scholar with less interest in the unique library in the vicarage. All in all she was devoted to the life of the village and resented leaving it even for London.

She had not been as happy in their early years when she had to accompany Godfrey to Washington DC where for two years he had been attached to the CIA at Langley, nor when he had headed the Central American station. During those years she would return home whenever she could in order to make sure that her house was well. She had always refused to lease it when they were serving abroad; she wanted no strangers living among her things. She preferred to know little of Godfrey's work and to share only what he cared to tell her. So she had been happy at Godfrey's appointment as C, not only for him but also because it meant that any risk of a posting overseas had finally passed. The presence of the constant police guard had at first disturbed her but she had grown used to it and she had made friends of them, as she did so easily with so many.

Her favourites among all his staff were Godfrey's driver, Webster and his taciturn Scots wife. She had the family down

142

to stay for two weeks each year and their two children, watched benevolently by Angela, raced around the garden as though it were their own.

So the years were passing happily and tranquilly, marred only by her inability ever to have children. One day she knew that Finches, which she had done so much to restore and enrich, would pass to Godfrey's nephew, a nondescript director in a minor merchant bank with a plain and nondescript wife and three plain and nondescript children. It was this lack of any family of her own – or as there might by now have been, any grandchildren – that aroused in her the only twinge of regret about her life. She certainly had none because she lacked the remarkable looks of her guest and contemporary, Marie-Claire, of whom during the past days she had grown increasingly fond.

But Angela remained concerned at the other's unhappiness although the tension that Angela had hoped might be eased by a few tranquil days had lessened. As the days passed Marie-Claire had seemed calmer than she had been when they had all been together at the Cambridge feast. Angela had decided not to speak again of Marie-Claire's affair unless and until Marie-Claire spoke herself. She merely provided the opportunity and waited. But after their talk in the summerhouse when Marie-Claire had confessed to the passion that was dominating her life, Marie-Claire had remained silent, although she had remarked several times how grateful she was to Angela for these days of peace and laziness. The change and the rest from her official life in Paris and the responsibilities of Gauville, she declared, were doing her so much good. She would like to stay, she said smiling, for ever, but as that was impossible could she stay perhaps until the following Monday and pass another weekend at Finches?

So it was arranged, and Marie-Claire spoke on the telephone with Bernard who pretended to have lost their fortune at bridge at the Jockey and who told her to stay as long as she liked although he missed her dreadfully. Marie-Claire told him that she had some message from Margaret Murray about one of the dogs at Gauville and Bernard said that he would enquire. He looked forward, he said, to seeing her relaxed and rested when she returned to their apartment in Paris on the Boulevard Suchet on the evening of the following Monday.

On the Wednesday in that week, Angela was obliged to go to Bath for a council meeting and full day's conference of the Red Cross, which was to be followed by a reception and formal dinner at which the national President was to speak. It would be a long day and a late night. She therefore arranged to have herself driven to Bath early in the morning; the car and driver would bring her back in the evening. She warned the police at the house not to expect her to return before midnight.

'I am sorry about this, Marie-Claire,' she had said earlier in the week. 'But I really cannot avoid it. Would you like to come?'

'If you will forgive me, no. I have so many official occasions to attend at home. If you do not mind I would prefer to stay in the garden and take the puppy for a walk. I shall be very happy here, so please don't worry about me.'

'I thought you would say that,' said Angela gloomily, 'and I do not blame you. I even have to make a speech at the dinner introducing the national President. Think of the horror of that!'

'You will do it delightfully and the President will be enchanted by you.'

'The President is a female and has never enchanted nor been enchanted by anything or anyone. Oh dear, it will be a long day. I shall have to leave here early in the morning and I shall be back late. Lock up when you go to bed but don't bolt the front door so that I can get in. And don't worry at being alone. The police are here all the time, of course. I shall see you in the morning.'

But when Marie-Claire waved goodbye to Angela on that Thursday morning she felt a curious sense of foreboding, as though the day held in store something unhappy, even that Angela's car might be involved in an accident. She dismissed these thoughts as morbid and silly and later in the morning was in the garden at the herbaceous borders, whose demands for attention seemed insatiable, when she had heard the telephone. She hoped that it might be Bernard from Paris with news of her dog at Gauville but it was the voice of Henry Makepiece whom she remembered Bernard had not much

144

liked. Then she heard him say that M Simonet was expected that evening at the vicarage and she knew that, as he had done so often, he was summoning her.

When Makepiece spoke the name there flooded over her the emotions that were always aroused whenever she received messages from him, revulsion at his presumption and delight at his need for her. In Paris the summonses were usually short and direct; this was obviously dressed up in the invitation to inspect the clergyman's books. Jacques Simonet, the scholar from Paris! That was *drôle*, but that he should have traced her to where she was staying with her friends disturbed her. Never before had he intruded into her separate life, as she never had into his. That he had gone to the lengths of approaching her here in England could only mean that his need to see her was urgent. She remembered what he had said to her about his enemies when last they had been together.

She told Makepiece that she would come to the vicarage to meet her friend.

When she had replaced the receiver she remained standing by the telephone looking out through the French windows to the peaceful garden. What could he be doing here? Why was he coming here to see her?

Anxious and troubled she collected the puppy and set off to walk in the woods and to think.

Since that night when she had left him to drive home to Gauville in the rain, she had turned over and over in her mind what he had said to her that afternoon, the story of the dead girl and of the people in London who were having him watched. His enemies, he had said, and she had seen that he had meant it. There was something far more sinister in his life than his explanation that the watchers were commercial rivals.

The puppy was worrying at her to take the stick from its mouth and she bent and took it from him, throwing it up the path in the wood, watching the dog scamper after it. Soon the puppy was back beneath her feet and she had to throw the stick again until a young pheasant suddenly rose from the undergrowth with a screech and a flutter and the puppy vainly bounded after it. She called the dog to come to heel but it ignored her and she walked on.

145

From the start of their affair and the sexual domination that he had established over her, she had always suspected that there was something strange in his background. She had told herself that for a woman of her age and experience and the wife of a distinguished official to get involved in such an affair with a man of whom she knew so little was madness. And if there was anything really sinister in his background it would be worse than madness. It would be a double betrayal of Bernard.

But she also knew that this mystery had been a part of his attraction for her. What was it that the Irishman Wilde had said – 'feasting with tigers'?

But when Jacques had told her about what had happened in London she had sensed that the danger had suddenly become closer and more serious, and that as soon as he had begun to speak about it to her he had regretted that he had spoken; he had told her something he should have kept to himself. For him to seek her out here, in the house of her friends, could only mean that he was desperate for help.

The cause of the tension from which she was suffering, and which had so concerned her husband and her friends, had been this fear for him, combined with the humiliating physical obsession. Now, in a few hours, he would be here and he had sent for her.

She stopped in her walk and sat on the trunk of a tree, which had fallen in the great gale, and rested her head in her hands, the tears falling through her fingers. The puppy stood at her feet looking up at her, his head cocked on one side. Then he jumped up, his forepaws in her lap and she lowered a hand and fondled his head. After a time she rose and turned back along the path that led through the wood to the garden.

She would return to the house. She would telephone Make-piece that she could not come. Then she would wait for Angela's return and beg her for help.

She entered the drawing-room through the French windows and picked up the telephone. But then she thought: what if he is in danger? What if he does need help? He must be desperate to do what he is doing. Would it not be better to see him? If she did, this time she would force him to tell her the truth about himself, make him tell her what he did and from whom he was running. Then she would do what she could to help him and send him away. Was that not less cowardly than just refusing to see him?

Slowly she replaced the receiver. She would go.

So she passed the long hours of the afternoon and early evening waiting, doing what she always did when he summoned her, feeling the shame at the longing she had for him, the longing to see him, to touch him, to feel him inside her.

At about five o'clock she went to her room and dressed carefully, spending time over her hair and her face. As she sat at her dressing-table she decided that in the morning whatever happened she would tell Angela everything, for it was certain that at some time Makepiece would speak of her friend's visit. She would tell Angela that she had gone to the vicarage and that Jacques had been there but that it had not been arranged by her. She did not want Angela to think that she had taken the opportunity of everyone being out of the house and Bernard in Paris to meet her lover. In any event at the vicarage it would be impossible to see Jacques alone for any length of time; the most that could happen was that they would be able to persuade the clergyman to allow them to talk for a moment privately. Then he could explain why he had risked so much in coming to her here in England. She would help him as much as she could but of one thing she was determined: the mystery must stop. She would get from him the truth.

At six she was finally ready. She was not hungry but she did not want to offend the housekeeper, Mrs Stack, so she put down the sink the supper that had been left for her without eating a mouthful, washing up the plates in the pantry. She left the house through the front door, locking it behind her and taking with her a key that Angela had given her. When she left, the police had not begun the evening patrol and she went unobserved through the grounds, through the gate in the wall and into the vicarage garden.

She was surprised to see no car in the drive. Jacques could not yet have arrived; she would have to pass the time with Makepiece. But when she knocked, the door swung open and

147

the hand of the man she called Jacques Simonet took hold of hers and pulled her into the dark hall of the house and closed the door behind her.

'I knew that you would come,' he said in French, as he gathered her into his arms and kissed her on the mouth. For a time she stayed acquiescent, kissing him back, his body pressed hard against hers. Then with a strength that surprised her, she broke free.

'You must not do that, not here. Where is the priest?'

'He is out. He said that he will not be back for half an hour. We are alone.'

'Why are you here? What are you doing here? The priest telephoned me this morning, telling me that you were coming and that you wanted to see me. He said that he wanted to show me some books or papers and that you would be here at six o'clock.'

'I told him to say that. It was to give a reason so that he could invite you, in case it were difficult for you to get away from your friends.'

'There was no difficulty. I am alone today. My hostess will not be back until late.'

That, he thought, will give me more time.

'But why are you here? You are running a great risk for both of us. The priest will tell my friends.'

'I know, but this morning I had to visit a place on business near to Chapel Iford, a town called Westbury, and I wanted to see you.'

'But how did you know I was here?'

'That, *chérie*, is my secret.'

He tried to take her again in his arms, but she turned from him and walked from the hall into the library. He followed.

'You look tired,' she said.

'I had to travel last night to be here in time for my business. I have been in London and I leave for overseas tonight. I shall be away for a long time. That was why I had to see you.'

In the library she noticed that the curtains were already drawn and that the lamps had been lit.

'Why are the curtains drawn?'

148

'In case someone called to see the vicar and saw us through the window.'

By the light of the lamps she could see better the tiredness on his face, the lines etched more deeply, the shadows darker under his eyes. She wanted to reach up and touch his face but she did not.

'How did you discover where I was?'

'I just did. Does it matter?'

'Yes, it does. Why have you followed me here, to my friends?'

Who are your friends, he thought, the friends who have armed police to guard them?

'To see you. I told you, I will be away for a long time.'

She turned away so as not to look at him, hoping he would not come too near to her. She had to be strong; she had to find out more.

'I do not believe you. You want something. You are in trouble again. Who is it that you are running from, Jacques? Why won't you tell me and then perhaps I will be able to help?'

Before he could reply she asked, 'Where is the priest? When will he be back?'

'So many questions,' he said. 'That is not like you. Makepiece had to make an unexpected call but he said that he would hurry back as soon as he could. Half an hour to an hour, he said, but that he might be kept longer than he expected. I said that I would explain. There is no one else in the house.'

He took her in his arms.

'We shall make love in a presbytery. It will be exciting.'

She broke away from him. 'Here?' she said. 'Are you mad?'

She looked into the pale blue eyes. Would they tell her what she wanted to discover? But they did not falter and she turned and walked from him.

'I do not believe that you came all this way just to see me before you go away. You have been away often enough before. You must have known how risky it was to come here. No, you have some other reason, I am sure of it.' She turned away from him again.

'Jacques,' she said, her voice breaking slightly. 'Please tell me the truth, for once tell me the truth. I cannot go on seeing you if you do not tell me the truth. Ever since you came back from that night in London something has been troubling you. What is the trouble that you are in?'

'There is none, I promise. That business in London I discovered was all nonsense. I was too dramatic. It was just that woman and I didn't want to tell you about her.'

'But you said there were people watching you. Who were they?'

'I was wrong. I was overexcited. I had been working too hard. It was only the woman. But don't let us talk of that. Let's talk about ourselves. I had to come to England on business in the West Country and I wanted to see you, Marie-Claire. I just had to see you before I went away. It is as simple and as romantic as that.'

He stretched out his hand to take hers but she moved away from him around the other side of the table laden with Makepiece's books.

'How did you know that I was here? Unless you tell me that, I cannot believe anything that you say. I must have the truth, Jacques.'

He was surprised by her persistence. In the past, even more than he, she had always avoided questions.

'The last time we were together in Casimir Perier when you told me about that girl, you were frightened. I saw it in your eyes. Ever since then I have known that something strange had happened to you. I believe someone wants to kill you. Why?'

'That is absurd.' His voice was harsh and his pale blue eyes clouded and darkened. 'I was not frightened. I am frightened by no one and no one wants to kill me. Who on earth would want to kill me? That scene in London was nothing. Just a woman, an angry woman. I could not tell you the full story. I was ashamed at having got myself involved.'

'Ashamed? Jacques Simonet ashamed of getting involved with a woman? I know you well enough to know that no woman could frighten you.' She was smiling at him, amused. He had never seen her like this before. 'I don't believe that the girl in London who died in your arms or in your bed frightened you but somebody did. You were frightened, you were really

150

frightened. What is it, Jacques, that frightened you? You must tell me.'

Very well, he thought, I shall and it will be of little use to you.

He said, 'In Casimir Perier I was exhausted. I had discovered that the woman whom I was with that evening was having me followed. I did not like that.'

'And she had discovered something about you, about what you do? Was that what frightened you?'

He had turned from her and had his back to her, his arms limp by his side. He had not expected that she would be like this. He had planned something gentler. This would make it easier to do what he had come to do.

'You want the truth? You really want the truth?'

He had spoken very quietly but there was a note of menace in his voice. Marie-Claire did not notice it. Suddenly she knew that at last she would learn the truth about him. She had not liked acting as she had, questioning, nagging at him. Whenever they had met it had been always to make love, to have the sex that was so satisfying for her, lying together on the bed or on the floor, enjoying each other. No man had ever made her feel as she had felt with him, the long drawn out feeling which he had never failed to arouse. But she knew that she had to do what she was doing. She would not retain her sanity if she did not learn the truth. As she looked at him she also knew that whatever it was that he was going to tell her she would never cease to desire him and she longed for the scene to be over and for him to take her in his arms and love her.

She replied, equally quietly, 'Yes, I want the truth, however much it may hurt. What is it that you fear, Jacques? Who is it that you fear? And why? For I know that something must have frightened you very badly to make you come all this way to find me.'

He did not reply and she waited. I will make it dramatic, he thought, if that is what she wants.

When at last he broke the silence he spoke as though to himself, as though she were not there in the room behind him.

'Do you really want the truth about me?'

'Yes, Jacques, I do.'

151

'Very well, you shall have the truth. But you will not like it.' He turned very slowly and faced her. 'I kill, for a living.'

'Oh my God!' she exclaimed, her hand raised to her mouth.

'I am paid to kill people. Now you know, Marie-Claire. You have had your wish.'

Very swiftly his arm shot out and grabbed her dress above her breast and he pulled her to him. As he jerked her towards him her eyes widened with fear as they stared into his, seeing for the last time those pale blue eyes that had first drawn her to him in that restaurant on the Boulevard de Capucines. She began to scream. Then both of his hands grasped her round the throat while hers beat vainly against his face and her body twisted and turned as she struggled to release herself from his grip, her legs and arms thrashing helplessly. But she could not prise herself free and the air drained from her, and her deep brown eyes that had so often looked at him in love began to start from their sockets; the pale beautiful face turned red and then monstrously black as the life drained from her.

He held her for what seemed an eternity before he let her go and she fell to the ground. He looked down at her, at the body of the elegant woman who had entered that room half an hour before and that now lay crumpled like a rag doll at his feet.

He took from his pocket his black kid gloves and drew them on and bent over the face at which he had looked down so often as she had lain in ecstasy beneath him and which was now so distorted and ugly. He made sure that she was dead and closed her eyelids. He picked her up and carried her to the top storey of the house and then up the steep stairs to the attic, which he had prepared earlier in the evening. She was very light and he had no difficulty as he pushed her body through the trap door, laying it on the plank floor of the attic. He clambered up after it, lifting the body again, stuffing it and packing it roughly into the open trunk, which he had made ready. He covered it with clothes that had belonged to his aunt and closed the lid, pushing the trunk into a corner of the attic under the eaves. He wiped with his silk handkerchief the clasp and any part that he had touched, and piled on it a broken chair and other furniture and some cardboard boxes. When the trunk was hidden among the junk he descended the stairs closing the trap door behind him and locking the padlock. He put the key in his pocket.

He re-entered the library and pulled some books from the shelves onto the floor. He rifled the drawers of the desk, scattering the contents, then took some miniatures from the walls and put them into his pocket. In the dining-room he pulled open the drawers of the sideboard and from the canteen he pocketed some of the flat silver.

Then he went upstairs. Earlier on that evening he had opened the drawers of the dressing-table in the upstairs bedroom and taken from them the few pieces of jewellery and had scattered clothing onto the floor. Now he pulled the body of Henry Makepiece, the neck broken by a karate blow, out of the bedroom in which Maitland had been resting and to which Makepiece had brought the tea. He placed Makepiece face down on the landing. With a pan and brush he swept the debris of broken cup and saucer from the doorway of the bedroom where it had originally fallen and scattered it around the new position of the body. From the kitchen he carried up a cup of cold tea and milk and poured it onto the floor beside the broken cup.

He knew that the stain of the tea in the bedroom would later be located and the place where Makepiece had died would be identified; all that he was doing would only serve to cause delay and perhaps give him the time he needed should he fail to catch the boat.

Finally he went through the kitchen and into the scullery and climbed through the window, which opened outward on a latch. Beyond lay the back path running close to the high wall that divided the vicarage from Finches. When he was outside he plucked some fibres from his jacket and put them onto the jamb of the window. He then closed it and, standing in the dark on the garden side, he worked at a pane of glass in the window frame with his knife. When he had loosened it, he pressed a heavy stone wrapped in his handkerchief against the pane until it broke silently into large shards. He eased out sufficient of the glass so that a hand could reach inside to raise the clasp.

153

When he was done, he made his way through the shrubbery and crossed the churchyard keeping low behind the grave-stones until he came to the back of the car-park of the inn. He waited behind the wall as a party came out of the pub and got into their car and drove away. Then he slipped over the wall and into his car.

By now it was past nine o'clock. He had plenty of time to cover the one hundred and eighty miles to the boat. Since Marie-Claire had said that she had been alone in the house and that no one was expected until late, he reckoned that he had at least three hours before it was discovered that she was missing. That was the minimum. If she had left her bedroom door open at Finches, then someone might see that she was not in the room and the alarm would be given, perhaps at midnight. But there was a good chance that if her door was shut and no one knocked for her late that evening, her absence might not be known until the morning. At the vicarage the body of Henry Makepiece would not be found before the cleaner came after eight o'clock.

Maitland struck north to Chippenham and joined the M4 motorway at junction 17, where he turned west; from there it was fast driving across the Severn bridge and on the motorway until twenty miles beyond Swansea. At eleven o'clock he had sixty miles to complete. From there on he drove slowly but before he reached Fishguard he pulled off the main road and stopped. The migraine from which recently he had been suffer-ing at more frequent intervals had returned. He swallowed the tablets he had been prescribed in Hong Kong and which now he always carried with him. He rested his throbbing head in his hands over the wheel and sat in the darkness.

It was after 2.30 that he drove into the car-park in the Lower Town. Before he locked and left the car he took a wrench and jack from the boot and, emptying his pockets of the miniatures and silver which he had taken from the vicarage he packed them into the holdall. Then he boarded the boat that sailed for Rosslare in Southern Ireland at 3.15 in the morning. Before dawn, and when the ship had cleared the harbour and was well out to sea, he dropped the holdall overboard.

Four hours later he disembarked, made a telephone call from

the call box at the port and by 8.30, at the exact time when Mrs Yates, the cleaner at the vicarage, discovered the murdered body of Mr Makepiece, he was collected by two young men in a car. To one he handed over the key of the Ford, which he had left in the car-park in Fishguard.

The man took it and said, 'It will be collected tonight at midnight when the boat from here docks on the other side and it will be driven to London.'

'Be careful,' Maitland replied. 'That will be the danger time.'

The man nodded and got out of the car which moved off with Maitland beside the driver on the road to Dublin.

Maitland was dropped in Grafton Street in the centre of the city. He bought a small suitcase, a ready-made suit and a shirt and changed in the store. He took a taxi to the railway station and left the case with the clothes that he had worn the night before in the left-luggage office. He took another taxi to the Shelburne Hotel and from there booked by telephone a club-class ticket on an Aer Lingus flight to Paris. Just after three o'clock, at about the same time the police had discovered the body of Marie-Claire in the trunk in the attic, he boarded the Paris plane.

On arrival he stayed on at Charles de Gaulle and booked on an AVIANCA flight to Bogota, which left Paris at 23.30. From Bogota the Syndicate's helicopter would lift him over the mountains to the estate thirty kilometres from the small town of Las Paza where at the Bona Ventura Hotel there had recently been registered the arrival of the Englishman described as Professor Edmund Hamilton.

FIFTEEN

Angela woke late, tired after her exhausting day at the Red Cross conference. She had not arrived home until just after midnight, and before she had let herself into the house she had chatted with the police patrol outside the front door. Once inside she had gone to the kitchen to make herself a hot drink. She had thought of seeing if Marie-Claire was awake but there had been no light under her door and Angela had taken her drink to her own room and was soon asleep.

She lay in bed remembering with an agreeable glow of satisfaction her speech at the dinner introducing the National President. It had gone down rather well, including her joke about the visiting firewoman from headquarters. The President had not really been amused but she had to pretend that she had. Angela looked forward to telling Marie-Claire about it later in the morning.

It was a quarter past eight when she came down to the kitchen for her coffee. 'Good morning, Mrs Stack,' she said to the housekeeper as she flung open the back door to let in the morning sunshine. 'Is Madame de Tourneville about?'

'I have not seen her yet. She was out early yesterday morning and spent most of the day in the garden. She took Angus for a good walk. If she's up I expect that she's gone to the wood.'

Mrs Stack poured Angela's coffee.

'I am quite exhausted after yesterday. All that listening and talking and trying to remember the names of people. Then I had to make a speech at the dinner.'

'I'm sure that you did it very nicely.'

It was said in tones that made clear that a sensible woman like Mrs Stack had little time for anything so irresponsible as a lot of grown women making or listening to speeches.

Angela felt defensive. 'It's a very worthy cause.'

'I am sure that it is, for those with the time for such things. I expect that it does some good for some.'

Mrs Stack was not a person for good causes and Angela knew that she would have to wait for Marie-Claire's return to have a good gossip about her day. She drank her coffee at the kitchen table and Mrs Stack kept herself busy in the pantry. Then through the open window came the sound of a siren, a noise rarely heard in that quiet village.

'Whatever is that? There must be a fire.'

Angela went over to the window and leant out but she could see no smoke and no fire engine. The siren stopped, and as she turned to speak again to Mrs Stack she saw framed in the open kitchen door one of the policemen from the guardroom in the stables.

'I have terrible news, Lady Burne. They have found Mr Makepiece. He's dead.'

'What?'

Angela looked blankly at the man. 'What did you say?'

'I'm very sorry to have to tell you but Mr Makepiece from the vicarage has been found dead.'

'Mr Makepiece dead!'

'I am afraid that he is.'

'Mr Makepiece! But this is terrible. Was it an accident, a heart-attack –'

The policeman interrupted her. 'It was neither, Lady Burne. I'm afraid that it is more serious than that. It appears that there was a robbery in the vicarage during the night, a break-in. The poor gentleman must have surprised the burglars and they killed him.'

'Killed him! Oh, my God.'

Angela sank into a chair, her hand at her throat. Even Mrs Stack was startled.

'The vicar? Killed by burglars?'

'When did this happen?' asked Angela.

'Sometime last night, Lady Burne. He has just been found.'

'Oh, the poor man. And in his own house?'

'Yes. He was found at the top of the stairs. We heard nothing in the guardroom or during any of our patrols. Mrs Yates went

157

over this morning as usual to clean the house and found him. She came running over to us.'

'Edith Yates!' said Mrs Stack, as though this information might alter everything. 'You know Mrs Yates. Is she quite sure that the vicar's dead?'

'Oh, yes, I am afraid that we are quite sure. We have been to the vicarage. He's lying on the landing where he fell. He must have disturbed the burglars. There's quite a bit been stolen. It looks as if they got in through the scullery window. We have radioed HQ at Trowbridge and a squad car has already arrived.'

'We heard the siren. We thought it must be a fire. Oh, that poor old man! What a terrible way to die!'

'One of my colleagues is over at the vicarage and the other is with Mrs Yates in the stables.'

'The poor man, the poor man,' Angela kept repeating.

'How was he killed?' asked Mrs Stack.

'It was not a firearm or anything like that, so of course there was no sound of a shot. It was a blow to the head or to the neck. The pathologist will be there soon. He will find out. I am sorry to have to give you such a shock but you had to be told. I must get back to the vicarage, my lady, in case they need me.'

'Yes, yes, thank you. I'll come with you,' said Angela. 'Where is Mrs Yates now?'

'She's in the guardroom in the stables. She is very distressed.'

'Mrs Stack, run across and bring her here and give her some tea. If I am not back when Madame de Tourneville comes in from her walk you had better warn her.'

Angela went with the policeman to the vicarage. The squad car was in the drive and a uniformed policeman was standing at the door talking into his radio. The policeman and Angela went into the house. From the hall she looked up the staircase. One of the Finches police patrol leant over the bannister.

'There is nothing that you can do, Lady Burne. I would not come up; the poor gentleman is quite dead.'   .

His relatives must be told, she thought; and then she remembered that Henry Makepiece had always said that he had none. But she thought that she should search his desk to find something, anything which might reveal the name of some lawyer or bank manager who ought to be informed. And the

Church, someone in the Church must be told. From the open door in the hall she could see papers and books scattered on the floor of the library, the rifled drawers of the desk and the blank spaces on the wall by the fireplace where the miniatures had hung.

'Look,' she said to the policeman, pointing to the wall. 'They have taken the pictures.'

'Like they took the silver from the other room,' he replied.

Angela was about to go into the library but the policeman took her arm and said, 'Better not disturb anything, Lady Burne. You had best not go in. The scene-of-crime officer will be here soon. There is nothing that you can do. I think you should leave, Lady Burne.'

Angela did as he had asked. 'I shall be in the house if you need me,' she said and leaving the policeman by the front door of the vicarage she went back to the kitchen in Finches.

Mrs Yates was sitting at the table, tears running down her face. 'It was terrible, Lady Burne, terrible. I came to the vicarage as I always do every Thursday and went into the kitchen through the back door and then I saw the broken window in the scullery. So I ran into the hall and I could see the mess in the dining-room. All the pieces from the sideboard strewn around the floor. I called out to the vicar that there had been a robbery. But he didn't reply. Sometimes he gets up late if he has been working at night in the library so I flew up the stairs to wake him. Then I saw him on the landing lying there, all crumpled. Oh, it was horrible.'

She began to weep again and rocked to and fro. Angela knelt by her chair and put her arms around her. 'It's all right, Mrs Yates. It's all right. You have had a bad shock. You must drink some tea.'

'Poor Mr Makepiece, poor lonely old man. He had such a sad life after his wife had gone.' Mrs Yates lifted her head. 'And to think it must have happened with all your police in the stables only a few yards away!'

Angela turned to the housekeeper. 'Is Madame de Tourneville back yet?'

'I haven't seen her. I'll go and warn Joe to tell her. He's

159

down at the end of the garden and he will see her when she comes back.'

I had better telephone Godfrey, Angela thought. He will have to be told. A murder in the vicarage a few yards from Finches! She tried to comfort the weeping woman.

'You have had a terrible shock, Mrs Yates. You must try and drink some tea.'

Mrs Stack returned with Joe, her husband.

'Mary has told me what has happened,' he said. 'I heard the siren. I thought it must be the ambulance or a fire in the village. But murder, and of the old vicar! I don't know what the world is coming to.' He shook his head. Then he said, 'I haven't seen the French lady. She must have gone out early.'

'Look after Mrs Yates,' Angela said to Mrs Stack. 'The police will have to ask questions. They will be coming from Trowbridge. There is only one squad car here at present.'

She went into the drawing-room and dialled Godfrey's office but he was at a conference at the Foreign Office. She told the Duty Officer to get him to telephone her as soon as he could.

'It's urgent,' she said. 'There has been a tragedy next door, in the vicarage. Ask him to call me as soon as he can.'

Her head was splitting and she went upstairs for an aspirin. When she had taken two, she knocked on Marie-Claire's door. There was no reply so she looked inside. The bed was made up, neat and tidy; Marie-Claire must have made it before she went out. Angela closed the door and went downstairs to join the others in the kitchen.

After another half-hour they heard the arrival of more police cars and a policewoman came to fetch Mrs Yates and led her to the vicarage. A young plain-clothes officer came and began to ask them what they knew, making notes in his book.

Angela explained that she had arrived back from the Red Cross conference in Bath at about midnight and gone straight to bed. She had heard nothing during the night, nor had the Stacks in the flat over the stables.

'Was there anyone else in the house or the stables, apart from this lady and her husband and the policemen?'

'Yes,' said Angela. 'I have a friend staying with me. She was in bed asleep when I got back last night so I didn't disturb her.'

160

'Can I see her?'

'She is not here at present. She must have gone out early for a walk in the woods. She often does that.'

'I'll go and look for her,' said Joe. 'I know the way she usually takes.'

The young detective wrote down carefully Angela's account of where she had been the day before and of Mrs Stack's day and evening after she had returned to the flat above the guard-room. No one had seen the vicar since earlier in the week.

Joe returned. He said that he had searched the woods but that there was no sign of Marie-Claire. Moreover the puppy was still in the kennels, which was strange since the French lady always took him when she went for her walks.

A new and sudden fear gripped Angela. The detective looked at her. She said, 'I am sure that she will be back soon. She often goes for long walks.'

'Can I see her room?' said the young detective.

Angela led him up the stairs. Why doesn't Godfrey telephone, she kept thinking. He must be told.

They entered the bedroom together. 'It does not look as if this bed has been slept in,' the young detective said. 'Unless she made it this morning when she got up. Does she usually do that?'

'I don't know. I can ask Mrs Yates who cleans each morning, except today, Thursday, when she goes to the vicarage. That may be why Madame de Tourneville made up her bed.'

On the dressing-table were the pots of the make-up which Marie-Claire had used before she had gone to her rendezvous. The detective opened the cupboards and looked at the clothes on their hangers.

'Do you have to do that? She is probably in the village shopping.'

'I must do what I think best,' the young officer said. 'Can you tell if any of her clothes are missing?'

Angela went to the cupboard and fumbled through the dresses. What did Marie-Claire wear when she was out walking? Usually those trousers and the walking shoes. Please God, they will not be here. But they were.

'Oh, my God,' she said. 'Oh, my God.'

161

'What is it?'

'It is just that I have found what she usually wore when she went for a walk. Of course,' she said desperately, 'I may be wrong. She could be wearing something else. I just cannot be certain.'

'Who is this lady?'

'A friend from France who is staying with me. I am sure that she must have gone out. She will be back soon.'

The telephone rang.

'It will be my husband,' she said and ran to the telephone in her bedroom. The detective walked to the door and stood so that he could hear what she said.

'Godfrey, something terrible has happened. Henry Make-piece has been found murdered in the vicarage. Yes, murdered during the night. They say there was a robbery and he must have disturbed them. None of us heard anything over here. That poor old man, such a terrible way to die.'

She paused. Her husband must be speaking, thought the detective.

Then she went on: 'And, Godfrey, there is another thing. We can't find Marie-Claire. Well, she is not in her room and her bed is made up. We thought she must have gone for a walk early. But Joe has been down to the wood where she usually goes and he can't find her. No, we haven't done a real search. Only Joe has been into the wood but he says there is no sign of her . . . I know, I know. I am probably panicking because of what has happened to poor Mr Makepiece and she might easily have gone into the village. But there is another thing, Godfrey. I have found in her closet the clothes she usually wears when we go on our walks. Oh, I hope I am being silly.'

In answer to a question from Godfrey she turned round and saw the young detective standing by the door.

'Yes, there is a plain-clothes man here with me in the room, from Trowbridge . . . Very well.' She held out the receiver. 'My husband wants to speak to you.'

'Oh, he wants to speak to me, does he?' The man took the telephone and said authoritatively, 'This is Detective Constable Simmonds of the Wiltshire police. What do you want?' Then

162

the expression on his face changed. 'Yes, sir. Of course, sir. I understand. He is over at the vicarage. I shall get him to telephone you immediately.' He wrote quickly in his notebook. 'Yes, sir, I have the number. I am sorry, sir. I'm new here and they didn't explain. Thank you, sir, I'll do what you ask immediately.'

He handed the receiver back to Angela. 'He would like to speak again with you, madam. I'll go and get the Chief.'

He ran from the room.

By lunchtime it had been established that Henry Makepiece had probably been dead for several hours longer than had first been suspected. The time of his death was provisionally fixed at between four in the previous afternoon and midnight. Then the place where he had fallen after the blow that had killed him was identified as more likely to have been in the guest bedroom and not on the landing to which they judged he had been dragged after he had been struck. Why that should have been done they were at this time mystified.

Attention was particularly directed to the presumed point of entry by the intruders and the glass and some fibres were despatched to the forensic laboratories in Bristol.

While this was going on at the vicarage during the morning, Godfrey, after speaking on the telephone to the senior of the officers who had come from Trowbridge, had arrived at Finches from London at 12.30. He was accompanied by the Head of Special Branch and preceded by the Chief Constable and the Detective Chief Superintendent of the Wiltshire Constabulary.

After Godfrey's telephone conversation with Angela and then the Inspector, enquiries were made in the village, but there had been no sighting of Marie-Claire. Cars were despatched along the neighbouring lanes. When they returned a large party was organised to beat through the woods and the surrounding countryside. They were at work during all of the late morning and afternoon but without success. No one had seen her.

It was three o'clock when the police in the vicarage, having laboriously completed their inch-by-inch examination of the downstairs and upper floors, finally turned their attention to the attic. They climbed the stair and, after sending for tools, broke the padlock. Standing with difficulty, their heads bowed beneath the beams of the low ceiling, they began to poke around the accumulation of boxes and junk and broken pieces of furniture. They found the trunk and pulled it into the centre of the attic. They broke the clasp and found within it the body of Marie-Claire, the beautiful face twisted and distorted and discoloured.

The parties still searching the woods and ditches in the countryside were recalled.

Later that evening, a distraught Bernard de Tourneville, who had been summoned from Lyons where he had been making an official visit, rushed through the Charles de Gaulle terminal to catch the plane for London. On the escalator he ran up the moving steps to get to the boarding gate for the plane to London. In his haste he brushed past a man, knocking from his hand the newspaper he had been reading. With a muttered apology Bernard ran on.

'*Merde*,' said the man.

The man himself was in no hurry; he had plenty of time to catch his evening flight to Bogota.

SIXTEEN

Later that evening, Godfrey and an attaché from the French Embassy were at Heathrow to meet Bernard de Tourneville as he was led from the plane before the other passengers had begun to disembark. Godfrey embraced him in the French fashion, their cheeks touching twice. Bernard nodded to the diplomat.

'I will travel with Sir Godfrey,' he said. 'You may return to London. I will send for you if I need anyone.'

Neither Godfrey nor Bernard spoke as they made their way to the car. It was not the usual Rover but a large Daimler, which Webster had collected from the Government car pool; it had a glass partition between the passengers in the rear and Webster and the Special Branch officer in the front. A police car led them as they swung out of the airport and onto the M4 motorway.

Godfrey pressed the button and the glass partition rose. He put his hand over Bernard's.

'I am sorry,' he said. 'I am dreadfully sorry. She was my guest and I did not protect her.'

'Tell me exactly what happened.'

'So far as they can tell she died last night, at about eight or nine o'clock.'

'How did she die?' Godfrey was silent and Bernard said, 'I have to know.'

'She was strangled.'

Bernard put both his hands to his face. He lowered them as Godfrey said quietly, 'She had not been attacked in any other way. Whoever killed her did so deliberately, intending only to kill. He must have come for that purpose.'

Godfrey turned his head towards Bernard who was staring

165

straight ahead of him. The lights of the oncoming cars in the other carriageway momentarily lit the taut drawn face so that Godfrey saw him in flickers as if in an old-fashioned film. They were travelling fast, the police car ahead with its lights flashing.

'Where was this?'

'In the vicarage, where you went to see the library.'

'What was she doing there? Where was the priest?'

'He too had been murdered, perhaps some hours before Marie-Claire. We think that he had been killed before she arrived at the house. His death was made to look like the work of intruders. The murderer was probably waiting for her.'

There was silence for a time and then Bernard asked, 'What was she doing there?'

'We do not know. She had spent the day at Finches alone, apart from the housekeeper who on weekdays only remains in the house until the afternoon. Angela had gone to Bath to a Red Cross conference and did not return until late. When she got back she thought Marie-Claire was asleep and did not go into her room. It was only after they had found Makepiece that later in the day they found Marie-Claire.'

'But why had she gone to the vicarage?'

'We do not know. Apparently there had been a telephone call in the morning and Marie-Claire had answered it. This could have been the message which led her to go to the vicarage in the evening. The housekeeper did not see Marie-Claire after leaving the house for her rooms in the stables.'

Both remained silent and then Godfrey went on: 'The police have established that she had been at her dressing-table at sometime after her room had been cleaned in the morning. She was wearing a flowered silk dress when she was found.'

The beam from oncoming headlights again lit Bernard's face and Godfrey waited until it was dark before he said, 'She must have known, Bernard, whom she was going to meet.'

'In Wiltshire?'

'It is surprising, I know. But the telephone call and her preparations and change of clothes suggest it.'

'She could have been visiting the priest.'

Godfrey did not reply. He knew that his friend did not believe that. He would say no more and wait to see if Bernard would speak about Marie-Claire's life. Angela was certain that Bernard knew or suspected why his wife had lately been so unhappy. If Bernard said nothing he would wait until they had arrived at Finches and then Angela could tell Bernard exactly what Marie-Claire had said to her on the Sunday in the summerhouse. Bernard broke the silence.

'I knew that she had become involved with some man and that she was very unhappy. She needed to talk to someone and she could not to me. I knew that she wanted to talk to Angela. That was the reason why I was glad that she stayed at Finches and did not return with me to Paris. If she had . . . '

He did not finish the sentence and Godfrey did not immediately reply.

Then Godfrey said, 'You are right when you said that she wanted to talk to someone and she did speak with Angela when they were together on the Sunday when I was at Chequers and you were at the vicarage. Angela believes that she stayed on because she needed peace and quiet.'

'And to stay away from the man she was seeing in Paris. But if she had come with me, she would be alive.'

Would she, Godfrey thought? If the murderer was her lover he had come to Chapel Iford to kill her and he would have killed wherever she happened to be. It was not a killing done in passion; it was a killing according to a plan, for the clergyman had been killed first and, the police were certain, by the same man. So if the murderer had come from Paris and if Marie-Claire had been in Paris and not in Wiltshire, then in Paris she would have been killed. But what if the lover was an Englishman living here in England whom she had arranged to meet? Was Marie-Claire's decision to stay on at Finches because she had expected to meet her lover? But it had been Angela's idea that Marie-Claire should stay. In any event, if the murderer was her lover, what was the motive for the killing? Why was it so important to silence her?

Bernard interrupted Godfrey's thoughts. 'What exactly did Marie-Claire tell Angela?'

'She will tell you herself when we arrive at Finches but Angela told me that Marie-Claire had said that she had met a man by chance and had become involved with him. The affair was making her very unhappy. She told Angela that the man was not a pleasant man and caused her great unhappiness but he had such a physical hold over her that she could not end the affair. She told Angela that she felt very ashamed – and that she loved you.'

By now they had turned off the motorway and the oncoming cars had become fewer but for a second a beam from oncoming headlights lit up the back of their car. Godfrey could see that Bernard had his hand over his eyes. Then it was dark again.

'Marie-Claire also told Angela that she thought that you knew.'

'That she had a lover? Oh yes, I knew that she had a lover and I knew that she was suffering. She had suffered once before, many years ago over Alexander Murray. That was over the manner in which Alexander had broken with her. But this, I could tell, was different. This suffering was far greater. I knew that for some reason the affair was shaming her bitterly. I had thought much about that. Why such special shame over this lover? Who could he have been?'

Godfrey did not reply. Yes, who could he have been?

Bernard went on, as though he was speaking to himself, 'In my position I could easily have found out who her lover was, but that I would not do that. If I had, she would be alive today.' Then he said louder, 'You see, my friend, the price that can be paid for behaving what is called like a gentleman.'

They did not speak again. As the two cars prepared to turn off the road at Chapel Iford into the lane that led to Finches the Special Branch officer knocked on the glass partition and Godfrey lowered it.

'May I suggest, sir, that you lower the blinds?'

Godfrey did so. Webster kept the Daimler close behind the police car and Bernard and Godfrey could not see the mass of pressmen who had already gathered and were now surrounding the gate; they only saw the flashes from the cameras against the drawn blinds as the car swept past the police barrier and up the drive to the house.

Only when they were safely inside with the front door closed behind them did Angela appear and take Bernard in her arms. In the drawing-room Godfrey brought whisky and soda while

Angela sat beside Bernard, holding his hand.

'Tell me everything that she told you,' he said.

Angela repeated all that Marie-Claire had said when they had sat together in the summerhouse that Sunday evening, and of Marie-Claire's despair over the physical hold that the man had held over her.

When Angela had finished, he said, 'So he came from Paris.'

'It would appear so,' said Godfrey. 'The police and immigration were alerted and of course your people. He may be still here but . . .'

Bernard completed Godfrey's sentence: 'He was probably away before she was even known to be missing. But the clergyman? He was found earlier.'

'Yes. An attempt had been made to make his murder look like the killing of the householder in the course of robbery. The pretence worked for a time, which is what the killer must have hoped might happen in order to gain time. It was only when it had been established that Marie-Claire was missing that the clergyman's murder came to be seen as something more.'

'And the man must have used the priest to approach her at Finches and invite her to the vicarage?'

'Yes. Then he killed him before she came. That is what we presently think. Henry Makepiece had to die because otherwise the killer could have been identified. How the clergyman was persuaded to entice Marie-Claire to the vicarage I cannot tell. There may be some link about which we are at present ignorant and we are making more enquiries. We shall know more tomorrow.'

Bernard took his hand from Angela's. He rose and walked to the fireplace. He put his whisky glass on the chimneypiece and stood with his back to the two of them.

Godfrey said, 'The actual killings were very professional. The man clearly knew what he wanted to do and how to do it. Whether or not there is a link with the vicar we do not yet know.'

Bernard did not look round as he said, 'It can only mean that my wife was having a love affair with a professional killer.' He turned to face them. 'And he murdered her while she was a guest of yours. All that he spared you was from murdering her

169

under your own roof. You in your position, and I in mine.'

Yes, thought Godfrey, we will certainly be hearing much of that.

Angela came over to Bernard. 'None of that matters, none of that matters in the least. What matters is that he killed Marie-Claire, the beautiful Marie-Claire.'

'SPY CHIEF'S GUEST MURDERED. DOUBLE SLAYING
IN COUNTRY VICARAGE.'

The headlines next morning were spread across the tabloids, the television carried pictures of Finches, the vicarage and of Godfrey. An old photograph of Henry Makepiece at a village fête had been found in the local newspaper but at first none of Marie-Claire. For the moment she was identified only by name. Bernard's official position in the French Intelligence Service had not yet been identified, only that he was a French diplomat.

In former times the activities, even the existence of MI6 was never published in the press and the identity of C was not known even in many quarters in Whitehall and Westminster. But that had all changed. Knowledge of the name of the current holder of the office was widespread and sections of the press felt little inhibition in publishing his name. When therefore in the early evening on the day that the bodies had been found a local stringer heard from his sources in the headquarters of the Wiltshire police at Trowbridge that Sir Godfrey Burne was the owner of the manor house that stood a few yards away just across the wall and that one of the victims was his guest, he had informed the tabloids in London and he and his source had been amply rewarded.

There was no question of restraint; the story of a spy chief and the murder of his own guest a few yards from his own door had been irresistible. Within two hours of the nationals being alerted, journalists and the cameramen had gathered in Chapel Iford. It was the first wave that Godfrey and Bernard had encountered when they had driven through the entrance to the drive, and it was there that the army was to remain encamped. Finches was under siege.

No request, no threat of D-notice would have stopped the

tabloids and indeed none was made. Godfrey had known from the first what to expect and he knew that it would not be long before there came the further twist to the tale, the revelation of the role of Marie-Claire's husband as the fellow Head of a sister intelligence service. Inevitably that would increase the sensation and the besieging army would be swollen by others from across the channel.

When the first headlines appeared, Harvey Thompson telephoned Finches. He did not ask to speak to Godfrey nor Angela, but left a message to say that he would be available should Godfrey wish to talk. In Whitehall the Home Affairs Committee of the Cabinet was meeting in the Cabinet Offices under the chairmanship of the Home Secretary. When the business was completed, the Home Secretary walked with the new Attorney General and the Chief Whip through the connecting door from the Cabinet Offices into Number 10 and then through to Number 11 and the offices of the Chief Whip.

The Home Secretary picked up a copy of one of the tabloids and threw it onto the table.

'Have you seen that?' he said.

'Yes, I have seen it. Quite a sensation,' said William Blaze. The Attorney picked up the newspaper and read it.

'It doesn't read very well. What is it all about?'

'I don't know,' said Blaze. 'I will find out. I shall find out all right.'

'So shall I,' said the Home Secretary grimly. 'It looks as if our friend the mandarin is in real trouble.'

On the other side of the river James Kent picked up the telephone and asked Michael Robertson, the Chief Clerk of the service, to come and see him.

When the two were together in Kent's room Robertson enquired, 'Is he expected this morning?'

'No. He has telephoned. He said nothing about his trouble save that he had asked Special Branch for anything they can discover about the clergyman, Henry Makepiece.'

'Makepiece is the vicar who was murdered?'

'Yes. C wants to know everything that can be obtained about Makepiece's background and whether he has any relatives. That was all he would say about the murders.'

171

'Nothing about Bernard de Tourneville's wife?'

No. He then enquired if anything had come in from South America. I told him that we had been told by Bogota that Hamilton had reached there at last. Why he took so long to get there I do not know. I also told C that the police had discovered the name of a London enquiry agent called Mason who, on the instructions of a Mary Traynor, had made some report on Maitland. Mason is abroad but he is due back this weekend when he will be seen. C considers that important, why I am unsure.'

'Will C be in the office on Monday?'

'I sincerely hope so. What has happened in Wiltshire, Michael, makes a bad impression.' Kent shook his head. 'A very bad impression. All this publicity involving the Head of the service is not good for the service. It is not good at all.'

SEVENTEEN

Paul Mason was not in the best of condition when on that same afternoon he was accosted at the immigration barrier at Heathrow by two men who asked him to accompany them to a near-by interview room. He was suffering from an appalling hangover.

He had only been away for two days and he had been in excellent form when he had arrived at Nice from London in the late afternoon of the previous Wednesday. At Nice airport he had hired a small Seat car and had driven along the coast, turning inland at Cagnes-sur-Mer and after consulting the map easily found the hotel, the Val d'Or in the village of Roquefort-des-Pins to which he had been recommended by his brother-in-law and partner Basil Davis. As he turned off the road up the drive he could see that the hotel was, as Basil had promised, a most attractive white house set deep in the pine forest. As he registered at the hotel desk Paul Mason had been feeling good, for here he was in this pleasant place engaged on a simple professional task for a client who had already paid a very handsome deposit – which, if the firm received not a penny more would be a most lucrative piece of business – but who could be guaranteed to settle the balance of the fee and, what was important, a hefty bill for expenses.

Mason Associates had few such clients; most took their time in settling the balance of their account, that is if they ever did. Long experience had led the firm to require a healthy deposit on receipt of instructions, well before work and expenses had commenced. But times were hard, business was slack and clients often proved unreliable. The cash flow of the partnership was also not improved by the woeful incompetence of the one woman whom they employed in the office; invoices were

173

regularly delayed in their dispatch so that often imagination and invention replaced any accurate record of expenses actually incurred.

But the job that had brought Paul Mason to Roquefort-des-Pins was a thoroughly desirable job, a quick run-of-the-mill matrimonial. As Paul Mason wrote in the register his correct name and address, reluctantly and only because the desk clerk had examined his passport, he reflected that this job was quite unlike some of their recent assignments, one of which had lately caused him considerable disquiet.

That had been an enquiry by a mysterious foreign girl who had hired Mason Associates to locate her boyfriend. She had conveniently supplied the name of the man whom Mason Associates had to find, and when such instructions were received to find a named person, the first step they regularly took was to look the person up in the telephone book, something that a surprising number of clients in their stress or distress never even considered. The firm had registered several profitable successes in the past by this simple procedure. But the man for whom the foreign girl was searching had not been so easy to find and probably never would have been found by Mason Associates if Paul Mason, unknown to his wife, had not been making up to a girl called Sarah Boyd, solicitor's clerk, whom he had met in the course of what Paul Mason called one of 'their regular matrimonials'.

In his pursuit of Sarah Boyd, Paul Mason had taken her to lunch on several occasions to the dining-room of the Coach and Horses in Shepherd Market off Piccadilly but from the amount of giggling that he appeared to inspire during these trysts, he began to suspect that his suit was not altogether prospering. But he persisted and he received his reward, but it was of a different kind to that which he at the time was seeking.

Shortly after the firm had received instructions to find Martin Maitland, Sarah, unasked, had brought with her to lunch a friend, a secretary Sally Greene, for whose lunch Paul Mason gloomily but correctly assumed that he was expected to pay. But his sulks rapidly disappeared when in the course of conversation between the two girls Sally Greene spoke of her new job round the corner in Bond Street and of her new boss whom

174

Sally described as 'dishy' and who was called Martin Maitland.

So through no skill and little industry on the part of Mason Associates, the foreign girl's quarry had been located. Paul Mason then set about the usual tasks, routine visits to St Catherine's House to examine the records of births, deaths, marriages and wills and the inspection of electoral rolls and old rating registers. Everything had seemed set for a satisfactory conclusion after some simple personal observation of the man's movements, commencing with following him from his office in Old Bond Street. This led to Maddern Road in Fulham and then, to his consternation, Paul Mason had found that the subject was already under observation by some other team who were watching both at the house in Fulham and the office in Mayfair. As Paul had later told Basil in the jargon the two of them affected when they discussed their clientele in the saloon bar of the Coach and Horses, he had not at all liked 'the cut of their jib'. Indeed these others had looked to him, he told his partner, singularly unpleasant.

The appearance of these rivals on the scene of what Paul Mason had understood was merely the location of a runaway lover in a run-of-the-mill scenario of a wronged and deserted girlfriend with which Mason Associates were only too familiar had alarmed him. They did not look, he had said to Basil, like the usual nervous husbands or furtive lovers whom Mason Associates were used to encountering nor did they seem like employees of another agency. When a few days later two men had confronted Paul Mason at the corner of an ill-lit street in Fulham, pushed him sharply against a wall and told him in no uncertain terms to back off, he had retreated smartly and the following day had rapidly submitted to his client a sketchy report, which was as far as the firm were prepared to go on a job that appeared to have some pretty unusual complications.

But the case he was now engaged on involving this agreeable trip to the South of France was the straightforward business of photographing and serving papers on an unsuspecting couple enjoying the sun and each other. Paul Mason had been informed by the client husband that the two lovers were to be found at a villa near Mougins, so no tiresome investigation would be necessary. By all accounts the place was too romantic and the relationship too new for the couple to want suddenly to leave the villa and if they did they would be easy to trace and to follow. Meanwhile he planned to enjoy himself on some of the handsome fee that the firm had already extracted.

At the hotel he had been allotted a room in a cottage a little way from the main building, which was reached by climbing a flight of outdoor stairs. It was not yet dusk and he had stood on the little balcony outside his bedroom sniffing the scent of mimosa and jasmine before he crossed the garden to the main dining-room. The waiter who served his dinner examined the tubby figure of the newly-arrived guest, with his receding dark hair and a full rather wet mouth, with ill-concealed disdain, which a more sensitive person might have resented. The waiter flipped the napkin exaggeratedly over the diner's lap, left him for an unconscionable length of time and when he returned presented only the most expensive menu. When Paul Mason chose an even more expensive wine to accompany the food, the waiter had reacted with studied indifference. Mason accepted his coolness without concern for he was determined to eat much and drink more, and if the service was to be slow and casual that worried him not at all. He addressed the waiter in execrable Anglo-French and laughed heartily at his attempts to explain what he required. The waiter with no hint that he might be amused and with no perceptible change of expression replied in impeccable English. It was accordingly late when Paul Mason, replete and satisfied, returned to his room and slept.

The next morning after a leisurely swim in the pool, he had driven to the estate near Mougins where the villa was situated and, leaving the car at the bottom of the drive outside the gates, which, he noted, were electrically controlled from the villa and connected by an entry phone, he had busied himself taking photographs of what could be seen of the house from the pine woods. He then skirted the property and climbing with some difficulty a wire fence made his way towards the house. He laboured up an incline into some oleander bushes in full bloom where he could see the lawn surrounding the large pool in front of the low ranch-like house.

There were two figures lying on the grass, a pretty blonde

176

woman, topless and wearing only the briefest of briefs, whom he could tell from the photographs with which he had been supplied was the subject of his enquiry; and a man whom Mason was relieved to note was grey-haired and as stout as Mason was himself. He, Paul Mason reckoned, would not prove troublesome and certainly not dangerous physically, which was a relevant consideration to the business of Mason Associates.

Using his zoom lens he was able to get some interesting shots of the two when from time to time they entwined themselves around each other before frolicking in the water. Then he withdrew down the slope, climbed back over the fence and walked to the gate. He put the zoom lens in the boot of the car, then rang the bell of the entry phone.

When to his relief it was answered by an obviously English voice, he had replied in English.

'I hope that you will forgive me interrupting your holiday. I tried to telephone but something seems to be wrong with your phone. It often happens down here, you know. But anyway I am the local representative of Dean and Harrison and I have been sent to enquire whether it would be convenient if I came and took one or two photographs of the inside of the villa. Our next tenant has asked us to send to him in New York some pictures and all we have is the brochure and that is not enough for him. You know what these New Yorkers are like.'

He laughed pleasantly into the entry phone, although he was standing uncomfortably on the tip of his toes in order to get his mouth near enough to the box. There was a pause; the person on the other end was obviously in conference.

'I assure you that I shall not be long and I would not disturb you if you are in the garden. It is the rooms which this tiresome client wishes to have photographed. Once again I do apologise for this intrusion.'

A little later the door swung open and Paul Mason drove up the short drive to the villa. The grey-haired man, now in a bathrobe, was standing at the door. Mason jumped out of the car as quickly as his bulk permitted him and grabbed the man by the hand.

He said effusively, 'I am so sorry about this and you are being most understanding. I shall not be long, I promise.'

They went into the hall, the grey-haired man leading.

'Please don't let me interrupt your swim. I know the house well and I can find my way around,' Mason lied. 'It is just the drawing-room and the dining area and especially the bathrooms. You know these Americans and bathrooms.'

The other nodded weakly. Mason could see the woman, herself now in her wrap, sitting on a chair by the pool.

'I do hope that you are comfortable here. It's a lovely place, isn't it, the best on our books I always say. And you are having splendid weather.'

He took the camera from its case. Then he started photographing, watched by the man. Mason took his time, apparently taking pictures of the drawing-room from many different angles and then slowly moving into the dining area. The man grew bored and walked out of the French windows and stood talking to the woman but still watching Mason, who had noted the doors leading from the drawing-room. They must, he realised, lead to the bedrooms for the whole villa was laid out on one floor.

He darted towards one and opened it before the man could speak, calling out, 'Just the bathrooms, if you don't mind.'

Mason took the photograph of the bedroom beyond which was the bathroom before the man had reached him. Very convenient, he had thought; male and female clothing. Then he bustled into the bathroom and again photographed. Splendid, an electric razor and all the lovely bottles on the basin. He came out rapidly.

'May I just take the other main bathroom?'

The man led him across the drawing-room to the other door and stood beside him as he took the pictures.

'I cannot thank you enough for being so considerate. I promise that you won't be disturbed again. And I shall report that phone. Up here it is usually incoming calls which don't get through and it is often quite spasmodic. Not like British Telecom, eh?'

He pumped the man's hand and slipped out of the front door to the car.

'Will you work the automatic gate. Otherwise I shall be with you all day and that I am sure you would not relish.'

He laughed heartily and waved as he drove off down the few yards of drive to the gate. He waited while the automatic gates swung open and then, leaving the car with the engine running now blocking the gates so that they were unable to close, he jumped out, ran back to the front door, rang the bell and thrust some papers into the hand of the surprised man.

'I was asked to give you these. Nothing important, I assure you.'

He then cantered back to the car and drove off, the papers now safely served, the photographs in the can and his task accomplished.

Vastly pleased with himself, he had driven rapidly away from Mougins towards Antibes on the coast. There he made his way to the Garroupe, spent the day eating, drinking, swimming and sunning himself on a mattress. In the evening he went back to the hotel, checked out and drove east along the coast to Monte Carlo where he passed the evening at the casino, losing two thousand francs inexpertly playing roulette. He had spent the remainder of the night in a brothel.

He was still fairly intoxicated when he handed over the car and took British Airways flight back to London. He breakfasted off champagne on the aeroplane and the accumulation of all this good living to which he was unaccustomed was the reason why he was not in the best of condition when he was accosted by the two men at the immigration barrier at Heathrow.

'What is this all about?' he asked truculently. 'I have nothing to declare. Why do I have to go with you? What do you want to see me about?'

'There's no trouble, Mr Mason, nothing to worry about, I assure you,' the taller of the two men said, showing Mason a pass. 'We are from Special Branch, Metropolitan Police. We just want to ask you about some work which your firm was asked to do a few weeks ago by a Miss Mary Traynor.'

'Who?' Mason asked unsteadily. 'Miss who?'

'Mary Traynor of Cavendish Mansions in Chelsea. That is what we understand the lady was calling herself at the time although we believe that she came from Brazil in South America. We understand that it may have involved you

179

discovering for her the whereabouts of a Mr Martin Maitland.'

'Oh, my God,' said Mason and he sank into a chair, which the other Special Branch man pushed towards him.

'I knew that job would mean trouble. What's happened? Why are you interested?'

'Mary Traynor is dead. No,' the Special Branch officer stretched out his arm and gently pushed Mason who had half-risen from his chair back into his seat. 'There's no trouble about that. She died of natural causes, a sudden attack. What we are interested in is the report which she asked you to make on a Mr Martin Maitland.'

'Maitland?' The effects of the breakfast champagne were wearing off and Mason began to feel sick.

'Yes, that, we understand, was the name of the man Mary Traynor asked you to locate. Doubtless we have found out as much as you did about him but we wish to confirm that at some time you did submit to Mary Traynor a report in writing on what you yourself had discovered. No such report has been found at the dead girl's flat and that is what interests us.'

'The office,' said Mason weakly. 'The office should have a copy.'

'We have been to your office in Shepherd Market, Piccadilly and spoken to Mr Basil Davis, who I understand is your partner and your brother-in-law. He says that you told him that you had sent Mary Traynor a written report on Maitland but for the moment he cannot find a copy. If I may say so, your office seems a little disorganised.'

The officer looked reproachfully at Mason who was now sweating slightly and mopping his brow with his handkerchief. He remembered that he had typed the report himself at home.

'Yes, you are right. We have been short-staffed, and of course I have been away.'

'But this,' said the other officer, 'would have been before you went to Nice.'

'Of course, of course. Yes, I did send a preliminary report. I remember now. I typed it at home.'

'Then you may have a copy at home. May we drive you there, sir, and see if you can lay your hand on it? It is rather urgent.'

Mason brightened. It would mean a free trip home.

'Yes, certainly. Of course. I am sorry, I am a little confused. I am not feeling very well.'

'Never mind, sir, we quite understand. We will soon have you home. These early morning flights can be very tiring and I expect that you have been working hard in Nice.'

But there was no copy of the report to be found when they got back to Mason's house in Lavender Road in Hackney. So, after he had doused himself with cold water and drunk some coffee, which his wife, Lelia, brewed for him, and relieved that on his immediate return he had to talk to the police about the Mary Traynor business and not to his wife about his trip to the South of France, he told the officers what he could remember had been in the report and of what little he had discovered about Martin Maitland, none of which seemed to surprise them.

What they were seeking was confirmation of the report received from Teresa Macdonald in BA that there had at some time existed some written report on Martin Maitland from the enquiry agent in London, which had been in Mary Traynor's possession. Although Paul Mason was unable to produce a copy, he satisfied the police officers that he had made such a report, which he had himself personally pushed through the letter box of the flat in Cavendish Mansions a week before Mary Traynor had died.

The significance of this for the Special Branch officers was that since this report had never been found, either Mary Traynor had destroyed it, which seemed highly improbable; or, and this was more likely, that someone else had removed it from Cavendish Mansions. If the latter, then it must have been taken by the person who had been with Mary Traynor when she had died. As the report was on Martin Maitland and as he had disappeared on that same night, it seemed conclusive that it was he who had been with the girl when she died and it was he who had taken the report.

When Mason went on to describe to the Special Branch officers the other watchers whom he had seen around Maitland's house and office and of how their appearance had effectively scared off Mason Associates from further enquiries into

181

Martin Maitland, he was taken to New Scotland Yard to make a statement. By then Paul Mason was thoroughly regretting his evening on the tiles in Monte Carlo.

By this time the police had been informed that a man travelling alone and answering to the general description of Maitland based on the photograph taken by the Germans in Padeburg was identified as having travelled to Paris on the early Air France flight on the morning on which Mary Traynor had died in Cavendish Mansions. The French link was thus established.

In Wiltshire, following house to house enquiries, the owner of Gate's Farm informed the investigating police that he had seen a man in a Ford Escort parked by the road near to the track on the outskirts of the Finches estate shortly after dawn on the day when Marie-Claire and the clergyman had been murdered.

Next a boy said he had seen a Ford car parked during the whole of that day in the public car-park by the pub in the village. Earlier, and before the significance of the type of car had been established, a patrol car from the Avon police had followed a Ford Escort being driven at a speed over the 70-mile-an-hour limit east along the M4 towards London. The police had given chase and stopped the car and taken particulars from the driver, an Irishman who gave the name of O'Brien. But he had been allowed to proceed and trace was lost. When the call went out for reports of the movements of any Ford Escort in the area, the registration number of the speeding Ford Escort was fed into the computer and the number was found to be false. By that time it had disappeared.

Then came reports from the Welsh Constabulary of a Ford Escort seen parked in the early hours of the morning after the night of the murders in the car-park in the Lower Town at Fishguard. Although no registration number had been noted, the police considered that this could have been the same car that had been stopped on the following morning driving to London.

It took a little longer for the Garda in Dublin to send a report of a man giving the name Jacques Simonet who had flown that same morning from Dublin to Paris.

At Godfrey's request passenger lists on flights to South America from Paris on the day after the murders were studied and lists made of all single passengers. One was a Mr Oscar Brandt, passenger to Bogota. A subsequent report from Teresa Macdonald in BA confirmed that this was a name used by Maitland.

Late in the evening of the morning when Paul Mason gave his statement it was discovered that the widow of the Reverend Henry Makepiece was Martin Maitland's aunt.

As Godfrey studied the reports that flowed in to him at Finches it began to fall into place. Maitland had been with Mary Traynor when she had died. Maitland had been Marie-Claire's lover. Maitland had killed Henry Makepiece and Marie-Claire.

As a result, here at home he, Godfrey, was now in the eye of a storm. Edmund Hamilton was in the field, already or soon to be where Godfrey had sent him and to where Maitland was now heading. All that Godfrey could do was to warn Edmund, and, with the press and television still encamped around his house, ride the storm.

EIGHTEEN

An hour after Teresa had left him in the hotel in Rio, Edmund went to the telephone. From the Embassy he got the telephone number of the Olivella family in Brasilia. When he had been connected, Edmund asked to speak to Señorita Pilar, saying that he had a message from Señorita Macdonald. He was told that the señorita was staying with friends and Edmund asked for and was given their telephone number. When he was through to this number, he repeated his request to speak with Señorita Pilar. He was told that she had left unexpectedly on a visit to the Argentine. Edmund sent for a car and was driven to the Consul's house in Rio. He asked the Consul to get a message through to the attaché in Brasilia asking him to inform Bogota that Edmund Hamilton was delayed and that he would not be arriving in Bogota for three days. He passed the evening dining alone and after he had dined he sat smoking on the balcony of his room listening to the music of the guitars around the pool below him. At midnight he extinguished his cigar and went to bed.

In the early morning he checked out of the hotel, booked a seat on a flight to BA and arranged to have a hire car at his disposal for the morning. He instructed the driver to take him to the university. There he worked for two hours and then told the librarian that he had discovered that he needed to do more research in Buenos Aires before he visited the library in Bogota and asked the man to cable the National Library of Colombia to inform them that he was delayed and that he would now be arriving there in three days' time. He took the car on to the airport. Then he flew south.

*　　*　　*

He did not return to the hotel in BA where he had stayed earlier in the week but spent the night in a small boarding house. The weather had again become wet and cold and he thought of the raincoat, which he had left in Teresa's apartment. He did not telephone, but taking his bag with him he went to her street and sat in a café where he could keep a watch on her door, drinking brandy and coffee against the cold. At about noon he saw her. She came down the street and let herself into the apartment. He stayed where he was for half an hour and then crossed the road and rang her bell.

When she answered the door he stood in the doorway looking at her and saw that the dark patches remained beneath her eyes. She looked tired and very vulnerable. She stared at him.

'As you are here, you had better come inside.'

He followed her in to the hall.

'Why have you come here? You are meant to be in Bogota. You are expected today.'

'I have warned them. I could not go until I had seen you.'

'This is not sensible.'

'Of course it is not. But I could not go without seeing you again. I was told in London, not by Kent but by C, that after I had gone north I might not be able to return. Kent does not know what I really have to do when I get to Colombia.'

She looked at him, surprised.

He said, 'Kent believes that all that C wishes me to do in Bogota is to check on Carlos and report to him on the Colombian station. But there is more to it than that. Carlos is to send me into the hills beyond Cali where a new group from Medellin have established themselves. C needs to locate them. He warned me that when I reach where I am to go, it could prove dangerous. That is why I had to see you again. I can think of nothing else but of you. Just of you – and of Pilar Olivella –'

'She is in BA,' Teresa interrupted him. 'We flew down together.' They were now in the sitting-room. She had her back to him, looking out the window. 'Why have you told me of the danger in what you have really been sent to do?'

He said quietly, 'I have fallen in love with you, Teresa.'

She did not reply and did not move.

He said again, 'I am in love with you.'

185

She did not turn to look at him but said, 'Do you know what you are saying? Oh, Edmund, you are a fool. You were sent here because you were meant to be so clever, so reliable.'

'I know that in our situation it is not sensible,' he said quietly. 'But it happens to be true. I cannot help it. And I think that you love me.'

She turned and faced him. 'Edmund, listen to me. You were chosen by London for a mission. I thought it was a simple mission but now you tell me that it is more important than what they told me. They chose you, Edmund, because they trusted you and relied on you. Now here you are, miles from where you ought to be and you are talking about love.'

'I know,' he said. 'That is what I came to talk about.'

She went on, 'You and I were given a job to do together, a professional job. As far as I knew it was to get you to see Pilar. We were to be pretend lovers so that I could get you into the place where you could meet her. And I did. But you mishandled it because you said that you became angry at how that woman looked at me! But for you and me it was pretending, play-acting, part of our professional job. Being good actors, as you said to me in the restaurant after we had first met.'

'I know,' he said. 'That was the start of it, at that restaurant.'

'It may have been for you. But what of me? Do you really believe that I want to become involved in a love affair with the man they sent from London and ordered me to help?'

He put out his hand towards her but she turned away again. 'You will ruin everything with this stupid talk about love. You will ruin what you were sent here to do and you will ruin me and my work and my life. Then you will go back to your university and your stupid books and documents – unless you get yourself killed. Leave me alone, for God's sake, leave me alone.'

He reached out and turned her until she faced him. Then he took her in his arms. But she beat on his chest with her fists and he lifted her so that she lay in his arms like a struggling child while she cried out. He lowered his face to hers searching for her mouth to kiss but she twisted her face from side to side. Still he held her, looking down at her until for a moment her head was still and he kissed her, finding her mouth, feeling the

186

wet of her tears on her face against his. She jerked away, again twisting her head from side to side but he persisted, kissing her eyes and her forehead and again her mouth. Then the struggling ceased and her hands slid behind his neck, and she looked up at him silent and grave. She pulled his head towards her and his mouth ever deeper into hers. He carried her through the sitting-room into the bedroom and for a moment stood with her in his arms above the bed. Very gently he lowered her and lay beside her, caressing her, unbuttoning her shirt, holding her breasts, moving his hand down as he pulled at the buttons of her jeans, sliding them to her knees until she kicked them off and she lay naked beside him.

They made love, he on top of her, at first solicitous lest he crushed the slight figure, until she clawed at his shoulders making him mount her and she cried out, whimpering. So it began and so it went on all day into the evening, pausing, lying in each other's arms until at night exhausted they fell asleep.

He woke to find her like a kitten curled against him, her small head on his chest, sleeping fitfully, now and then stirring and whispering but on occasion crying out as though in pain. When she did so he gripped her more tightly in his arms and whispered back to her, calming her until she quietened and slept silently.

When finally she woke the next morning, she went from the bed into the kitchen and she returned, naked, with a tray of coffee and croissants, which they drank and ate while she sat cross-legged on the bed beside him. Then she pushed the tray aside and they made love again; this time she the leader and he the led.

They were sleeping when late into the morning the telephone rang.

'Leave it,' he said but she shook her head and looked at the clock beside her. She picked up the telephone and spoke in Spanish and he knew that it was Pilar. As she spoke Teresa smiled at him over the mouthpiece. He had his hand on her naked breast.

'I am well,' she said into the receiver. 'What time did we arrange? Yes, I shall be free. I shall come to you.' She was still looking at Edmund. 'About three o'clock.'

187

She replaced the receiver.

'Do you have to?' he asked.

'You know that I must.'

They bathed together and when they had dressed Teresa opened some wine.

'We had better eat here and you must not leave the apartment. I do not want you to be seen.'

'What does the woman want?' he said.

'You know what she wants. She wants me and I want her story. She has told me a part but I am not sure that it was the whole truth and if it was, I am not sure how much it will help.'

'Let me speak with her. This time I would be more sensible. I do not like her being with you.'

She put her fingers over his mouth. 'You know that I will do far better than you ever could.' She took his hand. 'Leave Pilar to me. I can handle her.' She smiled at him, watching the look in his eyes. 'Do you not trust me, even after what has just happened between us? If you do not, you are even more foolish a man than you are clumsy an agent. So far, that is.'

When he protested she put her fingers again over his mouth. 'I only tease. When I get back we shall talk and make our decisions. What has happened between us does not alter the fact that you ought to be in Colombia.'

The serious expression had returned to her face and he leant forward and kissed her.

She went on gravely: 'Do not yourself speak on the telephone. I shall leave the answer-machine on and that way you will be able to hear any messages. There are bound to be some and they will be about you. If I need to leave a message for you, I shall pretend it is for the cleaning woman.' She brushed the hair back from his forehead. 'Do not look so anxious.'

And she kissed him again.

After she had gone the telephone rang twice and Edmund listened to the messages on the machine. The first was a long-distance call from the offices of the British Council in Bogota in Colombia enquiring whether Señorita Macdonald knew the whereabouts of Dr Hamilton, who had originally been expected yesterday in Bogota on a research project and had not yet arrived. Señorita Macdonald was asked to alert the Council offices urgently if she was able to help. The second, an hour or more later, was from nearer home for the caller gave a local number and asked the señorita to telephone urgently. Edmund had little doubt that this too concerned him. Two hours later that call was repeated.

He wandered restlessly around the flat, touching her possessions, lying again on the bed where she and he had lain together. It was late in the afternoon when at last he heard Teresa's voice on the answer-machine. The message was for Lydia, the cleaner, explaining that the señorita was delayed and that she was not to wait for the señorita, who would not be back for several hours.

He searched her desk in the living-room and found an airline guide. A flight left BA for Rio early in the morning; from there he could catch a connection to Bogota where he would arrive the following evening.

As Teresa had warned him not to use the telephone he could not reserve a seat but he would get to the airport very early and if necessary bribe his way onto a flight.

Then he took some of her writing-paper and wrote at her desk. He folded what he had written, put her name on it and slipped it into his pocket. He wiped off the messages on the tape, save that from her. Then he lay on the bed and waited for her.

It was not until midnight that Teresa returned. Once through the door she came to him in a rush and he held her in his arms. He could feel her trembling.

'I am very tired. I want a bath and some wine.'

He brought the bottle and glasses to the bathroom and sat beside her as she bathed, marvelling at her slim body as she lay in the scented water, the glass of wine in one hand resting on the rim of the tub. As she soaked and sipped the wine he said nothing but waited for her to talk when she was ready.

'Dry me,' she said, and as she stepped out of the bath he enveloped her in the large white towel, holding her to him, rubbing her gently, kissing the point of her shoulders and the

189

nape of her neck and her nipples. She took a wrap from the cupboard and taking his hand in hers led him into the sitting-room and lay on the sofa, he beside her.

'I am sorry for her,' she said at last. He made no reply but put his arm around her.

'Do you ever think how lucky we are, you and I and the ones like us, without all that anxiety and guilt, all that defensiveness and the justifying and that desire which makes the few like her want to believe that many feel as they do. Why do they have that need to convert others to feel as they do? The world would not last long if everybody did.'

He could not see her face, his cheek was against the side of her head, his arms around her and his hands cupping her breasts.

'Do you remember the birth laboratories and the incubators in *Brave New World*?' he replied. 'Perhaps that is what Pilar and her kind want – with just a few male drones to make the world go on.'

She made a slight grimacc. Then she said, 'I would like to bear your child.'

He held her more tightly and again kissed the side of her neck.

'Pilar was in love with Maria Santos, or Mary Traynor, as she called herself in London. You brought back to her Maria's death.'

'I am sorry,' he said, and she lowered her cheek so that it rested against his shoulder.

'After the wedding party in Brasilia, Pilar decided that she would come with me to BA. She is a woman of sudden passions. I suppose that is like all her kind. Have you met many?'

'No. Not that I know. She is attracted to you.'

'Oh, yes. I have become her latest passion. She keeps kissing me, very seriously.'

He held her to him more tightly.

'She promised that what she told me today was the whole story and I believe her. It does not take us much further. It only tells us more about the kind of man that Maitland is.'

'What was her story?'

'Last year Maria Santos' sister, a girl of sixteen, was taken by her family to the Palace Hotel in Baden-Baden. There was a man there who called himself Brandt and he seduced the girl. Pilar said that he had raped her but I suppose she would say that about a man. But Brandt, as he was called, did more; he got her onto cocaine. She became pregnant and Brandt disappeared. The girl had to be taken by the family to London for an abortion and later to the States for a cure for the drugs.'

'When did –'

She turned and put her fingers in front of his mouth. 'I must try and remember everything that Pilar said. Maria sent for Pilar who joined her in Germany. The two of them determined to find Brandt so that they could expose him. Eventually they got on to his track through a man called Josef whom they met in a lesbian club in Berlin. He was peddling drugs and was involved in some ring which ran the drugs across Europe, and they discovered that Josef knew Brandt who was part of the ring, more important than Josef. Their plan was to inform on him.'

'When did they plan this?'

'Soon after they learnt that Josef knew Brandt. So they met Josef several times at the club. Josef told them that their kind amused him and he wanted to photograph them together out of doors, making love, I suppose. They agreed because they wanted Josef to lead them to Brandt. He took them to the country, to a house near a place called Eyendorf to spend the day and take the photographs. Some, Pilar said, were just photographs of the two of them sitting together in the garden; others, she said, were less ordinary. But they succeeded, for they learnt from Josef that Brandt was in England where he called himself Maitland.'

'So then they came to London?'

'Yes. To find Maitland they hired a private detective.'

'Did Pilar remember the name?'

'It was a firm called Mason who traced Maitland to an office in London. But then came the trouble. The detective sent Maria a report which said that there were other people also interested in Maitland and who were watching him.'

'Who were they?'

'I do not know. The detective thought that Maria had hired

191

him to find some man who had abandoned her but the other people watching Maitland frightened him and he did not want anything more to do with it. That was when Pilar wanted to call it off.'

'Why?'

'She said that she knew about these drug people. Something once happened to her with these people when she was a girl. Pilar said that at some time she would tell me. I am curious to know.'

'What happened then?'

'She said that she had told Maria in London that it was too dangerous for them and she wanted to go home but Maria refused because by then she had managed to meet Maitland and had agreed to go out with him. This was on the evening of the night when Maria died.'

'So he was the man who was with Maria when she died?'

'It must have been. Pilar saw Mason's report on Maitland and Maria had it in the flat. When she found that Maria had died, Pilar searched for it but it had disappeared. So Pilar is sure that it was Maitland who was with Maria when she died. He must have found it and either destroyed it or taken it away. I have sent all this to London. That is why I am so late.'

Edmund rose and she held out her hand and he pulled her to her feet.

'Are there any messages on the machine?'

'Only your message for your cleaning lady, which was meant for me.' He did not tell her of the other messages.

'Then let us go to bed. I am very tired. We can talk in the morning.'

In bed they made love, but not like they had before. This time they loved each other slowly and gently. Afterward she was restless. He asked if she had a sleeping draught and she said that she had. He brought it to her. There would be time in the morning to make their plans, he said; it was important that she should sleep.

When she was asleep he remained awake, holding her, waiting and watching over her as the hours passed. Then, when it was still dark, he rose and dressed, and put the letter that he had written earlier on her dressing-table. He stood looking at her as she slept, trying to imprint on his memory every feature of her face so that it would be with him for ever. Then he slipped away.

When she woke it was late. She stretched out her hand but could not find him. She sat up, thinking that he was in the other room. Then she saw his letter. She ran over to the dressing-table and brought it back to the bed.

My darling, (she read) I am not deserting you but now I must go north. I shall think of you all the time. I have loved you from the moment when I saw you in the hall of the hotel. When it is all over I shall come to you whatever they may say. I am writing this while you are with Pilar. Soon you will be back and I shall hold you in my arms and we shall make love. Then, in the night, I shall go and you will read this after I have gone. Think of me as much as I shall think of you. I love you. Edmund.

She turned on the bed, crumpling the letter in one hand as she lay, her face buried in the bedclothes with the tears streaming from her eyes.

Although she had denied it, her love for him had begun as his had for her, on the first evening they had met when she had spoken so seriously at the restaurant of what he had to do. She had seen the amused look in his dark eyes and watched the way he moved his hands with their long fingers, expressively, constantly, quite unlike an Englishman. Later, when they had been at work together in the libraries in BA and Rio, she had admired the way he worked so authoritatively, seeking and hunting through the documents and volumes, rarely hesitating over what he needed to note and what to discard. She had been very aware how closely he had been watching her.

But she had belonged to the secret world since her time at the university and she knew that what was happening between them was contrary to every rule that she had been taught. She knew that she should never have allowed him to kiss her after they had danced together at the *asada*; when he had been lying on the bed in her bedroom, separated from her by the wall in her apartment the evening before they left for Rio, she had longed for him to come to her. She had dressed for him at the engagement party in Brasilia, proud to be seen on his arm and to be envied. All that she had wanted that evening was to have been able to dance with him until the sun had risen over that garden of cascades with the water that ran like necklaces of light down to the pools at the edge of the woods.

There had followed the scene with Pilar and his irrational jealousy which had led him to mishandle what he'd been sent to do because he had believed that Pilar might present a challenge to his relationship with her. She had to force herself to be angry with him but it had not altered what she felt.

When she had been warned by London that they were sending an academic, she had prepared herself for someone very different. But on their second night of dining together Edmund had spoken, only half laughingly, of how Byron had put pre-eminence on the battlefield and even in the debating chamber ahead of success as a poet. Edmund had claimed that unlike many academics he knew what Byron had meant. Later he had told her about his regret that he had left the service before he had a chance of working in the field. He would never have been content, he had said, if he had not been given the chance offered to him by C. Ever since he had revealed to her what was his real mission she had worried lest out of some wish to test himself he might try and do too much.

In her misery after his departure and her fear for his safety, she decided that she would speak to the man to whom she reported locally. After telephoning Pilar, who was due to visit that afternoon, she joined a group of friends, mainly women friends of her own age, for luncheon. Among the few men present was a young diplomat from the re-opened British Mission and she passed to him a message. At three o'clock she opened her front door to a man in his early forties. He had a pleasantly weather-beaten complexion and light brown almost red hair.

'Simon gave me your message,' he said in English. 'So our

194

friend has gone north at last. What I don't understand is why he had to come back here from Rio. I thought he would have gone on from there.'

'He decided that he ought to know Pilar's story before he reached Colombia.'

'So that was his reason.' He did not sound very convinced.

'Pilar is coming here this afternoon at four o'clock.'

'Then I will not stay long. What exactly do you want me to do?'

'I am anxious about him.'

'About Hamilton?' The man looked at her sharply. 'Why? What he has to do is not very difficult – just take a look at the Bogota station and report. He knows that he is not to get too embroiled.' He threw himself into a chair and stretched out his legs. 'I like that word "embroiled", especially in our business.'

'Has that been made clear to him?'

'Of course. His task is to pick up the gossip and check out friend Carlos.'

So he does not know, she thought. Then she remembered: this man was a Kent man and Edmund had told her that he was not. She regretted that she had sent for him.

'So why are you so worried?'

She had to reply.

'I am not sure. But I am.'

The man said nothing, placing his hands together, the fingertips under his chin. He looked at the tired little face of the girl sitting opposite to him. 'I suppose he spent last night here. Was that wise?' He got up from his chair and walked over to the window. 'It is very unlike you.'

'I know,' she said. 'But it has happened.'

There was a silence. Then he said, 'You will not be seeing him again. He has passed on to the Bogota station, or what is left of it.'

He thought, she knows more about what Hamilton has been asked to do than she is telling. Kent has guessed that there is more to it than what they have been told. C would not have sent a man like Edmund Hamilton merely to take a look at Carlos.

195

'I only wanted to see you to tell you he had gone north,' Teresa said.

She had already done that, the man thought. She does know something.

'The choice of Hamilton, I believe, surprised some,' he said. 'His academic work certainly provides him with reason to be wandering around but it did seem a little unnecessary to send a special man.'

'Pilar will be here soon.'

He saw that she would not say more. 'Don't worry. Hamilton's not a fool. Bogota is not the front line.'

'You sent London Pilar's story?'

'Yes. They have that.'

'If I learn more this afternoon I shall pass it on.'

'Of course. Don't worry about Hamilton. It is probably all quite unimportant.' He rose. 'In view of what has happened, from now on you must stay clear. Do you understand, Teresa?'

She nodded and turned away.

From the café at the corner of the street the red-headed man sat and watched the large Mercedes car draw up outside the apartment block. He saw the chauffeur ring the bell to the main door and wait until it had been answered before returning to the car and opening the rear passenger door to allow the smartly dressed woman to get out. She crossed the pavement and disappeared into the building. The Mercedes drove away.

It was silly for the girl to have become emotionally involved with Hamilton. But she would not see him again now. No one might see him again if he really did have some very special task.

He ordered more coffee and settled down for a long wait. He had better keep an eye on the girl.

Pilar had swept into the apartment on a wave of Chanel, and, throwing back her coat, took Teresa's face in both of her hands and kissed her on the lips.

'*Chérie*,' she said. 'Since you left me I have done nothing but think of you. But you look so pale and tired? You need a change. Why don't we go away together into the country?'

196

'I cannot get away. I have work to do, unlike you lazy rich people.'

Pilar was striding around the apartment. 'I like your home. It has character. It is even seductive. I am glad that you asked me here.'

'It has a good view over the city. Come and look.' Teresa had gone to the window; she wanted to see if the man with the red hair was at the café.

'I do not like cities,' Pilar said. 'I like the plains and the hills and that is where you and I ought to be. So why, little Teresa, will you not come away with me?'

She had her arm around Teresa's shoulder.

'I told you, I have much work to do. I have to do more research and write up my notes which I have been hired to do by Dr Hamilton.'

Pilar dropped her arm and walked slowly back into the centre of the room. Teresa came to her and this time she put her hand on Pilar.

'I know that he was clumsy and that you were right to be upset but he was only trying to discover what you could tell him about the man whom you and he were looking for. What was his name?'

'Maitland,' said Pilar. 'Or Brandt.'

'You told me yesterday about the discovery that others were interested in Maitland. Who could they be?'

Pilar sat and looked up at Teresa. 'Maria did not understand. I knew the kind of people they would be, drug people. I know what those people can be like. I have seen them – in Medellin. That was why I told Maria we must stop.'

'You have been to Medellin?'

'Yes, when I was very young. Before my father became a government minister he had a business in Medellin. He once took me with him on a business trip. It was the last time he went there.'

Teresa came and sat on the arm of the sofa above Pilar, resting her hand on the other's shoulder.

'What happened?'

'My father had taken me, his elder daughter, as company. I

197

was very young. We were dining together in our suite in the hotel when they came in.'

'They? Who were they?'

'Three men. One was a man called Consuero.'

'Who allowed them to come in?'

'The hotel. It must have been arranged. Two stood over my father and Vincente Consuero came and stood behind my chair and put his hands on my shoulders to prevent me running away. He said to my father that he was to abandon his business and leave Medellin and not return. Otherwise, Consuero said, Medellin would have me – now.'

Teresa took Pilar's hand.

'When he said this he put his hands over my breasts, gripping them. I remember that I screamed and the other two laughed. Then he ran his hand down between my legs. We left that night and my father never returned.'

Pilar got up from the sofa and stood by the table, playing with some flowers in a vase. Then she turned back to Teresa.

'I have never forgotten Medellin.'

Teresa came and put her arm around her.

'When the detective learnt that others were following Maitland and they had threatened him, I knew that they would be like those men in Medellin. That was when I told Maria that we should leave it alone.'

Teresa kissed Pilar on the cheek. 'We won't talk more about it. I am sorry that all this has been brought back to you, and all because of my professor. But he seemed so desperate to find the man whom he said was very evil.'

'They are all evil.'

'Let me make you some tea and then let us talk about something different. I shall show you the notes on which I am working.'

It was six o'clock when the red-haired man saw the Mercedes saloon collect Teresa's visitor. When it had passed down the street he paid the check for the innumerable cups of coffee and the single glass of brandy and wearily stumped off back to the Embassy. From her window Teresa watched him go. Then she packed a grip with some underclothes and shirts and, putting her passport and money into a shoulder-bag, she went down the stairs at the back of the block and into the street at the rear of the building. She found a cab and told the driver to take her to the airport where she waited for the next flight to Bogota.

At the British Mission in BA, the red-haired man was speaking on the telephone to James Kent in London.

'Our visitor should be in the north by now. You are right. I am certain that he is up to more than merely checking out our friend.'

'I have always known that,' said Kent. 'Well, it is C's business and no one else's. Does the girl know about it?'

'If she does, she's not telling. She got herself involved with the visitor. Quite unlike her. I have told her to keep clear of him.'

As he was speaking the young man who had been at the luncheon with Teresa's friends put a slip of paper in front of him.

'Simon has just handed to me a note. She is at the airport. I suppose she plans to follow him.'

'See that she is stopped,' said Kent. 'At once. And bring her back.' He rang off.

The red-headed man sighed. 'A job for you, young Simon. You are to bring the lady home.' As he spoke he was handed another signal. 'Hamilton has appeared at the Hyatt Hotel in Bogota. He's off on his frolic.' He tossed the signal on his desk. 'Mark my words, young Simon. It will all end in some gigantic cock-up. I am going home.'

While Teresa was sitting waiting at the airport she felt a man's hand on her shoulder.

'I am sorry. But you have to go home.'

She picked up her bag and followed him.

NINETEEN

The small aircraft bucked and danced as the rain lashed across the wings and fuselage. For much of the time it blotted out any view from the narrow windows but whenever they cleared Edmund peered out at the dark storm-tossed night spasmodically lit by spectacular flashes of lightning that illuminated the mountains over which the antiquated aircraft seemed to him to be flying perilously close. When the rain blotted out all vision he resolutely tried to stifle the pictures that kept crowding into his mind of a scene in a film of an aircraft slicing through the tops of the trees on the side of a mountain and ploughing up the undergrowth before it finally came to rest in a tangle of aluminium and gore.

He had forced himself to concentrate on his notes, which he had laid on his knee and which he had made in the library in Bogota. They were notes about a Spanish expedition that had set out from Bogota in 1539 and among whom could have been his forebear, Octavio de Coronado whose fate had never been known. He tried to conjure up a picture of the expedition, the soldiers in full armour suffering under just such a tropical storm as they struggled on foot through the jungle over which the aircraft was then flying. As the plane leapt and jumped, despite his fastened seat-belt his head almost struck the fuselage above him and he clung to his papers to prevent them scattering upon the floor. He even began to envy the men he was picturing, those bearded tough adventurers in their curved helmets carrying their pikes and heavy long-barrelled muskets as they cut and slashed a route through the jungle four hundred years ago. They, he thought, would have had their feet on solid earth! But at least in the cabin of the bucketing aircraft he was dry and warm.

As he shifted himself in his narrow seat, the pistol Carlos had given him pressed uncomfortably into his back. So much for the grand-uncle and the Great Game. He glanced at the twenty or so fellow passengers who looked supremely unconcerned, as though flying through a tropical thunderstorm was for them a daily routine. The steward, balancing himself on his toes with a tray of drinks held in one hand high above his head, kept up a regular and cheerful service. Edmund drank the fierce brandy the steward handed to him and felt better.

He had only spent forty-eight hours in the capital, Bogota, before he had set off on this stormy flight across the mountains. He had got away from BA on the 8 a.m. flight and had reached the capital of Colombia in the afternoon. During all the hours of the flight from BA to Bogota he had thought about Teresa, imagining her waking and finding him gone and reading his letter. Already the time he had spent with her in her apartment seemed a dream.

At the Hyatt Hotel he had been handed an envelope which had been left for him. In his room, he had opened the message addressed to Professor Hamilton. It read simply:

Welcome to Bogota. I hope that you will find the visit rewarding and your work in the library fruitful. I believe that you might find the life of Antonio Vieria 1608–1697 helpful. But perhaps he is of too late a period? I trust that we shall meet while you are engaged in your researches.

He had not been able to decipher the signature. The note bore that day's date and at the head of the piece of rough paper on which the message had been written was the name of the National Library, which the archivist in Rio had arranged for him to visit. He lit the paper over an ashtray and burnt it, crumpling the ashes.

Then, after he had unpacked, he rested. In the evening he did not feel hungry, had gone down to the bar for a drink –

and to a most unwelcome encounter.

When he had ordered his drink and was sitting alone at a small table reading a local newspaper, he heard his name and looked up to see standing in front of him a man whom he had not seen for over ten years, not since their time together as undergraduates at Cambridge. Seen that is in the flesh, because over the years Edmund had often seen him on the television screen presenting news and television programmes from every quarter of the globe. As Edmund regarded the figure that was now standing over him across the table never had he wanted to see anyone less.

'Edmund Hamilton! I haven't seen you since May Week '79! What the devil are you doing here?'

The speaker, Francis Maddocks, pulled up a chair and sat down. He was a slight, sharp-faced man, with a pointed beard and a rather vulpine face and thinning fair hair. Edmund had disliked him from the day they had first met, when he and Maddocks had, by coincidence, both decided to make their maiden speeches at the Union. Maddocks' speech had come first and when Edmund had spoken he had, to the great enjoyment of most of the audience, so successfully demolished Maddocks' argument and so wittily mocked Maddocks that he had thereby earned Maddocks' implacable hatred.

'Francis Maddocks! What an extraordinary coincidence! You are right, we haven't met for years, although I have seen you on the box often enough.'

'What you mean is too often.' Maddocks liked to have his fame acknowledged. Edmund could see that he was pretty tight. 'This is an odd place to meet! Fancy running into you in this godforsaken city. When did you get in?'

Before Edmund could answer he went on, 'I am here interviewing politicians for a programme we are making. I have been here for a week and it is a week too long.'

'I have only just arrived,' Edmund replied, resigning himself to a drinking session with this man whom above all others he would have preferred to have avoided. 'I have come from BA.'

'What brings you here?' Then before Edmund could reply, Maddocks said, 'Shall I tell you something?'

'Of course.'

'Well, when we left Cambridge, I was told that you had become a spook! Is that why you are here?'

Maddocks leant back in his chair and laughed. Edmund looked at him evenly and joined in the laughter.

'Whatever do you mean?' Edmund asked.

'A spook. You know, intelligence. That's what I was told.'

'What utter nonsense. When I came down I did go into the civil service for a short time but I spent my days running errands and making lists. There was nothing as glamorous as intelligence. Who could have told you such rubbish?'

'Someone in our crowd who were with us at Cambridge. I ran into some of them just after we had all gone down and I had started in the TV business. Perhaps it was a joke. You always were a secretive bastard.'

We were never in the same crowd, thought Edmund, never ever. But he would have to be careful with this man whom he so greatly disliked and whom he so little needed to meet on his first evening in Bogota.

'You have made a great success of the TV business. You're famous.'

Maddocks had looked gratified.

Edmund went on: 'But what bunkum about me. That crowd would say anything for a good send-up. I didn't stay a civil servant very long. Then I got a Fellowship at St Peter's.'

'Did you, by God?' Maddocks was impressed.

'Yes. That is the reason why I am in this part of the world. I am doing some work on sixteenth-century Latin America and the arrival of the Portuguese and the Spaniards. I have been down in BA and Rio and I have come here to do some more research.'

He hastened to bring the conversation back to Maddocks. 'But tell me about yourself. Your life is far more interesting than mine. Why are you interviewing Colombian politicians? Have another drink while you tell me about it.'

'Thanks. I will. Whisky.'

Edmund gave the order to the waiter.

'The programme people don't like it to be known what we are planning so you must keep it to yourself.'

'Of course I shall,' said Edmund gravely.

203

Maddocks leant forward, speaking in a whisper as though he was about to pass on a state secret. 'We are doing a programme about the drug trade and we have come out here to film the Colombian end. Between you and me, this programme could be dynamite.'

'Will you be going to Medellin or Cali?'

'Don't be a bloody fool. We're not going to risk our necks among those gangsters.' He leant back, looking over his shoulder to make certain no one had overheard him.

'Max and I – Max Pottinger is the producer and he and I have worked a lot together – well, we are looking at what the British Government is doing or rather failing to do over the international drug problem. They simply have no idea of its extent and they don't seem to care. It's a bloody scandal.' He drank and then again looked over his shoulder before leaning forward, his face close to Edmund's. 'Max thinks there may be something funny going on.'

Edmund tried to avoid the whisky breath and he pushed his chair back from the table.

'I ought to have guessed that it had to be drugs which would bring you and a TV crew to Colombia. But what do you mean – something funny going on?'

'Just what I said. Some sort of pay-off with someone pretty high up, probably police.'

'Do you really mean that?' Edmund added some water, a very little water, to Maddocks' drink. Was the fellow drunk or off his head? But then the ludicrous man probably believed what he was saying.

'I just can't believe it.'

'Well, you bloody well ought to believe it.' By now he was even more drunk. 'You know,' he said, shaking his head owlishly, 'you dons tucked away in your unreal world amid, what was it, your dreaming spires, drinking port on your High Table, you don't know half what goes on in the real world.'

'I suppose that we are a little out of touch,' said Edmund humbly. 'But won't you have to be very careful if you are going to make such appalling accusations? Won't you have the Corporation or the Broadcasting Commission or whoever it is down on you?'

'And the bloody laws of bloody libel,' Maddocks said gloomily. Then he cheered up. 'But Max thinks we can get round it. Just the hint, you know, without pinning it on anyone. We think it can be done.'

They had more drinks, Edmund pacing himself carefully and Maddocks drinking steadily. When finally they rose from the table to go up to their rooms Maddocks was almost affectionate.

'It was fun seeing an old mate again. You know, Hamilton, you're not as stuck up as you used to be. At Cambridge you used to be so bloody conceited, such a stuffed-shirt intellectual. You've changed, Hamilton – and for the better, old man.'

The lift had stopped on the first floor and before Maddocks stumbled unsteadily out into the corridor, he had added, 'We're off tomorrow, the whole crew. Home to Blighty. We have enough in the can and there's plenty of library footage we can use. That's what the bosses like, depth. If only they knew!'

He laughed jovially and had staggered out of the lift and down the corridor to his suite leaving Edmund to ascend to his modest room twenty floors above him.

The following morning, led by another bearded figure whom Edmund identified as Max and including a pallid and for once rather silent Francis Maddocks, the TV crew departed from the hotel in a suitable display of fuss. Edmund made his way to the library, had an agreeable talk with the Head Librarian, apologised for his delay in arriving and settled down with the books he called for and which, as in BA and Rio, were courteously and efficiently brought to him.

After he had worked for some two hours at his table, which was lit by a green-shaded reading lamp much needed for study in the gloom of the library, a short, overweight and heavily built man with a dark moustache and sweating profusely came and sat on the other side of the table facing Edmund. The newcomer placed a book on the table and began to read, turning the pages rapidly as though searching for something in the text. Neither spoke and when the man closed the book while he pulled a red bandanna handkerchief from his pocket to mop his forehead, Edmund was able to see that the volume the newcomer had been studying was a life of a seventeenth-century Jesuit, Padre Antonio Vieria SJ 1608–1697 by Charles Boxer. The man sighed heavily, closed the book and, leaving it on the table, rose and walked towards the reception desk. Edmund watched him leave the library and then idly picked up the book on Vieria and casually leafed through it, holding it so that its bottom end rested on his notes. As Edmund had expected, a piece of paper slipped down onto his notes and Edmund placed the book on top of it. Then, as though something had caught his attention in the text he began to make notes. After about ten minutes of writing he pushed the volume aside while he consulted others in front of him. Now and again he turned back to the life of Vieria, as though using it to check what he had written. Then he shut the book and left it on the table. At the end of the morning he gathered up his papers and left for the cafeteria.

As he drank his coffee, he read the message that had slipped from the book which the man had brought to his table. It consisted of one sentence: '6 Santo Spirito. 2200 hours.'

Back in the library Edmund worked solidly through the rest of the day and on his return to the hotel he obtained a street guide from the concierge. At 8.30 he took a taxi to a restaurant in the quarter where he was to have his rendezvous. When he had eaten, having memorised from the guidebook the way to his destination, and although by now it was dark, he walked. He had been told that in the city someone would be looking after him but he watched to see if he was being followed and could observe no one.

Number 6 Santo Spirito was a tall dingy house, with steps leading up from the short narrow street. As he climbed the steps to the front door he passed a young woman leading by the hand a wailing child who had apparently come from the house where he had been bidden. He waited until they had passed up the street and then rang the bell.

After a time, the bell was answered by the man he had seen in the library and Edmund stepped inside. Without a word the man closed and bolted the door behind them and led Edmund silently down a narrow hall to an ill-lit sitting-room in the rear of the house. For all the man's bulk Edmund noticed how silently and lightly, almost delicately, he moved on his small feet.

The room they entered smelt musty and was shabbily furnished but Edmund noted the number of books on the shelves and the prints on the walls. Still without a word the man poured Edmund some liquor from a large pocket flask into a tumbler and waved him into a chair.

Then he said in Spanish, 'I was expecting you, Dr Hamilton, three days ago.'

Although the room was cool and the man had been wearing no jacket and no tie, he was sweating badly. His shirt, stained at the armpits, bulged over the edge of his dark linen trousers; his skin was unhealthily pale and he looked ill, as though with a fever. His hand had shaken as he had poured from the flask.

'I was delayed. What do I call you?'

'Carlos. I had hoped you would be here sooner. Now there is not much time.'

Edmund made no reply and sat silent, watching the man sweat.

'I am alone here now on the Colombia station. Or almost alone.'

'Almost?'

'Yes. There is no one of any worth. There are still one or two but they are of little use. They are only good for observation here in the city, provided I pay them enough. The killings were not even made to look like accidents. They knew whom to target. As you can see, so far I have survived.' The man drank noisily. 'They know me. How important I am they do not as yet know.'

'Are you important?'

'Yes,' said the man simply. 'But I cannot go where you have to go.'

'Where is that?'

'I shall tell you in a moment.'

'Why did you send for me to come to this house? Was that wise?'

'It was necessary. I could not come to the hotel. I could not speak in the library. To meet here is as good as anywhere. I shall be leaving this house tonight but I shall be back and it is

207

here that you will be able to find me should it become necessary.'

'I passed a woman and child in the street.'

'They are mine.'

'I was told that I would be looked after while I was in the city.'

'That is so. But it is only in the city. In any event, why should they follow you – yet.'

There can always be leaks, thought Edmund, either through the embassies or even from London. It has been known.

'For the present I doubt they know anything of you. You are a scholar working on a treatise. You have reason to be here. That was my plan.'

'And C's?'

'Yes. He is my friend.'

'Some in London are worried about you. They say that you are drinking.'

'So would they if they were here.' He poured more of the liquor from the flask into his glass. He held out the flask to Edmund who nodded and Carlos filled his glass.

'Have you heard from our people in BA?'

'Yes, I was informed that you were on your way. And only just in time. But not from the one of whom you are thinking.' He added, 'She is very capable.'

She is more than very capable, much more.

'C sent you his regards.'

'We are old comrades. I am all right.'

'C said that you would instruct me. Kent believes that all that I am to do is to take a look at the station and report on you. Some of them believe you are no longer reliable.'

'C doesn't.'

'What is it you want me to do?'

'Pay a visit', said Carlos, shifting his bulk back again in his chair, 'to somewhere I cannot go. I am known and I have no one here I could send. That is why I asked C to send me someone, someone with a reason for going where I cannot. There is a meeting. Precisely where I have not discovered but it will be somewhere near to where I will send you. Their people are already gathering and among them C believes will be the man from London.'

Edmund looked at the ugly, ungainly figure, the sweat running from his forehead down his cheeks onto his black moustache and staining further the armpits of his shirt. But C trusted Carlos. C had recruited him, years ago when Carlos must have been slim and his eyes bright.

'You were shown the photograph?' said Carlos.

'Yes,' Edmund said. 'In Brasilia.'

It had not been a good photograph, just a hazy profile of the man as he passed up the stairs of the Weisses Rossel Hotel in Padeburg beside Heinrich Bucholz.

Carlos repeated once again, as though more to convince himself than to explain to Edmund, 'I told C that I cannot go where you have to go. They know my face and I can have no reason to be there. You can have good reason. C and I planned that.'

'What reason?'

'I will explain. As I have said, at this moment they are gathering.'

'In Medellin?'

'No. Near Cali. But they came from Medellin. It is there that they have their roots. London sent me some letters, with initials found on a paper which they got off a Libyan at Heathrow. The initials were BV and LP. They were very excited but C and I knew what they meant long before London sent them.'

'What do the letters stand for?'

'Bona Ventura and Las Paza.'

'What are they?'

'BV is Bona Ventura, an hotel; LP is a place near Cali, Las Paza. That was why I needed someone like you, with your qualifications.'

'Did you send for me?'

'In a manner of speaking. C and I arranged it. You can have a convincing reason to get in.'

'Why?'

'In Las Paza there is a small, little-known museum attached to a sixteenth-century church. It is nothing much, just a room with a few objects, artefacts they call them, and old weapons. There are also some documents and church records. The place dates from the earliest days of the Europeans and some of the conquistadors are buried there. I am told that it is difficult to decipher the inscriptions on the gravestones so few have shown interest in them. The priest is a scholar. He will be interested to meet someone like you.'

'Is that the reason why I can go in? Because I could have reason to look at the records and the graves?'

Carlos nodded and took a paper from his pocket. He consulted it, reading carefully. His hand was now steadier.

'At the library during your researches tomorrow, you must seek out the issue of February 1961 of the *History Review* published by the National University. In it you will find an essay by Francisco Michaelis on Pedro de Heredia. In that essay there is a footnote referring to a priest, Juan Moreno, and the records and gravestones in his church of St Ignatius at Las Paza. Have you heard of these records?'

'I have not. Is this genuine?'

'Certainly. The existence of these church records and this small burial place is known to very few Latin American let alone any European scholars. When you come across this footnote you must tell the librarian and say that you would like to pay a quick visit to Las Paza to look at the records and the graves. You must ask the librarian to warn the priest of the reason for your researches and that you come from the English university.'

'Will the librarian prove difficult?'

'I do not see why. He himself may not know about the church of St Ignatius but like the priest Juan Moreno he will be pleased to help a visiting scholar. Can you remember the reference I have just given you?'

'I can.'

'You are certain?'

'I am.'

As Edmund had with his note at the hotel so Carlos placed the paper in an ashtray and lit it with a match, crumbling the ashes in his fingers until they had become dust.

'How shall I get to Las Paza?' asked Edmund.

'There are evening flights on some days, one in three days' time. A small aircraft flies over the mountains. You must stay at the Bona Ventura Hotel. That may be more difficult but you must insist. It is, in fact, the only hotel and they will have to take you although they will not like it. Get the Hyatt to help if you have any difficulty. Tomorrow evening when you return from the library, instruct the concierge to book you on the flight and into the hotel. Let it be known why you only wish to make a short visit. Keep to your room at the Hyatt.'

'And when I get to Las Paza and when I have studied the records and the inscriptions, what then?'

Carlos shifted uneasily in his chair. 'Have you not understood?'

I want it spelt out, thought Edmund.

'Find the place where they are meeting.'

'Who exactly are they?'

Carlos drank again noisily from his glass. 'The people who control the centre. And the Europeans who have come. Some will be at the hotel. The meeting must be at a place near to there. Las Paza is not a large town, more a village cut out of the jungle and on the edge of the plains. You are to do no more, just locate the place. Others will decide what must be done once you have found it. If the man in the photograph is there, be careful. His English name is Martin Maitland.'

'I knew that. How do I communicate with London?'

'Only through me. But do not telephone from Las Paza. You must wait until you return. While you are there I shall get the Embassy to cable saying that you are to meet the Ambassador when you return. The hotel will read it. So they will know. It might help.'

Carlos stood and looked out of the window, moving back a corner of the curtain.

'If it is necessary,' Carlos said quietly, 'I shall try to get you out from there through the north, Panama or Nicaragua. But try to get back to Bogota. Then I can send you direct to Miami.'

I shall go south, Edmund thought, to the Argentine.

'And if you are not here to help me?'

The other shrugged. 'You will be on your own. There is no one else. You will have to do your best. What C wants from you is to get in, pick up the information and get out without being identified as anything other than the visiting scholar.

211

They will be suspicious as they are of all strangers but you must avoid giving them reason to know that you have been sent. When you have left Las Paza, they must believe that you came because of the records and the tombstones and nothing else. Otherwise, your journey will have been worthless and what is planned to follow when we know the place will fail.'

'What is planned?'

'You will learn in good time. When you are there, if you judge that anything is too risky you are to return, immediately. C also sent a personal message which I don't understand. It said, "Forget the grand-uncle." Does that make sense to you?'

Edmund smiled. 'It does.'

Carlos went over to a table and wrote. 'This is the telephone number of this house. You must memorise it. Telephone only when you are away from Las Paza. When you speak, ask for Carlos and when you are asked who wants to speak with Carlos, say that you are speaking on behalf of his cousin Cesar, Jaime's son. Do not speak if it is not I who replies. Learn the number and destroy this paper tonight.'

He handed it to Edmund. Edmund took the paper and studied it. He then tore it up and handed the pieces back to the man.

'There is one thing more.' Carlos walked to the sideboard and opened a drawer. Then he turned and handed Edmund a pistol with a silencer and a magazine. 'It is a Beretta. I am told that you know how to use it.'

'I had some training on the range in London some years ago.'

'I have not given you a shoulder holster. You must carry it in the waist of your trousers under your coat at the back, with the silencer in your pocket.'

'I know. I remember how.'

'Fit the magazine and keep it loaded, and keep it with you at all times.'

Edmund loaded the gun and, unbuttoning his jacket, put it into the waistband at the back and the silencer in his trouser pocket.

'That is all,' said Carlos.

'How shall I get back to the hotel?'

'I have arranged that someone will watch. When you leave

this house turn to your left and walk until you enter a square at the end of the street. In the square walk down the left-hand side and take the second turn on your right. On your right you will see a stationary taxi. It will be waiting for you. At the hotel pay him off, like any ordinary fare.'

'Including a tip?'

'Including a very handsome tip, as befits a prosperous foreigner. Good luck.'

He smiled, a diffident, embarrassed smile and Edmund began to like him. Carlos held out his hand. The palm, when Edmund took it, was wet and slippery.

At the library on the following morning Edmund had followed the instructions he had been given and he had shown appropriate excitement at his 'discovery' of the footnote to the essay referring to the existence of the museum with its records and the small burial ground of the conquistadors in the village of Las Paza. He told the librarian that the existence of this was almost unknown, certainly in the English-speaking world. He had added with a smile that it was conceivable that one of those inscriptions could bear the name of Octavio de Coronado. That in itself, he explained, would make a trip worthwhile.

The librarian had promised to inform the priest by telegram of the visit of the English scholar and of the reason for his interest. The airplane ticket had been booked but the hotel reservation had not been so easy. The Bona Ventura was reluctant to accept another guest. Eventually the manager of the Hyatt himself had taken over the telephone and had spoken with the manager of the Bona Ventura, telling him that he knew that there was accommodation because of a cancellation which had come through the Hyatt from London cancelling a reservation for a visitor from Tripoli in Libya who had been delayed. The message had been forwarded to the Bona Ventura by the Hyatt only an hour earlier. If the reservation for a distinguished English scholar was not arranged the licence of the Bona Ventura would be enquired into not only by the Ministry for Tourism but also by the Ministry of Education. The reservation for Edmund had been reluctantly accepted and the Hyatt manager had handed him a slip of confirmation.

So it was that at seven o'clock two evenings later Edmund had found himself sitting uncomfortably cramped in a window seat with the pistol pressing into his back as the aged propeller-driven aircraft forced its way through the storm and over the peaks of the mountains to Las Paza.

TWENTY

The thunder crashed directly overhead and the flashes of lightning lit the small airfield as Edmund stumbled down the gangway from the aircraft, and with the wind and rain whipping his face, ran to the airport building. When he had reached the door he stood aside as other passengers jostled to get out of the storm and he turned and looked back at the ridge of mountains in the distance. He watched as they and the aeroplane now parked in the field in front of him were illuminated by the brilliant flashes of lightning. He marvelled that they should have flown through such a storm.

When the last of his fellow passengers had pushed through the swing door he turned and followed them up a narrow stone staircase to the immigration area on the first floor of the shabby building that served as the airport of Las Paza.

Theirs had been an internal flight from Bogota and so the twenty wet and vociferous passengers pushed past the open immigration barriers and into the baggage hall to await their bags. When Edmund reached the open barrier he wondered why this small airport should have Customs facilities. Then he remembered C's warning about the possibility of a hasty departure and that the way would be by north. The only direct link from Las Paza overseas must be with Panama or Costa Rica. But Edmund had his own plans. Whatever his instructions, when he came out he was not going north and he was not going to London. First he would be going south to Teresa.

The baggage had not yet arrived when Edmund joined the noisy circle that had gathered round a low platform in front of a hatch festooned with strips of cloth through which their bags would eventually emerge. A man who Edmund had seen sitting across the gangway on the flight and who had helped

215

retrieve one of his papers which had fallen onto the floor of the gangway when the aircraft had bucketed particularly violently, appeared beside him.

'Have you a light, señor?'

He was a short man, clean shaven with a pointed face; he reminded Edmund of a ferret. He had a hat pulled low over his head and with his American-style raincoat he looked almost a caricature of the cinema gangster. When he spoke he smiled, showing gold in his teeth. Edmund pulled out a lighter from the pocket of his wet jacket and gave it to the man who took it, offering Edmund a cheroot from the packet he had in his hand.

'No, thank you. After the liquor I drank on the flight I have a slight headache.'

The other smiled his golden smile.

'On such occasions liquor is necessary. You have not made this journey before?'

As he lit his cigar the man eyed Edmund above the flame of the lighter.

'No, never before.'

'Staying long?' The man handed the lighter back to Edmund.

'Only a few days.' Edmund turned to peer over the heads of other passengers, looking for any sign of the baggage.

'I saw that you had difficulty with your papers on the flight.'

Edmund looked down at the sly eyes above the smile with its glint of gold. 'I had hoped to do some reading but I could hardly keep my papers steady on my knee. Did I look very unhappy?'

'Not in the least, señor. You appeared most composed. The British sang-froid, I said to myself. You are British, are you not?'

'I am, but how could you tell? I pride myself on my Spanish.'

'It is excellent, señor. I happened to see that the paper I handed back to you was in English and I was sure that you were not an American. I am always interested to see a stranger on this flight. It is a change, you know.'

'You take this flight often?'

'Once each month. At this time of year there are often storms. You are here on business?'

216

'My own business.'

A veil fell over the eyes of his questioner and Edmund realised that he had been foolish. He had no need to conceal the reason for his visit; rather he needed to broadcast who he was and what he had come to do.

'If you can call it business,' he said hastily. 'I am a scholar and I am engaged in some research. I have come to see the local priest, Father Moreno, and take a look at his records.'

The other did not immediately reply. Then he said, 'He is an interesting man is Father Moreno. But old.' He bent to look around the back of the man standing in front of him. 'At last. Here comes the luggage. Forgive me, señor,' and he slipped away.

The bags were pushed by hand through the hatch and piled onto the wooden platform. The crowd pushed forward to get at them. Edmund, able to see over the heads of the others who now surrounded the baggage as it was piled on the platform, waited for the appearance of his grip. He noticed that his was the last bag to appear and by then the Ferret had disappeared. He grabbed it and walked to the exit.

The thunder and lightning had ceased but the rain was still heavy and it was hot and steamy. He joined the end of a queue lined up under a shelter, the rain beating a tattoo on its tin roof as they waited for the taxis, old battered American saloons, which at infrequent intervals drew up to collect their fares. Edmund was wet from the dash across the tarmac to the airport; he was uncomfortable and tired. It was half an hour before his turn came.

'The Bona Ventura Hotel,' he said and climbed in. The taxi driver looked over his shoulder at Edmund and then put his head out of the window.

'Anyone for the Bona Ventura?'

Two men whom he had not seen in the queue approached the driver's door.

'Get in,' the driver said to them.

Edmund squeezed up against the side of the car as the others slid in beside him. Then the car moved off.

In the darkness Edmund could not make out the faces of the other two passengers, only that they were wearing caps with peaks such as he had seen in Eastern Europe and raincoats. All three of them balanced their bags on their knees. No one spoke.

After a time Edmund leant forward and enquired, 'Is it far to the hotel?'

'Ten kilometres,' replied the driver.

Edmund turned to the passenger on his right. 'Have you enough room?' he asked.

The man did not reply but shifted slightly. Nothing more was said until the car turned off the road up a steep and winding drive and drew up before the door of a low, straggling building.

As Edmund opened the door and got out of the car, the man who had been furthest from Edmund said, 'We will share the cost.' And to the driver, 'How much is the fare?'

He spoke Spanish with an accent; German, Edmund guessed.

'Seventy-five American,' the driver replied. Edmund was about to protest but the man had taken a clip of money from his inside pocket and peeled off three notes.

'Fifty,' he said to the driver. 'Now go.'

The car drove away leaving the three of them in the rain by the front entrance.

'That was exorbitant,' Edmund said as they got under the shelter of the porch.

'You may pay ten,' said the man with the clip of money.

'Certainly not,' said Edmund. 'I must pay my share.'

'If you wish.'

Before Edmund could reply the man pushed open the door and the three emerged into the foyer of the hotel. The two pulled off their caps, shaking and slapping them against their legs so that the rainwater dripped onto the bare wood of the floor. Edmund stood behind them blinking a little in the light. The man who had paid the taxi looked about fifty, with close-cropped iron-grey hair; the other, younger, was more hefty. In the light they appeared as German as they had sounded in the dark.

Edmund looked around the foyer, at the cheap wooden sofas and chairs, the few worn rugs scattered on the floor, the paint peeling from the walls, which were decorated with posters advertising liquor and cigarettes. About half a dozen hotel guests were sitting in the room, glasses in their hands. Edmund noted that only one was a woman. The room was dense with tobacco smoke but strangely hushed. As his fellow passengers walked ahead of him to the reception desk, the older man nodded to the people in the room but none spoke.

At the far end of the foyer Edmund saw that open doors led onto a verandah and a roofed passageway open to the gardens on each side and he could see the slanting sheets of rain silhouetted against lamplight beyond. While the two who had shared the taxi were at the desk registering, Edmund strolled over to the verandah and stood at the entrance and stared through the rain at the garden, which was faintly lit by lamps hanging from the roof of the passageway. He leant against the open verandah door and was conscious of the attention he was attracting.

From what he could make out in the dim light, the hotel consisted of a central block with cottages strung around a central swimming pool. The whole was laid out in a series of ovals. The innermost was the pool itself with its paved surround; next a border of flowering shrubs mounting to the height of the windows of each cottage but higher in the gaps in between; then the outer oval formed by the ring of cottages themselves, and finally the outer open passageway circling and giving access to the doors of the cottages and which ran left and right from where he stood at the entrance to the central block. This consisted of the hotel offices, the dining-room and bar, which he could see to his right, and the foyer through which they had entered the hotel. Next morning he was to see that the whole property lay within a compound bordered by tall trees and a high stone wall.

After a minute or so he turned and wandered casually back to the reception desk where his taxi companions were completing their registration. He waited behind them and heard the clerk tell a young porter, 'Number twenty-one.'

The porter took their bags and led them to the passage. They were sharing a room.

'My name is Hamilton. A reservation was made for me in Bogota.'

He had deliberately raised his voice so that people could hear what he was saying and the talk in the room behind him, which had risen while he had waited behind the two Germans,

219

became quiet again. He adopted the rank which had been given to him elsewhere.

'Professor Hamilton. I have the booking slip here.'

He handed over the slip which had been given to him by the manager in the Hyatt in Bogota. The desk clerk who had been writing took the paper from him and studied the ledger in front of him.

'When was this?' he asked.

'Yesterday. By telephone. I had been advised to come to this hotel by the National Library where I have been working. I have come to see a Father Moreno, to consult his records.'

The clerk again turned the pages of the ledger. 'I can find no reservation booked by the Hyatt Hotel. What was the name?'

'Hamilton. You must have the reservation. I was beside the Manager of the Hyatt when he telephoned. He spoke about the Ministry of Education. I heard the conversation.'

'Your passport.'

Edmund handed it to him.

'One moment. I shall check with the office.' The clerk disappeared into an inner room. Edmund turned to face into the room behind him, leaning against the desk. He saw that the faces of the people in the room were turned towards him, listening. They made no attempt to disguise their interest. The clerk returned.

'I find that we have the reservation. Two nights, for Professor Hamilton. There is a message which has been left for you. It is from the priest.'

The clerk pushed an envelope across the desk and turned the book for Edmund to sign. Edmund put the envelope unopened into his pocket and signed the book.

'My passport, please.'

'It will be returned to you tomorrow. It has to be registered with the police.'

The young porter appeared at his side and took from him his grip.

'Number twenty-six,' said the clerk.

Edmund followed the porter through the silent foyer to the verandah and into the passage. As they walked he heard behind him the conversation in the foyer resume.

The porter led him along the covered passageway until they reached the door of cottage number 26 which, with the pool in between, was at the end of the oval compound almost directly opposite the opening from the foyer from which they had come. The porter unlocked the door and switched on the light. It was a small room with whitewashed walls, furnished by a single bed, a chest, a hanging cupboard and a deal table and chair. The room was close and smelt damp. The porter threw the grip onto the bed and walked to a curtain on the far side of the room and drew it aside.

'The shower,' he said. Then he walked over to the air-conditioner under the window and switched it on. It did not respond and the porter gave it a kick but it remained silent. He shrugged.

'That usually makes them work. I will get it fixed, perhaps tomorrow. In the meantime . . .'

He threw open the window from which Edmund could see the shrubs and the pool with its paved surround and the entrance to the verandah beyond. The porter turned and looked at Edmund.

'You do not look like a Cuban. Are you an East German?'

'No, I am English.'

'I thought you were not a Cuban,' the man said, examining the notes Edmund gave him.

'I would prefer American. Have you American?'

Edmund gave him a five-dollar bill.

'The dining-room is opposite the reception. There is still an hour for dinner, then the kitchen closes. You must hurry if you wish to eat.'

'This rain,' said Edmund, 'is it going to last?'

'It will be gone by morning. You speak good Spanish for a foreigner.'

When he had left Edmund drew the curtains across the open window and went round the room, opening the drawers of the chest, testing the shower, examining the light fittings and the telephone beside the bed. He assumed that the telephone and perhaps the whole room might be bugged but he would not know how to find any device. He opened his grip and began to unpack. He noticed that the notes he had laid on the top of

221

his clothes when he had packed in Bogota were out of order and he remembered that his had been the last bag to appear at the airport. At some time on the journey someone had opened it.

When he had removed and hung his damp clothes on the three wire hangers in the hanging cupboard he looked at the message the clerk had given him at the desk. It was a note written in English under the heading, 'The Presbytery, St Ignatius' Church, Las Paza.' It was dated that day.

I am truly happy to welcome you to Las Paza. Señor Fernandez in Bogota has cabled to me of your interest in the parish records and the headstones in the graveyard. I shall be honoured to show them to you. Perhaps you will come to me here at eleven o'clock tomorrow morning. Take a taxi from the hotel. The church is well known and you should have no difficulty. I shall look forward to seeing you.

The letter was signed, 'Juan Moreno'.

Edmund took a shower in tepid water and put on a fresh white shirt and his spare jacket and trousers. He stuffed the pistol in the waistband at the back under the jacket. He measured the gap between the hangers in the cupboard and memorised the position in which he had placed his underclothes in the chest. Then he took his briefcase and walked along the passage back to the main building.

The foyer was now empty and he went straight to the dining-room. When he entered the half-dozen diners looked up and watched him. There was no sign of his two companions from the taxi. He was left standing for a moment until a young waitress came over and greeted him.

'Señor?' she said, smiling.

It was the first smile he had received since he had arrived at the Bona Ventura.

'You are alone?'

He smiled in return. 'I am.'

222

She led him to a table in the centre of the room and smiled again as she handed him a menu. She was young and pretty and he thought of Teresa.

'There is only chicken,' said the girl.

'That will do very well. Is there any wine?'

'Yes, but it is very expensive.'

'Never mind. I am tired and I need it.'

Before she returned with the wine he had opened the brief-case and taken out some of his notes which he laid beside him and made a show of studying. When she brought the bottle of Bulgarian red wine and had poured some into his glass and as he raised the glass to his lips, he saw at a table in the corner of the dining-room his friend from the aeroplane with the face like a ferret. The man was looking straight at Edmund who smiled at him but the man dropped his eyes, rose from his table and walked from the dining-room.

Edmund began to eat and looked around at the other diners. There were two pairs and a table of four at which was the only woman. They all appeared to be Europeans. There was no sign of the Germans. The room, like the foyer earlier, was curiously hushed.

He finished his meal and left the dining-room. The other diners remained at their tables and did not look up as he passed by them.

His room was a little fresher when he returned to it. He studied the clothes in the chest and the hangers in the cup-board. As he had expected all had been slightly shifted. He undressed, leaning the chair under the handle of the door. He thought of closing and bolting the window but he knew he would be unable to sleep in the stuffy atmosphere so he decided to leave it open. He took the pistol into the bed with him and left on the bedside lamp. He slept fitfully.

He woke early. The rain had gone and the sunlight streamed into the room. He put his head out of the window and over the border of shrubs he could see the inviting water of the pool only a few yards from his window. No one seemed to be about. He put the pistol in the pocket of his gown and went from his room down a path beside his cottage to the pool. As he swam he kept his eye on the gown but his solitary swim went undisturbed and he climbed from the water into the sunshine and dried himself and felt the delicious warmth of the paving stones beneath his feet. He stood examining the flowers and shrubs in the border around the pool. The sun was shining and everything was quiet and very peaceful. Then he remembered that someone had been through his bag during the journey and that someone had visited his room while he had dined.

Back in his cottage he dressed and again tucked the gun in his waistband under his jacket. He was becoming used to the feel of it. He walked to the dining-room but it was still too early and no one was yet about. Then the pretty girl appeared from the kitchen and he asked her to bring coffee to a table in the sun on the verandah. After about half an hour the men whom he had seen the previous night began to pass him in pairs as they went to the dining-room. He nodded to them but they ignored him. As they passed he studied their faces. There was no sign of the woman.

Then he saw the two who had shared the taxi. He got to his feet and greeted them.

'Good morning. Sunshine at last. That was a rough journey. I certainly did not enjoy that flight.'

The older man who had paid off the taxi replied, 'It is certainly a better morning. I trust that the fine weather will last.'

'I never paid you my share of the taxi last night. I am so sorry.'

Edmund held out a twenty-dollar bill. The man looked at it and then took the bill and put it in his pocket.

'Tell me, do the taxis here always make such exorbitant charges or did we run into a rogue? I have not been here before and I shall need a taxi later this morning to visit the local priest who has some documents which I want to examine for some research I am engaged upon.'

The man was staring at Edmund. 'It was late and there was a storm. It was to be expected that he would charge as he did.'

'Well, I hope my trip this morning won't be quite as expensive. My name is Hamilton. I am a professor, from England. Do you know this place well?'

224

The younger man had walked past Edmund and stood waiting for his companion in the doorway. The other was still facing him.

'I have been here before. The taxis are expensive. Now, if you will excuse me.' He did not give his name.

Edmund stood aside. 'I am so sorry, I was keeping you. But I like to pay my debts.'

The man with the grey hair looked at Edmund, then nodded and the two men entered the dining-room.

I shall remember you, thought Edmund; and doubtless you will remember me.

He went through to reception. The same clerk was behind the desk.

'I am Professor Hamilton.'

'Yes. How can I help you?'

'I am going to St Ignatius' Church later this morning to visit Father Moreno. I have to be there at eleven o'clock. Can you get me a taxi?'

'I can.'

'At what time should I leave?'

'I shall have the taxi here at half-past ten.'

'I probably may not have the time but is it possible to hire a car? I should like to see a little of the country.'

'I know of no one who hires out a car. But a taxi will take you where you wish to go.'

'Then it will have to be a taxi if I have the time.'

Before Edmund's taxi arrived at half-past ten to take him to Father Moreno no other guest had used the pool; no one had strolled around the garden; and by ten o'clock the whole place was deserted and as silent as had been the room that he had entered out of the rain on the night before. While Edmund sat on the verandah apparently working at his notes, two cars arrived and the guests were borne away. Edmund was left alone in the empty hotel.

TWENTY-ONE

Juan Moreno was an old man, his lined face the colour of parchment. Despite the heat he was wearing a long black soutane and he led Edmund through the small presbytery into the garden at the back of the house, bade him be seated and disappeared to fetch coffee. Edmund sat in a wicker chair basking in the sunshine, facing the garden with its mass of exotic blooms and clouds of brilliantly coloured butterflies, which hovered over the flowers. A constant procession of tropical birds, brighter than any kingfisher on the banks of an English river, dived down from the trees to a small pool to drink and then swooped back to perch in the foliage from which they had come. The only sound came from the call of the birds and the plash of water from the small fountain.

Father Moreno returned with the coffee.

'Your garden, Father, is enchanting.'

'It is said that some of these plants and flowers were originally brought here in the eighteenth century by the great botanist José Celestino Mutis. You have heard of him?'

'I have.'

'But I do not know if that is true. Remove your jacket if you so wish. It is already hot.' He poured the coffee. Edmund could feel the pistol against his back under his jacket.

'I am fine, thank you, Father. The sun and the warmth are a delight for those of us who are not used to them.'

'Ah, you English. You are so formal. But soon it will become much hotter and then you will relent. You come, I am told, from Cambridge?'

'I do. I am a don at St Peter's and as it is our Long Vacation I am taking the opportunity to do some research on a study I am doing on the sixteenth-century conquerors.'

226

'I do not know St Peter's College but many years ago I visited Cambridge to stay with a Benedictine who had been with me in Rome. We had become friends when he was at the English college and later the Benedictines gave him charge of their house in Cambridge. Like me, if he is alive, he must be very old. You speak excellent Spanish.'

'My ancestors on my mother's side of the family are Spanish. It was she who made sure that I could speak the language. The family connection is one of the reasons why I chose Latin American studies.'

'Your study, you say, is on the early conquerors? Is it confined to Colombia?'

'No. It will also concern the Argentine and Brazil.'

'Then it will need to be a very great tome.'

'I know, and it will take much time. I have much research to do. I have been working in both the Argentine and Brazil.'

'How did you learn of my modest records and of the graves here at St Ignatius'?'

'By chance. I was working at the library at the university at Bogota and I came across a footnote to an essay on Pedro de Heredia by Francisco Michaelis, which was published by the National University of Bogota in, I believe, February 1961. The note referred to a paper which you had given to a conference in Medellin in 1957.'

'That is long ago, but I remember the paper.'

'Apparently you drew attention to the little-known burial plots here at St Ignatius' in Las Paza, the headstones of which had become indecipherable but which you believed mark the graves of sixteenth-century Spanish soldiers. I was very interested since I had an ancestor Octavio de Coronado from Seville who, according to family tradition, had marched with Gonzalo de Quesada in an expedition from Bogota to the interior in 1539. His fate was never discovered. When I read the footnote about your paper I was greatly excited.'

The priest nodded, his tired old eyes never leaving the face of his visitor.

Edmund went on, 'Do you remember that scene in the *Poema del Cid* when the Cid becomes so excited at meeting his

227

sovereign on the banks of the Tagus that the great warrior ate the very grass at the King's feet?'

'I do.'

Edmund smiled at the priest. 'When I chanced on that footnote in the library of the university in Bogota, I did not quite fall to the ground and eat the *Review* in which Michaelis' essay appeared, but I confess that I did kiss it. I do not know what the librarian must have thought for I made rather an exhibition of myself. As you must know, scholars when they stumble on a discovery can behave very intemperately.'

Father Moreno did not smile in reply. His eyes were still fixed on Edmund, studying him with such intensity that Edmund began to grow uncomfortable. He did not like to lie to this old man.

'It is not always wise to be intemperate,' the priest said at last. 'Are you as intemperate a man as you confess that you are a scholar?'

Edmund smiled again. 'I hope not. If I am, I blame it on my Spanish blood.'

'It is good that you have that. It will help you in your studies to understand this strange country – and especially this unhappy corner of it.'

'Unhappy? It does not appear to be unhappy here in your garden.'

The old man was silent and then said, 'This is only an oasis. But I can understand your interest when you came upon that footnote. Few have heard of Michaelis and even fewer of Juan Moreno.'

He turned his eyes from Edmund and looked over the garden. Then he said gravely, 'It is many years since anyone has shown any interest. Nowadays few visitors come to Las Paza. It was not always so.'

'Why is that?'

The old man raised a hand to his brow and for a moment Edmund thought that the priest was about to make the sign of the cross. But he merely rested his forehead in his hand, the long fingers as slender as twigs and even whiter than the pallor of the skin of the old face against which they rested. The back of the hand was mottled with the marks of extreme old age.

228

'I cannot remember when any stranger last came to my church to worship, let alone to study my records. Some strangers come to the town, but only those who have been invited and they are not the kind who would come to visit me or my church.'

'Invited by whom?'

'By the new people. Since they have come my people have grown fewer. Nowadays they do not like to be seen coming to Mass at St Ignatius'.'

'Who are the new people?'

'The ones who have bought all the land, in particular the land around the estate of the Villa Rica where long ago I used to stay with the family who once owned it. The son and I were at school together and I visited often as a boy. But I am no longer welcome there.'

'The Villa Rica? That is a famous name for a house.'

'You remember that name?'

'Was it not the name of the place on the coast from which Hernán Cortés set out in 1519 on his march overland to Tenochtitlan and the conquest of Mexico?'

'It was. The Villa Rica de Vera Cruz.'

'But that is in Mexico, far to the north.'

'It is. When the Sanchez-Barba family came to Colombia over two hundred years after Cortés, they named the house which they built the Villa Rica. One of their forebears had been the godson of Cortés. The Sanchez-Barba became a famous family in this country.'

'Is the family still here?'

'No, none is left. They were bought out and driven away. For two hundred years the family had lived in the house which they had built, lived there through the time of the *audiencia* – do you know of that?'

'I do.'

'They were prominent through the years of the Viceroyalty and they joined the Great Liberator, Simon Bolivar, in the uprising in Bogota in 1810.'

'What happened to the house which they built?'

'The family stayed on, but the estate fell into ruin and more and more land was sold. Then a year ago the new people came.

229

They bought the villa and I am told that they have spent millions in restoring it. They bought all the land belonging to the people who had been given it in the re-distribution thirty years earlier. It was illegal but no one stopped them. They paid great prices.'

'Who are they?'

'They call themselves the Colombia Syndicate.'

'What is the Syndicate?'

'They say that they are mine-owners and plantation managers. They came from Medellin. They study the land and what lies under it. When I complain of what they have done to the people by taking the land, they tell the people that I am old and soured because the people are deserting the Faith.'

'Las Paza is not far from Cali, of which I have often heard. And of Medellin. Was not that the city where the bishops of Latin America proclaimed the Christian crusade against poverty?'

'That is so. Now it is known for something different.'

'So I believe.'

'Medellin and Cali. The message now they bring from those places is one of death and killing, and it is always the people who suffer at the hands of them all, the soldiers included.'

'Is the Syndicate connected with such people?'

The priest turned his old eyes from the garden back to Edmund, who in turn looked away, avoiding the old man's gaze, watching instead the flight of one of the scarlet-plumed birds as it dipped and drank and swooped away.

'Why do you ask?'

'Because of what you have just said.'

'No, they would tell you. Most certainly no. They say that they are interested in the land, the crops and the minerals. I never now visit the place where I played as a boy for they know that I accuse them of having corrupted the people. They reply that I am old and make up fantasies and that the people are happier not to believe and are glad to stay away from the church.'

'Where is this place?'

'Thirty kilometres from here.' The eyes of the old man were fixed on Edmund. 'Why are you interested?'

'I am only interested in your story.'

There was a silence and then the priest said quietly, 'How did you find that essay by Michaelis?'

'By chance, Father, by chance.'

'I am beginning to wonder,' said the priest. He stretched out one of his old hands and laid it on Edmund's arm. 'I should not have spoken as I have. At the Villa Rica they say that I am bitter and foolish and that I see spectres where none exist because my people have deserted my God. But why should you be interested?'

'Because of what you have told me about the Sanchez-Barba family. I would like to see the house which they built. My family too has a connection with Hernán Cortés.' The old man had turned his gaze away from Edmund and was for a time silent.

Then he said, 'That would not be advisable. No one now welcomes strangers in Las Paza. A foreigner at the hotel will have already aroused interest.'

'But it is scholarship which brought me to Las Paza. To see you.'

After a pause, the priest said, 'Was it, my son? Was it only scholarship?'

Before Edmund could reply he again put out his hand and gripped Edmund's arm with a strength he had not expected in one so old. 'As I said, I should not have spoken to you as I have. They are right. I am old and foolish.' He rose slowly to his feet. 'Whoever you are and whatever you have come here to do, I can only warn you. It would not be wise for any stranger to visit that place. Now as you have come to me as a scholar, we had better be about your work. Then, if you are wise, you will go home.'

Edmund too got to his feet.

'Come with me.' The priest without speaking further led Edmund through the garden along a path beside the pool until they came to a door in a high stone wall. He took some keys from the pocket of his soutane and opened the door. They passed from the garden into a tangled neglected plot of land over which the jungle had taken complete possession.

231

'First,' said the priest, 'let us look at what I can show you in the church.'

They spent two hours over the records, principally records of births, christenings and burials and the deeds of some conveyances and some letters on parchment. One was a letter dated 27 July 1606 from Cordoba, a letter from a mother to a Jesuit priest, José Molar, begging him to return to her as she was old and ill.

'The Jesuits of those times were great men. Now –' the old man shook his head – 'I do not understand some of their younger ones.'

There was no entry in the church records of burials or among the other scraps of documents which bore the name Coronado and when Edmund had finished his study of them Juan Moreno showed him the church plate and furnishings, a chalice inscribed with the sacred initials IHS, the name of the maker from Seville and the date June 1548. Finally he led Edmund into a small bare room off the vestry where on a plain wooden table laid out and marked with tags in fading brown ink were pieces of Indian pottery, some sixteenth-century copper coins and a helmet and breastplate of the same period. Along the length of the table lay a pike. It was not much of a show.

'They were found in the churchyard. They were displayed like this three-quarters of a century ago when I came here as a boy with my friend Luiz Sanchez-Barba.'

The heat was intense and the priest sat.

Edmund said, 'Now may I see the stones?'

'You go,' said the old man. 'You will find the gravestones on the far side. Only a few are visible. The jungle has the rest. I would like to pray. I shall wait for you in the church. It is cooler there.'

Edmund walked out into the heat and through the shrubs and jungle followed a line of gravestones that began near to the church and then disappeared into the undergrowth. The inscriptions were so worn that although he rubbed at the surface of each he could make out only the cross cut into the stone. On four only could he decipher dates – the earliest 1541, then 1604, 1675, 1742. The names were gone.

The jungle had taken over the bulk of the graveyard but as

232

Edmund stood up to his waist in the tangled rope-like vine and thorn and grass, with the sweat pouring from him and with his jacket still concealing the pistol in the waist of his canvas trousers, which had already been torn in one place, he felt that if he had been able to penetrate deeper into the jungle he might have come upon the grave of his ancestor Coronado. But he could not and he contented himself by imagining that the stone for which he searched was the stone with the date 1541. For Coronado had disappeared in the expedition of 1539 so Edmund stood on the ground by that stone and thought of the bones that lay in the earth beneath him; and then of the priest praying in the church. So he too prayed, for his ancestor and for himself and for Teresa.

He pushed his way through the undergrowth back towards the church. When he had reached the clearing by the door, he saw a figure standing in the distance beside the high wall and the gate through which he and Juan Moreno had passed from the garden three hours earlier. Then it disappeared but not before he recognised that it was the figure of the man with a face like a ferret.

Back at the presbytery the priest told Edmund he had no telephone to summon a taxi but that he would send him to the village by cart. While they waited for the priest's servant to get the horse from the field and harness it, they ate cold meat and a mess of manioc and drank some wine.

'I have one final request, Father. Is there any one in the village from whom I might be able to hire a car for a few hours? As I have come so far, I would like to see something of the country before I leave.'

The priest looked at him across the table over the remains of the meal. He shook his head. 'I suspected that it was not only scholarship which brought you to me. I have told you about the place. Is that not enough?'

'I have come a long way, Father.'

For a time neither spoke. Then the priest rose and walked wearily to his desk. 'You are foolish and very stubborn. But if I do not help, you will try someone else and you will certainly

233

be betrayed. With me, there is at least a chance.'

The priest wrote and handed the note to Edmund.

'Give this to Pedro Barra. He is a good man and he will do what you ask.'

'Have you a map of the countryside so that I could see where I might tour?'

The old man brought an old heavy atlas bound in faded red leather. He turned the pages. 'This is a plate of the district. The house I told you of lies to the south, in a valley in the foothills. It cannot now be seen from the road. To see it you should climb the hills.' He pointed with his thin white finger. 'Twenty kilometres from the village as you enter the foothills, there is a track. Follow this for two kilometres. If I remember right there should be some rocks on your left and behind them there used to be a clearing from which there lay a path up the hill. You must climb, bearing always to the left.'

He sat and repeated the gesture which he had made in the garden, putting his hand to his head.

'The path may have gone by now. We knew the forest well when we were children. When you reach the summit you will see the house beneath you. Do not try to go any closer.' He placed both hands palm down over the atlas.

'If you are detected and you are fortunate they may only stop you and turn you back.' He closed the atlas. 'If they find you they will know who showed you the way, but I am old and it does not matter what they do to me. If they are whom I suspect they may be, you will be in danger.'

'I understand.'

'I do not know why I help you. Perhaps it is because I hope that those who sent you may help my people.' He got to his feet and Edmund stood facing him. 'You remind me of my English friend, the Benedictine, fifty years ago in Rome. He too was headstrong. He and I tried to help the people hiding from the fascists and the Germans and he enjoyed the danger. You are like him.' Then the old man bent forward and took Edmund in his arms. Surprised, Edmund felt the frail body pressed against his.

The old man led Edmund out of the house to where the

horse and cart were standing waiting for him. Edmund climbed up beside the driver.

Moreno looked up at him and said, 'You did not find what you came for at the church. You may not find it where you now plan to go. Are you so determined? Will you not go home?'

Edmund smiled down at him.

'I shall go home, Father. Soon.'

The priest lifted his hand in a blessing. The driver waved his whip and the cart rumbled off. Edmund turned back and saw the old man standing in the centre of the dirt road. Edmund waved but the priest stood motionless. At the bend he was lost from sight.

Edmund stopped the cart at the outskirts of the village and gave the driver some money, sending him back to the presbytery. Then he walked along what served as the main street past the mean shops and houses until he came to the entrance to the yard to which Juan Moreno had directed him. He went through a gate and into a shed, which appeared to serve for an office. He asked the woman behind the counter if he could speak with Pedro Barra and handed to her the note from the priest.

While he waited he heard the clatter of a helicopter and he went to the door and looked up at the sky. The machine passed overhead heading south.

It had come from the airport at Bogota where in the afternoon it had picked up a single passenger, a man with striking blue eyes. When the helicopter landed in a paddock some thirty kilometres from where Edmund was standing in Pedro Barra's yard, the passenger hurried into the house.

As Pedro Barra led Edmund to the car in the garage yard, he said, 'The priest wrote that you are an historian from England.'

'I am. I have spent the morning with him at the church and now I would like to see a little of the countryside before I return to Bogota tomorrow on my way home to England.'

Pedro Barra looked at him. Then he said, 'You only require the car for one day?'

'Yes. I have to catch the eight o'clock plane to Bogota

tomorrow morning. I should like to keep the car overnight and bring it to you tomorrow at about half-past six and hire you to drive me to the airport. Taxis seem a little unreliable. Would that be possible?'

'If that is your wish.'

Edmund paid in advance in American dollars.

'Have you any particular place which you wish to visit?'

Edmund shook his head. 'No. I would just like to make a small tour.'

'These are troubled times, señor. I would not advise you to travel south. That way you would encounter patrols.'

'Army patrols?'

'Militia patrols, and they are often not in uniform. There are frequently bandits in the neighbourhood and sometimes the peasants gather in bands to protect themselves. If you are stopped by a patrol, do as they require. They are not friendly to strangers.'

'Thank you for your advice.'

Edmund started the engine and drove the car out of the yard, and with Barra watching he turned north. Outside the village he stopped the car.

He had a choice. He could either return to Bogota and report to London what he had been told by the priest and leave what followed to others. Or he could go on. To return and report undetected or at least unexposed, was what Carlos wanted. No trouble, that was what he had said. But when he had got back, what had he to report? A mysterious place which he had never seen? The suspicions of an old embittered priest whose people were deserting him? On the other hand, for a few hours he now had a car. Only a few kilometres down the road to the south lay a place that could be, might be, the control centre for which C was searching. If Juan Moreno's memory was right, he might be able to climb to the summit of the hill, see the house and get away unseen. Then at least he would be able to report personally on the lie of the land, which he would have seen for himself. Whatever Carlos had said, now that he was so near and had the opportunity which Moreno's memories and Barra's car presented, he could not be expected tamely to turn back. Above all, he did not wish to. He turned the car and drove south.

The small town of Las Paza and the out-lying village of St Ignatius lay in the Valle de Cauca some miles from the city of Cali, bordered on each side by the mountains. He drove through well-farmed plantations of sugar cane and tobacco and then, after a dozen kilometres, through a vast expanse of pasture, tall grasses which spread on either side as far as the eye could see. He met little traffic, an occasional ancient lorry or bullock cart meandering slowly in the centre of the road. After another ten kilometres the road entered the foothills and began to wind between the hills densely covered in forest. He slowed, searching for the track; several times he stopped fearing that he had passed it. Eventually he found it, the narrow overgrown entrance barely visible from the scrub which bordered it. He turned the car off the road, and it bumped along the scarred surface of the track as he swung the wheel trying to avoid the ruts and stones, some as large as boulders. He came to the outcrop of rock of which Juan Moreno had spoken and stopped. He got out of the car and pushed his way through the bushes and brambles beside the rocks and saw that beyond lay a clearing. He drove the car slowly off the track breaking through the bushes until it was into the clearing.

The hill and forest towered above him and he began to climb on foot. He could find no path but he remembered to keep bearing to his left. After half an hour of difficult struggling through the tangle of briar and undergrowth he came upon what must once have been a mountain path, and the going grew easier. The bush thinned and an hour later he reached the summit where he entered a belt of trees and pushed on out of the trees waist high in fern and bracken. Then, very abruptly, he stopped. He was on the edge of a precipice; a crevasse lay open almost beneath his feet.

He looked across it and on its far side he could see another line of rock, but lower than that on which he stood so that from where he was he could see beyond a vast plain and in the distance the mountains. At his feet was the gorge narrowly separating and dividing the two lines of hills, great walls of rock that fell sheer to a narrow valley at their base. In places trees

237

and bush clung to the sides of the rock partially concealing from the summit what lay below.

Edmund dropped to the ground, crawled to the edge of the gorge and peered down. There directly below him at its foot he saw the Villa Rica.

But it was more, much more than a villa; it was a great house, fitting snugly into the narrow valley between two walls of rock and half-hidden from above by the overhanging trees. He had to shift his position to get a better view and then he could see more clearly the shape and size of the extraordinary building that lay directly below him, neatly fitting into the valley at the foot of the two cliffs on either side. The centre of the house was a block built of stone in the Palladian style with a portico supported by pillars and steps. Flanking this centre block were two shorter and lower wings, at the ends of which walls swept forward at right angles close to the sides of the enclosing hills to meet at a gatehouse in a cross-wall, the whole forming a narrow rectangle. From this gatehouse there wound a long drive, and as the walls of the hills fell away it emerged into a thick belt of trees and ended at another gatehouse on the edge of the road. Behind the house he could see stables and outbuildings; beyond, walled gardens and a narrow fenced paddock. Figures were moving between both of the gatehouses and parked in the paddock at the rear was a helicopter. To land even a helicopter in the narrow space between those walls of rock would require considerable navigational skill.

For several minutes he lay looking at the amazing panorama beneath him. Suddenly he felt a blow in the small of his back and turning he saw that it had come from a jab with the barrel of a rifle. He rolled onto his side and saw standing above him a burly figure in a dark hat and a ruana or poncho cloak, a bandoleer across his chest, his rifle now a few inches from Edmund's face. Very slowly and deliberately, his eyes never leaving those of the man holding the rifle, Edmund got to his feet. As he did so the man worked the bolt and raised the rifle to his shoulder. Behind him Edmund could see two other men, similarly dressed and armed, emerging from the trees.

The man with the rifle pointed at Edmund's chest said, 'What are you doing here?'

238

'I have been walking in the forest,' said Edmund. 'I was lost and I found myself here.'

'Where is your permit to walk on this land?'

'Permit?' said Edmund. 'I did not know that I needed a permit.' He could feel the sweat running down his back. If they searched him they would find the pistol.

'How did you get here?'

'I climbed. I have come by car from the village. I left it below. I am a stranger, a visitor. I am staying at Las Paza and I wanted to see a little of the countryside. I was told about the house down there and I heard that it could be seen from the hill. Is that not allowed?'

'Where did you come from?'

'I am a professor, a foreigner, from England.'

'No, where in the village have you come from?'

'I am staying at the hotel in the town.'

The burly man turned to the others and they spoke together. Edmund could not hear what they said.

The man turned back to Edmund. 'Where is the car?'

'Down below, where I began my walk.'

'Take me to it.'

Edmund led him back to the trees. The man called to his companions, telling them to warn the gatehouse. Edmund and the leader of the patrol began to descend the path that he had found on his climb.

'How did you know of this path?'

'I came upon it by chance on my walk.'

It took them half an hour to reach the car.

'Get in.'

The man clambered in beside Edmund, putting his rifle between his knees. He took out a handgun from his belt and held it in his left hand, the hand nearest to Edmund.

'Drive,' he said.

Edmund drove slowly through the scrub and out onto the track. The man gestured to him to turn back onto the road.

'Turn left.'

So they were going to the house. Edmund glanced at the man beside him.

'I am sorry if I was trespassing. I am a scholar and I am most

239

interested in the history of that wonderful house. I suppose that you must be one of the gamekeepers?'

'Drive,' repeated the man. 'And be silent.'

They stopped at the first gatehouse at the entrance off the road that Edmund had seen from the hill. The trees wholly concealed what lay within.

'Give me the keys of the car.'

Edmund handed them to him. As the man got out, the gate-keeper came from the gatehouse; he too was armed with a rifle. They stood talking for a moment; then the man who had accompanied Edmund went into the gatehouse while the gatekeeper waited, his rifle trained on the car.

The leader of the patrol returned. He gave the keys to Edmund and said, 'Drive.'

The gate swung open, operated electrically, and they drove down the long winding drive to where the cliffs of the hills rose like walls on either side. As they approached the second gatehouse the gate swung open.

'Drive to the front of the house by the steps.'

Edmund did so.

'Get out,' said the man.

When they were out of the car the man gestured with his rifle towards the steps and Edmund began to climb. He knew that the man was standing at the bottom of the steps with his rifle pointed at his back.

As he mounted the broad stone steps, he looked up. Between the high pillars of the portico stood a tall bearded man in an immaculate white suit. As Edmund approached he threw aside his cigar; he was smiling.

When Edmund had reached the top, the tall man thrust out his hand.

'Welcome, Dr Hamilton. Welcome to the Villa Rica.'

TWENTY-TWO

'We are most flattered, Dr Hamilton, that you have honoured us with a visit. My name is Vincente Consuero. I am the Administrator here.' He took Edmund's hand. 'I must apologise for the manner in which you have been conducted here. We have, unfortunately, too many trespassers and you failed to warn us of your intention to visit.'

Edmund looked at the immaculate figure before him, very conscious of his own torn and dirty clothing.

'It is I', he said at last, 'who should apologise. I fear that I have been trespassing. I only heard of the Villa Rica this morning when I was in the village and as I leave Las Paza in the morning I thought I would drive over and walk through the woods and try to find it.'

'And found us you have. But why, Dr Hamilton, why did you not think of warning us that you would be coming instead of scrambling about over our hills and through our forest?'

'I fear I came upon the spur of the moment.'

Consuero was smiling. 'Ah, these sudden impulses. The hotel, I am sure would have been happy to have telephoned to us and you would have avoided your, I fear, somewhat undignified arrest.'

'I have not been back to the hotel since I learnt of the existence of the villa. As I said, I came on the spur of the moment. I apologise for my discourtesy.'

'Of course. But you will agree I am sure that in these troubled times it was perhaps a little thoughtless? As a result, instead of coming to us you have been brought to us. But was it, perhaps,' and still smiling he put his hand on Edmund's arm, 'just the whim of the absent-minded professor?' His smile broadened.

241

'You must forgive my little joke. Never mind, Dr Hamilton, all that matters is that you are at last safely here. We have you, as you might say, among us.'

He is enjoying himself, Edmund thought.

'I can only apologise for trespassing and for my thoughtlessness.'

Consuero waved his hand about him. 'Well, now you are having your wish and seeing this very remarkable house built so cunningly between these two walls of rock. The period, which probably you will recognise, is of the 1740s; the builders, the Sanchez-Barba family.'

'I have been told a little of its history,' said Edmund.

'Doubtless by that interesting priest, Father Moreno.' Vincente Consuero turned to face Edmund. 'He could not have given you good instructions since you strayed far from the road which would have brought you the sooner to us.'

'He gave me none, save that the house lay somewhere to the south. I only decided to explore after I had left Father Moreno. I drove into the hills and then I fear that I lost the way. I tried to turn the car and found a track. Then I thought the house might lie in that direction.'

'That was a pity. If you had followed the road instead of exploring little-known tracks and making so strenuous a climb, that would have led you straight to us and you would have avoided the tiresome but necessary attentions of my men. But let us overlook your misadventure and go inside.'

He led the way to the great doors.

'I fear that this afternoon I cannot show you over the whole of the house. It is the home of a foundation dedicated to the improvement of the resources of the land, much needed in our poor country. Today our mining engineers and soil erosion experts are holding their annual conference. As usual, they have taken over the whole place and I dare not disturb their deliberations, even for so distinguished if unexpected a guest as yourself.' He bowed to Edmund and stood aside as he opened the tall, massive doors.

'But I can show you the hall and the library and even offer you tea – which, if I remember right, is what an Englishman expects at this time of the afternoon.'

242

'How do you know who I am?'

'Report of any stranger travels fast in this part of the country. So I know not only your name, but' – Consuero closed the heavy wooden doors behind them – 'I also know what you are. Or so I believe.' He turned the key in the heavy lock. 'Yes,' he went on, 'we get few strangers and news of a foreigner naturally excites us.'

He took Edmund by the arm and led him across the black and white chequered marble floor into the centre of a vast octagonal-shaped hall. From the view that Edmund had obtained from the crest of the hill he calculated that the hall must run the whole width and length of the central block. Four wide pillars supported the ceiling two storeys high, at the foot of which stood like sentinels wax figures in sixteenth-century armour. There was no furniture, save for one table, and the white walls were bare except for one on which there was spread like a fan a crescent of spears and lances. Beneath were racks of arquebuses and muskets. Opposite this display of weaponry stood a narrow oak table with a large looking glass in a gilt frame hung above it. Consuero steered Edmund to the table and they stood close to it.

'It is extraordinary, is it not? Quite a folly, but on a great scale. The bedrooms are on the top storey above us and the living rooms are in the wings, which were of course added later. The main saloon is now the library, which I am able to show you. You have of course noted the ceiling.'

Consuero pointed to the ceiling and Edmund looked up to the fresco high above his head. It covered the whole of the ceiling, a circle of painted cherubs pointing their trumpets towards a central figure emerging from clouds, not a God but a bearded conquistador in armour.

'It has not the artistry of the Sistine Chapel but then there were no Michelangelos in the Spanish colonies in the eighteenth or any century. Nor, perhaps you will agree, anywhere else.'

'It is very fine.'

'It is a fair representation, would you not agree, of the conqueror of Mexico? Hernán Cortés was an ancestor of the

243

Sanchez-Barbas and so when they came here they brought him with them.'

'Cortés was the godfather of one of their ancestors, I was informed.'

'I am sure that you are right. You are the scholar; I only a humble administrator. If you have seen enough, Dr Hamilton, perhaps you would come this way.'

With the heels of his boots clacking on the marble floor, Vincente Consuero led Edmund away from the looking glass across the wide hall to a heavy mahogany door opposite the front door.

Before he opened it, he said, 'I am correct, am I not, to address you as Doctor and not as Professor Hamilton, as I believe some have done since your arrival?'

'You are quite correct. I have no chair.'

'Of course.' Consuero opened the door and stood aside to let Edmund pass. 'Originally this was the salon but later generations added the rooms in the rear and turned this into a library.'

The room was large, with the high ceiling of the period. Three sides were lined with heavy glass-fronted bookcases with panelling between each case. On the one unfurnished wall hung portraits. It was a dark room despite the light from two large windows, which looked out onto a formal rose garden in the square of the stable block that Edmund had seen from the crest of the hill. It was furnished with groups of formal gilt armchairs and settees. To one side was a Louis Quinze desk and in the centre a large table covered by a handsome cloth. On the table, surrounding a huge vase of flowers, were newspapers and magazines in several languages. In front of the tall marble fireplace had been set two chairs and another table on which was a tray with two silver teapots, two fine bone china teacups and a plate of sandwiches.

I was expected, Edmund thought.

Consuero waved him to a seat at the tea-table.

'Pray be seated and join me in your English ceremony of the tea-table.'

They sat facing each other.

'So you are a don at the beautiful college of St Peter's where, I am told, Sir Alexander Murray is now the Master.'

'He is. He has only recently been elected. We are very fortunate to have him.'

'I am sure that you are. He was your Ambassador in Paris, was he not?'

'That is so.'

'It was such a pity that you did not select another time for your visit, Dr Hamilton. I might then have been able to show you more of this remarkable establishment. Coming from your own beautiful, and of course older, establishment I am sure that you would have been most interested. Do you prefer Indian or China tea?'

'China, thank you. As I explained, I only decided to drive out here on the spur of the moment. I had come from Bogota to Las Paza and I was most disappointed with what there was to see at the church and in the graveyard. I have to return tomorrow. The trip, alas, has not proved worthwhile.'

'I am sorry. But I trust that in the end you will consider that your visit to Las Paza was not wholly a waste of time. At least you have seen us.' Then he said quickly, 'So you hired a car?'

'Yes.'

'From Pedro Barra.'

'Yes. When I began to walk I got lost.'

'Lost, Dr Hamilton? You cannot be much of a navigator, unlike your and my ancestors.'

'You know of my ancestors? There appears to be little that you do not know about me.'

'In my position I have to be well informed.'

'As administrator of the Villa Rica?'

'As administrator of the foundation and the curator of this great estate. We have an important position in this part of the country and we are interested in all that passes in the neighbourhood. Will you have a cucumber sandwich? They are, I am sure you will agree, the only tolerable sandwich to have at tea.'

He handed the plate to Edmund across the table. 'So you plan to return tomorrow to Bogota? And then to England?'

'Yes, to Cambridge.'

'Ah yes, back to St Peter's and to Sir Alexander. Tell me, am

245

I not right in thinking that Sir Godfrey Burne of your Foreign Office is a Fellow of your college?'

Consuero was smiling at Edmund who looked back at him levelly.

'Sir Godfrey is an Honorary Fellow.'

'Sir Godfrey is an interesting man. I first heard of him when he was *en poste* in Caracas many years ago.'

He knows a great deal, thought Edmund, and not only about St Peter's. This is a game which cannot last much longer.

'As you are the curator here –' Consuero bowed – 'may I ask if you could help me?'

'If I can, Dr Hamilton, I would be honoured.'

'I am engaged in research for a study I am preparing. I have been in Argentina and Brazil and it was in Bogota that I stumbled upon a little-known essay by Michaelis that had a footnote referring to Juan Moreno and his records and the gravestones at St Ignatius' which led me to come to Las Paza. I was most excited to learn of the stones since one of the reasons why I have made Latin American studies my speciality is that I have ancestors on my mother's side of the family who –'

Consuero interrupted him, speaking for the first time in Spanish. 'Which is the reason why you speak our language so excellently, a facility most appropriate' – he paused slightly – 'for the purpose of your trip.'

Edmund replied also in Spanish. 'It is. I have spoken the language all my life. As I was saying, on an expedition into the interior in 1539 was Octavio de Coronado who came from Seville to Colombia.'

Consuero held up a hand. On the third and little finger were heavy gold rings. 'Forgive me if I interrupt you once more. But let us speak English again. It is good practice for me.'

'You do not sound as though you needed practice and you appear to know our English ways. For instance, this tea.'

Consuero shrugged deprecatingly.

'But, as you wish. By all means let us talk in English. I was explaining what brought me to Las Paza. My ancestor disappeared into the jungle and when I came across this footnote I thought it might be amusing to spend a couple of days

246

here on the chance that I might discover his gravestone. And to look at Father Moreno's records.'

'"Amusing"? Ah, yes the English meaning.'

Edmund looked at him and then said deliberately, 'Interesting, if you prefer. Well, I could find nothing about Coronado, but then Father Moreno spoke about the Villa Rica and of the link between the Sanchez-Barba family with Hernán Cortés and why it was called the Villa Rica. Coronado also had served with Hernán Cortés. So I wondered if there were in the house any local records which someone would be kind enough to show me.'

'And then, Dr Hamilton, you went for a walk and unhappily lost the way.'

Consuero rose from the table and went to the window. 'Alas, I cannot help you. What documents there might have been must have been removed by the family when I purchased the house. But as you can see, I did retain some of the pictures. The Sanchez-Barba family preferred the money to their family heritage. Unlike the good nephew, Charles Surface, in your play *The School for Scandal*.' He walked and stood beneath one of them. 'They are not very distinguished.'

'You said, "I purchased". Father Moreno told me that the house had been bought by what he called the Syndicate.'

Consuero turned to face Edmund. 'I am inclined sometimes to become too proprietary,' he said softly.

'Why would the priest call it the Syndicate?'

'I do not know. We are a foundation and as you seem to be interested, Dr Hamilton, our foundation was established by a group of corporations, a consortium of miners and traders.'

'Originally based in Medellin?'

'You are correct. The Villa Rica is, I suppose you might say, our home. And I am its manager. Does that tell you enough?'

This had better end, thought Edmund, whatever the consequences. He got to his feet.

'I am disappointed that there are no local records but I knew that it was, as we say, a long shot. You have been very kind and hospitable. I have kept you long enough and I must return to the hotel.' Then he added, 'I am expecting to be telephoned from Bogota to be told when I am to meet my Ambassador tomorrow afternoon. He too is something of a scholar. It was a great pleasure to see at least some of this remarkable house. I must repeat my apologies again for trespassing on your land and on your time.'

Now the fooling must end. Edmund loosened his jacket and felt again the pistol in his waistband. He would not have much of a chance.

Consuero did not move. He was now in the shadows, his dark face above his light suit hardly visible. Edmund came towards him and saw that Consuero was no longer smiling. The two faced each other, a yard apart. Then the moment passed. Consuero suddenly turned and walked to a telephone on the desk.

'My guest is leaving,' he said into the telephone.

He led Edmund in silence back across the empty hall. He unlocked the great door and walked onto the portico. Edmund followed. Consuero turned back and stood between Edmund and the open door.

'Goodbye, Dr Hamilton, and bon voyage. Or perhaps I should better say, safe journey.'

He did not hold out his hand but bowed, and as he did so Edmund saw behind him in the shadow of the great door another man. Then Edmund bowed in reply and turned to descend the steps. As he got into the car, he saw that the man who had been in the doorway had now joined Consuero and was standing beside him.

The keys of the car were where he had left them in the ignition. Vincente Consuero and the man who had joined him were still standing between the pillars in the portico when Edmund turned the car into the drive. At the gatehouse the gate swung open and he drove on through the second gate and into the road on his way back to the Bona Ventura.

Consuero turned to the figure beside him and looked into his startling blue eyes.

'You watched him through the mirror in the hall?'

'I did,' said Maitland.

'Did you see enough of him?'

'Yes.'

'Have you ever seen him before?'

248

'Never.'

'He could not entirely conceal his surprise when I spoke of Burne. He is certainly a don at the college but I am convinced that he has been sent. Whoever he is, it is enough. Whether he is a fool or a spy, he must be dealt with. It will serve as a lesson to Burne.'

'It should have been done here and now.'

'No. I decided that nothing should happen in the house. No one must know that he has been here, save for Juan Moreno and Pedro Barra. They can be attended to later. Tonight you must deal with our visitor.'

'Tonight? I have been travelling much. Is that essential?'

Consuero looked at him and said sharply, 'It is. Hamilton leaves tomorrow. There must be no overt connection with us. His Embassy will send someone. I want as little trouble as possible. Tonight a break-in and a robbery at the hotel must be arranged and the man killed when he surprised the intruders. But the body of Dr Hamilton must only be found in the morning. You will know what to do. We shall talk further before the people go into dine. I myself leave later tonight in the helicopter for Medellin. You are to join me tomorrow. You have work to do this evening.'

TWENTY-THREE

As soon as he was through the second gate, Edmund put his foot down on the accelerator and pushed the Fiat to its limit, watching in the mirror the road behind him for the pursuit that he thought was inevitable. He laid the pistol on the seat beside him. He would drive through any patrol that might try to stop him.

For a second as he had begun to walk down the steps, he had thought that he might have succeeded in convincing Vincente Consuero that it had been out of genuine curiosity that he had wandered onto the estate of the Villa Rica, but commonsense told him that Consuero had been playing with him throughout the elaborate ceremony at the tea-table. Consuero must have been aware that Edmund's visit had not been in the cause of historical research. Why otherwise the mention of Godfrey Burns and Godfrey's service in Caracas? Consuero knew who Godfrey was and after the virtual elimination of the Colombian station he must have anticipated that Godfrey would send in someone from outside. And the only someone from the outside who had turned up at the Villa Rica had been Dr Edmund Hamilton.

So the only reason why Consuero had let him go must have been because he had thought it wiser to avoid the murder inside the actual home of the Syndicate of a foreigner who was to meet his Ambassador on the following day. Consuero must have decided to have Edmund killed either on the road or later that night at the hotel.

Edmund thought of Carlos, who had said that if Edmund was identified his mission would have been worthless and all that had been planned to follow from it would be frustrated. Carlos had wanted a location, nothing more. Well, Edmund had no doubt that he had been identified; the Syndicate would know that he was a spy sent from London and, moreover, a spy who had actually been across their threshold. Whatever Carlos wanted and whatever the consequences, that was now the situation. All that Edmund could do now was survive so as to be able to report what he had discovered.

And he had much he could report. For he had seen their people at the hotel and several of these he would be able to identify. He had seen the layout and some of the inside of their headquarters; and he had seen and talked with the man who was their leader. Martin Maitland he had not seen, unless he had been the man behind Consuero in the shadow of the door. If he had been, then he was the one whom the Syndicate would send.

At first Edmund thought of returning to the presbytery of the old priest or to Pedro Barra to seek refuge. But he had already put them in enough jeopardy. He considered lying up for the night somewhere in the woods before driving to the airport in the morning. But his passport was at the hotel. He could abandon it but then he saw in the driving-mirror that he was being followed. Immediately he slowed and saw that the car behind slowed with him; he accelerated again and the car followed, settling down some distance behind him. He knew now that wherever he went they would track him down. It would be better to choose his own ground and prepare. Despite the danger in which he was, Edmund felt a strange sense of exhilaration. When he had sat in the library opposite Vincente Consuero waiting for the confrontation that he had then expected, he had been surprised at how calm he had felt. Now he felt ready for whatever lay ahead.

The dusk, which came so swiftly, had fallen when he drove up the steep drive of the hotel and parked the Fiat under the trees. He saw the other car cruise slowly past the entrance to the drive and then stop. They knew now that he was safely home; so it would be at the Bona Ventura during the night and before he left on the early flight to Bogota that they must have planned to kill him.

He asked at the desk for the return of his passport. With it the clerk handed him a cable. It had arrived that morning, the

251

clerk said, after Professor Hamilton had left the hotel. Edmund opened it at the desk and carried it to the bar where he ordered a drink. The place was empty and he sat at a table and watched by the barman he began to read. It was from the Embassy as Carlos had promised.

The Hyatt has advised me where you are and I am cabling to confirm that the Ambassador has invited you to luncheon tomorrow to meet some academics with whom he believes that you would be interested to talk. Will you please confirm your acceptance as soon as you return to Bogota tomorrow morning. Roger Stapleton.

The hotel would have passed that on to Consuero; it would at least have confirmed what Edmund had said. Perhaps it may have played some part in deciding Consuero to find a killing-ground away from the villa.

He remembered that Carlos had told him not to telephone from Las Paza but if he were not to survive he decided that he must take the risk and try and pass on what he had discovered. He would send the name, the Villa Rica. That was all.

He went to the desk and asked to make a call to Bogota.

'I regret,' said the clerk, 'the lines are down. We cannot contact Bogota. It must have been the storm last night.'

Edmund turned away. For the first time a wave of fear came over him. He went to his room and lay on his bed. After an hour he got up and put out his pyjamas on the bed as though for sleep. He had his ticket and passport with him in his jacket and he checked the pistol. It was many years since he had fired a pistol and never in anger. He slipped the gun again into the waistband at the back of his trousers and kept the silencer in his pocket as he had since Carlos had given it to him. He picked up a book and some of his notes and, locking his room, walked back along the dimly lit passageway to the dining-room.

The pretty waitress led him to his table in the centre of the room. He took the chair and moved it so that he faced the door. There were few in the room, only two middle-aged men sitting at one table. They had not been there on the previous night. They looked like locals dining together. Soon they left.

'It is very empty tonight,' he said to the girl. 'Where is everybody?'

'We are not expecting many. There is a conference in the town. They will be back later.' She moved the knives and fork and side plate around the table and put them in front of him.

'It is chicken again.'

'Very well. And another bottle of that Bulgarian wine, please.'

But he drank little of it. He took his time over the meal, attempting to read but in reality thinking of what lay ahead. Now and then he looked up and watched the entrance. Halfway through the meal the man he had christened the Ferret came through the door and slid into his seat at the far side of the dining-room. He did not look at Edmund and both ate in silence. When he saw that the other had almost finished, Edmund shut his book, rose and wandered slowly over to the table.

'How are you? I saw you at dinner last evening.'

The man kept his eyes on the plate in front of him. Edmund pulled out a chair and sat down.

'I hope you don't mind my joining you. It is very dull here tonight. I gather everyone is out at some dinner.'

'So I have been told, señor.'

'And you, did you have a good day? Mine was most interesting.'

'I am glad, señor.'

'Yes, I spent the morning at the church with Father Moreno, examining his records. But they were of little interest to me. I tried to decipher the lettering on the gravestones but they are too worn. So my trip has not been very successful.'

'I am sorry, señor.'

Edmund leant across the table. 'When I was in the churchyard I thought that I saw you standing down by the wall. Was it you?'

'I?' The man looked at Edmund. 'Not I, señor. What would I be doing in the churchyard?' He forced a smile. 'I do not often visit graveyards if I can help it.'

253

'I was sure that it was you. Still, it was quite a distance away. But tell me, what do you do? What is your business here in Las Paza?'

'I am a traveller. I am the agent for some of the tobacco growers in the area and I travel between here and Bogota.'

'Do you ever go out to the Villa Rica?'

The man went on eating and then pushed his plate away. 'No. I have seen it – at a distance.'

'You should visit the villa. It is most remarkable. It is an extraordinary house to find in such a faraway place. I went there today and met the charming man who runs the place. He gave me tea, of all things. His name is Vincente Consuero. Have you ever met him?'

'I have not, but I have heard of him.'

'What exactly do they do up there at the villa?'

The man shifted in his chair. 'The villa is the headquarters of a group which owns much of the pasture and the mines to the north.'

'Any tobacco?'

'No, not that I am aware of.'

'You would surely know if there was?'

'Of course. As I said, I am not aware they grow or distribute tobacco on the estate at the villa.'

He put down his napkin and got to his feet. 'Forgive me, señor, I have to telephone. A business matter.'

'Of course. I hope it is a local call for the lines to Bogota are down.'

'It is.'

'Do you feel like joining me in the bar for a liqueur before turning in?'

'If you will excuse me, I have work to do in my room and I have to be out early.'

'A pity. I would have enjoyed talking about Las Paza and the church of St Ignatius and the Villa Rica.'

They left the dining-room together and separated, Edmund going to the bar and the ferret-faced man in the direction of the telephone beside the desk. Doubtless, thought Edmund, to report that I am safely here.

He ordered some brandy from the surly barman and lighting

a cigar he took his drink to a chair on the verandah. He poured the brandy into a tub of flowers by his chair and sat smoking. No one was about. After a time he got up and walked round the paving beside the pool and then around the outer circle of the passageway, noting the numbers of the rooms. He chose the place where he intended to wait.

The guests from the 'dinner in the town' had not yet returned and the hotel was silent and empty. Edmund came back to the verandah, threw away his cigar and told the clerk at the desk that he wished to be called at seven o'clock in the morning.

'Good night,' he said and walked back to his room.

He locked the door, switched on the light and threw open the curtains so that the light from the room fell on the oleander outside the cottage and almost to the surround of the pool. He placed the chair carefully out of any line of sight from the window and sat watching the door. He screwed the silencer onto the barrel of the pistol and held it on his lap.

An hour later Edmund heard the sound of cars arriving; then feet walking down the passageway and voices saying good night. He peered from the window and he could see figures in the passageway on the opposite side of the pool. Then he drew the curtains and pushed the pillow and some of his clothes into the bed, making as best he could the shape of a body. He turned out the light and waited another hour. Then, when all was quiet and with the pistol and his torch in his pocket, he opened the window and dropped silently into the bushes. From the outside he drew the curtains and left the window open. Following the line of the shrubs he crept slowly and carefully past the windows of the other cottages. When he had reached the end of the pool he took up his position, sitting between two trees with his legs stretched out before him, his back against the boundary wall, holding the pistol with the silencer in both hands. He was about fifteen yards from the window of his cottage.

As he waited in the dark he tried to recollect the training he had received on the range in London. He would have only one chance to fire and his life would depend on that single moment. Overhead he heard the noise of a helicopter as it passed low

255

over the silent, dark hotel where he lay waiting for Maitland. It was taking Vincente Consuero to Medellin.

In Martin Maitland's opinion there had been no need for the charade of the tea party; the man should have been dealt with there and then. But Consuero had decided on staging the break-in at the hotel in the course of which the academic would be killed. But it would be he, Maitland, who would have to do it.

While Vincente Consuero returned to the conference, Maitland went up to the room that had been prepared for him. He took the tablets that had been prescribed for him in Hong Kong for his migraine and lay on the bed. He slept little, took more tablets than he should and then went down to join the others. Consuero led him to the two Germans who were sitting together at a table in a corner of the room. They got to their feet when Consuero and Maitland joined them and bowed. All four sat.

'These colleagues are in the party which is staying at the hotel,' said Consuero. 'Friedrich has spoken with Hamilton and knows his room. He will remind you of the layout of the hotel.'

The older of the Germans with the cropped iron-grey hair said, 'The man is in room twenty-six. You remember the hotel?'

'I have been there several times but it is some time ago.'

Friedrich tore some paper from a notebook and began to draw. 'This may help you. Here is the foyer and the verandah. The swimming-pool is in the centre, surrounded by the cottages. Room twenty-six is here. Like the others, it has a window looking out over some shrubs and a flower border to the pool. You can walk from the verandah around the pool to the window of number twenty-six, which is approximately opposite the entrance to the verandah. The lights in the garden will be on but they are dim and give little light. The bed is in the centre of the room, the head against the right-hand wall as you look from the window. Yesterday I entered the room while he was dining. Last night he slept with the window open. The air-conditioner does not work and I have made sure that it was not repaired. The next-door room, number twenty-seven, is empty. There are no other strangers in the hotel.'

He handed the sketch to Maitland.

Consuero said, 'You will use the window?'

Maitland nodded.

'When they learn in the morning that Hamilton is dead, doubtless they will send someone from the Embassy at Bogota. So it must appear that he was killed by the intruders. The hotel has been warned. Force the front door and when you enter the room take what is necessary to make it appear to be a burglary. Bring to me all his papers and his passport. Any money I am sure that you will keep.'

Maitland did not reply.

'Leave the room locked with the key on the inside. Do the same to the empty room next door. On your way out of the hotel you will pass the office. Force the lock of that door and also the drawers of the office desk. There will be more money.'

Consuero looked at Maitland who remained silent.

'The cars taking those of our people who are staying in the hotel will be leaving after the dinner and the Final Session at which I shall be presiding. One car will drop you in the woods where the Jeep has been left for you. Wait for two hours and then proceed to the hotel. When you have completed your task, drive back to the woods and lie up until well into the morning. Then join the morning supply lorries and follow them to the villa. I do not want you driving into the estate during the hours of darkness.'

'Is the waiting necessary?'

Consuero spoke sharply. 'It is. His Embassy will insist on some investigation and probably seek to accompany the investigator. I will prepare the police but I want no risk of some witness noticing any vehicle returning to the villa late at night.'

He turned to the Germans. 'Whatever is heard, there must be no alarm at the hotel during the night and the body must not be discovered until morning. During the hours of darkness all must stay in their rooms and keep silent. Make that clear to everyone.'

Consuero looked first at the Germans and then at Maitland; all three nodded. He rose to his feet and said to Maitland, 'I

257

leave later this evening for Medellin. I shall send the helicopter back for you in the morning and you must leave by noon.'

'I shall not have slept all night and I shall not get back to the villa with the supply lorries until well into the morning. I have been travelling much.'

'The task will not be difficult. He cannot be a skilled man or he would never have blundered into here this afternoon. I need you at Medellin. You must be ready to leave at noon.'

Consuero turned on his heel and left them.

Maitland said to the Germans, 'Call me when you are leaving for the hotel.'

'You will not eat with us?'

'No.'

He returned to his room and dressed in black shirt and trousers and soft dark shoes. He put a black woollen balaclava helmet in his pocket and lay on his bed. Since the night in the vicarage, he had begun to have visions of Marie-Claire as he had taken her throat in his hands and before her beautiful face had become disfigured and distorted when he had squeezed the life from her. Before he had come to Chapel Iford he had not been concerned by what he had to do; but since he had killed her the image of her face and her body as she lay at his feet like a broken rag doll had kept returning. He had killed often, either in war or for money, as he had killed that officer in Germany. Josef he had killed because Josef had become drunken and had betrayed him to the lesbians. But it had only been after the killings in the vicarage there had begun these recurring visions, always of the face of Marie-Claire and the look in her eyes before she had died.

He tried to drive them away with other memories, of Fan Sen, the mother of his child in Repulse Bay; or of his boyhood with his aunt who had been kind to him. But with the image of the aunt there returned that of the widower whose neck he had broken in the vicarage – and that in turn brought the vision of Marie-Claire as she had died before his eyes and at his hands. When he had killed her he had no doubt that it was necessary but during the long hours on the flight across the southern Atlantic he had begun to wonder if she really had to die. Would she have proved such a threat to him or to the

258

others? But then he remembered the cold look in the eyes of the old man as he sat opposite him across the table in the stateroom in the junk in Repulse Bay, the accusation that his mistress had a husband linked to the French Security Service and the unspoken threat to himself. There had been no alternative.

Now he had this new task, the tall faceless agent sent from London. This was a contract on a man of whom he knew nothing, whom he had seen for the first time that afternoon through the glass in the hall. This one would never return to haunt him. But he had not slept since before he had left London for Chapel Iford, although he had pretended to in the room in the vicarage before he had killed Henry Makepiece. When tonight was over he would sleep and then perhaps the vision of Marie-Claire would fade.

The German Friedrich knocked on Maitland's door and, armed with his gun and the silencer and a jemmy, Maitland joined Friedrich in the car. They dropped him off in the woods beyond the estate and he clambered into the Jeep which had been left for him. He sat lowering his head between his hands on the steering-wheel, the pain of the migraine as severe as before. He forced himself to wait for the hours that Consuero had prescribed and then drove at speed to the Bona Ventura Hotel. He parked the Jeep in the drive and sat for a time listening. Save for a solitary light over the porch of the front door the hotel was dark and silent.

The door was easy to force, but his hand shook and he splintered the wood more than he need. In the foyer a single light was burning. He sank into a chair. He held out his hands. They were trembling and he clasped them in front of him, gripping them tightly together. Then he got to his feet and stood on the verandah, allowing his eyes to become accustomed to the darkness.

The garden, as Friedrich had warned, was only dimly lit but the moon shone intermittently through the clouds, reflected in the water of the pool. He walked around the edges of the pool, his step in the soft shoes making no sound. He went to the cottage opposite the entrance to the verandah and stood with his back to the pool looking across the border of flowers and low shrubs to the window. It was open, the curtains drawn across it. He went noiselessly round the side of the cottage and into the passageway to check the number on the door. He returned the way he had come to the poolside of the cottage and stepped through the waist-high shrubs and stood by the open window. Carefully he pulled back the curtain. He did not need his torch for in the moonlight; he could see the hunched figure under the bedclothes.

It was all so familiar, not the place nor the circumstances, but the similarity. He had done it so often. Again he saw the vision of Marie-Claire. His hands were trembling again and he steadied them as he raised his gun. Then he heard a voice from the wall behind him.

'Martin Maitland.'

Maitland should have dropped. Why he did not in the short time he had left he did not know. Instead he wheeled round and Edmund, holding the gun in both hands as he had been taught long ago on the range in London, fired from the darkness in the shadow of the wall. At first Edmund thought that he had failed. He should have fired when Maitland's back was towards him. He should never have called out. He steadied himself to fire again. Then he saw the figure slowly crumble and fall face forward into the bed of flowers and shrubs.

Although he had used a silencer on his gun, the smack of the bullet that had pierced Maitland had struck the cottage and Edmund, crouched against the wall between the trees, waited for the alarm to be raised. Nothing stirred. Then he heard the sound of the leaves and branches of the shrubs being brushed aside and the stems of the oleander snapping. Into the moonlight and onto the flagstones of the surround of the pool he saw Maitland crawling from where he had fallen.

Edmund could make out the white of the face as the head now and then turned this way and that like a labouring swimmer as the figure laboriously dragged itself on its belly towards the edge of the pool. There was no gun in either hand. By the time the hands gripped the rim of the pool the whole body was visible stretched out on the flagstones.

260

With a great effort the figure raised itself by the arms until the chest was clear of the ground. The head turned again first to one side then to the other, this time like a wounded beast. When the face turned to him, Edmund could see in the moonlight the eyes staring into the darkness in which Edmund was hidden, searching for the person who had struck him down. The head turned again and hung low on his chest between his arms and then was raised so that the neck was bent right back, the face staring up into the sky. The figure stayed motionless as though transfixed, caught in the moonlight. Then Edmund heard the man give a great sigh as though all had been consummated and his head dropped. With a last effort Martin Maitland pulled himself over the edge of the pool and slipped into the water where his body floated face downward, arms spread-eagled, leaving in the water spirals and on the stones stains of his blood.

TWENTY-FOUR

Edmund watched the pool as the body drifted lazily on the surface of the water, which was lit from time to time by patches of moonlight, as he waited for what must happen next. Either the sound of the bullet or the noise of Maitland's body falling into the water could have aroused the people in the nearby cottages. But no lights came on and the hotel lay as silent and dark as it had before he had fired. He decided to move.

To escape he had to get to the verandah and the foyer. He had a choice: either he could slip into the passage behind the cottages but onto which their doors opened; or he could keep to the cover of the garden and work his way around to the verandah. He chose the latter and began to move slowly and carefully, bent double and sometimes crawling as he made his way through the circle of shrubs outside the windows of the cabins towards the central block of the hotel. He was helped by the clouds, which had now begun to pile up in the night sky and move across the face of the moon so that the pool and the garden were now only rarely out of total darkness. When he had almost completed the half-circle back to the verandah outside the foyer, there was a longer break in the clouds and he had to wait among the tall oleanders before he broke cover and slipped into the entrance.

But he misjudged the gap in the clouds and when he was still moving he was momentarily caught in the moonlight. Still there was total silence, eerie and unexpected. But now he was inside the dimly lit foyer and he stood by a window, his back to the side wall waiting for the expected flood of light and the attack that would surely follow the discovery of the body floating in the pool. Peering through the window during one of the now infrequent intervals of moonlight, he saw for the last time the dark shape of the body as it lay in the water. Then cloud blanketed out the moon and he saw that from now on the darkness would last. Only the dim lamps under the roof of the open passageway cast pools of feeble light around the edges of the garden. Still nothing happened.

He looked around the room behind him and then backed across the foyer to the solitary lamp on a low table and switched it off. He used his torch, covering the beam with his fingers and found his way to the front door. When he had reached it he saw that it stood ajar where Maitland had left it after his clumsy forcing with the jemmy. Edmund slipped out and stood for another few seconds, scarcely daring to believe that undisturbed and undetected he could leave the killing-ground that Consuero had chosen for his execution.

He went down the drive keeping close to the border of trees towards where he had left the Fiat. Before he came to the car, which he had parked off the drive under the trees, he saw Maitland's Jeep. He tried the handle of the door. It was unlocked. Inside the cabin he released the catch for the hood and then moving to the front of the Jeep he leant over the engine and wrenched off the distributor head and the cable. When he reached the Fiat he pushed it back onto the drive and, jumping in, he let the car roll silently down the steep incline. At the bottom by the entrance of the drive to the main road he started the engine and drove away.

But he had been seen, or rather a figure had been seen. For in the hotel Friedrich and his companion had both heard the sounds of the bullet striking the cabin and the fall of the body into the pool. After a time Friedrich pulled aside the curtains of his darkened room and peered out. In the last beam before the cloud had blotted out the moonlight, Friedrich had seen the black shape floating in the waters of the pool and a shadowy figure go through the entrance to the verandah. He stayed watching and listening. A little later he heard in the far distance the sound of the engine of a car. That, he thought, was the man whom Consuero had sent returning to the villa after completing his mission. Friedrich returned to his bed. The morning would be the time, as Consuero

263

had instructed, for discovery. Until then the Englishman could lie where he had fallen.

On the main road Edmund drove towards the village. On the outskirts he pulled up and parked the car on the grass verge close under the wall of a solitary barn. He got out and crossed to the opposite side of the road and lay in a ditch from where, pistol in hand, he could watch for the lights of any approaching vehicle. By now there was no more moonlight. He looked at his watch. There were three hours before the dawn.

As he lay against the bank of the ditch watching the road he felt again as he had in the car when he drove from the Villa Rica, strangely exhilarated. He thought of the grand-uncle with his tales of the Raj and the North-West Frontier and the message that Carlos had given him from C. What had it been? 'Forget that grand-uncle'? Edmund smiled. He would never forget him now.

But as the night wore on he grew cold and very tired. He thought of all that had happened during that day; of the old priest's story and the climb through the forest and his arrest and the elaborate meeting with Vincente Consuero; and now the death of Maitland. His feeling of exhilaration left him. Although the night was warm he shivered and longed for sleep. Now all that he wanted was to get away and go to Teresa.

At first light he returned to the car and drove on into the village and into Pedro Barra's yard. He got out and knocked on the door of the house. Pedro Barra opened the door.

'I have come early.'

Barra looked at Edmund, with his pale face and dishevelled clothes and stood aside to let him into the house, bolting and locking the door behind them.

'We do not leave for the airport before seven o'clock.'

He walked ahead of Edmund into the kitchen. A pot of coffee was standing on the hob.

'Coffee?'

He poured and handed Edmund a mug. He did not look at

264

Edmund who took it and drank greedily.

'I know where you have been,' said Barra quietly.

'I had to see the place for myself.'

'That was your decision. Now they will stop you from leaving.'

'They have already tried. In the night they sent someone to kill me but they may not know that he failed. When they do find out, I hope that I shall have gone.'

Barra pulled up a chair and put it near to the stove. Edmund sat. Barra watched him silently.

Then he said, 'They are not yet looking for you?'

'They will be. No one followed me here. I must get to the airport.'

Barra walked to the window and looked out into the yard. 'And when you have gone, what then?'

Edmund at first did not reply. After a few moments he said, 'They knew that I had your car.' Again there was silence. 'You can come with me.'

'And my family? No, I cannot leave.'

Edmund placed the gun with its magazine and the silencer onto the table. 'I will leave you this.'

Barra looked at it and then put it in his pocket.

'And this.' Edmund pulled a roll of dollar bills from his jacket and peeled off several. Barra took them.

'I am sorry to leave you but I have to get back. I have to report.'

All Barra said in reply was, 'Wait here,' and he left the room. Edmund sat in front of the stove warming himself.

The woman came but she did not look at Edmund and said nothing. She put some bread and olives before him.

'Thank you,' he said and she left him alone.

At seven o'clock Pedro Barra returned.

'We had better go. Have you any luggage?'

'No.'

'Good.'

They got into the car and with Barra at the wheel they drove to the airport. When they came to the small building that served as the airport office, Edmund put out his hand. Barra looked at it. Finally, he took it.

265

'I shall do what I can when I get to Bogota.'

Barra shrugged and Edmund watched him as he drove away.

There were only a handful of other passengers. Edmund sat next to a window and no one came to the seat beside him. When they were airborne and he saw the mountains below him, Edmund called the steward and ordered brandy. At about the same time at the Bona Ventura they were taking the body of Martin Maitland from the pool where it had lain all night.

At Bogota Airport he telephoned Carlos but there was no reply and Edmund found a taxi.

'Six Santo Spirito,' he said.

The door on the other side of the cab opened and Carlos clambered in.

'Eighteen Bolivar,' Carlos said to the driver. The man looked at Edmund who nodded and they drove off.

'You have had an interesting trip?' asked Carlos, at the same time putting his handkerchief and his finger to his lips before wiping the sweat off his brow.

'Very,' said Edmund.

Eighteen Bolivar was a similar house in a similar street to the house in Santo Spirito. When Carlos opened the front door Edmund could see at the end of the passage the woman he had seen leaving the house in Santo Spirito when first he had come to Carlos. She was holding a small child by its hand. Carlos went to them and bent and kissed the child.

'I shall be taking you away tonight,' he said. 'All three of us are going on a holiday. So you must get ready.'

The face of the woman broke into a smile but she said nothing and gathered the child to her.

Edmund followed Carlos into the sitting-room, again a very similar room to the one in the other house, the same musty smell and identical lace curtains drawn across the window. Carlos went and returned with a tray of cups and coffee.

'You look tired,' said Carlos. 'Brandy?'

He took from his pocket his battered, thick leather flask with a silver top and poured the liquor into the coffee cups.

Edmund said, 'I have found the place. Have you a map?'

266

Carlos went to the desk and brought a map to Edmund. It was unlike the old atlas of the priest so at first Edmund had difficulty. Then he found it.

'It is near here, in the foothills, in a narrow valley, almost a gorge between two lines of hills. It cannot be seen from the road and only with difficulty from the air. There is a paddock where they land a helicopter but it cannot be easy. It is called the Villa Rica.'

'How many were at the house?'

'I do not know. Only half a dozen went there from the hotel. The rest were staying at the villa. The locals call them the Syndicate. They own the town and the hotel. Everyone is theirs.'

'You did well,' said Carlos.

'But they know about me. A patrol found me in the woods and took me to the man who is in charge. He is called Consuero, Vincente Consuero.'

'Oh, my God,' said Carlos.

'They let me leave. I suppose because they did not want to kill me there. They sent Maitland to kill me at the hotel. But for some reason he came without care, and I shot him. They will have found him by now.'

Carlos rose and with an agility surprising for a man of his bulk moved to the telephone and dialled.

'Stapleton,' he said. Then after a pause, 'He is back. He found the place but there is trouble. You must come immediately.' He replaced the receiver. 'Why did you go in?'

'Because I had to. Because I did.'

Carlos wiped his face with the bandanna handkerchief. 'Oh, my God,' he repeated.

Edmund drank his coffee and brandy. 'I need a bath,' he said.

'Down the corridor, facing you.'

'I shall be going south, to BA.'

'Do as you please,' said Carlos. He fell into a chair still wiping his face with his red handkerchief.

The bath water was as rusty as the chipped edges of the tub. Edmund heard Stapleton arrive but he continued to lie soaking in the brown water. Then he climbed out and wrapping a towel around him went back to the sitting-room.

'Carlos has told me,' said Stapleton and Edmund looked at the Englishman standing by the telephone in his neat suit. He had the map in his hand.

'I need clothes.'

'I will send some. You are to go to London at once.'

'I am going south, to the Argentine.'

'They will want you in London.'

'I do not care. I shall be in BA. They can find me there.'

'She wanted to meet you but she was turned back. Do you insist upon going to her?'

'I do. I shall leave today. There is another matter. Two men helped me in Las Paza: the old priest, Juan Moreno, and his friend, a man called Pedro Barra. They will be in danger.'

'I will do what I can.'

Edmund struck the table, rattling the coffee cups. Carlos poured more brandy from his flask.

'They will be killed unless you protect them. They helped me and I had to leave them to get back to report.'

'I said that I shall do what I can.' Stapleton was walking to the door. 'I must return to the Embassy to see what can be done.'

'It will be too late,' said Carlos. 'There is no point now. I told you not to go in.'

Edmund turned on him as though he would have struck his face but he checked himself and repeated to Stapleton, 'You must protect them.'

Stapleton did not look round but said over his shoulder as he opened the door, 'It will be up to the Colombian government now. I shall do what I can to persuade them.'

He went out of the room and Edmund heard the front door slam behind him.

'I am very weary,' Edmund said and poured more brandy from the flask into his cup. Carlos did not reply and sat as he had before, mopping his face with his great handkerchief.

Later, in the clothes that Stapleton had sent, Edmund left for the airport. He had not seen Carlos again. He boarded the 21.30 AVIANCA flight to BA. When he landed early next morning at the airport she was there to meet him. She ran to him and he lifted her high in his arms and then pressed her to him, kissing the tears off her wet face. Behind her he saw two men.

One, a red-headed man, said, 'We are from the Embassy. Kent wants you to return to London immediately.'

'I am not going,' said Edmund and with his arm around Teresa he brushed past them.

The red-headed man sighed. 'Did I not say, young Simon, that all this would end in some gigantic cock-up?'

As soon as Roger Stapleton had returned to the Embassy after leaving Carlos and Edmund, he spoke with the Ministry.

That afternoon three assault helicopters of the Colombian army landed on the strip in the paddock behind the Villa Rica. But Traffic Control at Las Paza airport had warned that very early in the morning, well before the soldiers had arrived, a helicopter had come in from Medellin and then, late in the morning, had returned. Vincente Consuero had come and gone. He had made his arrangements. At the Villa Rica the soldiers did much damage, shooting off the locks of doors, breaking others with the butts of their rifles. When they found no one in the house save an elderly married couple, the caretakers, who told them that there had been a conference of mining engineers and agronomists, which had ended at noon when cars had arrived to take them away, the soldiers in their anger did more damage, searching the rooms, ripping at the fabrics with their bayonets. Men from the platoon that had gone to the first gatehouse shot a woman and a child who had run in fear when the soldiers battered their way through the door.

When they had done at the Villa Rica the troops commandeered a light lorry from the stables and were driven to the Bona Ventura Hotel. There too they found only the staff. The soldiers were told that no one knew anything of any shooting during the night; the guests, a handful of engineers attending the conference at the Villa Rica had all left, as they had been expected to leave, early in the morning. There was no corpse at the hotel. Why should there be, the desk clerk enquired? The soldiers stayed on, drinking by the pool and throwing the empty bottles into the water. Then they went away.

But there were corpses in Las Paza, although the soldiers did not see them and in any event would not have been interested. For these corpses were matters for the local police and the civil authorities of the town. In the course of the night, as the Chief of Police later reported to the provincial Governor, a gang that had been operating in the neighbourhood had broken into one of the houses in the village in order to rob it. It was the house of one of the richer villagers, a man called Pedro Barra. In the upper storey the police had found the bodies of Pedro Barra and his wife, although they did not trouble to report that from the bloodstains found in the lower storey others had died before Barra and his wife. It was, reported the Chief of Police, just another in a series of robberies in the region involving an armed gang who had been robbing houses and even murdering and desecrating in the church.

For the church cleaner at St Ignatius Church had found that the church too had been broken into, the plate taken and the vestments strewn around the sacristy. Lying on the steps of the altar facing the tabernacle she had found the body of the old priest, Juan Moreno.

They had found him at his prayers. He had heard them walking up the aisle of the church behind him. He had not turned. He had no need. He knew who they were and why they had come. They had used their knives, slashing him repeatedly.

That was not the end of the arrangements made by Vincente Consuero.

In the evening of the day when Edmund joined Teresa in the Argentine, the police in Bogota were called to a street in the city. Neighbours had reported that just before nightfall there had been the sound of heavy firing. When the police arrived, a woman told them that in the dusk she had seen three figures, one that of a small child, coming from the doorway of a house opposite. All three were on the top of the steps when a car had cruised slowly down the street. The woman said that one of the figures, the largest of the three, had immediately flung itself in front of the other two as though to shield them. Then the firing had begun and the woman had hidden in her

270

house as the car sped down the street and disappeared round the corner into the square.

The police walked over to where the three bodies were lying bloody and bullet-ridden in the gutter at the foot of the steps which led up to the house. One was the body of a child; the second of a woman; and the third of a heavy, middle-aged man. By the side of his body there lay a battered leather flask with a silver top. It was empty.

TWENTY-FIVE

On the day when Edmund was due back in Bogota Godfrey waited for news. In the evening BA reported that Edmund Hamilton had arrived in the Argentine and for the present refused to come home. Stapleton had reported in Bogota that Hamilton had found what C had been seeking but that he had got into trouble. Later Stapleton signalled that the Colombian government had no alternative but to mount an assault. Like Carlos, Godfrey knew that it would be too late and he went home to bed.

He was woken by Harvey Thompson telephoning from the Foreign Office. The Foreign Office was extremely concerned. The British Ambassador in Bogota had been summoned to the Colombian Foreign Ministry to receive a complaint concerning the activities of a British citizen following an abortive raid on a house near to Las Paza. In the morning Kent told Godfrey that Carlos had been assassinated.

'Leave me,' said Godfrey.

The army of reporters laying siege to Finches remained. Bernard de Tourneville had gone, taking with him Marie-Claire's coffin for burial at Gauville. The funeral of Henry Makepiece had received its share of attention but the mourners had all been local and so it was Angela whom the cameras had pursued. They photographed her and thrust microphones into her sad face.

The press continued to speculate about the murders on the spy master's doorstep. The source in the Wiltshire police fed the stringer who in turn fed the nationals as the investigation of the murders in the vicarage followed the track of the man who had come and killed and gone. The last trace that the press had of the killer's escape was the journey to Ireland. There, as far as the press was concerned although not Special Branch, the trail had gone cold. The speculation, however, continued.

Terence Haynes was a young Spanish-speaking reporter who had been newly-recruited from Exeter University by Metropolitan TV to work on the preparation of their programme on the international drug traffic. He had been given the task of sifting any likely news stories that might come in from Colombia and on that morning his eye fell on a headline in a Bogota newspaper, which had been faxed by Metropolitan's local agents. It read: 'The English Connection'.

The report was about a government raid on an estate and house not far from Cali and the discomfiture of the army when nothing remotely connected with the drug dealers had been uncovered either in the house or in the neighbourhood. The army, according to the newspaper, had been sent on this wild goose chase because of a tip-off from an English visitor, a Dr Hamilton, who had recently been in the area but who had since disappeared. Terence Haynes included the story in his report to the daily production conference presided over by the producer, Max Pottinger, and attended by the presenter Francis Maddocks.

At the mention of the name Hamilton, Maddocks said, 'I know a Hamilton. I was at Cambridge with Edmund Hamilton.'

Max was under pressure; preparation for the programme was not going well. 'Thank you, Francis, but we really haven't time to hear about your old school friends.'

'I said I knew him at the university, not at school. If you're not interested it doesn't matter but Edmund Hamilton was certainly in Colombia when we were there. I met him in the Hyatt Hotel the night before we left Bogota. We had a drink together.'

Max remembered Maddocks' condition on the morning they had left. 'Several I expect, Francis. But the report says Doctor Hamilton.'

'He probably is a doctor, an academic doctor. He is a don. He

273

is also a stuck-up bastard. He said he was there doing some research. But when Hamilton went down from Cambridge, that is,' he explained patiently for the enlightenment of Max, 'when he left Cambridge, I heard that he had become a spook.'

'A spook?' Max stared at Maddocks who was lounging back in his chair, looking suitably pleased with himself.

'That's right, a spy. Well, what I was actually told was that Edmund Hamilton had gone into intelligence in the Ministry of Defence. Of course, that was a few years ago.'

'But you said that he was a don.'

'He is now. At Cambridge.'

'Cambridge?' said Max. 'Cambridge.'

Into his mind like a litany swum the names of his youth; Philby, Blunt, Burgess, Maclean, the Apostles.

He said quietly, 'Find Hamilton. Bloody well find me Hamilton.'

One of the production team, a girl called Sandra, telephoned the informant they used at the Ministry of Defence. He told her that he knew nothing of any Dr Hamilton but there was a rumour going around the Home Office about trouble inside MI6. The Chief Political Editor checked out the rumours and later spoke to Max.

'There is a major reshuffle in the government coming and everyone is concentrating on that. So I haven't found out much. But something is certainly going on over Burne, the Head of MI6. The Home Secretary is after his hide. No one has ever heard the name Hamilton.'

But they had in Cambridge. Max's reporter phoned in to say that Edmund Hamilton was a don at St Peter's College who was believed to have gone out to BA late last month.

'That's our man,' said Max.

'He's out there researching a book. The Master of his College is Sir Alexander Murray.'

'That pompous bastard? We had an interview with him in Paris last year.'

'There is something else. One of the Honorary Fellows at the college is Godfrey Burne, the head of MI6.'

'Christ!' said Max. 'The Cambridge connection.'

Terence Haynes brought confirmation from Bogota. Hamilton had certainly been in Las Paza, the place where the army raid had taken place.

'Well done, Terence. We'll use it, all of it.'

The programme was screened in the evening in the network's weekly current affairs slot. It received much attention. The critics considered that the programme had been most effective in probing the fiasco and the role of MI6 in Colombia and its effect upon the leadership of the service. On this, the programme included the extraordinary events at the Wiltshire home of its Chief. Francis Maddocks, it was generally felt, had been at his acerbic best in his commentary about 'the Cambridge connection' and especially effective about Dr Edmund Hamilton.

The next morning William Blaze telephoned the new Attorney General from the Chief Whip's office in Number 11 Downing Street to enquire if he had seen the programme. The Attorney had not.

'I will send round a video. It was devastating about the leadership of MI6. First that murder business and all the publicity. Then Burne's link through Cambridge to this fellow Hamilton in South America.'

'Who is Hamilton?'

'A friend of Burne's, a don at Burne's college who the Colombians say sent them off on some fool's errand, which ended in fiasco. I understand that the Foreign Office is highly embarrassed. Something must be done.' Then just before Blaze replaced the receiver, he added, 'By the way, the government changes will be announced tomorrow. Our friend is pleased.'

After he had spoken to the Attorney, Blaze asked Brian Pepper, the PM's Parliamentary Secretary, to come and see him and later they went together to the Prime Minister's room in the House. The Home Secretary was with the Prime Minister but Blaze and Pepper were called in and all four men conferred.

Godfrey began to collect together his private papers in his office. He knew that his usefulness to the service was at an end, and the summons he expected was not long in coming.

He was invited to call upon the Cabinet Secretary, Sir Leslie Crichton, at seven o'clock the following day.

At six Godfrey invited himself to Harvey Thompson's chambers in Albany.

'You have heard the news of the reshuffle?' Harvey said as Godfrey walked into the room.

'No.'

'It has just been announced from Number Ten. The Foreign Secretary has gone. The Home Secretary is succeeding him. So I shall pack my bags. What is your news?'

'I am summoned to see Leslie Crichton at the Cabinet offices in', Godfrey looked at his watch, 'half an hour. Either then or later I shall be led into the presence for the decencies to be observed.'

'So soon?'

'Yes. I have been involved in too many misfortunes, or blunders, as they would have it.'

'The man you chose for South America?'

'That is a part of the story. But he was the only man who could do what I wanted.'

'What went wrong?'

'He did more than was necessary. I do not blame him. He was in the field and he made a decision. Another might have been more cautious.'

'Were you wrong to have chosen him?'

'As I said, he was the only man who had a chance to get to where I wanted him and he found for me the place for which I had been searching. I suppose my man was at heart something of a romantic and as a result he went a step too far. Romance of all kinds is best avoided in my profession.'

'I can believe that.'

'Now he will pay a price, for the people he came up against will not forget him. From now on he will have a shadow watching and protecting him, searching beneath his car for the plastic box with the bomb. That was the legacy which I have left to him when on a summer evening in the garden of St Peter's I asked for his help. I hope that he will forgive me.'

'Those murders at the vicarage, the murder of de Tourneville's wife – that was all very mysterious. I never felt that I could ask.'

'I shall tell you one day.'

'How did this all start?'

'It began with an obsession conceived by one woman in the Brasserie Lippe in Paris and it was followed by the death in Chelsea of another. I hoped that the death in Chelsea might help lead me to the place which I asked Hamilton to find. In a way it did, but that death in Chelsea also led to the death of the other.'

Godfrey stood and looked out the window at the rain.

'I am sorry that you will be leaving the government but I can understand why. That new Foreign Secretary! So in the end that false man has triumphed.'

He looked again at his watch. 'I had better be off,' he said.

Webster drove Godfrey to Whitehall and Godfrey entered the Cabinet Offices through the security doors and walked up the steps over the internal bridge formed by the stairs between the rose brick walls of old Whitehall and the buildings at the corner of Whitehall. He waited, seated at the round table outside the Cabinet Secretary's room. Then he was shown in. An hour later Godfrey and the Cabinet Secretary went through the doors and passageway, which leads from the Cabinet Offices to Number 10, and into the Cabinet room where the Prime Minister was waiting. The obsequies were decently observed, as Godfrey had known they would be. Two days later Webster drove him to Finches for the last time.

The sunshine of that long summer had gone. It was cold and it was raining and the leaves swirled in the north-east wind as the car passed the empty vicarage. It would be long, Godfrey thought, before another could be found who would care to live in that house.

The car drew up in front of Finches.

'Goodbye,' Godfrey said to Webster. 'I will miss you.'

He went into the house to Angela.

'I knew he'd get the push after all the trouble over those murders,' said the Special Branch man as they drove back to

London. 'You can't have that with a man in his position. Nice old bugger, though.'

Webster said nothing.

On that evening in Whitehall James Kent was shown into the great room with the portrait of George III above the fireplace. The new Foreign Secretary did not rise, he did not even look up from the papers which he was busily signing. Kent waited, standing.

'Ah, C,' said the Foreign Secretary at last. 'Welcome. We are to celebrate. I think that you and I deserve it. I am taking you to dine at the Turf club. I hope you fancy oysters and champagne.'

And he laughed genially at the very thought that James Kent might not.